THE
PREDATORS

HAROLD ROBBINS

THE
PREDATORS

A TOM DOHERTY ASSOCIATES BOOK
NEW YORK

THE PREDATORS

Copyright © 1998 by the Estate of Harold Robbins

A Forge Book
Published by Tom Doherty Associates, Inc.
175 Fifth Avenue
New York, NY 10010

Forge® is a registered trademark of Tom Doherty Associates, Inc.

Design by Patrice Sheridan

Library of Congress Cataloging-in-Publication Data
Robbins, Harold
    The predators / Harold Robbins. — 1st ed.
        p.   cm.
    "A Tom Doherty Associates book."
    ISBN 0-312-85294-0
    I. Title.
PS3568.O224P7 1998
813'.54—dc21   98-5553
                                              CIP

First Edition: May 1998

Printed in the United States of America

0 9 8 7 6 5 4 3 2 1

THE
PREDATORS

PROLOGUE

For a thousand years, Plescassier was a spring in the Alps of France that sprayed its water on the earth; it was a sacred, worshiped spring until Man decided to take this natural resource and bottle it, ship it, and sell the water for profit around the world.

Suddenly there was a change in reason for and about Plescassier water.

BOOK ONE

TWO CENTS PLAIN

1

I looked down at the kitchen table. I stared at my math homework. This was hell. I could do arithmetic in my head, but when it came to algebra or geometry I couldn't get it. I wasn't stupid, but it just didn't make any sense to me.

I looked up at the kitchen clock. It was midnight. I looked out through the window. I had the window open just a crack. It was starting to get too cold in the room. I walked over to turn on the heat. I didn't blame my parents for wanting to spend the weekend in Atlantic City. It was always nice there on the beach, and they loved the ocean air.

I closed the window in the kitchen and turned on the radio. Guy Lombardo and the Royal Canadians were playing. The radio show came from the Pennsylvania Hotel at midnight every night. Real good music. Dance music. My parents loved this show. They loved to dance. I would bet that they were listening to it on the way home on the car radio.

I looked over at my pack of Twenty Grands. It was almost empty. I took one out of the pack and lit it. I started straightening my math papers to put in the loose-leaf folder when I heard a knock at the back door. Quickly I pinched out the cigarette and threw the butt out the window.

"Who is it?" I called. I knew it wasn't my parents—they had their own keys to the door. Maybe it was Kitty, but she hadn't told me she was coming back again. She had been down earlier in the afternoon. I had gotten laid twice before we went out and got Chinese. Besides, she wouldn't be back again—she knew my parents were coming home tonight. I heard a voice come through the door but I couldn't hear who they said. I called out again.

"Who's there?"

The voice was deeper and hoarse. "It's your Uncle Harry and Aunt Lila."

I walked over to the door to open the lock bolt. My father always insisted that I keep the bolt on the door when I was there by myself.

"Come on in," I said, surprised to see my aunt and uncle. "Mom and Dad aren't back from Atlantic City yet. They should be here pretty soon. They're probably slow because of traffic on the turnpike." I looked at my aunt. She looked like she had been crying. Uncle Harry stood and looked at me. "You want to come in and sit down?" I asked. "They'll probably be here any minute."

Uncle Harry and Aunt Lila came in the door. I closed the door behind them.

"Would you like a cup of coffee?"

The top of my aunt's head barely came up to my chest, but she put her arms around me and pulled me toward her. "My poor tatele." Her tears were wet against my shirt. "My poor tatele, what are we going to do?"

Suddenly, I felt a knot in my stomach. I pulled away from her. I looked over at my Uncle Harry. His face was flushed, but that was normal.

"What's going on?" I asked. I felt like I couldn't catch my breath.

"There was an accident on the New Jersey Turnpike. Your mother and father were coming back from Atlantic City," he said.

"Yeah, I know. Were they in an accident?" I asked, trying to figure out what was going on.

Uncle Harry's eyes spoke the answer.

"They're okay," I said, my voice quivering, fighting the truth. "Right?"

"The car went off the road, it was really foggy," he said. "The state troopers pulled the car out of the water, but it was too late."

"The car doors were locked and jammed. They couldn't get out," Aunt Lila said as she reached for me, tears streaming down her cheeks.

My legs were going out from under me. I reached for a chair and sat down heavily. I sat there staring at Aunt Lila. I felt Harry's hand on my shoulder. "I'll get you a schnapps. I know you're not old enough. But I think you need it."

I started to motion where he should go to get it. I think he was the one who needed a schnapps.

"Don't get up, Jerry. I know where your father keeps it in the kitchen closet," Harry said.

He came back with two glasses and the bottle. He sat a glass in front of me. "No thanks, Uncle Harry. You go ahead and have a drink, but I can't handle it right now."

There was silence as Harry poured himself a schnapps.

"What do I do now?" I asked.

"We have a lot to do," Uncle Harry said. "It's already Monday. As soon as your school opens I'll call them and explain that you won't be coming to school for at least a week. Then I'll need to drive you over to Jersey City to the morgue. You're head of the family and you will need to sign some papers. I called Kaplan at the Seventeenth Street Mortuary. He'll send a hearse to the morgue to pick up your parents as soon as the papers are signed."

"Harry?" Aunt Lila tried to get Harry to slow down, but he brushed her aside.

"Kaplan's oldest son will come over here in the morning and pick up the clothes for your parents to be buried in. Rabbi Cohen will do the services. We already have a family plot at Mount Zion Cemetery in Queens. We'll start calling all of the relatives right now and we should be able to get everyone here by Tuesday." Uncle Harry had everything planned but it didn't make sense to me. "Why wait? Why not have the services tomorrow?" I asked.

"But what about the family?" Uncle Harry asked.

"We haven't seen most of the relatives in years. They all think of you and Daddy as nothing more than cheap bookies. To hell with them," I said in disgust.

"Tatele, don't—" Aunt Lila started.

"No, Aunt Lila," I stated. "Why should we pay good money to take them all in Cadillacs to the cemetery?"

Aunt Lila began crying again. "It's a *shande*; they'll think we have no respect."

"Enough," Uncle Harry said in his bosslike attitude. He put his hand up to quiet Lila. "Jerry's right. They don't respect us. To hell with them."

"But, Harry . . ." Aunt Lila started to protest again. She looked over at Harry and then stopped. She knew his mind was made up.

I looked at my uncle. "What time in the morning do we have to leave?" I asked.

Uncle Harry took out his pocket watch and flipped the top open.

"If we're going to have the funeral tomorrow," he said importantly, "I'll have to pick you up at six-fifteen so we can drive over to Jersey City and back."

"I'll be ready," I said solemnly.

Aunt Lila reached across to touch Harry's arm. "The boy will need to get some clothes together so he can come home with us now. I don't want him to be alone tonight."

"Why not?" I asked.

"Tatele, don't you want to stay with us? You don't want to be alone in this house tonight," she said. "We love you and want you to be with us."

I looked at her. I knew she meant well, but I just had to be alone for a while.

"I'm not a kid," I said. "I'm used to my own bed. Besides, this is still my home. I want to be here."

Uncle Harry came to the rescue. "Leave him alone. Besides, he has things to do here. He'll pick out his parents' clothes for the service. He has to get his good blue suit out so he has something to wear."

"Uncle Harry, I wore that at my bar mitzvah. The moths have eaten that years ago. I have a brand-new suit that Daddy bought me just a few months ago." Suddenly everything seemed to choke up on me. I closed my eyes and took a deep breath. I didn't want to cry.

I remembered my father had taken me to Joe and Paul's to get a new suit. We had lunch together and then we went and got Mama a present for Mother's Day. I fought back the tears.

"Just one thing," Uncle Harry said. "Your father had a small briefcase that he always carried. By any chance, do you know where he kept the case?"

He was right. My father always had the briefcase at the apartment. It was the betting slips. I had sneaked a look a long time ago. He left it in his closet. "I can get it for you, Uncle Harry." I nodded and went into their bedroom and brought the case out to Harry.

Uncle Harry opened the flap of the case and looked inside. Quickly, he took out a bundle of bills held with a heavy red rubber band. He flipped the bills one by one with his thumb. He then put them back into the case and snapped the flap shut. "Good," he said. "You've saved me a lot of money, Jerry. Once I check the slips I won't have to pay a bunch of phony claims once it gets out that your father has died." He shook my hand. "You're very much like your father, Jerry. You're bright, just like he was." He turned to Aunt Lila and then back to me. "I can stay over with you, if you want."

"I'll manage, Uncle Harry. But thank you, anyway."

Aunt Lila came over and hugged me. She started to cry again. "You're a brave mensch," she said softly.

"Don't cry anymore," I said to her. "I love you both."

Harry grabbed my hand tightly. "You're a good boy." He shook his finger at me. "And just remember, don't smoke," Uncle Harry said in a fatherly way.

"C'mon, Uncle Harry," I said, and wondered if he had smelled the cigarette smoke when he came in.

He turned to Aunt Lila. "Let's get home to bed. We all have a very busy day ahead of us."

2

I closed the door and shoved the bolt and locked it tight. I walked over and sat down at the table. I pushed my homework papers to the floor. Fuck it, the hell with it. I lit another Twenty Grand cigarette. The smoke felt good in my lungs. I needed a good drag. I studied the Twenty Grand package on the table. The drawing of the great Kentucky Derby winner on the front of the package was really a beauty. That was one of the reasons that I bought Twenty Grands. They also cost less than Luckys or Camels or Chesterfields. But for some reason tonight I couldn't even taste the smoke in my mouth or nose. I stared blankly ahead at the white-papered kitchen wall. I remembered when my father and I had tried to roll that wallpaper on ourselves, but it was a mess. He finally got fed up trying to figure it out and hired the super to do the work. I nearly jumped out of my skin when I heard another knock at the door.

"Hold on, Uncle Harry," I hollered for the second time, pinching my cigarette butt and throwing it out the kitchen window.

"It's me," Kitty called through the door. "Hurry up, will you? Someone might see me."

I opened the door and Kitty breezed in by me in a thin pink robe. I closed the door and snapped at her. "Are you crazy or something? Your dad will kill you if he finds you dressed like that up here in my apartment."

"My father is fast asleep, and he thinks that his baby girl is in dreamland." She grinned. "I came down the fire escape and through the hall window."

16

"Kitty, I think you oughtta—"

Kitty was talking ninety miles an hour. "I thought I was a goner when your aunt and uncle showed up. I was just about ready to come in the kitchen window to bring you my present. I had to sneak back upstairs until they left."

"Kitty . . ." But I had a hard time finding my voice.

"At first I thought it was your folks, which would have ruined everything, but when I saw it wasn't them . . ." She stared at me finally. "Hey baby, what's the matter?"

I still had a problem finding my voice. I rubbed my sleeve across my cheek to stop the tears.

"What's the matter, Jerry?" she asked. A real concern had come into her voice.

"They've . . ." I reached for the kitchen towel to dry my tears on my cheek. "They were killed tonight in an accident on the Jersey Turnpike coming back from Atlantic City." By then I really was crying.

"Oh, my God." She pulled me to her. "You poor kid."

"I'm not a kid—you're only two years older than me." A sob made me shudder. I struggled to get myself together. "I'll be all right."

"Of course you will," she said softly, holding me tightly and stroking my forehead. A terrible pain seemed to engulf me as I cried.

I tried to pull away, but she still held me close until finally I was able to get my voice back. I looked at her. She was bare-assed naked under that little robe.

"What are you going to do now?" she asked. "You can't live here by yourself."

"I don't know. I'll probably have to move in with my aunt and uncle." I started to reach for my package of cigarettes from the table, but my hand caught accidentally on her robe and pulled it open. "Damn!" I said. "What the hell are you doing, Kitty? I can see everything that you've got!" I wasn't able to move my eyes from her nipples, which were sticking out.

"That's what the surprise was. That's why I sneaked down here," she said.

"Damn," I said. "We did it twice before dinner."

"Yeah, well I thought it'd be nice to do it again. After all, we don't get that many chances to be alone where we don't have to sneak around." She rubbed her hand against my fly.

"Cut it out, will ya?" I growled.

Still trying to open my fly, she nuzzled my cheek and whispered. "You're sad, and nervous. Maybe I could relax you a little bit and you'd feel better."

I pushed her away. "What kind of schmuck do you take me for? Don't you get it? My parents were just killed in an automobile accident."

She kept right on and got my fly open and slipped her hand inside my pants and held my cock tight. "Better tell him. He's still standing and hard." She pulled it out and she was right—it was standing at attention. "What do you call that?"

"I got a nervous reaction."

"That's bullshit," she said as she rolled her eyes. "I call it a hard-on and my pussy is aching for one more time."

I pulled her hand off of me. "It's not right. Besides, I can't really do anything right now."

Kitty stared at me persistently. "Don't be stupid," she said almost angrily. "How do you think we're going to make out when you're living with your aunt and uncle? Don't break my heart. This might be our last time."

I shook my head and pushed my prick back inside my pants. I felt stupid. My hand was soaking wet from my leaking pecker.

She started crying. "I just want to help you. C'mon, grab one of the Ramses from your dad's top dresser drawer."

I took her by the hand and led her to the kitchen table. "Let's sit down a minute. I'm not feeling that great."

One more time she reached for my hard-on. "I know I can make you feel better."

"You can only help by taking your hand off of my cock," I said. "Give me a few minutes to figure things out. I gotta figure out what to do next."

She pulled her robe around her tightly, and she sat down at the kitchen table opposite me. I took out a cigarette and offered her one. She took it and I gave her a light. She took a drag and then made a funny face. "I don't know how you smoke these cheap cigarettes."

I dragged some smoke through my nostrils. "I like them. And besides"—I picked up the pack and showed her the picture on the front—"I like the horse."

We both laughed. It helped.

"What do you want to do?" she asked. "Did your folks leave any money around the house for you?"

"My father left me a fiver for the weekend," I said. "He left his briefcase too, but Uncle Harry told me to give it to him and he took it home."

"What was in it?" she asked.

"Money and betting slips," I answered.

She stared at me. She was a pretty clever girl. She was nineteen years old, two years older than me. She was a sophomore at Hunter Business College and I was just in my senior year in high school. She had always been a horny little bitch from the day we moved in. Last year she had lifted her skirt almost over her panties when I was walking behind her up the staircase. She turned around on the step above me and smiled down at me. "You like that black curly pussy?"

I nearly fell down. I couldn't believe what she had said. That was last year and I was only sixteen and the only thing I had ever done was jerk off all the time.

"You're a big boy for your age," she said. "I have to get together with you." She paused and turned around to face me fully. "I wonder if everything you have is big," she said as she put her hand on my fly. She laughed and turned to go up the stairs. "I think you've really got a big one, Jerry. When can we start working it out?"

I was dumbfounded. I stared at her. "How did you know my name?"

"My name is Kitty," she said, ignoring my question. "Pretty soon you'll find out I know about everything that goes on in this place. My father is the owner."

She lived a story below me, and before I could even say anything more, she went inside her apartment. A second later the door to her apartment opened and she stuck her head out. "Don't forget to get yourself some rubbers," she whispered into the hall. "I'm not planning on getting knocked up."

Then she closed the door again and I went upstairs. It wasn't long before I learned that her father had bought the apartment house only about a month before we moved in. The next thing I learned was that her father was away at work all day in his real estate office. Two afternoons later Kitty called me to come down to her apartment and she screwed my brains out.

I kept on dragging on my cigarette and looking at her. It was hard to believe that I had been screwing her for a year. Suddenly I came back to reality. I really couldn't believe either that I had no parents. They were gone. I had no idea what I was going to do. My world had disappeared.

"What are you thinking?" Kitty asked.

"I don't know," I said. "Everything has changed. I've gotta get my parents' clothes out for the funeral tomorrow. I want to put them out on their bed. Then I have to get my own suit out."

"I'll help you," Kitty said. "Don't worry."

"Thanks," I said. "I guess we better get started."

I felt peculiar when I stepped into my parents' room. The choking in my throat began again. I began to feel a little dizzy. Kitty held my arm tightly. "It's all right," she said quietly. "It's all right. Everything will be okay in time. Why don't you let me get your mom's clothes out for you."

I looked at her. She made me feel better. "Thank you," I said. I pointed at the closet near the dresser. "My mother's clothes are in there." I moved over to the other closet on the other side of the dresser. "I'll get my dad's clothes out of this one."

She nodded and moved to my mom's closet. I decided to take out my father's good holiday suit. He always wore it for Rosh Hashanah and for Yizkor at the synagogue. I placed it carefully on a good hanger. Then I looked up on the top shelf, where he kept his hats. I also saw a cardboard shoe box. I took it down thinking that it was his patent leather dress shoes. I was wrong. The box was stuffed with rolls of bills. A roll of fivers, then a roll of tens, then twenties and a few hundreds on the bottom of the box. I looked up at Kitty, who had come over to see what I was doing. We were both speechless.

"Where did your father get that kind of money?" she asked, her mouth half-open.

"I don't know," I answered. "I know my father has worked for Uncle Harry for a long time. But he was only a runner picking up bets. Uncle Harry is the big-shot bookie. He handled all the connections with Frank Ericson, who is the boss."

"How much money is there?" she asked.

"I don't know," I answered, trying to figure out where my dad got this money. "Let's check it out." We split the rolls of bills and counted them.

After we had finished counting, I looked over at Kitty. "How much?"

"I've counted twenty-four hundred," she answered. "How much have you got?"

"I've got three thousand," I said.

"What are you going to do with the money?" she asked.

"I don't know. I guess I'll turn it over to Uncle Harry to keep for me."

"Don't be a schmuck," she said. "He'll only tell you that it was his money that your father held out from him."

"My father wouldn't do anything like that," I answered indignantly.

"It doesn't make any difference," she snapped. "It's money isn't it? And I bet your father would want you to have it. If you give it to your Uncle

Harry, you'll have to fight for it. He's a bookie and my father has told me all about bookies. They keep every dollar that they can get their hands on. You'll never see a cent of it if you give it to your uncle."

"What should I do, then?" I asked.

"Put it in the bank," she said.

"I can't do it," I said. "I'm only seventeen. I'm not old enough without one of my parents with me. I'm fucked. I'll have to give it to my uncle."

"Wait a minute," she said. "I'll put it in a safety-deposit box at my bank. After you turn eighteen, I'll take the money out of the box for you and you can open your own account."

"I won't have any time tomorrow to help you. I'll be busy all day with the funeral. My uncle will be here at six-fifteen in the morning."

"I'll hold it for you," she said as she watched me. "That is, if you trust me."

I lit another cigarette and stared down at the money.

"You don't have to worry about me," she said. "It'll be like sticking it in my pussy and whenever you want to make a withdrawal you'll know what to do."

Kitty had only one thing on her mind. "You're crazy," I said.

She leaned across the bed toward me. "The only thing I'm crazy about is your cock, and every time you stick it in me, it's like making a deposit in the bank."

"That's a romantic thought," I said sarcastically.

"There's nothing romantic about money or fucking, Jerry." She grinned and raised her hand. There was a Ramses between her fingers. "Sure you don't want to make a deposit right now?"

"Damn!" I said. "My parents haven't even been buried yet and all you want is—"

She interrupted me. "I'm sorry, but they are dead now, and nothing that anyone can do will bring them back. They can be buried a week, or a month, or a year from now and they will still be dead. But you're not dead. You're alive and you have to keep on living. You're a man now. You have to start thinking about your own life, not theirs."

I lay back on the bed. It was all crazy. I was getting dizzy from the accident, the money, and Kitty. I took a deep breath and sat up. I took her hand and led her from my parents' room to mine. Quickly, I opened my fly and my prick sprung out like a javelin. She dropped to her knees and covered my prick with her mouth.

3

The coroner's assistant took us downstairs in the morgue. He led Uncle Harry and myself into a room that held corpses. He opened the door of the refrigerated case, and pulled a body covered in a sheet out and pulled the sheet down so I could see the face. "Is this your father?" he said without expression.

I could hardly answer him. I was so nauseous. I just nodded.

He then opened the door of the next refrigerated case. He pulled the sheet down. "Is this your mother?"

I nodded and then threw up. The coroner was experienced—he held a pail under my mouth before I could let it go. Then he gently placed his arm around my shoulders. "I'll get you some smelling salts," he said softly.

I shook my head. "I'll be all right," I said. "I'm sorry. It's just that I never saw a dead person before. And it's my mother and father." I couldn't help it. I started sobbing again.

The coroner was a very kind man. He just patted my shoulders until I felt better. "Come with me into the office," he said. "You'll need to sign the rest of the forms so the mortuary can take your parents."

I got to his office and I suddenly realized that Uncle Harry hadn't come downstairs with me. "Where is my uncle?" I asked the coroner.

"Your uncle wasn't feeling too well," he answered. "We had him lie down on the couch upstairs, but he'll be down with us in a few minutes." He then picked up the telephone on his desk. "Jenny," he said. "Bring down the package of the Cooper things. Also check on Mr. Cooper and see if he feels like coming downstairs."

Jenny was a large black lady. As she walked in the door she was carrying a square cardboard box in front of her. Uncle Harry was right behind her. He still looked a little pale. Jenny walked behind the desk and placed the box on it. She then took a pencil from her thick black hair and opened her steno pad.

The coroner gestured to Uncle Harry to sit in the chair next to me. Uncle Harry was sweating and he took a handkerchief out of his pocket and wiped his brow.

The coroner opened the lid of the box. He looked at me. "These are your parents' belongings that were found by the police at the scene of the accident."

I looked at him silently.

"Yes, sir, we understand." Uncle Harry spoke for me.

Quickly he placed the contents of the box onto the top of his desk. "Jenny will give you a typewritten list of the contents in the box. Will you please let me know if there is anything that you remember of your parents' belongings that is not here?"

I looked down at the desk. I saw the jewelry, Mother's small diamond engagement ring, her gold wedding band, and a small thin gold necklace. I saw my father's large silver pocket watch and the diamond pinkie ring that he always flashed on his right hand. Then there was his wallet with his driver's license and some other papers that were still damp.

"Is there anything that you can remember they might have had?" the coroner asked.

"The only thing that I can think of is my mother's pocketbook," I said.

The coroner nodded and spoke to Jenny. "Make a note of that."

"We have a valise that is still very wet," Jenny said. "It was locked and we were not allowed to open it."

"That will be given to you when you are ready to leave," the coroner said.

"My brother always carried a couple of hundred bucks with him," Uncle Harry said.

The coroner looked up at him. "Nobody turned in any money. We went through all the pockets in his clothes and we found only a few ones and some coin change."

"I don't understand. He always had a couple of hundred hidden. You know, like pin money," Uncle Harry said.

"When accidents happen, no one can understand what happens," the coroner said. He opened a folder and took out several forms. "Now, all you have to do is sign these releases and we can turn everything over to you." He looked at Uncle Harry.

"There's one more thing," Jenny said. "A Mr. Kaplan is waiting to pick up the bodies."

"Is this what you would like, Mr. Cooper?"

Uncle Harry nodded. "Yes, he'll take them back to Queens."

Jenny then left the office. "All right," the coroner said. "Now both of you will need to sign these papers and everything will be in order." He looked down at me. "I'm sorry, Jerry," he said. "But, believe me, in time, everything will be okay."

We signed the papers and I shook his hand as I stood up to leave. We took everything from the cardboard box and the valise and the clothes my parents had been wearing and put them in Uncle Harry's Buick.

4

Aunt Lila must have stayed up all night calling the relatives. There were more than twenty men and women that came to the funeral and then to my apartment. Aunt Lila had also fixed the apartment for sitting shivah. She had wooden boxes for everyone to sit on and she had covered all of the mirrors and pictures. On the kitchen table she had placed several baskets of fruit and glass bowls filled with walnuts. She took charge of everything once we arrived home. I had to wear my yarmulke, but she told me it was okay if I took off my jacket. One of my other uncles, Uncle Morris, was kind of a rabbi, and he stood up and said kaddish for me. I couldn't help it—I started crying again.

Uncle Harry put his arm against my shoulder. "Let it go, Jerry," he said. "You're carrying a big burden."

Uncle Morris looked at him. "He's still a kid. It would be okay if he went and lay down on his own bed for a while."

"I'll be all right." I sniffed.

"No," Aunt Lila said. "You go lie down right now. I'll go turn the bed down for you."

Kitty had been at the funeral with us, and she also had come home with us to the apartment. She turned to Aunt Lila. "I'll help you."

I followed them into my bedroom and stretched out as soon as they had turned down the sheets. I turned and looked at Aunt Lila. "Thanks for your help, Aunt Lila."

"You try to sleep," Aunt Lila said, and turned to Kitty. "Here's two aspirin I have for him. Get him a glass of water and give it to him. I have to go back to the other room. I forgot to give the bottle of schnapps and Manischewitz to the guests."

She left the room and Kitty leaned over to kiss me. "I'll get the water for you in a minute. I just wanted to tell you that I put your money into the safety-deposit box already."

"Okay," I said. The money, for the moment, didn't bother me.

"I'll come up tonight and see you so you won't have to be alone. I'll really take care of you, Jerry. You don't have to worry," she said, and went to get the water for the aspirin, but I was out before she made it back.

It was almost dark when I awakened. I turned the lamp on beside my bed and sat up. Aunt Lila came into my bedroom. "Are you all right?" she asked.

"I'm okay," I said, standing up. "Is everybody still here?"

"No," she answered. "It was late and they all had a long drive ahead of them, so they left. Uncle Harry and I and your girlfriend Kitty and her father are the only ones here now. Her father seems to be a nice man. He wanted to come by and just give his sympathy. He said he liked your parents."

"I didn't know he even knew my parents very well." I turned to walk to the bathroom. "I have to go to the bathroom. I'll be out in a few minutes."

She saw the two aspirin tablets on my bedside table with the glass of water. "Take the aspirin now," she said.

I didn't argue. I swallowed the aspirin and went to the bathroom. I looked into the mirror over the sink. I looked lousy. Even my clothing looked wrinkled and uncomfortable. Quickly I got out of my clothes and stepped into the bathtub and pulled the shower curtain closed. I turned on the shower. The water felt great and refreshing. It made me feel a lot better. I dried myself quickly and put on a fresh shirt and pair of pants. Then I went into the kitchen.

My aunt and uncle, Kitty, and her father were seated around the table. Kitty rose as I walked in. "Jerry, I'd like for you to meet my father, Mr. Sam Benson."

Her father rose to his feet. He was a tall, heavyset man, six feet at least, maybe two hundred pounds. He held his hand out to me.

"I'm sorry, Jerry, about your parents' accident. I offer you my sympathy."

His hand was firm, but gentle. "Thank you, Mr. Benson. Please sit down again."

I sat down next to Kitty at the table. Mr. Benson looked at me. "My daughter tells me that you two are very good friends. She told me that she was tutoring you in geometry. Kitty was always good in math subjects."

I smiled to myself. Geometry wasn't the main thing she was tutoring me in. "She's been really nice, Mr. Benson," I said solemnly.

"I also found out something," he continued. "Our families have many things in common. Both of our ancestors came through Ellis Island at about the same time. My grandfather changed his name to Benson after he first arrived here because nobody could pronounce his name, Bramowickh. And your uncle has been telling me that your grandfather also changed his name from Kuperman to Cooper."

"My father never told me that," I said.

Uncle Harry shook his head. "It's not important anymore. That was a long time ago and now we're all Americans." He looked over at Aunt Lila. "It's been a long day. Is everyone else as hungry as I am?" he asked.

"It's the first day of shivah," Aunt Lila said. "We can't go out to a restaurant now."

Mr. Benson turned to Uncle Harry. "There's a great Chink restaurant just around the corner. We can get a whole family take-out dinner. Do you like Chinese?"

"I think it's great," Uncle Harry said. "But I can't go out for it."

Kitty looked at us. "I can go out for you."

Aunt Lila said politely, "We can't bother you, dear."

"It's no bother," Kitty said. "Just tell me what you would like."

Her father spoke up. "They have a great family dinner. It'll feed all of us. It's got everything: egg rolls, chow mein, chop suey, spareribs, dim sum." Quickly he took out a ten-dollar bill and gave it to Kitty. "That'll cover five dinners, plus a big tip. Ask one of the Chinks to help you carry it up here and tell him he can keep the change."

Uncle Harry gave Mr. Benson a fiver. "I'll split it with you. You have dinner here with us."

Aunt Lila got up. "I'll set the table."

I hadn't realized how hungry I had gotten. I ate like the Chinese were never going to cook again. I got a couple of Rheingold beers and two big Pepsis out of the refrigerator. Kitty, Aunt Lila, and I drank the Pepsis, and the two men drank the beers. The table was quiet as we all ate like crazy. Finally we were finished. Kitty smiled and put the fortune cookies on the table.

I started to take one and then I stopped. "I don't know if I want to take one. My future is pretty messed up right now."

Aunt Lila took my hand. "Tatele, today is already yesterday. Your tomorrows will be better. Let's all take one for a better day tomorrow and forever." She leaned over and kissed me. I looked at her. She was right. It was already yesterday. I took a fortune cookie and broke it open. I straightened the small piece of paper that had been inside. THE GODS OF FORTUNE WILL SMILE ON YOU. Then suddenly I was angry. I crumpled the little piece of paper and pushed the fortune cookies off the table. "What fortune am I going to get, what fortune did my father and mother get?" I said angrily. "An early grave. And I'm left in a fucked-up world."

"Don't talk that way in front of the ladies, Jerry," Uncle Harry said softly. "It's going to be all right, son. While you were sleeping I was talking to Mr. Benson and we worked a good plan for you."

I stared at him. "What kind of plan? You don't even have an extra bedroom for me to live in, and there's no way I can pay the rent for this apartment. I'm going to have to quit school, get a job, and live in a small room in some boardinghouse!"

"Jerry, it's not that bad," Uncle Harry said. "Mr. Benson has three months' security deposit that your father had paid him for the apartment. He has been kind enough to offer us a deal. He has a studio apartment open on the second floor. Your father's deposit will pay for your studio apartment for eight months."

"That's great," I said. "But where do I get money to live on? I gotta buy food and stuff."

"We've got that worked out, too," he said. "Aunt Lila gave me the idea. What time do you get out of school?"

"Two in the afternoon," I answered.

"You see, it's perfect. You can come work at my counter on the Square. It's the outside open counter across the street from Nedick's and down the block from S. Klein. It's the busiest store on the Square, and it's across from an IRT subway entrance."

"Fine," I said nervously. "What am I going to do for you?"

"I'm going to teach you how to work the counter, and you're a smart boy, you'll catch on fast. I'll make you a manager before you get out of school."

"Okay, Uncle Harry," I said. "How much do I get a week?"

"You're family." Uncle Harry smiled. "I'll start you at twelve dollars a week. That's a lot more than I pay the Puerto Ricans that work for me. And I'll give you a raise when you get more knowledge and experience."

"Is that the store where you have your office?" I asked. "Where my father used to check in his slips every evening?"

Uncle Harry flushed. He didn't like for other people to know that he was really a bookmaker. "Yes," he answered.

"Why couldn't I just take over my dad's job?" I asked. "I know how it all works and I'm a real genius when it comes to doing numbers in my head."

Aunt Lila gave me the answer sternly. "One, you're too young. Two, you have to finish school, so you can't start working at seven in the morning until three in the afternoon. Three, there are a lot of tough men in that work. Your parents wanted a better life for you."

I didn't say anything for a moment. I looked at them. "I'm not ungrateful for all the help that you are giving me. But I feel I should be doing more to take care of myself."

"Grow up, Jerry," my uncle said gently. "You still have time. First, you serve two cents plain before you make up the egg creams," Uncle Harry said prophetically.

"It's not that bad," said Kitty. "You will still be here in the same house where everybody knows you. Plus you don't have to change schools. It'll all be fine, Jerry."

I turned to her. She was sitting next to me. She nodded, smiling. Then I felt her hand hidden under the tablecloth slipping inside the buttons of my fly.

I jumped up quickly. I didn't need to come in front of all of them. I looked down at Kitty. "I'm going to wash the dishes."

She rose up and smiled again. "I'll help you."

5

Sitting shivah for the week was impossible for me. I didn't have time to mourn. Even Aunt Lila agreed that I couldn't stay in my apartment for a week and not go out into public. I had to move into my new apartment.

The studio apartment on the second floor had not been rented for a long time. It was unfurnished and everything needed to be painted, the walls, ceiling, trim, and windows. The ancient wooden floors had dried and splintered. Aunt Lila suggested that we cover the floor with the new linoleum that looked like real wood. She said it was easy to take care of and it was also not expensive. Mr. Benson said he would give me the paint for the apartment, but I would have to paint it myself. He said he couldn't afford to pay two schwartzes ten dollars to do the painting. Kitty volunteered to help me.

Aunt Lila picked out pieces of furniture that I already had that might fit into my new room. It wasn't easy because the studio room was only twenty by twenty-four and most of the furniture that my parents had was for bigger rooms. But it was Mr. Benson who finally helped me out. He said he knew an honest secondhand furniture dealer who would buy the extra furniture from the old apartment and would also give me a good price on a small Castro convertible sofa that I could turn into a bed at night. It had only been used for three months, but I could still get a good deal.

Meanwhile Aunt Lila asked two ladies from the Hadassah to take out my parents' clothing. When I asked Aunt Lila how much I would get for their clothes, she got very upset and said that the old clothing would be sent to the poor Jewish people in Europe and that it should be a mitzvah for me to give it to them. It didn't make good sense to me because I wasn't especially well-off myself. But I said it was fine anyway.

Aunt Lila cleaned the small kitchenette. She scoured everything. She said before she started cleaning it was so dirty even pigs wouldn't live there. But she finally was satisfied with the kitchen. Then she told me how to clean the white tiles in the bathroom with a mixture of muriatic acid, Lysol, and water. With a little more supervision from her I was also able to clean the white bathtub and toilet. Fortunately, I had a shower curtain from the old apartment and more than enough towels, pillows, and bed linens.

The most difficult part of fixing the apartment was the painting. Kitty really helped me, but it took an extra day to complete because of all the time we took off to get laid. After we had finished the painting, the furniture was delivered and Aunt Lila helped us move all the dishes and cutlery. She organized the dishes in the closet and the cutlery in the drawers. I couldn't use the closet in the studio because it was too small, so we kept my parents' armoire to keep my clothes in. Finally, it was all finished.

By the end of the week, Kitty and I were sitting in my new apartment. We lit up a cigarette, and looked at each other. "What are you going to do now?" she asked.

"What do you mean? I have to go to school on Monday and then afterward I'll go to Uncle Harry's counter and go to work." I looked down at my hands. They were red and the skin was cracked from cleaning the bathroom. "I was stupid," I said. "Aunt Lila told me to use heavy rubber gloves, but I didn't listen to her."

"That's not important," Kitty said. "How much money did you get from all this, the furniture, the insurance?"

"I don't know yet," I answered. "Uncle Harry is talking to the insurance people and he's going to let me know what they say. Your father is going to get me the money for the furniture."

"Jerry, when are you going to learn?" Kitty said in exasperation. "They are both crooks. My father will screw you out of the furniture money. Did you get any receipts or bills? And your Uncle Harry is the biggest crook in the world. Did you see any of the insurance policies or did Uncle Harry just take them?"

"He's got them," I said. "He said he would take care of it for me. He said not to worry, and he would make sure that I would get everything that was coming to me."

She just shook her head. "You better not waste any time. Ask Harry to show you all the papers and at the same time ask my father for all the invoices on the furniture," she said.

"That's insulting. I can't do that," I said, not believing what she was saying. "Uncle Harry is family. He's not going to screw me. And it's not a big enough deal for your father to make any money on."

"I know my father," she said. "He's a nickel-and-dime hustler, he takes anything he can grab. He even tried to grab my ass once, but I told him if he ever went after me I would get my mother after him. He didn't want any part of that."

"Where's your mother?" I asked. "I never saw her."

"She divorced him, and now she's married to a real rich guy. She lives over on Park Avenue. I have lunch with her a couple of times a week, and dinner with her and her husband once a month. He's nice," she said, nodding. "He slips me a hundred each month and my mother pays for all of my clothes."

"That's pretty good," I said. "Why don't you live with your mother?"

"The courts," she answered. "That was the agreement for the divorce. My mother is Jewish and my father is Catholic, and the judge was one stupid son of a bitch. He was Catholic and gave my father custody of me. But that's only until I am twenty-one. Then I can tell him to go fuck himself."

"You still have two more years," I said.

"I know," she said. "That's why I'm always trying to plan ahead."

"I wish I could plan ahead," I said. "I'll be eighteen in January. Then I have to register for the draft and by the time I graduate from high school I will probably have to go into the army."

She shrugged. "I'm getting hungry," she said. "Would you like to go down to the Italian restaurant for some spaghetti?"

"I'd like," I said honestly. "But I don't have enough money. Aunt Lila was going to bring dinner for me."

"Give her a call and tell her that you'll just have a sandwich," she said. "And I'll treat."

I telephoned Aunt Lila from the drugstore on the corner. It worked out fine—while I was there I bought a dozen Trojans for a quarter.

* * *

Kitty had been right. Her father screwed me on the furniture. He gave me only three hundred dollars for the family furniture. I told him that was crazy. It was only a year old and it had cost my parents fifteen hundred dollars, plus my bedroom set with a dresser. It had to be worth more than three hundred dollars. Mr. Benson was very smooth. He told me that the Castro alone cost seven hundred dollars. He said the furniture man had to pay to have everything moved out of the apartment and into the apartment. By that time there wasn't much left since the big heavy furniture we had in the old apartment was not very good in the market right now. He handed me the three one-hundred-dollar bills and told me that he had spoken to Uncle Harry about it and he thought it was a fair deal. He said if I wanted to I could go over and talk to the secondhand furniture man myself, but his warehouse was at the end of Brooklyn, and that was a half a day subway ride for me to get there. I decided that it wasn't worth it. There was nothing I could do now. Uncle Harry let him screw me. Mr. Benson smiled at me. "Don't worry so much about money, kid," he said. "Don't forget you're not paying rent for eight months. By that time, you'll be a manager at Harry's counter."

"Yeah," I said sarcastically.

"And don't forget, Kitty will always be helping you out," he said. "She likes you, I know. That's why she's always coming up to your studio."

That got my attention. I looked at him to see if he had any real idea of what Kitty and I had been doing, but I couldn't tell. He was too smooth.

6

I caught up on my schoolwork by the second week after the funeral. I managed to do just enough to get a passing grade. After that first week back at school, I started going to Uncle Harry's store on the street corner.

When I arrived the first day he was sitting behind a dirty-looking old desk with his big belly hanging over the top. It was just about four o'clock. He glared at me. "You took your own sweet time to finally get down here."

"I had to catch up on my homework," I answered.

"That's a good excuse," he snapped. "But from now on I want you here no later than three-thirty or you can go look for another job. And I want you here early while I'm training you."

I stared at him. "What are you getting mad about?" I asked. "I haven't even started working for you here and you want me to go out and get another job. Okay," I said. "I'll go get one." I started heading toward the door of his office.

"Wait a minute!" he yelled. "Don't be so hot under the collar."

"Look, I'm not the one that started this," I said. "You're the one that's acting crazy."

"You don't know how difficult it is without your father here," he said. "I have to do everything myself, and I'm worn out."

"I'm not doing that great without my mother and father but I'm trying the best I can," I said.

"Okay, okay," he said. "Calm down, and I'll take you downstairs and show you around."

34

"Okay," I answered. "Hey, Uncle Harry, one of my teachers asked me if my parents had any insurance. I told my teacher that they had some insurance but I didn't know exactly how much. But I told him that you were taking care of everything. He offered to take a look at the policies if I wanted him to. He said he was pretty good at that kind of thing."

"Fucking bastards," Uncle Harry swore under his breath. "Everybody's nosy. They can't mind their own business."

I watched him without speaking.

He opened a drawer from his desk and took out some papers held together with a paper clip. "Here's all the information. Your father had what they call a funeral policy from our shul. It covers the cemetery costs and funeral expenses. This policy paid for everything. Kaplan's arrange-ment for the coffins, opening the graves, and paid all the *alte* men at the service to help the rabbi with the kaddish and the ceremonies. Kaplan also took care of the hearse and the two limousines we needed."

"What kind of insurance policy is that?" I asked. "Wasn't there any money left for me?"

"That's not the kind of policy your father carried. There would have been money for you if it had been a society policy. Your father didn't expect to die this early, we had the plots for all the family, what was necessary? This was an old policy that had been taken out by your grandfather for his sons."

"Then there's nothing for me?" I asked.

"The funeral expenses came to two thousand one hundred dollars," Uncle Harry said. "Here's the papers. You can keep it, they're yours." He was silent for a moment. "You'll be getting about two hundred dollars from the automobile insurance."

"The car was only two years old," I said. "I remember what Daddy paid for it. Six hundred and fifty dollars."

"It's junk now," Uncle Harry said. "You're lucky to get two hundred for it."

I sat and thought for a moment. "It's really sad. All that my parents have left from their lives is five hundred dollars. What happened to all of my mother's jewelry and my dad's other jewelry? I can't find anything."

"Gone," Uncle Harry said. "Before we ever got to see anything. The cops probably took all the expensive stuff out of the valise. You remember, the coroner told us that nothing else was found."

"Shit," I said dejectedly. "It's not worth dying."

"Get it out of your head," Uncle Harry said. "Now, come downstairs with me and learn your job."

7

"Why don't you get a telephone?" Kitty asked as she rolled out of bed and crossed the room to get a Pepsi from the small refrigerator.

I waited until she came back to bed. "I don't need a phone," I said, taking a swig out of the Pepsi bottle.

"It's stupid to run down the stairs just to use the phone," she said. "I called you a couple of times at the drugstore, but by the time they got upstairs to get you, I got bored and hung up."

"How many times was that?" I asked.

"Enough," she said, "to let me know it was a pain in the ass."

"Why are you complaining?" I said. "I'm the one that has to run down-stairs to the phone."

"Why do you want to be so cheap?" Kitty said. "Suppose I got the hots for you and wanted to call you for a quickie," she purred demurely.

"That's stupid," I said. "I don't even get home from work until nine o'clock. I'm gone all during the day."

"I could call you when you get home," she said.

"What for?" I said. "All you have to do is knock on the door."

"Jesus," she exclaimed, and turned the last of the Pepsi from the bottle upside down and poured it over my balls!

"You've gone crazy!" I shouted as I leaped from the cold, sticky liquid. "Look what you did to my sheets. Now I'll have to take them to the self-serve laundry."

"Don't be a jerk," she said. "I'll lick all the Pepsi off your cock and balls,

36

then I'll make you come on top of the Pepsi, and that will make it just perfect."

She was right. It was perfect. Later, after we got out of the bed, I made some instant coffee for us. That was good, too. She looked around. "It's Sunday. Don't you have any of the newspapers?"

"What for?" I asked. "I don't need a whole newspaper. I read the sports page from leftover papers at Uncle Harry's counter. All I care about is how the Yankees are doing."

"Don't you know that there is a war coming?" she asked.

"I hear the bullshit on the radio about it," I said. "But I'm not old enough yet."

"You're going to have to go into the army," she said. "You're getting really close to the age."

"So? There's nothing I can do about it," I answered nonchalantly. "What are you worried about?"

"I just don't want you to go to war and get killed."

"That's a stupid thing to say," I answered. "We're not even in a war yet. I'm not going to worry about it until I have to." I took another cup of coffee. "Is the self-serve laundry open today?" I asked.

"Don't worry," she said. "I'll do them for you tomorrow. How are you doing on your job?"

"It's not bad," I answered. "But it's kind of boring."

"What do you mean?" Kitty asked.

"The counter kind of like runs itself. Uncle Harry has a Puerto Rican agency that sends him all the help he needs. Those guys do all the dirty work. Uncle Harry watches the cash during the day and he has a cashier girl that just sits in a chair and collects money. She leaves at seven, the same time as Uncle Harry, and then I handle the cash until we close at nine. The only time it gets really busy is when the Puerto Ricans are on the dinner break, and I'm by myself. It's the only time I get to go into action."

"The cashier girl, what kind of girl is she?" Kitty asked.

"Fat," I answered. "Zaftig, Uncle Harry calls her."

"Is Uncle Harry screwing her?" Kitty asked.

I looked at her. "You've got a dirty mind."

She laughed. "You still didn't answer my question."

"How would I know?" I said. "The only thing I know is that she goes up to his office at lunchtime to do the books. When I get to work she's always sitting in the cashier's chair."

"He's screwing her," Kitty said positively. "Does she keep the books in the betting department?"

"How the hell do I know?" I said, annoyed with her prying. "My job is working at the counter, serving two cents plains and egg creams and Cokes in small glasses. Then I sell cigarettes, cigars, and candy bars. But I heard from Buddy, this nigger guy thats worked for Harry for a long time, he runs the numbers for Harry. He said that my dad used to keep the accounts."

"You never told me that Harry was running numbers," she said.

"I didn't think about it," I said.

"Taking numbers is pretty good money. Why didn't you ask for a job doing that?" she questioned.

"It's a nigger's job. Buddy covers all the coloreds in the area and he told me that if I tried to do his job, I wouldn't live a minute," I said. "They don't like white people taking money from them. He said they'd never give me a dime, 'cause they'd be afraid they'd never see it again."

She was quiet for a minute. That was unusual.

"Why are you so nosy about Uncle Harry's business?"

"Maybe he needs a bookkeeper now that your father isn't there," Kitty said.

I couldn't even believe what she was saying. "You want to work for Uncle Harry?"

"I could use a little extra money." She laughed.

"Little is what you'd get," I said. "He pays the spicks thirty cents an hour for a fourteen-hour day. He's only giving me twelve bucks a week, and that's because I'm family and he knows that I wouldn't steal any money from the cashbox."

"Your Uncle Harry is a funny guy," she said as she looked off as though she were in a dreamworld. "You look at him and think that he is some kind of a poor slob. But that's not the truth at all. He's got a good booking operation and he runs numbers, too, and he also has the hottest corner in town for drinks and stuff. It just goes to show you, you can't judge a book by its cover."

"You sound like you like him," I said.

She shrugged. "He's like my father," she answered. "A real prick. I like to study people like that. They're interesting."

"You told me that you didn't like your father."

"I don't," she answered. "But sometimes I wish he wasn't my father. He has one hell of a cock. Even my mom said so."

"Is that all you ever think about? Cocks?" I said. "Sometimes you are really too much."

"Well, that's why I went after you." She laughed, reaching for my prick. "After all, if you want to be an important lady, you got to grab a man with big balls." She laughed.

8

Buddy was a tall, very light-skinned black man. He had strong, big shoulders and big hands. He always sat at the back of the counter while I ate my dinner that Aunt Lila sent me every evening. Tonight it was boiled chicken and matzo ball soup.

He stared over at me. "How can you eat that shit that she sends down here for you? I notice that she ain't giving Harry stuff like that."

"I don't know what they eat for dinner," I answered.

"They eat out at restaurants most of the time," he told me. "That's where Harry meets up with his connection. He settles up with them for the betting and the numbers."

"You mean it's not his book?" I asked.

"It's his book all right," he answered. "But he has to operate under the okay of the Mafia."

"You gotta be kidding. They're Italians," I said. "Harry is Jewish."

He waved his hand. "Don't mean nothin'." Buddy smiled. "He can't touch the numbers anywhere in this city unless he got the okay from the wops."

"I can't believe it," I said.

"You can believe it," Buddy said. "The Mafia controls the whole city."

"How'd you get to know so much, Buddy?" I asked.

"Niggers know street business," Buddy said. "I live up in Harlem and everybody there knows how it works and what's going on. But we mind our own business, and that's how we stay alive."

I finished my dinner and washed off the plate and the pot that Aunt

Lila had sent me. Then I walked over behind the counter and lit a cigarette. I was glad that Uncle Harry wasn't here because I never smoked in front of him. There wasn't much action tonight. Mario the spick was handling the business with no problems. He would give me the cash and I would give him back whatever change was needed.

I turned back to look at Buddy. He was still sitting at the back of the counter, where most of the customers couldn't see him. "When do you get your dinner?" I asked him.

"I eat before I come down to settle up the numbers with Harry," he said.

"Then why are you hanging around here?" I asked. "There's nothing happening down here at night."

"It's my job," he said.

"What job?" I asked, surprised. "There's no business for numbers now."

Buddy laughed. "I'm your bodyguard."

"What the hell for?" I asked. "Nobody ever bothers us down here."

"You never know." Buddy smiled. "Why do you think Harry is always carrying a gun? You just never know."

"I didn't know Harry carried a gun," I said.

"They hit on him a couple of times," Buddy said. "But he was smarter than they were. He's a tough man, your Uncle Harry."

"Yeah, but why would I need a bodyguard?" I asked. "I'm not carrying any money like Harry does."

"Nobody knows that," Buddy answered. "And you might be an easier hit."

"What can you do about it?" I asked him.

He took a small revolver from his pocket. "This helps a little," he said easily. "I also have my special slicer."

I stared down at his other hand. He had a straight razor encased in a white ivory holder. Quickly he moved the weapon, and the razor was now held against his fist. He smiled at me. "This is a special." He looked at it, admiring it. "No matter how many times someone might hit you. All you need is one shot. Hit him once, anywhere. It doesn't make any difference. It will cut through any part of him."

I watched him as he slipped the knife back into his shirt pocket. "Where did you learn how to use that?" I asked.

"Two years in reform school," he said. "That will teach you a lot of things besides readin' and writin'."

I didn't say anything for a moment; then I asked, "Can you teach me about handling a razor?"

"You planning on cutting somebody?"

"No," I said. "I just want to learn."

"Your only day off is on Sunday," Buddy said.

"It's okay with me," I said. "You can come to my place."

9

During the day the corner counter store was always jumping. Hundreds of people were going in and out of the subway station, traveling to and from home to work. They all needed a drink, cigarettes, or a snack. We didn't serve real meals, only snacks. Uncle Harry had made a deal with the two restaurants on the street that he wouldn't even sell wax-paper-wrapped cold sandwiches. I found out that the real business was between seven and nine in the morning, when people were going to work, and between five and six in the evening, when they went home. Uncle Harry was always there during the rush hours. He would pace around and start counting the money as soon as the crowds let up. By seven in the evening Aunt Lila would pick him up in the car and he would go deposit the money at the night depository of the bank. She would also send me dinner when she came by to pick him up.

During the day there were usually five countermen. After Harry left there was only one counterman besides me. It always slowed down after seven in the evening. Mario, the late counterman, was a good workman. His main job was to clean the counter and all the syrup pumps and glasses. He never spoke very much. He didn't speak very good English; it was kind of a mixture between Spanish and English. So most of the time I would just shoot the breeze with Buddy, because the only thing he had to do was sit there and watch me. It was Buddy who taught me more than anyone. It was Buddy who told me my uncle had a girlfriend set up in an apartment in one of the houses in the next block.

I was shocked when I heard this. I really couldn't believe that Uncle Harry was that interested in women. He never said anything to me about other women. "What kind of a lady is she?" I asked, curiously.

Buddy smiled, his big-face smile. "She's somethin' else."

"What do you mean?" I said.

"She dances up at Small's Cabaret at night," he answered. "She's got real talent and everybody that goes there likes her. She wants to be a big singer someday and your Uncle Harry pays for her singing lessons."

"Small's Cabaret, isn't that up in Harlem?" I said.

Buddy nodded his head.

"I thought only coloreds entertained there."

"She's a chorus girl," Buddy said. "She's really cute."

"But I thought only coloreds could work there," I said again.

"You're a stupid Jew schmuck." He laughed. "Harry likes black ass. The girl he used to take care of was black."

"Jesus," I exclaimed. "When does he have any time to see her? He works all day, and I know Aunt Lila doesn't let him out of her sight at night."

"Not all day," he said. "He takes a few hours off every afternoon. You know when he says he's going to go settle with the wop bankers. That only takes him about a half hour, then he scoots up to his girlfriend."

"I wonder if Aunt Lila knows about it?" I asked.

"No way," Buddy answered emphatically. "Harry's real smart about his business, private and public. Nobody can get anything on him. Even the cops leave his book and numbers alone. He pays off everybody."

"Then how come you know all about his business?" I asked.

"We niggers hang together," he said. "A pimp I know up on St. Nicholas Avenue told me the whole story about Harry. He told me to look after the girl, too."

"She's a whore?" I asked.

"She's straight," he answered. "But the pimp told me that she was his sister and he wants her to be a big star someday. He wants her to be like Billie Holiday or Lena Horne—they got big at the Cotton Club. He said Harry can help her be a star."

Before I could ask any more questions the counter started getting busy. I went over to help Mario out. Even Buddy had to step in and help us out because we couldn't handle the rush. I looked at my watch. It was almost eight o'clock. We never had been this busy. "What's going on tonight?" I asked one of the girls sitting at the counter drinking a Coke.

"Overtime," she said. "We're making army coats. The boss just got a big rush order from the government and he had to put us all on overtime until the end of the month."

"What time do you start in the morning?" I asked her.

"Six," she said, and rolled her eyes.

"That's rough," I said.

"Once I get up I'm okay," she said. "I can use the extra money. I have two kids to take care of."

"What about your husband?" I asked.

She stared at me. "He's been gone a long time. Disappeared. No hubby, no money." She threw down a dime on the counter.

I gave it back to her. "This is a treat on me."

She looked at me. "What time do you get off?" she asked.

"Nine o'clock," I said.

"Damn," she said. "That's late. I live in Brooklyn. I have to take the subway and bus to get home. It takes over an hour."

"That has to be a drag."

"It sure is," she said. "Maybe you'd like to come to Brooklyn some time. It's nice there. I live near Prospect Park."

"That's nice of you to ask," I said. "But I'm stuck here trying to study for my finals when I'm not at work. I'll be graduating from high school this year."

She stared at me. "How old are you?"

"I'll be eighteen in January," I said.

"You look a lot older," she said. "In fact, you look real good. I would have never guessed that you weren't twenty."

"Thank you," I said.

She turned to go over to the subway entrance, then looked back at me. "I'll see you," she said, and waved at me.

"Check," I said, and started wiping the counter.

Buddy was standing next to me. "She got the hots for you," he said.

"That's cuckoo. She doesn't even know me," I said.

"Maybe she don't know, but her pussy do." Buddy laughed. "I know those Polack girls that work at the factory. They all like to fuck like minks."

"How do you know?" I said. "Polacks are just like everybody else."

"That's right." Buddy smiled. "And everybody's got to have a national pastime. And they ain't got baseball. Gettin' laid is their national pastime!"

10

The next day when I got to work, I put on my apron and went straight to the counter and began to make two egg creams for a couple of hackies waiting there. I picked up the single that they gave to me and then took it over to Fat Rita at the cashier's chair. "Two creams," I told her.

She pushed ninety cents back to me and I looked at her. Her eyes were swollen and her mascara had been running down her cheeks. I gave the change to the customers and then I went back over to her. "What's going on, Rita?" I asked.

"Your fucking uncle is a prick," she said.

"What did he do?" I asked.

"I'm fed up with him. Not only did he screw you out of money that he owed to your father from bets that he had already turned in before he died, but now he is trying to screw my brother out of his business. I tell Harry every day that my brother will pay him the money that he owes as soon as business picks up for him. Things are very slow right now," she said, sniffing, crying, and collecting cash from the Puerto Ricans all at the same time.

"Why does your brother owe Uncle Harry money?" I asked.

"My brother is a jerk," she said. "He owes a grand for bets he made. Bad bets. I even told Harry I would pay off the markers at ten dollars a week. But Harry said no, the bankers want the money right now."

"Gee, Rita, what are you going to do?"

"My salary is only twenty-two dollars a week and I just can't give any more to Harry," she said. "Harry said that my brother will have to give his business up; if he doesn't he said that the bankers would take care of him." She sniffled some more. "Harry said he didn't want to see my brother thrown in the street and offered to pay him thirty a week and he can work for Harry."

"Is your brother's business any good?" I asked.

"Fair. Eddie was just managing to make a living until he got stupid and began playing the horses," she said, and pulled out another handkerchief.

"What kind of business is it?" I asked.

"Seltzer water," she answered. "He has a small truck. He bought his own bottles and then he filled them with seltzer. He has a good name for it, Coney Island Seltzer. He was just beginning to get new customers. He delivered the bottles of seltzer to the customers' apartments."

"I don't know what Harry could do with that kind of business," I said.

"I'm sorry, but your uncle is a pig. He grabs everything in sight, whether he needs it or not," she said.

"You're not going to quit?" I asked her.

"I'm not that crazy," she said. "It's not a bad job and I need the money."

That Sunday after I had talked to Fat Rita, I figured out that Uncle Harry not only kept a nigger girl, but he was also ripping off Fat Rita's brother out of his business. I kept staring at my homework trying to concentrate. But I couldn't think about anything but what a prick Uncle Harry was. I already knew he was ripping me off. But he and Aunt Lila were my only close family now. I had no choice. But the rest of it was too much.

I remember when my parents were alive I could never understand why my father was working with Harry even if he was his brother-in-law. Aunt Lila had to know what was going on. After all, she had lived with him for over twenty-three years.

I lit a cigarette and opened the Frigidaire to take out a Pepsi when the doorbell rang. I opened the door. It was Buddy. He smiled at me. "I got you a present," he said.

I let him in. "What the hell are you talking about?" I said.

"Can I get a Pepsi first?" he asked.

I handed him the bottle that I was holding in my hand and walked back over to the kitchenette to take out another one. "Okay," I said when I returned. "What's the big surprise?"

He took a swig out of the Pepsi bottle. He then pulled a small rectangular box out of his pocket. He put it on the table in front of me. "Open it," he said.

I looked at him and then at the small box in front of me. I had to cut the box open with my fingernail and then I opened it. I stared down at the straight razor with a beautiful white ivory holder. I swished the razor open as I had seen Buddy do; the light from the window shone off the stainless steel blade. The blade felt cold as I held it in my fist. "You're crazy!" I said. "You had no business blowing so much money on this beautiful knife for me," I said.

He was still smiling, like a kid. "You didn't even say thank you to me."

"Thank you. I just can't believe it," I said as I looked at the knife. "But I still think you're crazy. This had to cost a lot of money."

"I'm not crazy," he said. "I need your help."

"You got it," I said. "Tell me."

"My friends up in Harlem don't take much to Harry runnin' a numbers business. They say that running numbers is a black business no matter where it happens to be in the city. It won't sit anymore for your Uncle Harry to pay off the wops."

I looked at him. "What could I do about it? I just work for him."

"You're his nephew. He'll listen to you if you tell him that the Harlem bankers are going to step on him," he said.

I looked at him. "He'll know that the only person I could get this information from is you," I said. "He'll fire you."

"Don't matter," he said. "I won't be there anymore. And without me there won't be any numbers business."

I shook my head. "If it looks like trouble, he'll run right to the wops."

"It won't do him any good. The wops and niggers already made their deal," he said. "But if he okays the deal, I can still work out of his store and he'll get a piece of the action. That's better than getting himself killed."

"You're kidding . . . killed," I said. "It's not that much money is it?"

"That's not the point," Buddy said. "It's the principle of it all. It's about turf."

I thought about it for a few moments. It really didn't matter whether I liked Uncle Harry or not, he was still *mishpuchah*. I looked up at Buddy. "Okay, I'll talk to him. But there's no guarantee. He might just throw me out just as easily."

"Harry's not stupid," Buddy said. "After he finishes screaming and hollering, he'll see what's happening and he'll okay the deal."

"This is my family, Buddy, like it or not. I'm taking a big chance," I said.

Buddy looked at me like I was full of it. "There's something in it for you. I took care of you and got the okay to give you a grand to give to Fat Rita's brother as an investment. You'll have paper on it." He laughed as he said it. A big, down-deep laugh. "That'll really screw Uncle Harry. He never had any paper from Eddie, and he's lost all of it."

I stared solemnly at Buddy. "I hope it all works out."

"It will work out," Buddy said confidently. "Don't you see, it would only take a minute to go to Harry's wife and tell her the whole story about Harry's brown girlfriend."

"I wouldn't want Aunt Lila to get hurt like that," I said.

"Just do your job and nothing will happen." Buddy smiled. But his smile was cold.

"Buddy, you're a shit," I said.

"It's just a living, son," he said. "Now, come on, let me show you how to use that blade."

11

It went just like Buddy said. Uncle Harry's face was beet red and he was screaming and yelling and pounding on his desk until the glass on the desktop was broken. He looked down at it. "See what you made me do!" he yelled. "This piece of glass cost me fourteen dollars."

I looked at him and began to laugh.

He stared at me. "What's so funny, Mr. Wise Guy? Haven't you caused me enough trouble already?" he said. "If only your father was here! You wouldn't be laughing."

For the first time in my life I didn't call him "Uncle." "Harry," I said. "Don't be a fool. The wops aren't going to start a gang war for you. You're just small potatoes. Besides, they've already made the deal with the niggers."

Harry's eyes began to bulge out of his sockets. "I'll kill that little bastard Buddy. He's the one that screwed me!" he yelled. "He's out. He ain't going to operate out of this store."

"That's not going to bother him. He can call in his numbers from any phone booth. If you give the okay, they have already agreed to give you a piece of the action," I said.

"I'm not going to forget this," he said. "Someday I'll break his ass."

"If you try," I said, "he'll send your girlfriend up to Aunt Lila. Then you are really in the shithouse."

This was the final blow. He sat down in his chair out of breath. He shook his head, as if he couldn't believe what he had just heard. After a few moments he looked at me again. "You know that, too?" he said almost in a whisper.

I nodded.

"Are you going to tell your Aunt Lila?" he asked.

"No," I said. "That's none of my business."

"I'm just human," he said. "Even your father had problems."

I cut him short. I didn't want to know. "That's none of my business, either," I said. "My father is dead."

"Are you fucking Kitty?" he asked.

"Whether I do or not is none of your business," I answered. "Just as I have told you. Fucking is your own business."

He sat silent for a moment. "Were you fucking Fat Rita?"

"Uncle Harry, are you deaf? Did you hear what I just said?" I asked incredulously.

"Then the nigger must be fucking her," he raced on. "Why else would he arrange for you to get a grand to pay Eddie. That's how much Eddie owes me."

"Because Eddie told Buddy and me that my father gave him two grand to start his seltzer business. Buddy said that I deserved a partnership in his business," I said.

"I would have given you a partnership in his business if I had gotten it," Harry said.

"Would you, Harry?" I said. "You were trying to take over Eddie's business for just the thousand that he owed you. You never even told me that my father gave Eddie any money."

"I forgot it. I would have told you about it when I got the seltzer business," he lied.

I shrugged. "It's all over now. We can all go back to work."

"Good," Harry said, resigned to the situation. "Will Fat Rita be okay now? Is she coming back to work?"

"Yes," I said. "She's happy now."

"I'll give her a two-dollar a week raise," he said. "And what about Buddy, is he going to work until you close?"

"He told me that he would," I answered.

Harry sat there quietly for a moment. Then he looked down at the broken glass on his desk. "I'll have to get the glass top done."

I didn't speak.

"It'll cost fifteen dollars," he said.

I still didn't speak.

He looked up at me. "How do you know that Eddie will be fair with you in business?" he asked. "I know about gamblers. They never stop. No matter what he told you, he won't stop. Sooner or later he's going to be in the same mess again and he'll be shoveling your money down the sewer. There are plenty of bookies who will take your money."

"He's not going to hold the money," I said. "Fat Rita will take it and put it in the bank for him. I've asked Kitty to check on the accounts and I will get my share each month. Fat Rita will keep his."

Uncle Harry looked at me appraisingly. "How did you get to be so smart?" he asked.

"I wasn't so smart," I said. "I learned from you."

12

Sunday was the only day the store was closed. So this was the first day I had a chance to go to Brooklyn and have a look at Eddie's garage where he kept his truck and machinery that filled the seltzer bottles. I wanted Kitty to come with me, but she had a family affair at her mother's place. So I went alone.

I ran into Buddy on my way to the subway. I asked him to come with me, but he said that Sunday was a big day at church for him. He was an usher and took care of the collection plates for the reverend.

I started to laugh. "I never knew you were so religious."

He smiled. "Takin' care of those collection plates for the good Lord is important," he said. "The pastor gives me ten percent of the money that's collected."

"Is it big money?" I asked, curious.

"Not much," he said. "About ten dollars every Sunday. But the best part is that I get to know all the young girls, and their parents trust me 'cause I'm a man that works in the good Lord's service."

I shook my head. "You don't bother the girls?"

"Now, I didn't say that," he said, smiling. "Me and the pastor have an agreement. I don't chase his pussy if he don't chase mine." He laughed his loud, rumbling laugh and was on his way.

*   *   *

Eddie and Fat Rita were waiting for me at the subway station. Eddie seemed nervous. We walked to the garage, which was only a few blocks from the station. It was on a long street with nothing but one-story buildings. They looked like a lot of storage buildings and cheap manufacturing businesses, most of them producing sweatshop housedresses. We arrived at a building that had two doors that would open wide enough for a small truck to drive into.

Eddie had his small wooden sign over the top of the garage doors: EDDIE'S CONEY ISLAND SELTZER. Eddie looked very different than his sister Fat Rita. He was a tall, thin man, about six feet tall, but his arms were long, almost touching his knees. But his face was just like his sister's, round and with a dimpled chin. He seemed very proud of his business. He told me a hundred times how grateful he was to me for helping him out of this fix. I was surprised to learn that he was not married and that he lived with his sister. I also found out that he had worked for the man who owned the seltzer bottle place for almost ten years. About three years ago, the old man wanted to retire. He was tired of working the long hours and he thought that the soda pop business, with their cheap bottles that could be bought in grocery stores, would put him out of business eventually. The old man and his wife sold Eddie the business for five grand. That included the truck, the stock of seltzer bottles, and the machine that filled the bottles with seltzer and capped them. He and Fat Rita pooled their resources and bought the building as well as the business. And it was my father who gave them the two grand to buy all the supplies.

I stood in the garage and began to figure out how much everything in the business was worth. I wasn't very sure of the values of all the things, but one thing I did know was that Uncle Harry was really trying to steal Eddie blind for the thousand that he owed. Just my father's investment alone was worth more than the debt.

I turned to Rita. "About how much business does Eddie do a week?" I asked.

"The average is about fifty dollars a day plus the deposits on the bottles, which is about a dollar fifty. We never have to return the deposits, because people just turn in their empties and Eddie gives them full bottles. Once they make their deposits Eddie has their business forever. The old *Yiddelach* like their fifty cents for a quart seltzer." She smiled. "Eddie does real well. He makes twenty-five dollars a day and he is picking up more customers every week. He works six days a week. He takes off Saturdays because the Jews wouldn't like it if he worked on the Sabbath. He makes one hundred and fifty dollars a week. After expenses, truck servicing, gasoline, electricity for the place, and special materials for filtering the water and salts to make the seltzer, plus sterilizing the empty bottles leaves him one hundred dollars a week."

"Do you keep all the accounts?" I asked.

"Now I do," she said. "Eddie will give me all of the receipts at the end of the day, and I'll deposit it in the bank the next morning."

"And what do I get out of it?" I asked.

"We figured that ten percent would be fair," she said.

"That's not much," I said. "At that rate it will take three years to get the money back that my father invested."

"Then how much do you think would be fair?" she asked.

"I don't know," I said. "I've asked my friend Kitty to take a look at the books. She's graduating as a CPA. Why don't we wait until the end of the month. Then she'll figure out something that will work for everybody. But I know that ten dollars a week is a joke."

Fat Rita's eyes narrowed. "If it weren't for me you would never have even known that your father put money into this business."

"I saved Eddie's business before Harry grabbed it," I said. "After all, would Harry even keep Eddie working for him if he had taken over? And if he did, he'd only pay him twenty-five dollars a week at the most. And Buddy told me that he was going to hire a black man to take over Eddie's job and pay only fifteen a week."

"They wouldn't be able to run the business," Eddie said.

"Then Harry would sell it. He'd be able to get at least five grand for all the machinery, bottles, garage, and truck," I answered. "Harry is not a schmuck. He always has everything figured out. Don't forget he was going to get the whole business for only a grand."

They were silent.

"How much did the old owner pay you a week?" I asked.

"Twenty-five bucks, but I didn't have to do all of the work. He did fifty percent of the work preparing the bottles and seltzer. I made the deliveries and pickups, and sold to new customers," he answered. "Now I'm doing everything inside and out. And don't forget, I put three thousand dollars of my own along with what your father put in. I also put a lot of money fixing things up. The old man had let a lot of things wear down."

"Do you have receipts?" I asked.

"No, I just did it," he answered.

"I understand you've put a lot of work into this, but I just don't think ten dollars a week is enough. But let's wait and let Kitty try to work it out for us. We'll find a fair agreement."

"Isn't Rita entitled to something for the work that she's doing?" Eddie asked.

"Rita is entitled to a salary, too. Maybe it would be better if we just worked out a payment plan and you give me interest on the two thousand that you owe me. Then I'll be out of the business and you'll own the whole company."

Eddie turned to his sister, and then he looked at me. "The only problem is, some weeks I sell less than I expect. Then I might not be able to pay what I owe you for the week."

I decided that we were going around in circles. "Let's not worry about it right now. Just keep working and doing what you're doing, and we'll figure the right way for everybody. Once Kitty goes over the books we'll know more."

"You're not trying to take this business away from him?" Fat Rita said, crying.

"Don't be silly," I said, trying to comfort her. "What the hell would I want with his business? I don't know a damn thing about it. All I want is to get the money that's due me and then we'll all go our own ways."

"And what about the thousand that Buddy arranged for us?" she asked.

"I've got nothing to do with that. That's between you two and Buddy. But I know one thing—he won't break your back. He knows how tough it is. He'll work with you." I smiled at them. "Just relax. Everything will work out if Eddie takes care of business and stays away from the horses."

"I'm out of that," Eddie said.

"Good," I said. "Now, how about having a bottle of Eddie's Coney Island Seltzer. I'll treat," I said, reaching in my pocket and handing Eddie some cash.

13

I was listening to *The Eddie Cantor Hour* on the radio when Kitty came in. She had her own key to my apartment now, so I didn't even realize she was in the room until I heard her voice. "What are you doing in bed this early?" she asked.

"Trying to sleep," I answered. "After I got back from seeing Eddie and Rita at the Coney Island Seltzer factory I was tired." I shrugged and stopped for a moment. "I guess I'm worried," I said. "I don't know if I did the right thing or not."

She looked at me. "What did you arrange with them?" she asked.

"I told him that I didn't want any part of their business. All I want is the money my father invested and I'll be satisfied," I answered.

She laughed. "You're not a very tough businessman. Your Uncle Harry would have taken the shirt off their back as well as the business."

I looked at her. "I'm not my Uncle Harry. And maybe I'm not a businessman, but I wouldn't feel good if I ruined them. I told them that you would meet with them later and work out a decent deal for all of us."

"That's work," she said. "What do I get out of it?"

I laughed. "How about seven inches?"

"That's no money," she snapped.

I opened my fly and took out my cock. It was already hard. I waved it at her. "Isn't this better than money?"

She laughed and fell down on the bed. She put her hand firmly around my cock. Slowly she began to massage it. "Too bad, we can't fuck," she said tauntingly.

"Why not?" I asked.

"I've got the curse," she answered.

"So what's the big deal?" I asked. "You can still suck me off."

"Oh yeah, but what's in it for me?" she said.

"Don't act like you don't enjoy it," I said.

"All I get is a mouthful of salty cum, if that's all we do," she said.

"What do you mean if that's all we do—you said you had the curse."

"You can fuck me in the ass," she said.

"You gotta be kiddin'," I said. "I don't want to hurt you. I've heard it's painful for a girl."

"It won't hurt," she said confidently, starting to take off her dress. "Just run down to the drugstore on the corner and get a jar of Vaseline."

"You're sure?" I asked.

"Do you want to fuck or don't you?" she asked sarcastically. "Yours is not the only cock in town."

14

Kitty was the greatest. It was the first time I really understood how much she meant to me. I would do anything for her now. When I licked her ass, I knew it was the sweetest ass in town.

We stretched out naked in the bed. I was sweating bullets and I pulled a towel to dry me up. I smiled at her. "I love ass-fucking. It's the first time I've ever done it. It's really great."

She looked at me. "Wash your prick," she said. "It's covered with Vaseline and it's messy. When you finish, we'll talk about what I get out of the seltzer business."

"How come you never told me about ass-fucking before?" I asked.

"It's not called 'ass-fucking,' " she said angrily. "It's sodomy. And that's a bigger sin than fucking. I can't even confess that to my priest."

"If it's that bad, why do you do it?"

"I'm crazy, I guess," she answered. "I'm horny all the time and I can do anything I want with you because you're Jewish and you don't have to go to confession."

"You mean you wouldn't do it with another Catholic?" I asked.

"Don't ask stupid questions," she said in an annoyed voice. "Clean up and let's talk about business."

I went to the bathroom and stepped into the tub and turned on the shower. A moment later she was in the shower with me. Before we were finished, I heard the doorbell ring. I looked at her. "Do you think that your father is looking for you?" I asked.

"My father's out of town," she answered. "It has to be someone for you."

I grabbed a towel and wrapped it around my waist. I left her in the bathroom while I went to the door. "Who's there?" I asked.

"Buddy, you asshole, open the door." His voice sounded urgent through the door. "I'm in trouble, let me in."

I opened the door. Buddy was standing there, still in his Sunday clothes from that morning. There were also two pretty black girls in their Sunday clothes standing beside him. I let them in and closed the door. "I have some Pepsis in the fridge," I said. "Give me and Kitty a minute to get some clothes on."

By the time we were dressed, Buddy and his girlfriends were at the kitchen table smoking and drinking up all of my Pepsis. Buddy had already met Kitty from the time she had stopped over at the counter when I was working.

He introduced the girls that were with him, Diana and Arletta. They were daughters of the reverend at his church. "I've got a big problem," Buddy explained. "The reverend told me to take his girls home, and instead I took them over to my place. We smoked a little ganch and it got a little wild and we all screwed."

I stared at him. "You screwed both of them?" I asked.

The girls giggled. "Why not?" he asked. "They both wanted it. Don't forget, they're sisters and they are used to sharing."

"Oh, brother," I said. "So why don't you just take them home? There shouldn't be any problem."

"I can't do that," he said. "He'll kill me. He told me to take them home at noon." He looked at his watch. "It's now eight o'clock. He'll know I was out with them all day."

"So what do you want me to do?" I asked.

"I thought maybe you could take them home."

"You're out of your fucking mind," I said. "What will keep him from killing me?"

"You're a white boy," he said. "The reverend won't kill a white boy. He'll figure that you're straight."

"No way," I said.

"Jesus," he said. "I'm really in trouble now. Man, you got to do this one thing for me. I'm too young to die."

Kitty began laughing.

"What's so funny?" I snapped.

"Maybe I can help the girls out," she said.

"How?" Buddy asked.

Kitty turned to the girls. "You both go to school?"

Arletta nodded. "We both go to George Washington High School. I'm graduating this year, and Diana will graduate next year."

"Good," Kitty said. "I can tell the reverend that I had told them they would have a very good chance to get into Hunter College, and that I asked them to come for a school enrollment seminar."

"That's brilliant." Buddy's smile reached clear across his face. "I'll get the cab fare for you."

"How much is cab fare?" Kitty asked quietly.

"About ten dollars up and back," he said.

She smiled. "That's for cab fare. My service is worth fifty bucks."

"You're out of your mind," Buddy said.

"It's cheaper than getting yourself killed," Kitty answered.

Buddy shook his head. "That's a lot of money."

"I know what you do," Kitty said. "You make a lot of money."

"Okay," Buddy said. "I quit. You'll get your money."

Kitty held out her hand very politely. "Now."

Buddy looked at me. "Your girlfriend's really a ball breaker." He took out a roll of bills from his pocket and peeled out the fifty and one tenner.

15

Buddy sat down at the kitchen table again after the girls had left. He looked down and sighed. I took one of his cigarettes from the Lucky Strikes package. I dragged the smoke into my lungs. They tasted better than the Twenty Grands I smoked. I looked over at Buddy again. He still had his head.

"You gotta be tired after all that fucking," I said, and laughed.

"Nah, not really," he said.

"If you're worried about the girls, Kitty will work it all out. She's very smart," I said.

"For fifty bucks, she better be smart," Buddy said, and leaned back in his chair. "I'm gonna have to get another job."

"What do you mean? I thought everything was fine now," I said.

"It is, but I have another problem. I've got to get something that will keep me out of the draft," he said.

"What are you worried about? They're not after you, are they?" I asked.

"I'm twenty years old and I've been one-A for over a year now," he said. "They're cleaning up in my neighborhood. The local draft board is pulling in us niggers like flies."

"So what? There's no war and I think it's going to be a long way off, if ever."

"Maybe," he said. "Sooner or later, either way, it ain't good for me. Twenty-one dollars a month won't even keep me in cigarettes." He stood up and looked down at me. "I'm going to quit the job over at Harry's."

"Wait a minute," I said, shocked. "Do the guys know that you're leaving the numbers route?"

"They okayed it already," he said. "They've got me a job over at the Brooklyn Navy Yard. I'll have a numbers route over there."

"Harry will go off the wall. He won't have anybody to stay with me till closing time."

"Fuck him," Buddy said. "Let him give you some more money. Kid, you can handle the whole thing yourself. You've got no problem, I showed you how to use the blade."

I looked at him. I was eighteen and I had just got my notice to show up at the draft board. I was sure that I would be 1-A. I was healthy and I didn't have a family to support. "Maybe I should start looking for a defense job myself," I said.

"Maybe," he said. "They goin' to get all of us. And it ain't going to be easy for niggers and kikes. None of the services like us."

I took a deep breath. "I'm not going to worry about it now. I'm okay." I opened up another Pepsi. "What the hell! Christmas is coming in a couple of weeks and everything will be peaceful and merry."

I never realized I'd be so wrong, so fast. Later, after Kitty had come back and we were in bed together going at it pretty good, an announcer cut into the regular music on the radio and announced that the Japanese had bombed Pearl Harbor that morning and the war was on.

I looked down at Kitty. Suddenly there were tears in her eyes. And I had lost my hard-on. We both knew our lives would never be the same.

16

Everything was screwed up by the time I got to work the next afternoon. It was a madhouse. For the first time I saw Uncle Harry himself working at the counter, because only one of the spicks showed up to work. The others had taken off. There was no way they were going to take any chances of being picked up by the draft board. Most of them were over draft age and had never showed up at the draft board to pick up their card.

Harry screamed at me. "You're late! You knew I needed your help today!"

"I came down after school as usual, Uncle Harry," I said, tying an apron around me.

"Where the hell is Buddy?" he yelled. "He's usually here by this time."

"I don't know," I answered. "Maybe he went to enlist."

"Not that boy," he said. "I heard a week ago that he was going to get a defense job."

"Where'd you get that?" I asked, while selling a taxi driver a pack of cigarettes.

"I have connections," he said smugly.

I looked at him. I knew his connection. His little black girlfriend. I turned to Fat Rita behind the register. "What's with Eddie?" I asked. "How is he with the draft?"

"He's okay," she answered. "The draft board gave him four-F because his right leg is crooked and shorter than his other."

Harry looked at me. "What's the status with you?"

"I don't know," I said. "I'll graduate at the end of the next month, and I know I'll have to report to the draft board as soon as I graduate. I figure I'll be one-A for sure."

"I remember once that your father told me when you were a kid you had asthma," he said. "Maybe that will keep you out."

"I'm not sure of that," I answered. "I never heard anything about it."

"Maybe we can talk to your draft board." He looked at me. "A little chicken schmaltz might grease the wheels a little."

I laughed. "Uncle Harry, they don't even know chicken schmaltz in my draft board. The district is all goyim."

Harry looked at me. "Money is money. It talks in any language."

I shrugged.

"Can you handle the counter with José and yourself?" Harry asked. "I have to run over to the Puerto Rican employment agency and get us some new help."

"We can manage for now," I said. "But I don't know if we can handle the six o'clock rush hour when all the factories are out."

Fat Rita called down from the cash register. "You get in trouble, I can help out."

"I won't be too long," Harry said. I watched him go up to his office. I didn't see him after that. He always left by the back door that was downstairs from his office.

Things quieted down after Harry left. I looked over at Fat Rita. "Has it been busy all day?" I asked.

She nodded. "Everyone is talking about the war. Everyone was shocked by the news."

"Same for me," I said. "That's all we talked about at school."

She paused for a moment. "Has Harry ever said anything about letting me go?" she asked.

"I've never heard anything," I said. "Why should he? He just gave you a raise."

She looked at me. "He's been talking to your girlfriend," she said. "I know that she is graduating with a CPA certificate this month. I thought he might have said something about her taking over the books that I do. After all, I'm not a CPA."

"She's never mentioned anything to me about it," I said. "And I'm sure she would have said something. Besides, he wouldn't be willing to pay CPA prices."

"I was just curious," she said. "She's been up to his office every morning this week. She always comes in about eleven o'clock."

I knew that Kitty had said that she could do Uncle Harry's taxes. But she hadn't told me that she was talking with Uncle Harry about it. I thought for a moment as I took care of the customers at the counter. I turned back to Fat Rita. "I'm sure that you don't have anything to worry about. You know everything about his business." Then I heard Buddy call back from the end of the counter.

"Gimme a Pepsi and a pack of Luckys," he called.

I brought them over to him. "When did you come in? What's going on with you?"

He opened the pack of cigarettes, took one out, and lit up. He took a deep drag and a swig of Pepsi. "I've been fucked!"

I stared at him. He looked down. I had never seen him upset like this. "What happened?"

"The boss at the navy yard told me since the war had already begun he could not put any new people on."

"That seems crazy. With the war on wouldn't they need more people than ever?" I said.

"Right," he said. "But they don't want niggers."

"You check that out with your friends?" I asked.

"That's the first thing I did," he answered. "But they had an answer. The wops control all of Brooklyn's shipping yards, including the navy yards."

"Now what are you going to do?" I asked.

He shrugged his shoulders. "I don't know yet. Maybe I'll blow town. I've got no family keeping me here."

"They'll track you down because of your draft card," I said.

"Not if I go to another town and change my name." He smiled.

"You'll still need a draft card, won't you?" I said.

"Yeah, but that's easy," he said. "I can get any card anytime I want. Another draft card, even another driver's license."

"I don't know," I said. "There's always some way that they can catch up with you."

"Yeah," Buddy said as he nervously tapped his fingers on the counter. "I guess I'll just have to figure out another angle."

It was four-thirty now and the taxi drivers were starting on the new shift. There were two taxi garages down the block from us and we always got busy selling cigarettes and candy bars. A number of them asked for

Harry, but I told them he would be out for a while; they said that they would come back later to see him.

Fifteen minutes later the counter was empty. "Boy," I said. "Things really died down."

"Word travels fast if Harry's not here to take bets from the cabbies," Buddy said.

"It's not like Harry to miss this time of the day. These are his big bettors."

The six o'clock rush hour started and Harry had not returned. Buddy and Fat Rita and José all helped me when we got busy.

Fat Rita looked at her watch. "It's almost seven," she said. "This is my quitting time. I don't know what to do. If I don't go now I'll miss my ride. And I'll be too late to get dinner for the family."

"It's your time," I said. "Go on home."

"What should I do with the cash in the register?" she asked. "Harry always takes part of it to the night deposit at the bank."

"I'll keep everything here," I said. "It'll still be here when he gets back."

I watched her waddle over to the subway entrance and go down the stairs. I turned to Buddy. "Where do you think he's gone?"

Buddy laughed. "He hates Hitler. Maybe he enlisted."

I laughed. "Not Harry. He may be Jewish but he ain't that crazy." I went to the register and opened it. "A hundred and forty bucks," I said.

"There has to be more than that," Buddy insisted. "Press the lever on the side of the cash drawer. It'll slip out."

I did what he told me. He was right. The cash drawer came out. There was nothing but bills there. Quickly, I figured how much. Over a thousand dollars. I slid the cash drawer back into the register. "He's crazy to keep all that cash here."

"He's a bookie," Buddy said. "He uses that money to pay off bets."

It was almost nine o'clock and a light snow was just beginning. I started closing the glass shutters. Buddy and José were helping me. I was still trying to decide whether I should take the money with me when we closed up. I saw Aunt Lila pull up in their car in front of the store.

She got out and came over to me. "Where's Harry?"

I leaned over and gave her a kiss on the cheek. "He went to the agency to get some new Puerto Rican help, because nobody but José showed up for work today. He's not back yet," I said.

A taxi pulled up behind their car at that moment. "Here I am," Harry called out hurriedly as he got out of the cab.

17

Now that the war was on, everything was changing. More than ever women were taking over jobs that men used to do. Here, at the counter, Uncle Harry hired young Puerto Rican girls instead of the boys he used to hire. Buddy said that Harry got the better of the bargain. Not only did he pay the girls less than the boys, he was always able to talk one or two of them into giving him a fuck. They didn't complain. They needed the job. The only other opportunity they would have was to work as cleaning women. That paid even less than Harry paid, and they could only work a day or two a week. At least this was steady work.

Graduation day for me was on the twentieth of January. When I woke up that morning, Aunt Lila had a big special breakfast prepared for me. I had made a 3.0 grade average. It wasn't great, but it was better than flunking out.

Aunt Lila and Kitty were coming to the school for the graduation exercises. Harry had to keep the store open; as he said, without him "nothing would work."

Aunt Lila gave me a nice Arrow shirt and Kitty gave me a bulky sweater. She said that would keep me warm, since it was cold at the counter at night now when the windows were open.

After I got my diploma, Aunt Lila dropped Kitty and me back at the apartment house. She told us that she was going to go by and pick Harry up a little early and surprise him. She said she had gotten Harry an Arrow shirt, too, and she wanted to give it to him.

I looked at Kitty and she looked at me. We both had the same thought. I ran into the apartment and called the counter. Fat Rita answered at the register.

"Where's Harry?" I asked.

"Upstairs," she said. I could hear her gum clicking against her teeth. "He's got one of the spick girls with him."

"Get upstairs and tell him that Aunt Lila's on her way down there," I said.

"I can't do that," she said fearfully. "He'd kill me if I went up there."

"It'll be worse if you don't call him," I said. "There goes your job."

"I don't care," she said, starting to cry. "I'm afraid. You know his temper."

"You call him," I said firmly. "He won't be angry. He'll thank you for it. Believe me."

She hesitated a moment. "Stay on the phone," she said. "Don't hang up. I'll go up and knock on the door."

I held on for almost two minutes. She came back on the phone. "Everything's okay," she said.

"Thanks, Rita," I said, and hung up the phone.

I turned to Kitty. "She got him."

"Good," she said, and pulled an envelope out of her purse and held it in her hand. "This came for you this morning in the mail just before I went to your graduation."

I looked down at it. An official draft board envelope. I opened it and took out the note. They didn't lose any time. I was ordered to take the draft card and go directly to Grand Central and take my physical.

I handed the letter to Kitty. She glanced at it quickly and then looked up at me. "You were expecting it."

"Yeah," I said. "But not so soon. I haven't even had enough time to decide what I want to do."

"If you're one-A," she said, "you have no choice, anyway. They just send you to the army or navy. But if you're lucky and get four-F, then you stay here and get yourself a real job, not a crummy one like at Harry's."

"What kind of job?" I asked. "They don't train you for anything at high school."

"There's a lot of jobs," she said. "Just read the classifieds in the newspaper. All the good jobs are for the men that are left here. Maybe you don't realize it, but men are a real property—in demand."

"Maybe I can get a job fucking some rich society dame," I said kiddingly.

"You can't even handle what you've got," she said laughing, going along with the fun. She reached for my fly. "You have just enough to keep me satisfied."

We got out of our clothes and rolled onto the bed. I really liked Kitty; she made everything fun. I hoped I made her happy, too. Now that I had graduated we'd have a lot of time to do things together. That's what I thought, but we never had a chance. By the middle of March I was in the army.

BOOK TWO

PART ONE

ONE FRANC A LITER

1

France—1914

Jean Pierre heard his father and grandfather screaming at each other from behind the heavy, ornate library doors. He pressed his ear closer to the door, but then Armand, the heavy butler, pulled him abruptly away from the door by the collar and dragged him upstairs to his bedroom. He pushed him inside the room and slapped him twice on the face. "You never eavesdrop when your elders are speaking!" he snapped.

"But they were talking about a war!" Jean Pierre said. "I love wars."

"You're still young. You don't know anything about wars," Armand said. "Now you wait up here until you are called downstairs."

Jean Pierre watched as the butler closed the door behind him. He muttered at the butler under his breath. "Son of a bitch! I know why he has a job in this house. He sucks my grandfather's cock and lets my father fuck him in the ass." Still muttering under his breath, he walked to the window that overlooked the beautiful flower garden in the front of the villa. He continued wondering what they were talking about.

"Papa!" Jacques said. "Why are you so afraid? If we do have a war it will be over quickly. A matter of months."

Maurice looked at his son sadly. "Jacques, you're stupid. There is never a war that is over in just a few months. I remember when the French were fighting the Prussians when I was only twelve years old. Your grandfather took me and ten men with four wagons in the middle of the night to bring water into Paris because the Prussians had cut off the water supply. The French are never prepared, even then, as well as now."

"So what?" Jacques replied. "That's how we became rich and started a whole new business."

"You don't understand, Jacques," his father said. "Those were different days. Now Briand, our premier, is an egoist. I have to believe that he had Jaurès, the pacifist, murdered so that he could get us into the war. Don't deceive yourself, Jacques, the Prussians will beat the whole of Europe. We can't beat shit. Even our football teams can't win a game."

"But Briand is not in charge of the government; Poincaré is the president," Jacques answered.

"You must learn, Jacques, to read between the lines. He will become president within two years. Then all Europe will have to beg America to save us," Maurice stated.

Jacques looked at his father. "Perhaps we should ask his mother to let him live with her in Switzerland until this is over."

"You know the agreement we have made with her. Besides, I do not want my grandson in the company of that whore." He shook his head. "No, she would never agree to Jean Pierre living with her. She only agreed to bear the child, not to raise the child."

"The Rothschilds still have family in England. Maybe we should ask them to take Jean Pierre," Jacques suggested.

Maurice shook his head. "The only thing the Rothschilds are interested in is money."

"We have money, too," Jacques answered arrogantly. "Don't forget we own all the bottling plants for our water. That's more valuable than all of the Rothschilds' assets!"

"And don't forget that the Rothschilds are Jews," his father said.

Jacques also remembered that his father's name was Maurice, and he always felt uncomfortable because he thought it looked too Jewish. Maurice had tried to have his name changed to François, but his father, Jacques's grandfather, refused. He would not allow it because Maurice's wife's father was named François. He was a lowly drayman, who worked for Plescassier driving a wagon. The only reason there had been a marriage was because Maurice needed a strong lower-class girl who could breed a healthy son for him. The marriage was made because of the inheritance laws. Plescassier must always remain in the family. When Jacques married, he too married for the same reasons. His wife had given him two sons, Jean Pierre and Raymond. Jacques gave her and her family twenty thousand louis for a divorce. They parted amicably. His wife was not unhappy; at the time she married Jacques she knew he was homosexual, as his father and grandfather had been. She also knew that she could never be satisfied until she found a real man.

She agreed to relocate in Switzerland with twenty thousand louis for herself and five thousand louis for her family. She soon found many companions and opened a bar and café.

"No, not the Rothchilds," Maurice boomed, his voice echoing in the high ceilings of the room. "We will send him to Quebec, where I have distant cousins," Maurice said. "With a little money, they will care for him."

"But what about Raymond?" Jacques asked. "The boy is only three years old."

"There is no problem with Raymond," Maurice said coldly. "The boy is physically and mentally retarded. You know what Dr. Meyer said. The best thing we could do for him is to place him in a nursing facility that cares for children of his kind."

"But, Papa," Jacques pleaded. "He is our family. We can't desert him like that."

"Again you don't remember what Dr. Meyer and all the other specialists said. He will not live more than nine or ten years at the most. The kindest thing we can do is give him the best care available."

Jacques sat quietly. He felt small in the big chair. Tears filled his eyes. "He's still just a baby," he said. "Only God can know his future. A miracle could happen and he could be healed."

"There's always hope, Jacques. If a miracle occurs, the nurses can help and he can come home to us," Maurice said. "The child is a problem for us. We cannot show him in society—they would insult us behind our backs. Our business would slowly go down. I know these bastards. They can be cruel."

"But Jean Pierre loves his little brother," Jacques said.

"Jean Pierre will be going to Canada until the end of the war. He will be told that Raymond is too small to send away. By the time Jean Pierre comes home he will have completely forgotten about him."

Jacques looked up at his father. "*Vous êtes vraiment dur,* Papa," he said.

2

It was not the *Queen Mary* or the *Normandie*, but it was a large and comfortable ship, even if it was Irish. Its name was the *Molly Machree* out of Dublin. Jean Pierre sighed and looked up at Armand as he leaned on the railing. "Why didn't Papa book us on one of the big French boats?"

"The war," Armand said. "The Germans and the French are at war. But Germany is not at war with the Irish Republic. So our ship is safe to cross the Atlantic."

"But we're going to Quebec," Jean Pierre said. "That's part of France, isn't it?"

"Not anymore," Armand said as he shook his head. "It's British now."

"But they all speak French!"

"History. It's a never-ending story," Armand said. "Come, let's go to the cabin and get washed up. Soon we will have dinner and after dinner we will be able to see the Rock of Gibraltar as we sail into the Atlantic."

It was ten o'clock when they passed the Rock of Gibraltar, and then Armand put him to bed. They had two small adjoining rooms. He didn't know what time it was when the clanging ship alarm awakened him. He ran to the door to Armand's room. He banged on the door. There was no answer. "Armand! Armand!" he shouted. Still, no answer. Quickly, he pulled his trousers and shirt on. He could hear people running through the corridors. He ran out of his room, but he could not understand what they were saying because everyone was speaking English. He ran toward the barroom. One of the sailors picked him up and took him into the dining

76

room. Another sailor quickly slipped a life jacket over his head. The sailor gestured with his hand. "Stay here!"

Jean Pierre looked around the room. There were many people waiting in the dining room, all wearing life jackets, some seated, some standing, waiting for instructions from the staff. They were told only that everyone should stay in the dining room. There was nothing to fear; they should not forget that this was an Irish vessel and Ireland was not at war with anyone.

Jean Pierre was not afraid. He was still looking around for Armand. Not seeing him anywhere, he slipped out by one of the small doors leading to the deck. He had come out underneath a staircase. He was hidden in the shadows. Looking out, he saw two large searchlights covering the whole side of the *Molly Machree*. He turned and saw where the searchlights were coming from: a small German warship.

He stayed under the staircase and watched a motorboat bring a number of German sailors over to the *Molly Machree*. The Irish captain saluted them as they came aboard and the officer saluted the captain. They then shook hands. They were all speaking in German, so Jean Pierre didn't understand what had been said. The Irish captain nodded and made an order to his men. Then those men and the German sailors went off together. Once they had gone the Irish captain and the German officer went to the bar and had a few drinks.

Jean Pierre sat under the staircase. He was able to understand that the Irish and the Germans must have an agreement. But he was still angry about Armand. When his father learned about Armand's behavior, that would be the end of Armand. His father would destroy him. He heard some noise from the deck. The Germans were back carrying cases of things. Wine, whiskey, food. Jean Pierre couldn't see exactly what they were taking, but it seemed to keep them happy.

An hour passed before the Germans had transported their goods and had disappeared into the darkness of the Atlantic Ocean. Then slowly Jean Pierre stretched and listened to the engines of the *Molly Machree* begin softly. Jean Pierre stayed under the staircase another hour as the other passengers returned to their cabins. Then he stood up and went back to the barroom.

The barman was the only one left. He stared down at Jean Pierre. "What the hell are you still doing here?" Then he realized that the child didn't understand him. But he was a proficient barman. He spoke a few languages, one of them French. He repeated his question in French.

Jean Pierre was happy to find someone who could speak his language.

He began to tell him what had happened from the time that he heard the alarm.

The barman then called the purser, who also spoke French. The purser said he would take Jean Pierre to his cabin and try to locate Armand.

The purser opened the door to Jean Pierre's quarters. He then put the key in the door to Armand's room. He tried to open it. The door moved slightly, but not easily. The purser then threw his weight against the door. This time it opened enough to turn the light on in the room before it shut again.

But it was Jean Pierre, whose eyes were younger and faster, who could see what had happened. Armand was lying on his stomach on the floor with a knife stuck through his heart from the back. The blood was still seeping onto the rug.

3

The telegram came to Jacques at Plescassier's sales office in Paris. It was from the executive vice president of the Irish Atlantic Shipping Lines.

The message was simple:

DEAR MR. JACQUES MARTIN: We are sorry to inform you that the tutor of your son, Mr. Armand LeBosc, has had an accident and perished. We are also pleased to let you know that your son, M. Jean Pierre Martin, is well and not very distressed by this sad affair. We have placed your son into the care of the purser, Mr. Benjamin O'Doul, who speaks French fluently and is the father of three sons of his own. I would like to ask that you please give me the information concerning your son's care once we land in Quebec. Mr. O'Doul will be informing you about any news pertaining to your son.

> With all respect, sir,
> Thomas T. Watts
> Executive Vice President

Waving the telegram, Jacques walked into his father's office. He dropped the telegram on the desk in front of his father. He waited but one minute to complain to the old man. "Armand, the crazy asshole! You were the one that wanted him to take care of Jean Pierre!"

Maurice looked up from his desk. "What are you complaining about now?" he said calmly. "He's dead! There is no longer a problem."

"We don't know what he may have taken with him when he got on the ship. He was always a crook and a thief," Jacques said.

Maurice waved his hand in annoyance. "Nothing," he said. "Armand was not that crazy. He knew there would be a large bonus when he delivered Jean Pierre to Canada."

Jacques was silent.

Maurice looked up at him. "Now give the information to the vice president concerning the location of the school in Montreal that we have arranged for him. The boy seems to be in very good care. We don't have time to dwell on this. When you finish come back in here and we will find the money to buy the Cabernet farms and the winery that Prudhomme has offered to us this morning."

"Wine isn't like water," Jacques said. "We don't have to grow the grapes."

"But wine brings more money than water," Maurice said. "Water is only a franc a bottle. Good Cabernet can bring you ten francs a bottle."

4

"It won't matter whether the British bring their entire army into France. They are all stupid. Hindenburg has been put in charge of the German army in the east of France. That means they will wipe out the entire French and British armies in France. The son of a bitch is a genius like Bismarck. What will we do when he occupies Paris?" Jacques was angry as he spoke to his father.

Maurice smiled. "We'll open more cabarets so the Boche can see the cancan. Then we will open more brothels and let them all get venereal diseases. Last but not least, we will give them all the sweet boys they love. They will not last long in Paris."

"Papa, you're old-fashioned. The new German is not like that!" Jacques answered.

"Maybe the army is more modern," Maurice answered. "But the Germans never change."

"Regardless," Jacques said. "I feel I must do something to help save our country. I'm going to enlist in the army."

Maurice was upset. "Now you're being stupid. Do you want to get killed?"

"That will not be a problem," Jacques answered confidently. "General Pétain has offered a captain position in supplies. I will be in charge of all the wines and the champagnes. I will be in the general's office. Everyone knows that the general's offices are the safest. I will not see combat, Papa."

Maurice looked over at his son. "What will you do about your petit ami, Louis? Do you think he will stay here by himself once you are gone?"

"I thought I might take him along with me as my orderly," Jacques answered.

"You are more stupid than I thought," Maurice said. "In one week you would both be discovered to be homosexual. How long do you think it would take the army to find out about you? Then you will be court-martialed and discharged by the army. Your life in society after that will be ruined. You would disgrace our entire family publicly."

"Then what can I do, Papa? I love that boy."

"Give him a job at the winery in the mountains in the Alpes Maritime. Give him a title. Assistant manager. A good title—after all, he is a very bright boy. He has a diploma in accounting." Maurice nodded, pleased with his plan. "Now that I think of it, it's a good idea."

Jacques stared at his father. "*Merde!* You want to fuck the boy yourself!"

"What's wrong with that, Jacques?" Maurice smiled. "After all, you will be away in the war. And I could keep him in the family. There's nothing like a little incest to keep us all together."

The first snow of the winter in Montreal laid a thin icy blanket over the campus of St. Xavier. The final bell rang dismissing the math class. The room emptied quickly as the boys ran to their dormitories. Jean Pierre was the last boy in his room. The other three had already arrived.

Jean Pierre placed his books on the top of his wooden chest, then turned and sat down on the edge of his hard bed. He suddenly realized the three other boys were watching him. He stared back at them, not speaking.

Alain, the biggest boy in the room, looked at him as he spoke. "You're French, not Canadian. You can't even speak English."

Jean Pierre stared defiantly. "You're speaking French," he said. "Not very good French, but none of the Canadians know how to speak French properly. But, somehow, I manage to understand you."

Joseph, the intellectual boy of the room, spoke nastily to Jean Pierre. "We all know why you have been shipped here. Your father didn't want everyone to know that you are a homosexual. We also know about your man friend on the ship being murdered because someone was jealous."

Jean Pierre stared back at him. "How do you know about any of this?"

"Everyone in school knows about it," Alain taunted.

"Who told you about it, you prick?" Jean Pierre said angrily.

"The officer from the ship told the headmaster, who told all the teachers. Of course, then some of the kids found out about it." Joseph sneered. "Would you like to suck any of our cocks?"

Jean Pierre controlled his temper. He looked at them. "None of you have cocks big enough to play with."

This made Alain angry. He ran across the room to Jean Pierre and tried to hit him in the face. The blow didn't reach Jean Pierre's face. Jean Pierre was too quick. He rolled onto his back, so that his face was out of reach. He quickly kicked Alain in the testicles with his left foot, a maneuver he had learned in the Le Savate in the French gymnasium class.

Alain doubled over, clutching his groin. He fell to the floor and began to cry.

Jean Pierre looked down at him without moving from his bed and then turned to the others. "Do any of you know any more terrible stories about me?"

They all returned the stare, but remained silent. Then Joseph knelt beside Alain to see if he could help him in any way. He looked up at Jean Pierre. "You didn't have to do that. You might have ruined him for life."

Jean Pierre laughed. "Nobody ever got killed by a kick in the balls."

Paul, the shortest of the boys in the room, watched without speaking. Finally, he looked curiously at Jean Pierre. "How do you know so much about sex? You are not really that much older than the three of us."

Jean Pierre smiled smugly. "I'm French. All the French are experts in every kind of sex."

"There are other kinds of sex?" Paul asked, wondering.

By now the other three boys were waiting for Jean Pierre's answer. "I'm not going to become your teacher. You'll just have to learn on your own time."

Alain spoke, still on the floor. "He doesn't know anything, that's why he won't teach us."

"Could you at least teach us something to start us off?" It was Joseph who finally asked. The room was filled with curiosity by now.

Jean Pierre looked at them. "Begin masturbating."

"How can we do that?" Paul asked. "Our pricks are too small."

"It's very easy," he said as he unzipped his fly and began stroking himself. "It doesn't matter how small your prick is, it still feels good. Haven't you ever watched the older boys in the shower use the soap to rub their pricks to make them hard until they are ready to shoot out?"

The other three boys followed his motions. Soon they were all feeling the first tinglings of ecstasy. "How old are you really? Your prick is bigger than ours," Paul asked.

"I'll be ten," Jean Pierre said, "in a few months. But my father had to tell the school authorities that I was younger so I could get into this school. But it's not too bad. I'm learning very fast about English. The headmaster is giving me two classes a day."

Joseph looked at him. "You mean that you've been speaking and understanding English?"

Jean Pierre nodded. He watched the others closely. "Sometimes," Jean Pierre added as his phallus was becoming hard, "it feels good to let another boy hold your prick and rub it."

"That's for fags," Alain said. "My father told me never to let another boy touch me."

"I saw a picture of a girl sucking a man's penis once," said Joseph.

"I walked in on my parents one time while they were doing it. I watched until they caught me and my papa yelled at me to get out of the room," Alain said.

Jean Pierre walked over to Paul. He knelt down, watching the boy stroke his tiny penis. He bent over and with his tongue touched his penis and looked up at Paul. His eyes were glistening.

Alain and Joseph in unison yelled, "That's so gross! That's for fags!"

"I'm not a fag," Paul yelled back, and quickly pulled up his pants.

"You two should try it, you might like it," Jean Pierre said to Alain and Joseph.

"Let's go outside and play." Joseph shrugged and put on his coat.

Jacques sat up in bed and reached for a cigarette from the silver case on the bed table. He lit the cigarette from his sterling silver lighter next to the silver case. He inhaled the smoke deep into his lungs. Then he coughed and turned to Louis, who was lying naked and sweaty on the bed beside him. "Jesus!" he gasped.

Louis smiled up at him. "Am I getting to be too much for you? Don't forget I'm only twenty."

"Don't be a liar, you little whore." Jacques laughed. "I know how old you are. You couldn't even get your diploma in accounting until you were twenty-five years old. I saw your university papers."

"You really are a sneaky bastard," Louis said.

Jacques slapped him across the face. "You don't speak language like that to me, or I'll throw you out on the street where I found you."

Louis did nothing more than shrug. "I'm not afraid of you," Louis said. "You can do whatever you want to me. But your father has already offered me a position at the new winery that you bought."

"I suppose you are already having an affair with my father," Jacques said angrily.

Louis stared at him. "Why not? You knew I liked older men when I met you. You even watched me when I had that adventure at the masked ball on Bastille Day. You even let me do two of the German consular officials."

"Oh, shit!" Jacques yelled. "I don't know why I even bother with you."

"I know." Louis smiled devilishly at him and buried his face in Jacques's groin. After a moment he looked up into Jacques's face. "You always told me that I was the greatest cocksucker you ever knew."

Jacques snuffed the cigarette out in the ashtray next to the night table, then got out of bed and went to the bathroom. He sat down on the bidet to wash his genitals and bottom. Afterward he stood up and toweled himself and splashed some eau de cologne on himself.

Louis was still sitting in the bed watching him. Quickly, Jacques pulled on his trousers and a fresh shirt and slipped into his shoes. Then he turned to Louis. "Get up and take all your clothes and leave this house," Jacques said savagely.

"You can't do that to me," Louis said. "Your father wouldn't let you."

"You stupid little whore!" Jacques snapped. "Do you think that my father will even bother with you? He has a dozen boys prettier than you." He tossed down a thousand francs onto the bedsheet next to Louis. "Now get the hell out of here!" He went to the door. "I'll be downstairs in the living room," he said. "If you're not out of here in an hour, I'll have the two coachmen throw you out!"

Maurice entered the library and called to Jacques, who was reading the last edition of the newspaper in the living room. "I just heard that you had your petit ami thrown out of the house."

"I couldn't stand the little whore," Jacques answered. "He was beginning to believe that he was the head of the house." He looked at his father. "How did you hear about it so quickly?"

"He came to my office when I returned from lunch. He told me that you struck him and then threw him out of the house. He said that you were insanely jealous and he was afraid for his life."

"*Merde*." Jacques spat the word. "I should have beat the shit out of him."

"He wants me to send him up to the winery as the assistant, which he had been promised," Maurice said.

"No, Papa, absolutely not. He gets nothing," Jacques answered.

"He said if we do not give him the position, he wants fifty thousand immediately or he will tell the newspapers about the fact that we have collaborated with and paid the Germans to turn the winery over to us."

"The little bastard," Jacques swore.

"What do you think we should do with him?" Maurice asked.

Jacques thought for a moment. "Give him the job."

"What good will that do?" Maurice answered. "It will only give him more power over us."

Jacques smiled. "Only for a month. He will feel quite secure by then. I'll speak to the Germans about his threats. The Germans don't want any more trouble than we do."

"Then what will that accomplish?" Maurice asked.

"The Germans are our partners," Jacques said. "They are used to this kind of thing. He'll disappear in a little while. We'll wash our hands of the whole situation and no one will even remember him."

5

The snow and sleet had turned the streets into sheets of dangerous and slippery ice. Paris was impossible. People were slipping on the sidewalks; horses pulling drays and carriages were falling and falling again as they tried to dig their hooves into the solid sheet of ice. Traffic was at a complete standstill.

Maurice and Jacques stood at the bay window that looked out onto the street. "It's hell!" Jacques said.

"What do you expect?" his father asked. "It's always the same. A savage storm in the early part of the year. January, February, or March. It's the cycle, what can we do?"

"We should build a villa in the South," Jacques said. "Nice and Cannes are really beautiful. The beaches, the Mediterranean, the water, all are magnificent. We could even buy a little yacht. Then we can go over to Corsica or down the coast into Italy and on to Portofino."

"It's just pissing out money," Maurice answered. "What business could we do there?"

"The English, the Germans, and even the Scandinavians are going there for winter vacations. There are big hotels being built. It means big business," Jacques said. "The cost of shipping our bottles of Plescassier water will be a quarter of what we have to pay to ship it to Paris. There are also local wines that are not all that bad. We can buy land very cheap now back from the coast a few miles; we could build a winery and have our own vineyards for one-tenth of what it cost us in Cabernet."

"You are out of your mind!" barked Maurice sarcastically. "I am too old to build a project like that and you are planning on going into the army."

"Not anymore," Jacques replied. "Pétain did not get his promotion to general. He is still a colonel. Joseph Jaures has been appointed commander-in-chief of all French forces and Haig has been appointed to the same position in the British forces in France."

"Meanwhile, the Boche are making fools of all of us. They say that Italy will be joining us soon, but the Italians can't fight anything. They will just be another problem for us," Maurice said, turning to his son. "Now what are you planning to do with yourself?"

"I do not know General Jaures, and Pétain has returned my letter of service, so I'm clear." Jacques smiled. "I have decided to become a real businessman. I want to be a multimillionaire. Not only in France but in England and all of Europe."

Maurice laughed. "And how do you plan to do this? You still have the little whore that is blackmailing you at the winery in Cabernet. The minute you do anything he'll make sure that he becomes a part of your business. And then if you don't include him, he will tell the world about your tastes."

"He is the first plan I have developed," Jacques stated. "I have made arrangements with two Corsicans—"

"I told you before, don't tell me. I don't want to know of any plans like that," Maurice said.

Jacques looked at his father. "You're getting soft, old man. I remember when you would have done far worse."

"The world is changing," Maurice said quietly as he stared out the window. "I don't know if I can change along with it."

Jacques had never seen his father like this before. He walked over to him and patted him on the shoulder. "You're doing pretty good, Papa." Jacques smiled.

Maurice sighed. "I worry," he said. "A friend of mine who has a very important position with the German embassy has approached me with an interesting proposition. He says that it won't be long until the Germans occupy most of western France. He has offered to pay us one million louis to allow Bayer, a German company, to distribute our Plescassier water to the officers' clubs and restaurants here in France and also to distribute the water in Germany."

"What are they really offering to us?" Jacques said. "Germany can easily use up all of our production and then what are we left with? A company that has no water to sell in France." He lit a cigarette. "Then the Boche will own our company."

"That is what I believe also," Maurice said. "The world is changing and I am not fast enough to keep up. I worry. I don't know what to do. If I don't work with them, in time, they will take everything from us and we will get nothing."

"There is a way," Jacques said. "Let me meet with your friend. I'm sure we can develop a better agreement."

Maurice looked at him. "But he's not like us. He is married and has children."

"That's his problem, not ours." Jacques laughed. "Just let us all meet together."

"What will you be able to do?" Maurice asked curiously.

"I know a small water company, Campagne. They are almost bankrupt; they have asked me to assist them, even buy them out." Jacques looked at his father. "I can buy the company for two hundred thousand louis. Then I can merge it into Plescassier and, voilà, we have enough water for Germany and France."

"But is their water as good as Plescassier?" Maurice asked.

"With today's chemistry, it could be better," Jacques answered.

"But would it be natural?" Maurice asked.

"It will not seem any different," Jacques said. "The Boche have no taste. They would drink piss and think it is champagne."

6

It was not until the middle of April that they were able to go to the south of France. Maurice decided that they should stay in Nice, because that was the largest city in the Alpes Maritime. The best hotel at that time was completely booked, so they went to the new hotel, Hotel Negresco, that had just been built by a rich American, Frank Jay Gould, who had moved to France after being ostracized by his family for marrying a Ziegfeld girl. Jacques and his father had rented the two largest suites on the top floor of the hotel. Maurice traveled with his man Hugo, who acted as his nurse, but also served other special needs that the older man desired.

Jacques, who traveled alone, had a suite at the other corner of the top floor. It also consisted of a large bedroom and bathroom, a living room, and a smaller bedroom and bathroom for any servant that might be necessary. The hotel was luxurious and had many conveniences. The American made sure that the two Frenchmen were very appreciated. He had a private telephone installed in each room, even in the bathrooms. This was extraordinary since the average French hotel only had a telephone on each floor and a telephone concierge would call for you at your door and take you to the telephone. After you finished your call, he would escort you back to your room and hold out his hand for an extra gratuity, even though the hotel bill already included a normal gratuity for services.

They had dinner at the hotel restaurant. They were very pleased that the cuisine was authentic French by one of the best chefs. They complimented the hotel manager and he arranged for them to meet the patron, M. Gould.

"I think I'll take a walk before I go to bed, Papa. I'll see you in the morning," Jacques said.

Maurice turned to go to his room. He was tired after his dinner and wine and cognac.

The streets were still crowded as Jacques stopped at a small outdoor café. He decided he would have one more cognac before turning around and going back to the hotel to bed.

The garçon approached the table. "Your pleasure, monsieur?" he said with a twinkle in his eye.

Jacques looked up into his eyes. "Perhaps you would be my pleasure," he said lightheartedly. "For the moment I will take a cognac."

"Oui, monsieur, I am Pierre and I will take care of all of your pleasures." He turned and went to the bar.

Jacques thought about the boy's good looks. He wondered how his mouth would feel on his penis.

Pierre set the cognac down on the table in front of Jacques, lightly touching Jacques's hand as he set the glass down. "Monsieur, are you alone here in Nice?"

"No, I am traveling with my father and doing some business," Jacques answered as he lit his cigarette. "Do you work here every day?"

"No, monsieur, I work here only part-time. I sometimes show tourists around our beautiful town when I am not working," he answered.

Jacques looked at him directly. "Maybe you could show me some things tonight, when you leave the café?"

"That would be very enjoyable; in fact, I can leave now if you would like. I think I could show you a few things that would only cost you around twenty francs," Pierre answered, meeting Jacques's eyes.

Jacques could already feel himself getting hard. He hoped he hadn't misread the boy. But he had seen plenty of male hookers on the street.

Pierre went back to the kitchen and took off his apron. He appeared back at Jacques's table. They walked off onto the boulevard. They walked and talked for about a half an hour. Pierre suggested that they turn off onto a side street.

As they were walking down the darkened street, Pierre suddenly pushed Jacques into a doorway. He pulled at the zipper on his pants and Jacques's penis sprang forward. Pierre slapped the phallus until it was stinging and throbbing with pleasure.

Jacques pushed Pierre's head down onto his erection until he could feel it in the boy's throat. He muffled his scream as he felt himself ready to come. He could hardly keep his balance.

Pierre quickly turned around and pulled his pants down. Jacques rammed his penis deep inside the boy. They both collapsed in the doorway.

D uring the next few weeks they covered all the Côte d'Azur from Monte Carlo to St.-Tropez. After they returned to the hotel they went down to the bar and found a very crowded room. They were greeted by M. Gould. He quickly found them a table.

Maurice had a pastis. "No one here knows there is a war going on," he said as he motioned around the room. "The Germans are all over Monte Carlo and Nice. They have their families come down to vacation with them. Cannes has the English, *c'est la même*. From La Napoule through St.-Tropez there are all Scandinavians. I don't see anything for us down here."

Jacques had a cognac and a cigarette. "You've not been watching the same things I have."

"You're so smart," Maurice said sarcastically. "What have I not seen?"

"The whores, male and female—they will destroy the German army here faster than any battle. Syphilis is rampant here. So Nice and Monte Carlo are not for us."

"Then what is good for us?" Maurice asked.

"We build a villa in Cannes. I located a hill just behind the town of Cannes. The cost is very low. The owners are afraid of the war and want out. I also heard about four thousand hectares of farmland partly on the side of the hills in Bandol, not far from St.-Tropez." Jacques ordered another cognac. "I already have our specialists from Cabernet analyzing the farmland to see if we can grow grapes. I've had a builder seeing if we could construct a winery."

"And the answer?" Maurice asked.

"It will work," Jacques answered. "In addition to this, I see great growth in the Côte after the war. I hear plans of many hotels and businesses here. I plan to make Plescassier water the first water sold in the entire Côte and also to become the biggest distributor."

Maurice looked at him. "And where will you get all the money to do this expansion?"

"I will begin negotiations with the American, Monsieur Gould, and the German company, Wasserman. I will offer them fifteen percent of the company and profits and they will jump at the idea." Jacques lit another cigarette. "There is only one small problem."

"What's that?" Maurice asked.

"I have the clap," Jacques said. "I was stupid, I know. But he was a pretty young boy I met on an evening stroll."

"Fleming has a cure for it," Maurice smiled.

"*C'est vrai*," Jacques answered. "But it's annoying."

7

Jean Pierre entered the headmaster's office. He bowed politely. "Bonjour, Monsieur Barnett."

The headmaster remained in his chair behind the desk. He spoke to Jean Pierre in English. "It is June, Jean Pierre, and the term is finished. Another week and the school will be deserted. Do you have a program for the summer? I haven't heard from your father."

"I haven't heard from him either," said Jean Pierre.

"But you do have enough money to get you through the summer. I just have not been given any instructions where you are to go when school is closed." Mr. Barnett rose from behind his desk and faced Jean Pierre. "Have any of your classmates invited you to their home for the summer?"

Jean Pierre shook his head. "No."

Mr. Barnett leaned back against the desk. "Very strange. Many of the pupils will have one or another of his classmates spend the summer with him."

"No one has asked me," Jean Pierre answered without any rancor. "I think that they feel I am French and not really one of them."

Mr. Barnett nodded. "I had the same problem when I attended school in Canada. Many of my classmates didn't like me because I was American. My spoken English was better than theirs, of course, and they didn't like it."

"I have the same problem because of my French. They think I look down at them," Jean Pierre answered.

Mr. Barnett looked at him. "Do you?"

Jean Pierre smiled. "In a kind of way. They seem like such children. They are always asking me to explain life to them."

"Well, Jean Pierre, you do seem older than they," Mr. Barnett said. "How old are you exactly."

"Ten years and five months," Jean Pierre said proudly.

"You are bigger than most boys in your class," Mr. Barnett said, and met his eyes. "I spend the summer with my family in the United States. We spend summers in an area called Cape Cod, with a home on the beach near the Atlantic Ocean. Do you think you would like to spend your holiday there? Your English would be better almost immediately."

Jean Pierre met the headmaster's eyes. He knew the look. He had seen it many times when his father or grandfather saw another man. "I would like it very much," he answered. "But I do not have permission from my father."

"Perhaps I can send a telegram to your father." Mr. Barnett smiled at him. "I'm sure when I explain the situation at school, he will approve."

"My father probably is not at our home in Paris. The last letter that I did receive," Jean Pierre said, "he and my grandfather were planning on spending the summer in Nice. I am supposed to write them at the Hotel Negresco in Nice."

"All right, Jean Pierre. I will try to reach your father as soon as possible and I will let you know of the answer." Mr. Barnett held out his hand to Jean Pierre and spoke in confidence. "Don't speak to anyone here in the school about our conversation, Jean Pierre."

Jean Pierre shook the headmaster's hand. He felt the man trembling slightly. He smiled and looked up at him. "I'll be careful. No one will hear anything from me. Thank you, Monsieur Barnett."

8

All the students had left the school by the second day of July. The school was being refurbished by workmen who were painting, repairing, and fixing the wear and tear of the last year. Several of the younger teachers were staying on the campus to supervise the work.

Jean Pierre walked through the lonely and empty halls. He really was surprised, but he did miss his classmates. He was very relieved when he received the mail on the morning of the second from his father, who approved of his summer plans. His father had also enclosed two hundred dollars American. He immediately went to Mr. Barnett's office and gave him the check. He also gave the letter from his father to the headmaster. "My papa is very smart. He is sending the money so that I am no financial problem for you."

Barnett smiled. "Your father is very intelligent, but he did not have to worry about the financial support for you. I have invited you as my guest, and of course, I planned to pay all of the costs."

Jean Pierre smiled back at him. "Thank you. I am very grateful to you."

"Have you packed your valises yet, Jean Pierre?" Barnett asked.

Jean Pierre laughed. "I've been packed since your first invitation."

Barnett gestured to him. "Come here behind the desk with me. I would like to show you how we're getting there."

"I'm not worried," Jean Pierre said. "I know the right way."

Mr. Barnett raised his eyebrows. "How do you know?"

"I went to the railroad station and collected all of the routes to Cape Cod," Jean Pierre answered.

Mr. Barnett looked at him smugly. "Did you collect a train route to Detroit, Michigan?"

Jean Pierre was flustered. "Monsieur Barnett, I don't understand. On the atlas, Detroit is next to the Great Lakes, which is in the upper center of the United States, and we are going to Cape Cod near the Atlantic Ocean. That's exactly the wrong way to get there."

Barnett laughed. "Don't be silly. We are going to the ocean, but first we are going to Detroit. Mr. Henry Ford has made new improvements on his Model T and I have bought one. We will collect the car at his factory in Detroit and then we will drive to the coast."

Jean Pierre was excited. "That will be really a long drive. It's great. I never imagined a trip like this."

"I think it will be wonderful." Barnett laughed with Jean Pierre. "Now come here behind the desk and let me show you the photographs of the automobile and the map of our route."

Jean Pierre went and sat beside him behind the desk. Barnett had the literature of the automobile and the maps spread out before them. He placed one hand on Jean Pierre's shoulder and with the other hand he pointed out the auto and the route.

Jean Pierre felt the headmaster's hand pressing his shoulder against him. He said nothing. He felt it was comforting in a strange way. Kind of like family.

Barnett turned his body slightly against him. Jean Pierre felt the headmaster's leg pressing against him. He looked up at the teacher, smiling. "You're strong," he said.

"Yes," Mr. Barnett replied. "I'm very strong."

"I'm glad," Jean Pierre said. "My father is strong, and you remind me of him."

Barnett relaxed and moved slightly away from him. "You will need a visa to enter the United States. Do you have one?"

"I don't think so. I was only planning to stay in Canada on my student's passport," Pierre said, feeling worried. "Will I have any problem?"

"No, Jean Pierre, I don't think so," Barnett replied, at the same time squeezing the boy's shoulder. "I am a good friend of the American consul here. Tomorrow we'll go there and see him."

"Thank you, Monsieur Barnett," he said. "I don't know how I could do these things without you."

"It's nothing," Mr. Barnett said softly. "I am very fond of you, dear boy. As a matter of fact, I think it is time that you call me by my Christian name in private. My name is Elisha."

Jean Pierre looked at him. "I don't know. Someone might overhear us."

"Nonsense," Barnett said. "We'll be careful. Now call me Elisha."

"Elisha," Jean Pierre said, and smiled.

9

The Canadian Northeastern Railroad had a direct express that traveled between Montreal and Detroit. There were only three stops in Canada before the train crossed into the United States. They were Ottawa, Toronto, and then Windsor. Windsor was where the customs and formalities occurred before entering into the United States.

The trip was a total of six hundred miles. Barnett was an experienced traveler and booked a cabin for both of them which was very comfortable and had an upper and a lower bunk. The two days they spent on the train were very enjoyable.

Jean Pierre and Elisha both agreed that the food on the dining car was better than the food at the school. Barnett allowed Jean Pierre his privacy and did not attempt anything that might upset him. By the time they arrived in Detroit Jean Pierre was completely relaxed with sharing a room with his teacher.

Jean Pierre had never seen a city like Detroit. It was nothing but factories. The Ford Motor Company seemed to own the whole city. There were factories to manufacture automobiles that seemed almost five streets long, and at the end of each there would always be a brand-new black Model T Ford waiting to be driven onto a railroad car sitting on the track.

What had really astonished Jean Pierre was how rapidly the automobiles seemed to be arriving, one every five minutes, ready to be driven. Another thing that surprised Jean Pierre was that most of the workmen were Negroes. In France he had only seen a Negro occasionally. The other workers who were not Negroes were farmers who, it seemed, had never lived in the city before. They spoke another English, which was almost impossible for him to understand.

Jean Pierre looked at Barnett as they were walking through the factory. "I don't understand it. At home every workman must dress properly, even with the smallest position. Shirt, trousers, jacket, like a suit. These men wear overalls with a belt or suspenders and an undershirt that looks dirty. I guess Monsieur Ford does not pay them much money to live on."

Barnett laughed. "These men are some of the best-paid workmen in the world. Ford pays them as much as five dollars a day, some even more. He only wants them to produce. He doesn't care how they look. If they are good, he will pay them whatever they want. He is manufacturing almost fifty percent of the automobiles in the world."

Jean Pierre shook his head. "They don't look like the best-paid workers in the world."

Barnett smiled. "Don't worry about it. It's the American way."

The next day Barnett took Jean Pierre to the sales department of the Ford Motor Company, a few streets over from the factories. The sales department was in a large one-story building that seemed to be nothing but windows with one automobile after another on display.

They entered the main door of the building and were greeted by a young man who took them directly to a sales manager's office. The sales manager was also a young man and introduced himself to Mr. Barnett. Barnett nodded pleasantly to the salesman, opened his briefcase, and handed a large envelope to him that contained the sales contract already paid for in full. The manager was pleased.

"Mr. Barnett, your car is ready for you," he said. "If you will kindly follow me I will take you to it."

They walked through a maze of brand-new autos and finally came to an area where automobiles were being cleaned and polished by black workmen. The sales manager checked the slip he held in his hand. He called to one of the workmen. "Car number 11,931, please."

In only a few short minutes, the workman drove the automobile to them. Jean Pierre had never seen a car like this. It was shining inside and out. It had a canvas top, and between the body of the car and the top was a celotex attached to leather squares which served as a protection from rain that might spill into the automobile.

The sales manager turned to Barnett. "There are several extras that you can buy that might be helpful. First, I suggest that you buy an extra tire because it will be more convenient in case you have a flat on the road. Second, you will need a set of Ford tools in case you have to repair anything on the road. Third, you can purchase a Ford jack that can help you lift the car. Lastly, four cans that won't rust or corrode to carry distilled water for the radiator or battery, and two cans in which you can carry gasoline in case there are no gas stations as you travel. In some areas," he explained, "there are no gas stations for many miles. Also, it would be a good idea if you carried several quarts of Ford oil if the engine begins to dry out."

"Nobody ever told me about all of this," Barnett replied, annoyed.

The salesman shrugged. "Usually it is not necessary to have this, because most trips are short and in an area where service is available," the sales manager explained patiently. "But as I understand, you are driving to the Atlantic Coast. That's almost halfway across the country, at least one thousand miles. The roads are not always the best, and gas stations may not be handy."

Barnett looked at him. "How much will all of this cost?"

The sales manager had the answer. "Two hundred and fifty-one dollars. Plus another thirty dollars for someone to teach you how to drive, as well as how to fix any problem you might have on the road."

"But the automobile cost four hundred and thirty dollars to start with. Now this makes it even more expensive," Barnett said.

"It would be very expensive if you got caught on the road a hundred miles away from any help," the sales manager countered. "Believe me, Mr. Barnett, having these extras is the right way to go."

"I guess so," Barnett said. "But I guess I will have to stay an extra day in Detroit."

"Yes, sir," the salesman answered. "But since you are a very good client, I would like to invite you and your son to dinner this evening."

"Jean Pierre is not my son," Barnett explained. "He is from France on his first visit to the United States. He is a student in my school. His father and I felt that it would be very educational for Jean Pierre to travel to the U.S."

"I'm sure it is a wonderful adventure." He held out his hand to Barnett. "I'm Robert Johnson."

Johnson shook hands with not only Barnett but also with Jean Pierre. Then he turned back to Barnett. "Will dinner at seven-thirty be convenient? I will pick you up in my car at the hotel and we will go to a very good seafood restaurant near the lake."

"I think that would be perfect," Barnett said. "Thank you very much."

Jean Pierre walked alongside the headmaster as they were returning to the small hotel where they were staying. He looked up at Barnett. "That's a lot of money you paid for all the extras."

"Johnson said it might be necessary," Barnett said gruffly. He was already angry with himself that he had agreed so easily with the sales manager.

"In France, my papa and grandfather would have bargained about the price," Jean Pierre said.

"That's not American," Barnett said. "In America value is always more important than the bargain."

They walked the rest of the way to the hotel in silence.

Jean Pierre noticed that evening that Barnett took more time than usual dressing for dinner. Robert Johnson was right on time. The restaurant was very pleasant and the sales manager was a very good host. They arrived back at the hotel about ten o'clock.

Barnett suggested to Jean Pierre that he return to his small room located next to the headmaster's and go to bed since the next day would be a very busy one. Jean Pierre agreed and thanked the sales manager for a very nice evening.

Barnett then offered Johnson a cognac and cigar in the bar of the hotel. Jean Pierre returned to his room and undressed slowly. He finally stretched out on his bed and began reading the pamphlets from the Ford office. After a while he fell asleep.

The room was dark when Jean Pierre awoke. He heard some noises in Barnett's room. Silently he walked over to the door that separated the two rooms and slowly opened the door and peeked through the crack.

The two men were nude in bed. They were in each other's arms. They were kissing passionately. Jean Pierre smiled as he saw Johnson bend over and begin to kiss the headmaster's penis. Jean Pierre quickly put his hand across his mouth and closed the door quietly. He didn't want them to hear him laughing. It was not an unusual scene for him to see. There had been many times that he had watched his father and Louis enjoying the same exercise. Happily he went back to bed and fell asleep smiling.

10

They spent three more days in Detroit. Barnett said it was because he had to learn more about the automobile and get experience driving before they went out on the road. Jean Pierre said nothing. He thought that he knew better. Barnett was enjoying his affair with the Ford sales manager. The two of them had met for lunch and dinner every day.

Jean Pierre had been patient. He spent more time at the hotel reading and learning about America. He was anxious for the trip to begin to Mr. Barnett's home. Mr. Johnson had already routed their trip home, to save time.

He told them to take a lake ship that would take them to Erie, New York. That would save them almost a week on the way home. The roads would be better traveling through New York to the Maine coast and then from Boston to Cape Cod.

Jean Pierre was fascinated as they traveled. The United States was a very different country from France. Each state was like its own separate country with different customs and almost a different language. But each one was American. About fifty percent of the roads were asphalt or concrete and the rest were hard packed-down dirt.

There were not many hotels along the way so they spent many of the nights on the road at boardinghouses. Since most people thought that they were father and son they were given only a single room. At first Barnett seemed to be embarrassed at their arrangement, but when he saw that Jean Pierre was not concerned about it, he began to relax.

It took them almost three weeks to reach their destination. They went through Boston, which was a large city, and then drove south to Cape Cod. The headmaster's family had a summer home in a small village on the coast called Hyannisport. It was a very popular seaside town for the very wealthy from Boston. Jean Pierre also learned that most of the families were Irish Americans who seemed to control the local politics in Boston. He also discovered that the Barnetts were a very Irish family.

After Elisha and Jean Pierre left Detroit, Elisha acted very interested in Jean Pierre, and it was not long until Jean Pierre satisfied Elisha. Under the older man's instruction, Jean Pierre learned even more about his sexuality. He learned how to please and how to be pleased. He and Elisha agreed on everything except sodomy. Elisha explained to Jean Pierre that his anus was too small to allow the headmaster's large penis inside him. Jean Pierre enjoyed their intimate times together. He felt very grown-up. But when they arrived at the Barnetts' home everything changed.

Jean Pierre had his own private room on the third floor of the house. Next to him were the rooms of Elisha's younger sisters. There were three sisters, and Elisha was the only son. Elisha was thirty-one years old and the son from Mr. Barnett's first wife, who died a year after Elisha was born.

Mr. Barnett did not marry again until ten years later. Elisha was eleven years old. Then came the girls. Elisha's sisters seemed to be born every two years. By the time Elisha was twenty and at Harvard University the girls were five, seven, and nine years old. All of the girls were older than Jean Pierre and very curious about him.

There was only one bathroom on the third floor and Jean Pierre was always the last in line. While they were in the hallway the girls would speak to him in French and he would answer them in English. The girls were very friendly to him; still, they felt that he was much younger than they were, even though he was eleven years old.

They would pack a lunch each morning and spend the day at the beach. Jean Pierre loved the ocean. It was something he had never seen living in Paris. The beach and the sun were heaven for him. In a few weeks he was very darkly tanned. He had the habit of turning down the top of his bathing suit so that his chest would also become dark. When Elisha saw him like that in front of the girls, he made him put the top back up.

Elisha's room was on the second floor below the girls' and Jean Pierre's. It was also a very large room with its own private bathroom. The master bedroom belonging to Elisha's father took over three-quarters of the second floor. The parlor, the dining room, the kitchen, and two small servants' rooms were on the ground floor.

After a while, Jean Pierre began to miss Elisha. Elisha had many friends and since he had his own automobile he would usually go out in the evening. There were times when Jean Pierre would be around when one or another of Elisha's friends was there, but Elisha always treated him as a child. He wondered if Elisha enjoyed himself with his friends as he had done with him.

Unfortunately, most of the young boys he met on the beach were always playing American games, football, baseball, and they seemed to take no interest in teaching him their games.

Jean Pierre wrote to his father each week. He told his father about the way the Americans lived. He also was very proud to tell him that he was speaking English like the Americans, using slang as well! He would also write to him about the information in the American newspapers and he was depressed by what they said about the Germans seeming to conquer all of Europe. He also explained that the Barnetts were an Irish family and they were always pleased when there was a story about the Germans winning a battle against the English. He didn't think that they had any animosity against the French.

Jean Pierre learned a great deal about the girls since their voices easily carried into his room from the rooms next door. He knew that Rosemary, the oldest, had a boyfriend. In France he would be called a fiancé. Rosemary and the boy would go to the movies twice a week, he would meet her on the beach in the afternoons, and they had dinner with his family on Sunday.

Maureen, the middle sister, was what they called in English a tomboy. She always played the boys' games, baseball and football. And she would wrestle with any one of them on the sand at the beach, and would challenge them to a swimming race on the surf.

The youngest, Kathleen, was just fifteen, and everyone called her Kate. She was the most beautiful of the three girls and was already well developed. She was tall, almost as tall as her oldest sister, and her face looked older than her years. She was a quiet girl; she would read a book while they were on the beach. She would spend time alone in the ocean and then she would come and sit down next to Jean Pierre and speak French with him.

Jean Pierre would speak French back to her, even though he knew her accent was not that good. But he was very grateful for her company because the younger American boys did not want to be bothered with him. She would ask him about his life in France and how it was different from America. She also told him that he was more grown-up than the boys her age. He was also taller, and when she first met him she thought he was at least fifteen years old. She was curious about her brother bringing him to Cape Cod for the summer. She said that her brother was strange and usually spent all of his time with older men.

He said nothing about Elisha to her. Quickly, he learned that she knew very little about her brother's life, only that he was a teacher and was a very brilliant scholar at the university. But she thought he was very selfish and had never even offered to take them for a ride in his new automobile.

One evening at dinner Jean Pierre, with courage in his voice, spoke in French to Elisha. He felt more comfortable for some reason in his own language tonight.

"After dinner it might be pleasant if we could all drive into town in your car. Maybe we could even have an ice-cream soda. I'll treat. My father sent me some money."

"How do you know that I don't have another appointment?" Elisha said, annoyed.

"We wouldn't be very long," Jean Pierre pleaded. "The girls are excited about your new car."

Mr. Barnett looked at his son. "I think it would be a nice thing for you to do and I'll pay for the ice cream."

Elisha had no way out of it. After dinner, at seven o'clock, they all climbed into the car. Elisha growled at Jean Pierre: "It's your idea, you crank it."

Jean Pierre was silent. He stood in front of the Ford and set the crank into the operating hole. He held up one hand so that Elisha could know when it was ready. Elisha nodded. Jean Pierre turned the crank. Nothing happened. Instead the crank snapped backward, slamming at the back of Jean Pierre's right hand. He looked up and knew that Elisha had done it deliberately. But he said nothing and held the crank again. This time Elisha turned on the ignition and the motor started humming. Jean Pierre returned the crank to its place and climbed up in the seat next to Elisha. He placed his hands on the back of the seat and turned to the girls as the automobile began to move. "What do you think about it?"

"It's wonderful," the girls squealed almost in unison.

But Kate had seen the back of his hand. "What happened? The back of your hand is black and blue."

"It's nothing," Elisha called back to his sister. "Things like that always happen when you crank an automobile."

Jean Pierre laughed. "*Pas de probleme*," he said.

It took only fifteen minutes until Elisha parked the car in front of Giovanni's Italian Ice Cream Parlor. The store was very attractive. It was paneled in mahogany and all the tables and chairs were in white imitation leather. They sat down at one of the large tables, Jean Pierre next to Elisha. Giovanni, the friendly store owner, came over and stood next to the table. "I have-a made a fresh-a strawberry ice cream today and I make-a sundae with strawberry syrup, topped with-a whipped cream."

They all ordered Giovanni's strawberry treat except Elisha. He ordered a new soda that had just been shipped in from the South, Coca-Cola. Giovanni opened the small, icy bottle and put a straw inside. Elisha sipped it and smiled while the others waited for their sundaes. "This is really good. It seems to give you a lift when you are tired." He seems to be in a better mood, Jean Pierre thought.

The girls didn't answer. All they wanted to talk about was Elisha's automobile. They thought it was wonderful. Elisha smiled with all the compliments and then he turned and saw a friend of his standing outside of the ice-cream parlor. Elisha excused himself and walked outside to his friend.

Rosemary looked at Jean Pierre. "I don't know why my brother even bothers with that silly man. My friends say that he is nothing but a sissy."

Jean Pierre looked back at her. "What exactly is a sissy? We don't have this word in French."

Rosemary answered him. "A sissy is a boy who acts like a girl. He doesn't play any of the games that boys play and also he never goes out with girls."

Jean Pierre nodded to her. He knew more about that boy than they knew about their brother. The sundaes finally arrived. They were large and delicious. Jean Pierre thought that American ice cream was better than French ice cream. The American ice cream was made with real cream and milk. With each sundae a glass of water was served. Carbonated water. Jean Pierre looked at Maureen. "I didn't know there were sparkling water springs here."

Maureen laughed. "There are no springs on Cape Cod. It's only ocean. All salt water."

"Then where do they get sparkling water?" he asked.

Giovanni overheard his question. "We have tanks. Compressed air comes out of tubes and goes into the water and it comes out here." He turned and pulled the spigot forward and the bubbling water flowed out.

Jean Pierre smiled. "Thank you," he replied. He took a deep breath— the Americans were so smart.

Elisha came back into the ice-cream parlor. He turned and looked at Rosemary. "Jonathan has just invited me to a friend's birthday party and I said I would join him. I'll leave you enough money to take a horse carriage back home."

"Father will ask us why you left us alone and didn't make sure we were home safely," Rosemary said angrily.

"Tell Father that I have to meet the professor that is sponsoring me for an associate professor job at Harvard this fall," he answered, ignoring her anger. "And you know how important that is to me."

They were all silent as Elisha went outside and walked off with his friend to the automobile. Jean Pierre turned to Rosemary, his face flushed. "Is it true that he will go to Harvard this fall, not to St. Xavier?"

Rosemary shook her head. "I don't know. Nobody ever knows what Elisha is doing."

11

Kate kept her eyes on Jean Pierre as they rode home in the carriage. It was near ten o'clock when they climbed up the steps to the porch. Jean Pierre looked at the girls. "I'm going to sit outside awhile. I'm really not sleepy."

The two older girls went inside. Kate turned to him. "Do you mind if I stay with you?"

Jean Pierre nodded. "That would be nice."

She sat down on a chair opposite Jean Pierre. For a while they didn't speak. "You're not happy?" she quietly asked him.

"I'm okay," he answered.

"Are you upset because Elisha may not go back to your school with you?" she asked.

"I don't understand it," he replied. "Why did he invite me to come down here with him, if he knew that he might not be returning?"

Kate looked at him. "Do you love my brother?" she asked.

He stared back at her. "That's a stupid question."

"It's not the only time my brother has brought a boy home to spend the summer with him. And then after the season Elisha sent the boy off to his own home." She reached for his hand. "I'm sorry," she said. "You're not like the other boys were. They were all fresh and common."

"He never told me that he ever brought anybody else home with him," he said.

"I knew that you were different from the rest. You never went downstairs in the middle of the night to his room," she said, still holding Jean Pierre's hand. "Sometimes I think that Elisha is a sissy like many of his friends. But I just can't believe that about him." She paused. "After all, he is my older brother."

Jean Pierre looked into her eyes. He could see a faint touch of her tears welling up in the corner of her eyes. "Not your brother," he said. "Elisha is not a sissy. He's a very kind man and a very good teacher."

She took her hand away. "Are you still going back to St. Xavier in the fall?"

He shook his head. "I don't know. I have to write to my father. I would like to go home to France. I don't like the school that much. I don't have many friends there."

"I could talk to my father," Kate said. "My father likes you and he could get you into a very good school in Boston. You could live with us and you could help all of us with our French lessons."

This time it was he who took her hand. "Kate," he said, "I'm only eleven and I still have to do what my papa tells me."

She looked down at their hands and then up at him. "I guess it's time to go to bed. It's already after ten. My father likes us to be in bed by now."

"You go ahead," he said. "I'll stay down here for a while. I'm not sleepy."

"Are you going to wait up for Elisha?" she asked. "Maybe he'll let you know what he's doing. I haven't heard anything for sure about him moving to Harvard."

"Then why did you all think that he was going?" Jean Pierre asked.

"I think Maureen overheard our father talking about it. But nobody will know for sure until Elisha tells us," she answered.

"That's funny," he said. "My father knows everything that I do. In France parents always know what their children are planning to do. I guess the Americans are different."

"Americans are not different," she said in a positive voice. "It's Elisha. His mother died when he was only a year old and he was raised by nannies until he was almost eleven years old. Father never had time to take care of him because he was away on business. It was not until Father married my mother that Elisha began to live with a real family."

"I lost my mother before I even knew her. I was very young, my father told me. But my father and my grandfather always made a home for me." He smiled at her. "I was lucky, I guess."

"You were," she replied. "My mother passed on when I was four years old. I remember her a little bit, but I always had my big sisters to take care of me."

"Then we were both lucky." He smiled.

She got out of her chair. "Okay." She laughed. "Now I'm really going to go up to bed."

"Bon dodo," he said, and laughed.

12

It was after midnight when Elisha returned home. He walked up the steps of the porch and was almost opening the door to enter the house when he saw Jean Pierre sitting on the veranda chair. He stared down at Jean Pierre. "What are you doing up so late?"

"I wasn't sleepy," he said. Then he looked up at Elisha. "How was the party?"

Elisha shrugged his shoulders. "It was okay, I guess. But most of the boys there were pretty stupid."

"Then why do you bother with them?" he asked.

"What else is there to do here?" Elisha replied, and opened a package of cigarettes and took one.

Jean Pierre watched him. "Could I have one, please?"

Elisha lit his cigarette. "You can't smoke. You're too young."

"My father gave me cigarettes when I was nine years old," Jean Pierre lied. But he had smoked cigarettes that Armand had given to him once in a while. He looked up at Elisha. "Well?"

Elisha gave him a cigarette. He watched Jean Pierre light it expertly. "Damn!" he said. "You can smoke."

Jean Pierre let the smoke flow from his pursed lips. "The girls tell me that you are going to be a professor at Harvard."

"The girls talk too much," Elisha said angrily. He dragged on the cigarette. "Nothing has been agreed to yet."

"But you do want to go?" Jean Pierre asked.

"It would be very important for my career, Jean Pierre, if I got an associate professorship at Harvard," Elisha answered. "Harvard is one of the best universities in the United States. Of course I would go."

Jean Pierre put out his cigarette with his shoe. "You will go," he said. "I'm sure."

"But, if I do go, it doesn't mean that you shouldn't return to St. Xavier. I will know whoever becomes the next headmaster. He will be a very good teacher, I assure you."

"It doesn't matter so much about that," Jean Pierre said. "I'm lonely. I want to go home to France. Canada or the United States aren't comfortable for me."

"But what about the war?" Elisha asked. "Germany seems to be running over France. What are you going to do if they take your country?"

"I'm French," Jean Pierre answered quickly. "I learned to speak English; I guess I can also learn to speak German as well."

"You'll have to write your father for permission," Elisha said.

"I know," Jean Pierre answered. "But I'm not worried about his answer. After all, he is French and he will understand my feelings."

13

He felt a draft as the door to his bedroom opened. He sat up in bed and looked toward the faint light that was shining from the open door and then disappeared. He felt rather than saw a white gown coming to him. "Who is it?" he asked.

"Kate," whispered the voice.

The moon was shining through the open window and he could see her standing next to his bed. "What are you doing?" he asked, also whispering.

"I'm upset," she said, sitting down on the edge of his bed.

"Your father will be angry if he finds you here," Jean Pierre said.

"He won't find us," she replied. "He sleeps through everything. He can't hear anything from his bedroom."

"Why are you upset?" Jean Pierre asked.

"Elisha says that you are going back to France," she said. "But I don't want you to go; it might be dangerous because of the war."

"I just spoke to Elisha and told him I wanted to go home tonight after he came home. I thought you were already asleep. When did you talk to him?"

She was silent.

He tried to see her face in the dark. "Did Elisha come to your bedroom?" She still didn't answer.

"Does he come to your bedroom often?" asked Jean Pierre quietly.

He could hear her begin to cry.

He took her hands from her face. "What is it?" he asked softly. "You can tell me, we're friends."

She looked at him. "You won't tell my sisters or anyone else?"

"I promise," he answered.

"Every summer since I was twelve," she whispered.

"Do you think that he ever went to your sisters' room?" he questioned.

"No," she replied. "They always shared a bedroom. I was the only one in a room by myself."

"Did he do anything to you?" he asked curiously.

"Not really," she said.

"Then why did he come to your bedroom?"

"He always takes out his big thing. He wanted me to watch while he would massage it and it would get even bigger. Then he made me massage it until it spit out juice all over my hands." She began to weep again. "I told him I didn't want to do it, but he paid no attention to me."

"Did you ever want to do anything?" he asked.

"He wanted me to take it in my mouth or rub it against my behind," she said huskily. "But I never let him do it, Jean Pierre. I told him I would scream and everyone in the house would know what he had done."

He sat silent for a moment and looked at her. "It's something that a lot of boys like to do."

She looked at him. "Do you?"

Jean Pierre shrugged.

"Did Elisha show his thing to you?" she asked.

"Of course," he answered. "I told you all boys want to do it."

She sat quietly for a moment and then shook her head. "I'll never understand boys."

"You don't have to now. When you get older you'll understand everything. Isn't that what our parents always tell us?" Jean Pierre said, laughing.

"I guess the French and the Americans are the same. That's what they always tell us," Kate answered, giggling. "Do you really have to go back to France?" she asked again.

"It's my home," he said.

"Oh, Jean Pierre, I'll miss you," she said. "We have so much fun together and you're so wise."

"I'll miss you, too," he replied. "But we'll stay in touch with each other."

She leaned down and kissed his cheek and went back to her room. He sat on the bed and thought for a while. Then he went to the small desk near the window.

He wrote a letter to his father. He wanted to go home.

14

Jacques sat at the dinner table facing his father. He held an envelope and a letter out across the table toward him. "It's a letter from your grandson, the selfish little prick!"

Maurice read the letter quickly, then looked at Jacques. "What are you so excited about? I remember when you were a child, you pestered me to bring you home from the vacation camp that I paid a lot of money for. You were homesick. So why be angry because your son is homesick?"

"You know how much it cost to send him there," he answered. "Going to Canada and the United States is even more expensive than going to a French vacation camp."

Maurice laughed. "We can't afford it. We are really poor. Jacques, don't be an ass. The best place for Jean Pierre is to stay there. Not only for his education but his learning about a new world. A world that will someday control everything in business."

"The Americans are stupid," Jacques said. "There's nothing Jean Pierre could learn from them," Jacques snapped at his father.

"Jacques," his father said soothingly. "They are not stupid. Mark my words, in a very short time they will chase the Germans out of England and Europe."

"Their President Wilson said that he will not bring America into the war," Jacques said.

"Their President Wilson is a very brilliant politician, and what he wants is a second term. Do you think he could become president again by telling

people he wants to bring them into a war? Only the stupid European countries want to rush into war. If we had been intelligent we would have never
gone to war against the Germans. We have forgotten what they did to us
in the Franco-Prussian War. We were thankful then to get some of our
country back."

Jacques looked at his father. "You have no faith in us."

Maurice laughed again. "My dear son, the French are not warriors. They
are lovers." He leaned back in his chair and reached for a cigar. "We can
bring Jean Pierre home when the war is over and then we can teach him
about our business. And there will be no interference from a war to bother
him. By that time he will be maturing into a man and we will make sure
that he is one of the most respected and successful businessmen in all the
world, not only in France."

15

The League of Nations—1919

A light mist was covering the streets of Paris. Jean Pierre came into the house, placing his umbrella in the stand next to the door and hanging his cap and raincoat next to a mirrored wall with clothes hooks. It was nearly five o'clock as he went into the library.

As usual, his grandfather was seated in his large comfortable leather chair; a small table next to him held his cognac and a Baccarat ashtray, where his cigar smoldered. He looked at his grandson. "You seem very excited."

Jean Pierre held out an envelope. "Read this letter and you will know why I am excited."

Maurice smiled as he took the letter out of the envelope. "If it's a letter from that American girl you correspond with, your father will not be that thrilled."

"Grandpapa, please, just read the letter."

Maurice read the letter quickly. He looked at Jean Pierre in surprise. "The Americans are offering to let you be translator for them at the first League of Nations meeting to be held in Paris."

"Yes," Jean Pierre said with obvious excitement.

"Why did they choose you? It's very strange. You have just turned sixteen years old." He held out the letter as he spoke. "This is a task for someone more mature."

"No, Grandpapa, almost five years in American schools in Boston has given me a very good knowledge of the language in the States."

"That's true," he said. "But that doesn't tell me why they chose you."

"Did you read the signature on the letter?"

Maurice glanced down at the signature and then looked up at Jean Pierre. "It says that it's from the head of the translation committee, one of President Wilson's assistants."

Jean Pierre was growing impatient. "But the name, Grandpa," he said. "Elisha Barnett. He was my first headmaster who then arranged for me to live with his family in Boston while I finished my schooling in the U.S."

"And the American girl? She is his sister?"

"But only he will be in Paris, not her," Jean Pierre replied.

Maurice looked at him. "Did you have an affair with him?" His voice expressed curiosity.

"Not really, Grandpapa," Jean Pierre answered. "He had many friends closer to his own age."

"Then what did 'not really' mean exactly?" asked Maurice.

"We played," Jean Pierre answered. "I masturbated him and sometimes pushed my hand into his derriere."

"Did you have an affair with his sister? The girl you correspond with?"

"No, Grandpapa." Jean Pierre smiled. "We were very close friends and I think she tried to find out if Elisha seduced me."

"She didn't try to seduce you herself?" he asked.

Jean Pierre laughed. "No. She is almost five years older than I am, and besides, she always liked American boys who were athletic."

Jacques walked into the library. "I just heard your last words. Who was athletic?"

"American boys," Jean Pierre said. He held the letter out to his father. "I've been offered a position during the League of Nations' Parisian congress."

Jacques read the letter. He stared up at his son. "But this is from the American delegation?"

"My former headmaster from Canada, whose family I lived with in the States, has offered me this position as a translator for one of the American groups."

Jacques turned to his father. "I don't like it. Jean Pierre is French, not American. He should not work for them."

Maurice shook his head. "No, Jacques, you told me that you wanted Jean Pierre to become a worldwide businessman. Without the United States he will never become what you want him to be."

Jacques looked down at his father. "I don't see how it could benefit him to work in the League of Nations."

"You're not thinking, Jacques." Maurice continued looking at his son. "Remember just a few years ago, you laughed because the States were starting to sell Coca-Cola here in Europe. Do you also remember that I wanted you to make a deal to distribute Coca-Cola here in France? And look at it now. Coca-Cola is the favorite drink for young people and is second only to beer."

Jacques stood shaking his head. "How will it help our business?"

"America will be the next market for us," Maurice said very assuredly. "Maybe not in my time, and maybe not in yours, but in Jean Pierre's time, when Plescassier is his own, he will send our water to the States. If today he works in the American delegation, he will make contacts and acquaintances who might be helpful when Plescassier becomes the most successful bottled water in the world."

Jacques turned to Jean Pierre. "And what do you think?"

Jean Pierre answered, "I'd like to do it."

Jacques stared at his son. "Are you in love with your former headmaster?"

Jean Pierre laughed. "I'm too young to fall in love."

16

The Second World War—1940

JEAN PIERRE

Jacques leaned back comfortably in his leather-stuffed chair behind the antique ornate desk in his Paris office. He asked his secretary to call his father in his villa in Cannes. That was one thing he had been pleased about. Finally he had been able to persuade his father to retire in the south of France, where there was no pressure from the businesses and no nasty Paris winter weather. After all, his father was eighty-six years old, and even though he was bright and sharp as a tack, there was no reason to put up with the everyday pressures of the business world, especially with all the disruptions that the war had created in France.

The butler at the villa answered the telephone. "Villa Plescassier."

Jacques spoke into the telephone. "Hugo, is my father about?"

"Monsieur Jacques," the butler answered. "I am sorry but Monsieur Maurice is taking a nap."

"Could you please ask him to call me when he is awake. I will be leaving the office in a few minutes. He can call me at home."

"Oui, Monsieur Jacques," the butler answered politely.

"*Merci,*" Jacques said, and put down the telephone. He buzzed his secretary and stood up and reached for his overcoat.

The secretary came into his office. "Monsieur?"

"I'm going home. If Jean Pierre calls ask him to call me there. You can let him know that Monsieur Weil, the banker, will be joining me for dinner."

"Oui, monsieur," she said, and helped him on with his overcoat and then held the door open for him.

His limousine was already waiting for him in front of his office building on the Champs-Elysées. Robert, his chauffeur, was holding the door to his large Citroën open.

Silently, he stepped into the automobile. Quickly he picked up the afternoon paper that Robert had left for him on the seat. The news was grim. It was June the third and the German Luftwaffe had chased the British army of almost four hundred thousand infantry along with a large French army troop across the English Channel into England. There were several other stories, including General de Gaulle taking control of the French army in England and naming it the Free French Army.

He was thoughtful as he watched Robert crank the motor. He was pleased that he had bought the Citroën with its old-fashioned crankcase system. The new automobiles with the electric starting systems had many problems and fell apart very quickly. He was startled when the door next to him swung open.

Jean Pierre laughed at his father's surprised face. "I'm French, Papa," he said. "Not Boche."

Jacques was angry. "Why are you here so early? I thought you were still working at the army headquarters."

Jean Pierre pointed to the new stars on his uniform. "I've just been appointed a captain."

"Who made you a captain?" Jacques asked. "There's no one in the head-quarters." He pointed to the headline in the newspaper. "Maréchal Pétain is meeting with the Germans for an armistice."

"General de Gaulle promoted me," Jean Pierre said.

"How can he do anything? He's already fled to England."

"He has asked me to join him. He wants me to work in the intelligence division. He is impressed with my knowledge of language with the British and the Americans."

"The Americans are not even in the war with us," Jacques said with disdain.

"De Gaulle has told me it's only a matter of time," Jean Pierre answered. "I'm leaving tonight for London."

"You will not leave. I forbid it," Jacques answered adamantly. "I am your father and I will not allow you to go."

Jean Pierre looked directly at Jacques. For the first time Jacques heard anger in his son's voice. "You have nothing to say about it, Father," Jean Pierre snapped. "I'm thirty-seven now, not the child you sent to Canada."

Jacques looked at his son. "I love you," he said. "I don't want anything to hurt you."

"And I love you, Father," Jean Pierre said. "I'll be okay. Don't worry."

For a moment they embraced, and then Jean Pierre spoke. "I have to be on my way, Father. The British are bringing a transport plane to take my intelligence group to London."

17

Maurice awakened slowly from his nap at five-thirty. He rolled over on his bed and pressed the button on the night table to call the butler. By the time he had sat up and put the pillows behind his back, the butler was already there with the afternoon tea.

The butler placed the tray with its legs across his lap. Quickly he poured the tea in the cup and added a little milk. Then he took the sterling silver cover and lifted it off of the small plate of cookies.

"Merci," Maurice said, and saw the note that had been left by the telephone. He sipped his tea for a moment and then gestured to the butler to call Jacques. He had already eaten the first cookie by the time the call went through.

"Why have you gone home so early?" he asked Jacques.

"I've invited Monsieur Weil, the banker, here for dinner. I thought it would be an appropriate time to rearrange our bank loans. Interest is still low and I know the rates will go higher now that the Germans are in Paris and Pétain is already negotiating an armistice with the Germans." Jacques's voice sounded depressed.

"And what did the Jew bastard say to that?" Maurice asked.

"He agreed with me," Jacques said. "He also suggested that I borrow even more money."

"That's strange," Maurice answered with curiosity. "Weil is never anxious to lend us more money. Usually we have to kiss his ass for it."

"Monsieur Weil is worried. He has learned that the Nazis are already slaughtering the Jews in the other countries that they have occupied," Jacques said. "Now that Pétain has capitulated and is begging Germany for an armistice, he is afraid that the Germans will destroy France like they have the other countries that they have been in. He is giving his best customers the opportunity to borrow more money."

"Then what does he plan on doing, if he is frightened of the Germans? He's not going to loan out all of his money. He is a Jew—he will keep plenty for himself," Maurice said sarcastically.

"You're smart, Father," Jacques said. "Weil is smart as well; he has already sold his property in France. His family has been sent to Switzerland, and he has made a business partnership with a private Swiss bank. He plans to finish all of his business and will be in Geneva in two weeks." Jacques laughed. "I thought he was nuts. France is not like other countries. The Germans have too much respect for the French."

"He's not that crazy, he's a Jew," Maurice said. "France was crazy to believe in Pétain. He gave the country away for free."

"Are you afraid, Father?" Jacques asked. "Do you want to return to Paris?"

"I'm not that crazy," Maurice answered. "I am safer here than in Paris. The Côte d'Azur will always be a recreation area. There's no reason for a war to come here."

Jacques paused for a moment. "Jean Pierre has gone to England with de Gaulle. He has promoted him to captain."

Maurice laughed proudly. "The little son of a bitch is smarter than all of us. He will be important with de Gaulle, he speaks as the Americans do, and he will be a great asset to them. In time de Gaulle will become the savior of France and in time president."

"But Jean Pierre hasn't even stepped into the business world," complained Jacques. "He's spent his life just having a ball. He has fucked more men than I have ever dreamed."

Maurice laughed out loud again. "You're just jealous of your son. Now he's a man. He sees into the future. He's the new generation."

"Damn!" Jacques swore. "And what generation are we?"

"The last generation," Maurice answered. "It won't be long until our generation will be a memory."

18

Jean Pierre tasted his pastis, then held his glass to Louis, the lieutenant who shared the apartment. The officers had to share apartments because there was not enough space to house all of de Gaulle's intelligence department. They had all cursed Pétain because he did not really like de Gaulle or his men and had made it very cramped and difficult for them. There were too many times that de Gaulle had disagreed with Pétain publicly. Now that de Gaulle had gone to Britain, Pétain called him a traitor for not supporting the armistice.

Louis tapped their glasses together in a toast. "Cheers," he said. "I am sorry that I am not going to be with you."

"That's the luck of the draw," Jean Pierre said. "You know how the names were called. You'll make it on the second flight."

"But I will not be with you," Louis said, his voice breaking. "I love you, Jean Pierre, and I know that you will find another friend the minute you are away from me."

"Louis, don't be silly," Jean Pierre answered. "You're young, only twenty-two years old, and you have many years to be with me when we are in England."

"You don't love me the way that I love you." Louis was already crying.

Jean Pierre reached out to Louis and stroked his chest. "Stop the tears. We still have time to love. I don't have to be at the airfield until midnight."

Louis kissed Jean Pierre on the lips and reached to open his trousers. Jean Pierre's penis came out, already hard. Louis bent down and slowly

126

spread his mouth over Jean Pierre's throbbing penis and tried to swallow him completely.

"Slow down a minute," Jean Pierre said huskily. "We might as well be comfortable. The bed is still here. Let's take off our uniforms."

"I love your cock!" Louis mumbled, his mouth already filled with saliva.

Jean Pierre pulled him toward the bed while Louis was trying to drop his trousers. He grabbed his derriere. "I want to fuck you, I don't want to just come in your mouth. I want to be inside of you."

Quickly, they got out of their clothes. Jean Pierre rolled Louis on his back. Jean Pierre reached over to his night table and took out a jar of Vaseline. With his fingers he smeared Louis's anus with it and then covered his penis.

Louis moved up to Jean Pierre's mouth, his tongue probing wildly. Then he whined like a cat as Jean Pierre shoved his penis deep inside of him. Slowly, Jean Pierre began to slide his penis in and out until he settled into a pulsating rhythm.

Jean Pierre reached down with his left hand and clasped Louis's hard penis and held it close against his belly and felt the semen dripping from Louis's penis between them.

"For God's sake, come!" Louis gasped, grabbing Jean Pierre's testicles and squeezing them.

Jean Pierre felt the orgasm tearing through his body. He lost his breath as he felt the semen pouring from him. "I can't breathe!" he shouted.

"I felt the hot cum inside me," Louis said, kissing Jean Pierre. "Now you will really have to marry me. I'm pregnant!"

Jean Pierre smiled, kissed him, and held him close to him. "You are my lover!" he said. Then he looked at Louis. Louis was already asleep. Jean Pierre smiled and closed his eyes.

19

Jean Pierre stretched as he looked at his wall clock. It was ten o'clock. It was almost time for him to get ready to leave. The telephone rang. He was curious. He wondered if de Gaulle had changed his plans.

Louis woke as Jean Pierre picked up the telephone. Jean Pierre recognized the voice. It was his father.

"Your grandfather is in the hospital at Sunny Bank. He has had a stroke and the doctors think that he may not live twenty-four hours. He has begged that you come to his side."

"Jesus," Jean Pierre said to his father. "When did this happen? I know that you speak to each other every afternoon."

"The butler found him on the floor when he went upstairs to take his dinner to him," Jacques replied. "I already have two tickets for the Blue Train. It leaves here at midnight; we will be in Cannes by eight. I have already asked Robert to pick you up at your apartment and then take us to the station."

"Father," Jean Pierre said. "Have you forgotten that I am supposed to leave for London at midnight?"

"Your grandfather is more important. You just cannot go to London. Call your colonel, your superior officer. He is a Frenchman. He will understand the love of your grandfather."

"Of course, Father," Jean Pierre answered. "I will try and arrange it." He hung up the phone and looked at Louis.

Louis looked solemn. He already knew what had happened. "Jean

Pierre," he said. "I am sorry about your grandfather. Perhaps I can take your place on the plane. Just give me your pass and I am sure that Colonel Nicol will understand the situation."

Jean Pierre looked at the younger man. "You will do that for me?"

"I told you that I love you," Louis said.

"You are wonderful, but why are you so sure that the colonel will agree with you?"

Louis laughed. "Maybe you're more of a baby than I am. Colonel Nicol loves my cock and asshole more than anything."

"You little bastard!" Jean Pierre laughed. "And I thought that I was your one and only true love."

"You better hurry, Jean Pierre. Take your shower and I will repack your valise with civvies, because I understand that the whole German army vacations in Cannes. You will have to be careful," Louis said.

"Okay, General," Jean Pierre kidded. "I will straighten you out when I see you in London."

20

Jean Pierre waited in the car while Robert went inside the house and came back with two valises. A moment later Jacques came down and quickly got in the automobile. He embraced Jean Pierre. "My son, my son," he said in a husky voice.

Jean Pierre looked at his father. He had never seen his father so pale, his face so drawn. His eyes were still filled with tears. "Father," he whispered as the car began to move out into the street. "Please, Father, try to remember, Grandpa is a very strong man and he will survive any illness."

Jacques looked into his son's face. "Your grandfather is over eighty-six years old. Time wears out even the strongest of men."

Jean Pierre was silent as he looked at the busy crowds walking down the sidewalk. He took a deep breath. The people looked sad. Maybe all of France was depressed and ashamed because of the Germans' easy victory over them. "Damn," he muttered into the window.

"What did you say?" his father asked.

"I can't believe it," Jean Pierre said. "I should have gone on that flight tonight. Instead, I am on my way to the train going to Cannes."

"I'm glad you didn't take the plane," Jacques said. He looked at his son. "You were able to get out of your flight with no problem?"

"My friend Louis took my place," Jean Pierre said.

"So it was easy. And I thought that de Gaulle was very disciplined with his soldiers." Jacques shrugged.

"It was Louis that called and explained the problem." Jean Pierre smiled. "The colonel simply accepted the change."

"You're smiling." Jacques looked at his son curiously. "There is something peculiar. I thought that Louis was your lover."

"I, too, thought that he was my lover," Jean Pierre answered, still smiling. "But I was wrong. He told me that he and the colonel have been lovers for many years, since he was sixteen." He reached for a cigarette inside his coat pocket. "So, Papa, that is how I made it here so quickly."

"Are you upset about this news?" Jacques asked.

Jean Pierre dragged at the cigarette. "No, Father. He's still a chicken. I have had many like him before and there will be many others. *C'est vrai,* Papa."

It was ten o'clock in the morning when the Blue Train moved into Cannes. Jean Pierre looked out from the window. He turned to his father. "The station is filthy, just like the train. Plus we're late—it usually takes eight hours from Paris. Tonight it took almost ten hours."

Jacques looked at his son. "Don't be silly. The schedule is not controlled by the French Railroad anymore. It's the Boche army. If you noticed, that is why we stopped six times for the German soldiers on the way from Paris."

"There are no porters to help us with our valises," Jean Pierre grumbled. "All the African porters have been taken by the Germans for slave labor. But we are not cripples, Papa. We can carry our own valises."

"Stop grumbling," Jacques said. "Just remember we're Frenchmen, and we are alive. Now let's look for Grandfather's butler, Hugo. He said he will be at the street in front of the station until we come in."

Hugo was there. Quickly he placed their valises in the front seat next to him in the Renault while Jacques and Jean Pierre climbed into the tight seat in the back.

Hugo called back to them. "We will go to the villa first so that you can both have a bath and breakfast. By the time you are ready I can take you to the hospital."

"Why can't we go to the hospital first?" Jacques asked anxiously.

"Sunny Bank does not allow visitors until eleven," Hugo answered. "And also Dr. Guillemin wants to see you before you see your father."

"It doesn't sound good to me," Jacques said with concern. "He is my father and we should have the right to see him whenever we want."

"There is one more thing," Hugo interrupted. "If he should become ill or have an accident, he has left a large legal envelope that the monsieur had a *notaire* prepare and deliver to you. I now have it in the small safe in my room. I will give it to you the moment we arrive at the villa."

21

Jean Pierre showered and dressed and went to his father's room. Jacques was already dressed and seated at the small desk near the window. He had already opened the large envelope and begun to read the letter his father had written and signed before the *notaire*.

Jean Pierre looked down at his father. Once again he saw his father's face was drawn and pale, with the hint of tears. "Father," he asked, "is there anything I can do to help you?"

Jacques shook his head. "No, nothing can help. Grandfather knows it all. He knows he will go and he has told me everything that he wants us to do."

"He is very brave," Jean Pierre said.

"First, he wants us to bring him to our farm in Plescassier and place him in the small family cemetery next to his father and his grandfather. Before he is buried, he wants us to give him a room at the Athenaeum in Cannes and all of his friends can come to visit him for the last time. Then on the third day, he has requested that we will all go to Plescassier and spend time remembering the love we all have for each other."

Jacques read the last few lines of the letter out loud:

"I love you, Jacques, my son, and Jean Pierre, my grandson, and also Raymond, my grandson who has gone before me.

Au revoir, my children, when we will all once again be together.
Love from your loving father and grandfather,
Maurice"

Jacques looked up at his son. This time they both felt the tears in their eyes. Again they embraced.

Then the telephone rang. It was Hugo. "Dr. Guillemin is downstairs in the library, *messieurs*."

D r. Guillemin was a young man, much to their surprise. They all shook hands. Jacques liked the doctor's handshake. It was firm and strong. "I am surprised, Doctor. You're younger than I expected."

Dr. Guillemin smiled. "I was four years as a resident in neurosurgery at the Hospital de Lyons. Then I was ordered here as captain in the Army Medical Corps. Now since the surrender, I have heard nothing from Pétain's headquarters. I have accepted the offer from two hospitals in Cannes and I was allowed to open my own office and practice."

Jean Pierre nodded. "I am not surprised that you have not heard from General Pétain's headquarters, and I guarantee that you will never hear from him. If you still want to join with the French, please, get in touch with me in General de Gaulle's office in London. He has formed the Free French Army."

The doctor seemed not to be interested in Jean Pierre's suggestion. "At the moment," he said, "I want to bring you up to date on your father's condition." He looked directly at Jacques as he spoke. "The butler, Hugo, found him on the floor beside his bed. Brilliantly, Hugo called the ambulance right away and had him taken to the hospital. If he had touched your father, he might have perished before we got him to the hospital. The hospital called me after your father had been brought in. I examined your father quickly and realized that there was a purple clot from the top of his head to his right cheekbone. His pulse was weak, and his breathing was labored. He asked me to please contact you and your son. I immediately put him on oxygen and then called the technician to do an X ray of his skull. By this photograph, we observed he was hemorrhaging in his brain. The carotid artery was torn and was bleeding like a waterfall. Then there were three other supporting blood arteries that had also torn apart. Your father is in a coma right now. He may awake for a few minutes, but we don't know. But I can tell you that there is no medicine that will help

him. Anything that I might give him would only bring more damage. All
I can suggest is that we pray that he does not have to live with pain."

"My grandfather can overcome anything. He will come out of this, too,"
Jean Pierre said, almost pleading with the doctor.

Dr. Guillemin stared at him. "Only by the grace of God. There has been
significant damage."

They all sat in silence for a moment. After a few minutes, Jacques called
for Hugo. "Cognac and Monte Cristos for all of us, including you, Hugo.
I appreciate your kindness for my father."

Hugo left the room for the cognacs and cigars. Jacques turned to his son.
"Now it's just the two of us, my son." Then Jacques turned to the doctor.
"When can we go to the hospital?"

"Right away, *monsieur*," he answered. "The nurses would have had time
to clean him and make him comfortable."

Hugo came back into the library. He filled the glasses and passed out
the cigars. He looked at Jacques and Jean Pierre.

Jean Pierre lifted the brandy snifter in a somber toast. "To Grandpa with
all of our love and also for his love and care for us."

The arrived at the hospital at 11:10. Maurice was lying quietly on his
bed. The blue stain across his skull down into his face was frightening for
Jacques and Jean Pierre. Suddenly, Maurice's eyes flew open. His blue eyes
seemed to search the two of them.

"Father!" Jacques said. "We are here with you!" But there were no words
from him. Only a small stream of white spittle as he tried to open his
mouth.

The nurse standing at the door called, "Dr. Guillemin!"

The doctor quickly stood next to his patient's bed. He held Maurice's
hand and took his pulse. There was none. Maurice's hand fell limply to
the sheet. Gently, the doctor closed Maurice's eyes and closed his mouth.

He turned to Jacques and Jean Pierre and spoke softly. "I am sorry, but
he is gone."

Jacques took his son's hand. They both had tears in their eyes. Jacques
looked up at the wall clock.

Maurice had died at 11:15.

22

The Athenaeum in Cannes was a cold stone building. There were fine private rooms for personal family viewing and a number of other rooms that were larger and held ten to twelve corpses on only cement slabs. There were groups of wooden chairs placed around the slabs for each sorrowing family.

But Maurice's private room was the finest decorated room and the most tasteful of all the rooms in the building. The chairs were plush, made of the finest wood and most expensive velvet. In each corner of the room there were scented candles that gave a soft, warm light and took the chill out of the room.

Jean Pierre was the first to enter the room early the next morning. He looked at his grandfather. He couldn't believe how extraordinarily the mortician had worked. His grandfather's face was clean-shaven, his hair combed neatly; and even more extraordinary, the blood clots on his face had been completely erased. Maurice was wearing his finest silk evening clothes, with a white Irish linen shirt starched to perfection and his black silk evening bow tie. He lay there looking as though he were still alive. His mahogany coffin was lying on a rack covered with a velvet cloth.

Jacques entered the room and stood next to Jean Pierre. He peered down at his father and then he looked at Jean Pierre. "Father loved dressing up. He was a very handsome man."

"Yes," Jean Pierre said, and then sat down beside his father in the chairs in the first row, where they waited for the first guests to arrive.

The cardinal of the Alpes Maritimes was the first. With him came the archbishop of Nice and Cannes. Joining them was the priest of St. Mary of Cannes, the largest Catholic church in all the diocese. Jacques and Jean Pierre shook hands with all the churchmen and then knelt before the coffin while the cardinal gave the mass, assisted by the altar boys from the church.

It was 120 kilometers to the mountains where the natural springs of Plescassier sprang from the earth. Next to the springs was a small farmhouse set on two hectares. One-half hectare was on the west side of the farmhouse, which held the tiny family cemetery where all of the Martin ancestors rested silently in peace. There were simple gray marble headstones marking each grave. Each headstone carried the name of only men. There was never a female that rested in this cemetery.

It was four in the afternoon when the graveside services began. There were approximately seventy mourners there, mostly Plescassier springs and bottling-plant employees. The priest that was the head of the small Église de Plescassier parish began the mass and immediately Jacques paid homage to his father and Jean Pierre gestured as the coffin was lowered into the ground. Finally a single white rose was tossed on the coffin by each mourner and then the earth was placed over Maurice's final resting place.

Silently, the mourners left the cemetery. Jacques and Jean Pierre waited until Maurice's headstone had been securely placed at his head. Then Jacques gestured to his son and pointed at the ground. There were small footstones in the earth next to Grandfather, and their own names had been lightly chiseled on them.

It was dusk when they finally went back to the old farmhouse. Jacques spoke to Samuel and Therese, who had taken care of the grounds. They lived beneath the farmhouse, in a small apartment that used to be the cellar. Jacques asked them to prepare the master's room for him; Jean Pierre would use the room that used to be his room when he was the son in this house.

Therese, her eyes swollen with tears, said that she had a lovely *côte de boeuf, pommes frites*, fresh, whole baguettes, and a delightful 1937 Bourgogne that was from their own vineyard. Samuel turned to them as he spoke. "We had expected that you would stay here, so the two rooms have been prepared since we first learned of Monsieur Maurice's passing. Now that the house is your own, we hope that you enjoy it as your ancestors have."

After dinner they moved into the small living room. They sat in the old-fashioned overstuffed armchairs. Jacques took a large cigar and lit it.

He leaned back in his chair and thought a moment. "We must plan for our future," he said, waving his cigar as he spoke. "I am fifty-seven years old and twenty years older than you."

Jean Pierre looked at him. "But you are a young man, Father."

"But it's not so long that I will retire at the age of sixty-one. It is the year that every one of us has turned over the company to our next inheritor. And that is you, Jean Pierre. In the year 1945 you will be the president and owner of Plescassier."

"You're only forgetting one thing, Father," Jean Pierre answered, and smiled. "There is still a war going on."

"War or not," Jacques said in a strong, forceful voice. "In 1945, whether the war is over or not, you will leave the service and take over your born responsibility. We have all had to make sacrifices, Jean Pierre. This is what our ancestors have lived and died for."

Jacques met his son's eyes. "You will do as we all have done. You will select a beautiful woman, who will bear you the heir for the next generation."

"Jesus, Father," Jean Pierre said. "You were only twenty years old when you married your wife and she became pregnant *tout de suite*. I hardly think at thirty-seven I can start having affairs with a woman. I've spent my life with handsome men."

"You'll manage, Jean Pierre. We all do. Your grandfather was thirty-one years old when I was born," Jacques said with finality.

"Balls," Jean Pierre answered.

"You better make sure that you get a male heir." Jacques laughed, not as a joke. "Female heirs won't do a thing for you. Without a male you cannot inherit Plescassier and you will lose everything for yourself and all of your ancestors. Our name will be lost forever."

"Okay, Father, you know I will never destroy our family," Jean Pierre replied. He had known that this day would come. He had resigned himself to this fact a long time ago. "But first I will return to General de Gaulle and work to help the Free French save our country."

"Just remember, my son, you are the only heir," Jacques said. "You stay close to the general's side. You can be a hero, but don't go into the trenches."

"Yes, Father," Jean Pierre said, and leaned toward his father as they both embraced.

23

It was ten days before Jean Pierre was able to return to Paris to his quarters in the old building that had been General de Gaulle's office. It was eerie as he walked into the building. The offices were totally empty. He walked through the hallway to the back offices, where the remaining officers were.

There were seven of the sous-lieutenants who looked up in surprise as Jean Pierre walked through the door. Three of them spoke at once. "Jean Pierre!" Then all of them gathered around him.

One of the senior officers grabbed his hand. "You're alive!" he exclaimed. "It's a miracle!"

"What's a miracle?" Jean Pierre asked. "Nothing happened to me. It was my grandfather who passed away."

One other young officer, Alain, looked at him. "We had been notified that you were killed when the plane was shot down over the Channel by a German Messerschmitt fighter. We were told everyone on the flight to England that night had perished. We had just received instructions from the Department of Defense to notify your family."

Jean Pierre sank into a chair. "All of them?" he asked. The senior officer nodded.

"My God!" Jean Pierre said. "I need a drink. When Colonel Nicol learned of my grandfather's illness, he gave me a pass to go and be with him. He ordered Louis to take my place on the flight."

Alain shook his head. "They never notified us of any change," he said. "You were fucking lucky!"

"But not Louis," Jean Pierre said quietly. "I feel guilty now."

"Don't be stupid," Alain said. "This is war."

Jean Pierre sat quietly for a moment. "Whom do I see for my orders to go to London?"

The eldest of the officers looked at him. Rene was a heavyset man and almost totally gray-haired. "No one," he answered. "There are no staff officers here. We have had no communication with de Gaulle."

"Then what do we do here? Just wait until the Boche arrive and pick us up and either execute us or send us to a prisoner-of-war camp?" Jean Pierre said angrily.

"You are the senior officer here now," Rene said. "We have made arrangements to rent an old fishing boat to take all of us to Dover. We have only one problem: Between all of us we don't even have half of the money to pay the fisherman. And unless we pay it all up front, the fisherman, a fucking Spanish bastard, will not take us anywhere."

Jean Pierre looked at him. "I have all of the money that we need for the boat."

The other officers stood up and saluted. "Merci, Capitaine. If we can meet with the fisherman tonight, we'll be able to leave by tomorrow night."

"I'm ready," Jean Pierre said. "Just let me know how much money we need."

Jean Pierre had dinner with his father at the villa in Paris. Jacques had been surprised to see Jean Pierre when he came into the office in the Champs-Elysées. "What happened?" Jacques asked. "Have the Boche taken over your quarters?"

Jean Pierre laughed. "Don't be silly, Father. The Germans have not found us yet."

"Then what are you doing here?" Jacques asked. "Are you now going into the stupid underground and get yourself killed?"

"No, Father," Jean Pierre answered.

"You can't even get to England now. I read in the papers that all of de Gaulle's staff is with him already," Jacques said. "You're fucked. If you want my opinion, I think you should go back to Plescassier, dress like the local farmers, and lay low until this war is over."

"There are eight of us here now," Jean Pierre said, ignoring his father's advice. "We have found a Spanish fisherman who will take us to Dover tomorrow night."

"The Channel is terrible by boat. Nothing but storms, and now the Luftwaffe is patrolling the Channel and will sink every little boat from Calais to England."

"I'm sorry, Father," Jean Pierre said. "I have to go. My friend Louis, who took my place on the plane, is dead. And all of the others on that plane. Shot down over the Channel. They were stunned at headquarters when I walked in; they thought I was on that plane, because none of the transfer papers had reached them. So I must go. It is my duty for allowing Louis to go in my place."

"You are really stupid. What good will it do now, even for de Gaulle, even for France, even for me, if you are dead?" Jacques said. "I will not allow it! You will not go on a fisherman's boat in the dead of night, not even if you fly with angel's wings."

"Nothing else matters, Father," Jean Pierre shot back. "I have made up my mind."

"You can't do it." Jacques began to get angry with his son. "If anything happens to you, what would I do? I am left alone and without an heir. Do you have so little concern for your own father?"

"First, my father, I will not die." Jean Pierre laughed. "You are worrying for no reason."

"Monsieur Weil, our banker, was caught at the Swiss border and executed. The Boche show no mercy. They catch you on the Channel, you won't be given a chance to even escape. They will kill you," Jacques said, still upset.

Jean Pierre reached for his father's hand. "Then, Father, you can save the family again. You are still a man with all of his sexual power. You can make three women pregnant in a month. Then the family will be saved."

Jacques looked at his son. "You are just a crazy child, Jean Pierre."

24

The Spanish fisherman's boat was rancid with the smell of dead fish. Even the Frenchmen who didn't smoke cigarettes were smoking to try to kill the horrible stench. One after the other they emptied their stomachs over the side of the boat. An hour and a half outside of Dover they were hailed by a British patrol boat. Within an hour the Frenchmen were taken by the British boat the rest of the journey and the Spanish fisherman was on his way back to France.

A week after Jean Pierre arrived in General de Gaulle's headquarters, he was assigned to work with the U.S. Army platoon at the American embassy. The platoon, despite being a small group, had many duties, including protection of the ambassador and his family, and covering messages and telephone and radio transmissions to and from the State Department in Washington, D.C. Jean Pierre didn't think his job was too important in the beginning, but it wasn't long until he realized that his real work was collecting all of the intelligence information in and out of the embassy.

The two officers in charge of the platoon were a colonel and a major. However, Jean Pierre reported to only one man, Lieutenant Bradford Norton. He had been promoted in the field from sergeant. Brad, as he preferred to be called, was liked and well respected by all of the men.

Jean Pierre had a great deal of respect for the lieutenant even though he was several years younger. They worked together well and a deep friendship began to develop between the two men. It wasn't long before they discovered that each led a homosexual lifestyle. They became lovers.

Because Jean Pierre was rich, he was able to live a very good life in London. He was wealthy enough to rent a beautiful apartment near Hyde Park. He could easily walk to the de Gaulle headquarters, and within a quarter of an hour he could walk to the American embassy.

Jean Pierre and Brad were having dinner at the Mayflower Hotel several months after they had met. Jean Pierre looked at Brad. "I want you to move in with me."

Brad laughed. "That would be wonderful," Brad said. "I would love it; however, if the army ever found out about our relationship, I would be court-martialed, thrown in an army prison for at least three years, and given a dishonorable discharge."

"Why would anyone else have to know?" Jean Pierre asked. "We won't be here forever. And after the war you can come to France with me to live. Our life will be heaven in France."

"What kind of work would I do in France? I don't know the language that well. Jean Pierre, it takes money to live," Brad answered.

"Money is not important." Jean Pierre laughed.

"What? You have enough money to live like that?" Brad asked.

"I have enough money to even live in America without working. The important thing is I love you! I want us to be together," Jean Pierre said.

Brad looked at him and then lifted his glass and held it up to Jean Pierre. "I love you, too!"

They both drank from their wineglasses. Jean Pierre spoke first. "To our troth!" Under the table Jean Pierre placed his hand inside Brad's thigh. He could feel Brad's hardening phallus.

PART TWO

TWO FRANCS A LITER

1

Jerry in the Army and Out

Friday the thirteenth is always an unlucky day for me. It was a frozen day in February 1942. I was standing bare-assed naked in Grand Central taking my medical checkup for the army. There were at least twenty doctors who I had to see, and they looked into every hole in my body, from my ass to my nose and ears. Finally, it was over. I dressed and was seated at a small table across from a fifty-year-old doctor who had my medical history report in his hand.

He read it carefully and every few minutes looked at me over the top of his glasses. Finally he spoke. "You're Jewish?"

"Yes, Doctor," I answered.

"I'm Jewish, too," he said.

I nodded silently.

He got out of his chair and then took a small black instrument with a light on the front and peered into each of my ears. Then he went back to his chair and sat down.

The doctor continued reading my report. Then he opened a heavy medical encyclopedia and began studying it. I looked behind me to see if anyone was waiting to see the doctor. All I could see was the line of draftees standing in another line. They looked like cattle in a Clark Gable movie being taken to the slaughter. The doctors were impersonal; they didn't give a damn about the draftees. They would pass them or reject them. They didn't care which way.

But I thought I was in good shape. I turned back and watched the doctor. I began to tap my fingers. He finally looked up at me. "Do you have any problem hearing?"

"No, sir," I answered.

He took a deep breath. "Jerry," he asked, "when did you have your mastoidectomy?"

I thought for a moment. "I don't remember, Doctor," I answered. "I was very young."

"You must have been," he replied. "The perforation in the eardrum is almost completely closed. You're lucky you didn't have to have an operation on the other ear. You might have been deaf by now."

"What does all of this mean?" I asked.

"Nothing really," he said. "If you had had an operation on the other ear you would be four-F."

"But, Doctor, I heard if you have a perforated eardrum and can't hear as well as others you could get your head blown off," I said.

The doctor chuckled. "You'll only be classified one-B. Noncombat."

"What does that mean?" I asked.

"Maybe cooking, or mechanical work, maybe a clerk," he answered. "I really don't know what they will do with you."

"I know what I would like for them to do with me, Doctor," I said. "I would like them to let me stay home."

"You have no patriotism, Jerry. You should want to kill Adolf Hitler," the doctor said.

"I'm Jewish, Doctor," I said. "Not a hero."

The doctor filled out a new form and handed it to me. "This is a notice that will put you into a noncombatant class. You're not one-A, nor are you four-F. You will be one-B and you will need to come back tomorrow morning and take a few tests. I have recommended you for automobile mechanic repairs in the Quartermaster Corps."

I looked at the doctor. I then read the form for a moment, and then I realized what a wonderful kindness he had done for me. I turned back to him. "Thank you, Doctor. I'm really very grateful. Thank you very much."

He smiled at me and patted me on the shoulder. "You remind me of my own son. He's still in medical school and I only pray that this lousy war is over before he has to go in."

"Thank you, Doctor," I said again. "And I hope that everything is good for your son."

I felt pretty good as I found my way to the exit. Then I heard a voice behind me that I recognized. It was Buddy. I crossed the aisle to him. "What the hell are you doing here?"

It was the first time I had ever seen him look unhappy. "I've been drafted."

"Did you get your physical yet?" I asked.

He lit a cigarette and inhaled. The smoke came out from his broad nostrils. "I'm perfect," he said. "One-A." He looked at me. "How about you?"

"One-B," I said.

"What the hell is that?" he asked. "I never heard of it."

"Neither did I," I answered. "But I'm not complaining. I've got a pretty safe job. The doctor recommended me for the auto mechanic corps."

"What the hell do you know about being a mechanic? You don't even know how to drive!"

I stared at him. "Let's get out of here," I said to him. "I've got an idea!"

We left Grand Central and walked to the corner of Lexington Avenue, where there was a cafeteria. We grabbed a couple of coffees and sat down at an empty table.

Buddy tasted his coffee. "It's hot as hell."

"Give it time to cool off," I said. Then I showed him the form the doctor had given me.

He read it and looked at me. "What good is this going to do me? I got nothing like that." He pulled out a slip from his pocket and waved it in the air. "My doctor gave me a one-A."

"What's happened to you, Buddy? What happened to the smart hustler I've always known? What did that examination do to you? Scare the shit out of you?" I asked.

"What the hell can I do?" he asked.

"Don't you remember about that old black man that forged things that you introduced me to? Remember when he made licenses for Eddie to make the seltzer and also the license for him to drive the truck and sell the bottles?" I asked.

"Yeah, I know him."

"Is he still in business?" I asked. "You told me that he made Social

Security cards, driver's licenses, and sixteen-year-old birthday records for fourteen-year-olds so they could get a job."

"So?" Buddy asked, deep in his misery.

"So let's go see him in Harlem. You said he was an artist," I said, waving the 1-B paper in his face. "Let's let the artist copy this and make you an auto mechanic like me. And we'll be in the army together."

"You're forgetting one detail," Buddy said.

"What's that?"

"You're white. I'm black."

"Your skin's almost as light as mine. If anybody asks we'll say you're Cuban."

Buddy was silent for a full minute. Then he smiled for the first time that day. "I must be crazy," he said. He stood up and took out his money clip. "Let's go. I got money for a cab. The sooner I'm one-B and white, the better."

2

We both passed the tests the next day and by that evening we were on the bus to Fort Dix in New Jersey.

We passed a lot of pig farms and five hours later we arrived at the entrance gate of the army base. By now it had begun to rain and sleet. The temperature was dropping rapidly.

There were about twenty draftees who stepped out of the bus in the miserable and freezing weather. There was a big sergeant, who thought he was a general, who greeted us. He was a nasty bastard. He didn't give a damn that we were all soaking wet, cold, and tired. First he made us line up, and then he made us reline up again according to our height. This put me in the middle at about five feet eight, and Buddy ended up at the end of the line at six feet two.

Then the sergeant had us face him and he called out from the list of names. As we answered, he filled out our names on another form in his three-ring black notebook. Then once again he called out our names and we had to place an X next to our name in the black book. Finally, he took us to a long table where we received our uniforms. After that he took us to a small barracks, where it was as cold as the outside. He assigned each of us a bed. Behind our beds was a shelf holding two books, and below the shelf was a small cabinet with two doors on the front.

"The books will give you all the information about your dress code and other information you will need about the army. I will leave now and I will see you at reveille, which is at oh five hundred hours, at which time you should be completely dressed. Good night."

One of the draftees called to him. "Sergeant!" He saluted when he spoke.

The sergeant snapped at him almost before the word was out of his mouth. "Draftee, you do not salute noncommissioned officers. Only officers of lieutenant and up."

"I am sorry, Sergeant," said the draftee, quickly dropping his hand. "I wanted to ask when we might be having dinner?"

The sergeant laughed at him. "You're out of luck. All of the dinners are served at eighteen hundred hours. But you will be able to have breakfast in the morning."

"How about the heat in this place, Sergeant?" another draftee said.

"You're in the army now, son! You better start taking care of yourself. 'When's the food? Where's the heat?' " he mimicked. "I'm going to tell the officers we just got a busload of pussies! Figure it out for yourself!" he shouted, and briskly turned and walked out of the barracks.

After he had left the barracks, we all looked at each other. Buddy shook his head. "The army stinks!" He looked out the window of the barracks. Outside on the far corner was a rack of large garbage cans. While he was looking he saw a soldier in a white cook's uniform come out carrying one of the cans.

I got up and started trying to find where the heater was installed.

Buddy turned to look at his newfound friends. "If any of you have a few bucks to lay on me, I bet I could bring us all a little dinner."

It wasn't long before Buddy was the first corporal in our platoon.

3

It was the first weekend I spent at Fort Dix. In only one day of boot camp, my muscles and entire body were nothing but pain and agony. I bought and used up two bottles of Sloan's Liniment. No one in the platoon could stand near me because of that smell.

When Sunday arrived, it was supposed to be an easy day. But that was only until noon. Then the usual drill began. It was six o'clock before I could shower and have my dinner. By that time I was wiped out and had stretched out on my bunk for a little rest.

I fell asleep and began dreaming instantly. I began to dream about my last Friday night at home. Kitty had come up to my apartment. I had all of my things packed in my cheap valises that I had bought because Kitty had said she would keep all of my nice things until I returned. And then she began to cry.

I pulled her to me and wiped the tears from her cheeks with a hand-kerchief.

Then she looked up into my eyes. "I don't know how I'll live without you. I'll think of you every day. I'm so frightened that you will get killed or wounded, Jerry." She began to cry even more. "What if you lose a leg or an arm? If that happens I'll take care of you."

I chuckled, trying to lighten her mood. "You don't have to worry about anything, except getting my cock shot off." I grabbed her and put her hand inside my pants. It was hard and she made it even harder. I moaned as she stroked and held my phallus. I reached under her dress and pulled her panties down. The inside of her legs was already wet. I spread the lips of her vagina and probed her with two fingers and gently manipulated her clitoris.

She began to squeeze my balls and then jerk my penis. She repeated this until I couldn't hold it any longer—my semen shot out like a cannon. I lifted her up and threw her on the bed.

She was tearing her clothes off and I began to smear her breasts with the juices of her vagina. My prick was still dripping and I held it over her enlarged clitoris. As the drops fell she moaned in ecstasy. Suddenly, I was hard again. I fucked her like there was no tomorrow.

I looked at the clock. It was seven o'clock. We were lying on the bed smoking a cigarette. I turned to Kitty. "Aunt Lila is making dinner for us. We are supposed to be there by eight o'clock."

Kitty said nothing. She leaned over and kissed me and reached for my prick. "Just one more time before we go over to her place."

"There's no way I can get it up again," I said. "I'll grab a shower and then we can have dinner. I'll get my strength back and we'll come home and fuck our brains out."

She laughed as I started for the shower. "You don't have to fuck your brains out, honey. All you need is a hard cock and a wet pussy."

Suddenly, I awoke from the dream. It was real. That had been my last night with Kitty. But it was still just a dream. It was the first time I had a wet dream in the army.

4

The back room of the barracks was filled with smoke. This was the weekly poker game. It was always at night after dinner. At twenty-two hundred hours, army time.

Sergeant Mayer, the head of our platoon, looked across the table. "I'll raise," he said, chewing on the butt of his cigar. He threw another quarter into the pot.

Buddy was crazy. He didn't hesitate. "I'll meet you and raise you another quarter."

I looked down at my cards. I had a great hand—ace of spades high—but I had to live with the sergeant for another eight weeks. Mayer was a mean son of a bitch. Poker was his game. He organized the game every week. It was how he picked up extra money. Sergeants didn't make much money.

I saw the look on Buddy's face. He was hot. I tried to give him the high sign to lay off. But Buddy didn't give a damn. I laid my cards facedown on the table. "I fold," I said.

The sarge raised Buddy another fifty cents. But Buddy didn't stop. He threw two dollars down on the table. "See that, Sarge."

"You're one dumb son of a bitch," the sarge said, eyeballing Buddy. He chewed on his cigar and thought for a moment. "I'll see you and raise you five bucks!" he said, waving the five-dollar bill in the air.

Buddy covered the five-dollar bet.

The sarge spread his cards on the table. He had four aces. And one of them was the ace of spades that was in my hand. I whistled out loud.

"Shit!" Buddy swore, showing his hand. Three queens.

The sergeant pulled in his winnings and started gathering the cards. "This ain't no game for kids," he said.

Buddy walked away in silence. I looked back at the table. The sarge was turning over all the hands of cards. When he turned over my hand, he saw my ace of spades. He hesitated for a moment, looked up, and nodded at me. I knew I had done the right thing.

Buddy and I walked out of the barracks over to the baseball diamond and sat down on one of the benches. "That prick is a cheat!" Buddy scowled as he lit a cigarette.

"He's also our sergeant," I said. "Remember, he made you corporal. Look, we've been here two months, and I've learned a little bit about him. He's Caesar here. He likes you. Don't push him and he'll be nice to you."

"I saw him palm one of the aces," he said.

"So, you learned one thing," I said.

"What's that?" he asked.

"Don't bet dollars in a quarter game. On our salaries, you can't get crazy." I took out a cigarette and lit it. Boy, when you're outside, the smoke tastes good.

"Heard anything from Kitty?" he asked.

"Nothing. Her telephone was turned off," I said. "As a matter of fact, I've heard nothing from anybody in New York." I dragged on my cigarette. "Next week they're shipping us out to auto mechanics school in Detroit. I'm thinking about running over to New York City for a day to find out what's going on before we go."

"You're even stupider than I am. One day out spells AWOL. They dump you in the crapper for six months and there goes everything. You're fucked," Buddy said. "Besides, if they find out that my papers were copied from yours, we both will be in federal prison for years."

I decided to try to phone Kitty again before I turned in. There wasn't the usual crowd lined up at the telephones. It was late. About midnight. I threw in my dimes and gave the number to the operator. A moment later she told me that the telephone number I had given her was disconnected. I thought for a moment and then asked her to call Uncle Harry's number at home.

At least that number was working. I could hear the telephone ring. After six or seven rings there was no answer. I hung up and collected my dimes and walked back to the barracks. I didn't understand. Uncle Harry and Aunt Lila never stayed out this late, and the telephone was right by the bed. Even if they had been asleep they should have answered. I made up my mind that I would telephone earlier tomorrow evening.

As I entered the barracks the sergeant yelled at me from his room.

I knew the sarge's voice so I ran as fast as I could across the barracks to his room. He was still in uniform. It must be something important, so I stood at attention and saluted. "Yes sir, Sergeant," I said.

"Asshole," he snapped. "You're over two months in the army and you don't remember that you don't salute a noncommissioned soldier?"

I dropped my hand. "I'm sorry, sir," I said.

He shook his head in disgust. He handed me a telegram. "This just came in from the company's office. I got it after the card game. I looked around for you but didn't see you."

"Thank you, Sergeant," I said, tearing the telegram open. It was from Fat Rita.

DEAR JERRY. VERY IMPORTANT. CALL ME. TEL. NO. JA1-5065. WILL BE AT THAT NUMBER DAY AND NIGHT. SIGNED. RITA KASTENBERG.

I put the telegram in my shirt pocket.

The sergeant was curious. "Was that from your girlfriend? The only time they telegram you is if they are knocked up or need money."

"She's not my girlfriend," I answered. "She just worked at the same place that I did." I hesitated a moment, then asked the sergeant: "I know it's late, Sarge, but could I get permission to use the phone again? I won't be too long."

"Sure you can go. I just hope she ain't knocked up!" He laughed.

I went back to the pay phones. I was lucky. Only a couple of other guys were there, but it seemed like it took forever before they were off the phone. It was 0100 army time before I could call.

Fat Rita answered. "Jerry?" She sounded as if she had been crying.

"I got your telegram. What's going on?" I asked.

"Harry took over my brother's business, Jerry, and he sold it out from under us," she said, sniffing.

"How did he get control of the business?" I asked.

"He got Eddie back to betting on horses. Then when Eddie couldn't pay off his markers he took the business."

"What about my money?" I asked.

157

"I asked Harry about it and he said that it was his money because your father skimmed the bets when he was working for him," Rita said, starting to cry.

"The son of a bitch!" I swore. "Wait until I tell Aunt Lila about this. After all, my father was her brother."

"Your uncle didn't tell you?" she asked. "You won't even be able to talk to her. She's in the hospital dying of cancer. They say it could be any day."

"Jesus," I swore again, and hit the wall with my fist. "Harry never told me. He knows that I love Aunt Lila. He should have told me."

"He's way ahead of you," Rita said. "He's even got your girlfriend, Kitty. He moved her into the apartment and kicked out the schwartze. He also moved Kitty into his office with him and made her the manager since he spends a lot of time at the hospital. The first thing she did was give me two weeks' notice."

"I'll get the son of a bitch on the phone and straighten him out!" I said, almost shouting.

"Save your nickel," she said. "You'll never get him. He's spending the night with Kitty and they changed the telephone number at the business."

"I'm really fucked," I said. "I'm being shipped out next week to another camp and I can't even get a one-day pass."

"There's nothing we can do here," she said. "But a friend of ours has set us up with jobs at Kaiser's. Eddie and I are planning to leave for California the minute I get my severance pay."

"Damn!" I said. "It seems like the whole world has gone crazy."

"Ain't it the truth!" Rita answered. "But Eddie and me appreciate what you tried to do for us. As long as we stay here I'll let you know about your Aunt Lila."

"Thanks, Rita," I said. "You're a real friend."

"I love you, Jerry," she said. "Just don't get yourself killed in the war and I'll pray for you. Good luck."

"And good luck for the two of you, Rita. I really mean that. So long," I said, and hung up the receiver.

It took me a half an hour to make my way back to the barracks. It was dark; all the lights had been turned off. Through the windows, the street-lights showed some of the bunks as I walked into the barracks. I could see Buddy sitting up in the dark on the edge of his bed, his legs dangling, a cigarette glowing from his lips. "Where the hell were you hanging out?"

"I was on the phone," I answered.

"What was goin' on?" he asked.

"My Aunt Lila is dying in the hospital," I said.

"I'm sorry," he said. "She is a very nice lady. I liked her."

"That's only part of it," I said. "Uncle Harry got Eddie into the horses again and when he couldn't pay his markers he took his business."

"The next thing you're going to tell me is that Harry took over your girlfriend, Kitty."

"You're right," I said flatly. "But Harry kicked out his colored girl and moved Kitty into the apartment. Then he made Kitty the manager of the business. The first thing she did was fire Fat Rita."

"And what about the money you had in Eddie's business and the money Kitty had stashed in the bank for you?" Buddy knew everything I had done.

"Gone," I said. "He says that it's all money that my father skimmed off from him."

He took a deep breath and squashed out his cigarette in an ashtray. "You're fucked."

"I don't give a damn," I snapped. "AWOL or not, I'm going over to the city and I'll give them both hell. You taught me how to use a knife."

"And you spend the rest of your life in the can," Buddy said. "Let me take care of it for you. I can get in touch with a couple of friends of mine from Harlem. They will do something quietly and you will be as clean as an angel."

"I don't know," I said. "It's not the same thing."

"The same thing might look like the electric chair," Buddy said. "You should get into your bunk and get some sleep. By the morning you will cool down. In a week we're moving out of here to Detroit and yesterday is another world."

I looked at him as I thought. Finally, I nodded in agreement. "You know, you're a pretty damn smart son of a bitch!"

Buddy laughed.

I walked over to my bunk, stretched out, and went right to sleep.

5

We arrived in Detroit, but not at a regular army base. We were sent to an automobile school at the Willys Overland factory. This was the company that manufactured the jeeps, shipping them to the armed services by the hundreds every day. Outside the factory, the army had built large Quonset huts which became the barracks for the two hundred soldiers assigned to the school. It was not too bad. Much better than the training camp at Fort Dix. At least here we only had an eight-hour day.

It was Buddy's heaven. He had a crap game running every night and booked the horses all day long. I wondered how he ever got his auto mechanic lessons done. But he managed to do it all.

After being in Detroit for two weeks, I was worried. I hadn't heard anything from Fat Rita and I wanted to know what was happening with Aunt Lila. It was a Sunday evening when I placed a call to her. The phone rang a few times before she answered.

"Rita?" I asked.

"Jerry!" she exclaimed. "I've been trying to get in touch with you for the last week but the stupid army wouldn't give me any information. All they would say is that you will get a postal number before you go overseas and I could write you at that time. They said it would reach you wherever you went."

"I haven't got it yet," I said. "When it comes through, they'll just send it to my family."

"I guess they'll send it to Harry," she said softly. "Your Aunt Lila died last week. I thought about you and wished you could have been there. I liked your Aunt Lila and I went to her funeral."

I was silent for a moment. "Harry's a prick," I said. "He's a relative. The army would have let him call if they knew it was about a death. He didn't give a damn because he knew that I loved her."

"He didn't want to see you," Fat Rita said. "He had Kitty with him at the funeral, all dressed in black. He knew that you would have killed them."

"Why was she in black? She's not even in the family," I said.

Fat Rita took a deep breath. "She is now! Two days after the funeral they got married."

"Jesus! She's only half his age!" I exclaimed.

"I worked for him for nine years," she said. "He always had young girls. Rosey, his little black girl, was only seventeen when he took her in."

"I had to be stupid," I said. "I never knew he liked them that young."

"It's over," Fat Rita said quietly. "Now we can all get on with our lives and to hell with him. I'm so glad that you called me tonight because tomorrow we will take the train to California."

"Okay," I said. "I'll find a way to keep in touch with you and Eddie. Have a good trip, and good luck. And thanks for giving me the news."

I put the telephone down. It wasn't Harry alone that I was angry with. I was even angrier at Kitty. The bitch! She turned everything I had, my money, her pussy, over to Harry. Love at first sight, I guess.

6

Buddy and I did well in the mechanics school. As a matter of fact, we were real experts. They decided to keep us in Detroit as teachers for each new mechanic platoon. In six months we were promoted to sergeant and each of us was put in charge of a teaching section. I was motor repair and rebuilds. Buddy had the best part of the work. He was in charge of painting all parts and exteriors of the jeeps. He wanted to paint the jeeps black, but the army only called for olive green, so his artistic endeavors came to nothing. As sergeants we were entitled to use a jeep on every third weekend leave. It was immediately after our promotion that we requested leave.

The sergeant gave us the weekend pass. We used one of the older jeeps and Buddy drove us into town. Downtown Detroit was all black. The tenements were filled with black families who worked for the automobile factories nearby. They were not building automobiles now, only tanks and engines for airplanes and PT boats. The blacks had nothing but money. They were paid high hourly wages and as much overtime as they wanted.

Buddy knew exactly where he was going: a tenement that seemed to look a little better than the others. Painted. Cleaned. As we walked up to the entrance, a big man was standing guard at the door. Buddy spoke up to him. "My cousin, Leroy, in there?"

The guard seemed to know Buddy. "He's downstairs in the club."

"We'll go down to see him," Buddy said.

"Not so fast," the guard said. "He's working out a new show an' he don't want nobody to bother him."

"You call him and tell him that his cousin, Clarence, is here," Buddy said. "He'll see me. I sent him the girls for the new show."

I looked at Buddy. "I didn't know you had those connections."

He winked. "In the black world, all of us stick together."

The guard came back from the telephone. "You can go down and see him. You know the way?"

"Tell me," Buddy said. "I'm new in town."

He followed the guard to the back entrance of the building. Then he led us downstairs and into an empty kitchen behind the club. We could hear a piano and the beat of the drums as we walked into the club itself. There was a long bar and about thirty tables that could seat about ninety customers. One wall of the club was a small stage, a dance floor, and a place for a small group that could sit close to the piano and drums.

There were six black girls in rehearsal costumes and they watched as we came in the room. Leroy was a big, handsome black man sitting at a table near the drummer and the piano player.

Leroy started toward us. He waved at the girls. "Take ten minutes." Then he held his hand out to Buddy. He grasped Buddy's hand and pulled him toward him in a big bear hug. "Clarence!" He smiled. "The last time I saw you, you were hanging on to your mother's skirt." He laughed again. "Now, here you are in Detroit in the army."

"I grew up a little since then, Leroy." Buddy laughed. "It's great to see you doing so wonderful."

"I have some backup." Leroy smiled. "The Purple Mob are my partners. Real good friends." He took us to the bar. "What'll you have?"

Buddy gestured to me. "He's my friend, Jerry Cooper. We've been working together for about three years."

Leroy took my hand. Practically broke it. "Clarence is a friend of yours, you a friend of mine. We all have a shot of Canadian."

"We'll take ours with ice and water," Buddy said. "We're not used to the hard stuff. Just beer."

Leroy smiled. "Okay. We'll have a beer. Now what else can I do for you?"

"How did you like Rosey?" Buddy asked. "She was really a star at Small's."

Leroy looked at him. "Were you fucking her?"

"No," Buddy said. "She was kept by Jerry's uncle for a few years. Then he threw her out."

"Why?" Leroy asked. "Was she stealing from him?"

"No way. She was straight," Buddy answered. "We just want to talk to her a little. Jerry thinks that his uncle was screwing him on some things."

Leroy looked at me. "Do you know Rosey?"

"I never saw her before," I answered. "But I think she might be able to help me with some information."

"Okay," Leroy said. "But you can't talk to her until after her show tonight. I've got her starring in the show tonight and this is her first solo performance. I don't want her to get upset."

"It's okay, Mr. Leroy," I said. "You tell me when you want me to talk to her and I'll be here."

He turned to Buddy. "Why don't y'all hang around here while we go through this rehearsal. Then I'll take you out to dinner."

Buddy and I sat at the bar and nursed our beers. Leroy worked with the chorus line until it was perfect to his taste. He left the girls and came back to us. "Okay fellas," he said in his deep baritone voice. "Let's go to my place first. You'll meet my wife while I get a shower and a new change of clothes. I'm the boss, and I have to look my best."

We followed him out of the club. The guard at the door was already at the curb with a shiny black 1940 Cadillac limousine with the door open.

"We have a jeep," Buddy said. "We'll follow you."

"No way." Leroy smiled. "You'll come in my hog. Give the keys to the jeep to Johnson. He'll take care of the car for you."

Buddy gave the keys to the guard. "Hide it," he said. "It's government property. I don't want us to get canned for lettin' somebody else drive it."

Johnson smiled. "Don't worry. I have all the tricks to keep a car safe."

"Thanks." Buddy smiled, and tried to hand Johnson a fiver.

Johnson shook his head. "No sir, you're in the family."

Buddy sat in the front seat with his cousin. I sat in the back. I had never been in a new car like this. It rode like I was floating on a cloud, and the upholstery was like regular furniture. The smell of the new car was like heaven. Pure pussy.

Buddy looked back at me. "Like the car?"

"Fantastic!" I answered. "I never have been in a car like this."

"They ain't many of them around," Leroy said. "When the war started, all the new cars went to the big shots in the government. I paid for this one under the table." He laughed his big laugh. "That usually gets you what you want."

"It's great, Mr. Leroy," I said.

It took us only about fifteen minutes to get to Leroy's house. It seemed like a newly constructed apartment and there was a driveway that led to the apartment entrance. A tall uniformed doorman opened the car door for us and then drove the car away. There were two elevators, each on one side of the building, each with its own elevator operator. Leroy's apartment was on the top floor. Ninth floor. Penthouse apartment west.

Buddy looked at his cousin as we walked to his door. "Leroy!" he said with admiration. "You are one dickety nigger. How did you ever get so smart?"

"Connections," Leroy said, and smiled. "With connections you can own the world."

7

Leroy's penthouse was something else. The living room was at least forty feet long, with windows that covered one whole side of the room that opened to a terrace that looked over the river to Canada. The furniture was beautiful. It looked like a picture in a magazine. There were expensive antiques, leather easy chairs, and a large sectional sofa, with oil paintings on every part of the walls.

Leroy saw the astonishment on my face. "It's a beautiful place, isn't it? My wife, Carolyn, decorated it herself. She went to Chicago, New York, and Europe and bought all of these things."

"It's great," I said.

Buddy was staring with his mouth open. "This ain't like no black folks' house I've ever seen."

"My wife ain't black." Leroy smiled. "I met her in Paris where she was a showgirl at the Moulin Rouge."

"Is she here?" Buddy asked.

"She'll be home in a minute," Leroy said. "She has an interior decorating and furniture store over in Grosse Pointe. That's where all the bigwigs in the auto business live. They love Carolyn's work; she's done most of their homes. But it takes about a half hour for her to drive home. She'll be here soon."

"You doin' pretty good," Buddy said, still gawking.

Leroy smiled. "You soldiers get a drink over at the bar while I get dressed. Just relax an' enjoy."

A small man wearing a white waiter's coat came into the room and went behind the bar. "I'm Julian," he said in a soft voice. "I'm the butler. What can I serve you gentlemen?"

"Rheingold," Buddy said.

"Same for me," I said. "Thank you."

He filled our glasses and set out a plate of peanuts in front of us. "Is there anything else I can do for you gentlemen?" Julian said.

"We're fine, Julian," Buddy said.

"The door to the terrace is unlocked if you would like to go out, gentlemen," Julian said. "If you need anything else just press this button on the bar."

"Thank you," I said.

Buddy looked at me. I followed him out to the terrace. Buddy shook his head. "I never knew that Leroy was so loaded."

"He seems like a nice man," I said.

Buddy laughed. "You didn't know him when he was young. He was really tough. He was the collection man for the Purple Mob. Then when he made his mark they turned him over to the cabaret business and he ran all the games in a secret room behind the showroom."

"He still seems like a nice man," I said.

"He really is." Buddy smiled. "If you don't give him any trouble."

"I'm an angel." I laughed. Then we heard Julian open the front door and looked toward the doorway. Leroy's wife came into the room. He was right when he said she wasn't a black woman. She had skin that looked like ivory, platinum hair, and beautiful blue eyes. She was a beautiful lady who looked like a model off a magazine cover.

Buddy was up on his feet. He was off the terrace and into the room before she could get through the living room. I followed him but I was not as fast as he was. "Carolyn, I'm Leroy's cousin, Clarence."

She shook his hand. "I'm happy to meet you." She smiled back. "You sound like you're from New York," she said in a sultry voice. "I was born in New York, too."

Buddy laughed. "I guess we're all New Yorkers, then. This is my friend, Jerry Cooper."

I nodded and held out my hand. "It's nice to meet you, ma'am."

She held my hand. It was warm. "You can call me Carolyn." She smiled. "What brings you to Detroit?"

"We're working over at the jeep factory in the army. When we're finished here we'll be shipped overseas," I rattled off. I couldn't keep my mind on what I was saying, she was so beautiful.

"Jerry's too modest," Buddy chimed in. "We're both teachers here and we'll probably be here quite a while."

"Good." She smiled a radiant smile. "We'll be happy to have you here. Most of our friends have already shipped out." She turned to leave the room. "I'm going over to check with Leroy about what the plans are for this evening. Just relax at the bar and we'll both be back real soon."

Buddy looked at me after she left the room. "Man, she's really a knock-out. Cousin Leroy has done himself proud."

I looked at him and went to the bar. "She's a star. I'm surprised she never wound up in Hollywood."

Leroy had just come into the room and had heard me. "You're right, kid." He laughed at me. "We went to Los Angeles on our honeymoon and the first night we were at dinner, one of the big producers at MGM wanted to take us over to the studio the next morning and give her a screen test. But she said no, no. She was staying with her man Leroy in Detroit."

"You're a lucky man," Buddy said.

"Don't I know it!" Leroy agreed. "You fellas like surf and turf? We got the best place in town. We'll have dinner and then we'll all go back to the cabaret and see the show."

"You're the boss." Buddy laughed.

The restaurant was great. It was on the waterfront and we were seated on a corner that looked over the river to the lights of Windsor. From the way the maître d' acted I could easily understand that Leroy was an important man here. The steak and lobster we had was something I had never had before. I never tasted anything so good. By nine o'clock, Leroy had us back at his cabaret. The show began at midnight. By that time, I was bombed on beer and had to piss every twenty minutes. I was half asleep in my chair when Carolyn tapped me on the knee. "Showtime!" She laughed.

I shook my head to clear it. Then I realized that Leroy and Buddy were not at the table. I looked at Carolyn. "I guess I dozed off," I said.

"You were fast asleep," she said, laughing. "They left me here to make sure you didn't fall off the chair."

"I have never eaten or drunk like that in my entire life," I said. "The army never feeds us like this."

"Leroy went backstage. He always does that when a new show is open-ing. He wants everything to be perfect. Buddy followed along with him."

She smiled. "Buddy was checking out the girls. He looked horny, like he hasn't seen a girl in a long time."

"This is the army, ma'am." I laughed. "You don't get much time off for girls. This is the first time we got off since we went into the army at Fort Dix."

She placed her hand on my thigh and moved it up to my fly under the tablecloth. I felt my hard-on growing against the touch of her hand. She smiled at me. "I guess that you haven't gotten off in a long time."

I lit a cigarette and kept my hands on top of the table as I inhaled and then slowly blew out the smoke. I looked over at her. "You be careful with that hand or I'll get it off in my pants right here."

She took her hand away and reached for a cigarette. I held the light for her. She looked into my eyes. "I'm happy that you're not a fag," she said. "I hear that a lot of soldiers get queer and I wondered whether you and Clarence were a team."

I laughed. "No ma'am. We like it the old-fashioned way."

"Good," she said, letting the smoke lightly drift from her lips. Then she looked away. "I see them coming back." And again she looked at me. "We'll have another moment sometime, when there is no pressure."

I didn't have a chance to even answer. Leroy and Buddy were back at the table. Leroy turned to his wife. "I don't know." He shook his head. "I'm worried about the show."

Carolyn kissed his cheek and snuggled up to him. "You always worry about every new show, darlin'. They'll be great. I know it."

"All the same, we better keep our fingers crossed," said Leroy, and he gulped a double shot of Canadian.

The show was great. Maybe because I had never been to a cabaret or seen a stage show in my life. The only singers or dancers I had ever seen had been in the movies. The show lasted almost an hour and a half. After the show was over the stage was rolled up and it became a dance floor. It was unbelievable to me.

Carolyn smiled at me. "Would you like to dance, Jerry?"

"I'm sorry," I said. "I don't know how. I've never danced before."

Buddy laughed. "You have a lot to learn, Jerry. I've been dancing since I was three years old." He turned to Carolyn. "May I?"

"For a cousin, you're very formal." She laughed easily. I watched them go out on the floor. I'd never seen a dance like that. If I had to hold a girl that close on the dance floor, I know that I would come all over the place. Lucky I didn't get up and try to dance with Carolyn.

Leroy was watching them. He looked over at me. "Ain't she beautiful? And she's the best dancer I ever knew. Everybody loves my Carolyn."

"There's no doubt about that," I answered.

He was still looking at me. "Have you fellas got a room in town yet?"

"No, sir. We hadn't even thought about it," I said.

"We have a couple of extra bedrooms in our place," he said.

"Thank you," I said. "But we wouldn't want to put you out."

"You wouldn't be." He smiled. "I'll have to work late—the back room is busy tonight. But you can go home whenever you want."

Carolyn and Buddy came back to the table and heard Leroy's invitation. Buddy looked at me. "I have a date with one of the girls when she gets off. I thought I would just hang out here with Leroy."

"That's great for you," I said. "But how will I get to their place?"

"You can get a taxi," Buddy said. "I'll need the jeep."

"I'm not going to be staying here too much longer," Carolyn said. "I have to get up and be at the shop at nine o'clock in the morning. He can come with me when Chuck drives me home."

"If it's no trouble?" I asked.

"No trouble at all," Carolyn said.

"I want to have time to talk with Rosey before we go back to the barracks," I said.

"You'll have time tomorrow." Buddy laughed. "She asked me over tonight. I'll make sure that you see her about noon tomorrow."

"Okay," I said.

Buddy looked at me. "Do you have any extra cash on you?"

"About a hundred," I said.

"Let me borrow it." He smiled. "I feel lucky tonight. There's a hot poker game in the back room."

"You better be careful," Leroy said to him. "Those men are pretty sharp."

"Poker's my game." Buddy laughed. "You never really played poker until you've played in New York."

"You a big boy now," Leroy said. "I ain't going to worry about you like your mother."

"I'll be careful, cousin," Buddy said. Then he turned to Carolyn. "Do you mind if I go for the game right now?"

"I don't mind." She smiled. She turned to Leroy. "I'm waiting for the bottle of champagne."

Leroy laughed. "I almost forgot. Every time I open a new show we have a bottle of champagne to celebrate."

It took a half an hour for us to finish off the bottle of champagne; then Leroy kissed her and left for the back room. Carolyn looked at me. "It's time to go." She smiled.

I helped her on with her mink coat and followed her out of the club. Chuck was there with the big Cadillac sitting at the entrance. He held the door open for her and I followed her into the backseat. Chuck closed the door, and soon we were moving into the light traffic. Before I knew it she opened my fly and was rubbing her thumb over the tip of my penis.

She laughed. "We're lucky. We have no pressure now." She quickly bent on her knees in front of me and took my prick in her mouth and sucked it as she moved up and down my shaft. Her mouth was like a volcano. I exploded in less than a minute. She looked up at me as she swallowed the hot cum that was still flowing from my penis. It seemed forever until I could stop shuddering in ecstasy.

Still holding my phallus in her hand and smiling, she dabbed the corners of her mouth. The semen was glistening as she gently patted my cock with the handkerchief. Finally she sat back up on the seat and lit a cigarette.

I took her cigarette from her lips and dragged on it and then gave it back to her. "The inside of your mouth was on fire."

She laughed. "If you think that was hot wait until you feel my pussy."

I looked at her. "Don't you think that Chuck will squeal on you?"

She pointed with a finger to the front. I hadn't even noticed, but somehow she had pressed the button that closed the drapes on the window between the chauffeur and the passenger. "Besides," she said confidently, "all of them love me. I'm the one that pays them and gives them all the little extras that they want."

"But in the apartment it won't be so safe," I said. "Leroy might show up at any time."

She shook her head. "Leroy never comes home when a new show opens. It's a real big night in the back room. Leroy watches to make sure he gets his share. He probably won't be home by the time I leave in the morning."

"I'm still nervous," I said.

"That's what makes it even more exciting," she said. "But I've got everything under control. Chuck calls me the minute that Leroy is ready to leave the club. He always drives Leroy home at night because Leroy is carrying a lot of money and they put it into the night deposit at the bank."

I looked at her. "I don't know which one of us is crazier, you or me."

She laughed again. "It's been a long time since I tasted a white man's semen. It's lighter than the black man's. The black man's is thick and sweet, like molasses."

"Carolyn," I said. "You're making me nervous. After all, I was invited to stay here by Leroy."

"So did I," she said. "And I'm here with you."

The automobile was slowing down. Carolyn pressed the button and the curtain went up. "We're home," Carolyn said, then looked over at me. "You better close up your fly before you get out of the car."

8

When I woke up, I was in a real bed, not an army barracks bunk. I took a deep breath. Carolyn's perfume was still in the air and the scent of her pussy still clung to the sheets. I sat on the edge of the bed and I lit a cigarette. The smoke from the cigarette filled the air and smothered all of the scents that lingered.

But not the memories of the night. I never knew a girl could have so many desires. She took my cock and put it between her breasts, pressed and pulled me until I shot out under her chin. She then cupped the semen and rubbed it on her face. Then she taught me how to drive the Hershey highway and she masturbated her own clitoris until we both collapsed together in a wave of orgasms. I thought it was over for the night and then she bent over my prick and licked off the brown stain that covered it.

I felt completely drained by the time she finally sat up in the bed. Silently, she took a cigarette and lit it and handed it to me. Then she lit another one and inhaled. She looked at my face, not speaking. She searched my eyes and then she smiled. "Thank you," she said in a husky voice. "It has been a long time since I have loved like this."

"I don't understand," I said. "You have a good strong husband. I can't believe that he doesn't make love."

She crushed the cigarette out in an ashtray sitting on the bedside table. "Leroy is a great man and I know that he really loves me. And I do love him. But to him I am a white goddess in a black world. And he's old-fashioned. Only straight sex. Maybe he allows me to suck him once in a

173

while, but then he always apologizes to me for allowing him to be such an animal. To him, sex like that is only for the black whores."

"Did you ever talk to him about it?" I asked.

"I can't. I can never destroy the world he has made for us, even if it is not real," she said, and lit another cigarette. "He gave me the money to begin the decoration business. But the business is in my maiden name; he didn't want any knowledge out that I was married to a black man. That is why the business was started in Grosse Pointe. In fact, he has never even been in the store even though it has been his money that bought all of the beautiful things on the trips to Europe. The business has been very successful and we have become the number one decorator in Detroit. He's a wonderful man and I can't hurt him. I really love him but I am only human. I have my own needs."

"You're making a mistake. You have to tell him the way you really feel and how you need him; otherwise, sooner or later, he will learn about what is going on without him. You can never take the chance that you did with me by bringing me into your bed," I said. "He walks into this room and finds us and we're both dead."

She got out of bed and pulled on a kimono. She looked down at me. "You're very wise for being so young."

I looked up at her. "I am not only young, I'm also a coward."

"Then why did you come with me?" she asked.

"You are the most beautiful lady I ever saw," I said. "And you can tempt a stone statue into life."

She smiled and bent over and kissed me. "You're a very sweet man," she said, and left the guest room for her own bedroom.

It was only after I had awakened in the morning that I saw the card on the night table. It was her business card with her private phone number. On the back of it was a small note:

Please call me. I also have a small apartment in Grosse Pointe that I use when I have to work late. Also, look in the top drawer of the night table. I left something for you. This is in case Clarence lost all your money. C.

I opened the drawer. There were ten one-hundred-dollar bills. I hadn't seen so much money since I found the money in my parents' bedroom with Kitty. Then suddenly it dawned on me. Words I had heard from Buddy. "Sweet man." That was Harlem for gigolo. I tried to figure a way in which

I could give the money back to her. But there was no way. If I left the money in the drawer it would be discovered by one of the servants and that might make trouble. So I put the money and her card in my pants pocket. Then I went into the bathroom and showered, which was heaven sent, nothing like the barracks. I went back into the bedroom, got dressed, and went over to the dining room for breakfast.

Julian came into the dining room. "Did you sleep well, sir?" he asked.

"Very well, thank you," I said.

"Clarence telephoned while you were still asleep and he asked me to tell you that he would be here about two o'clock," he said.

I looked at my wristwatch. It was eleven-thirty. "Thank you, Julian," I said.

"Is Mr. Leroy or Mrs. Carolyn still around?" I asked.

"No, sir," Julian said. "Mr. Leroy is still in the club and the missus left for work at seven-thirty." He walked to a side table and poured a glass of orange juice and a cup of coffee and brought them over to me. "Would you like some eggs, sunny-side up, sausages, and hash browns?"

"That sounds great, Julian," I answered, my mouth watering.

"Thank you, sir," he said with a small smile. "You young men need all your strength to fight the wars."

I looked after him as he went to the kitchen. The smart little son of a bitch. He knew. And I knew right away that I would have to slip him one of the C notes that Carolyn had given me.

9

I found a copy of the book *Gone with the Wind* on a bookshelf in the living room. I sat at the bar and began to read it. I had seen the movie and I remembered that Clark Gable was great in it, but I never even knew that it was a book before a movie. Not that I would have read it, because I was never into reading books. The sports pages and the comic strips were all that I read. I started the book and I couldn't believe there was more of a story than in the movie. I was fascinated, and wondered if I could find it in the army library because it was a large book and I could never finish it while I sat here.

It was two o'clock before I knew it. As I was reading I heard the doorbell and looked at my watch. I couldn't believe it.

Julian went to the door and Buddy entered the room with Rosey on his arm.

He and Rosey walked over to the bar where I was sitting. He introduced Rosey to me and asked Julian to bring some bottles of beer.

Rosey said in a small voice, "I only drink champagne."

"Then bring us a bottle of your finest champagne," Buddy commanded.

Julian answered quietly. "Only mister and missus can open the wine cellar. I'm sorry, sir."

I saw him glancing at me out of the corner of his eye. He wanted me to back him. "Buddy and I will just have beers, and maybe you can find something else that the lady can have."

Julian turned to her. "I can make you some Lipton's orange pekoe tea or chamomile tea, miss," he said. "Chamomile is very healthy."

"I'll just take a beer, thank you," she answered.

He smiled politely. "Thank you, miss." He turned and walked toward the kitchen.

I walked into the kitchen after Julian. "Thanks for all your help, Julian," I said, and shook his hand. He felt the paper in my palm.

He smiled. "You're very welcome, Mr. Jerry."

I turned and walked back into the bar.

"They pretty stingy when they not here," Buddy said as I sat back down. "Leroy is stingy in that club of his. He wouldn't lend me a hundred bucks to stay in the game after I had a run of bad luck."

"That's his business," I said. "And he already told us that he has partners. He ain't in the business to lend money to players in his own game. He has to answer to his partners."

Buddy continued his complaining. "But I ain't just a stranger. I'm family."

"You told me he always tried to keep your mama from findin' out when you got into trouble," I said. "He's given us everything since we got to town. On account of you he let me stay here, and I'm a complete stranger to him."

Buddy stared at me. "You're right. I'm just being stupid."

Rosey looked at him. "Leroy is a great man. He'd give you his shirt off his back if he thought you needed it. He didn't make any of the girls fuck him, even when they wanted to, but the back room is something else. That's another world and you know which other business I'm talking about."

Julian came with a tray and went behind the bar. There were two bottles of Rheingold and a glass of champagne. "I found an open bottle of champagne in the refrigerator, miss." He smiled at her, then looked again at me as he opened the beer.

I returned his smile. The C note I had slipped him went a long way. "You were really great in the show," I said to Rosey as I sipped my beer.

"I'm surprised." She smiled. "You don't look any thing like your Uncle Harry."

"Harry isn't anything like me, because he was only married to Aunt Lila, my father's sister."

"Your Aunt Lila must have been a great lady. She had to put up with a lot from Harry," she said. "He is nothing but a liar and a cheat. I couldn't even believe some of the bullshit that he put your auntie through."

"Well, it's over now," I said. "You're through with him and I'm beginning to feel that I won't have any contact with him ever again, since my Aunt Lila is gone."

Buddy turned to her with a serious face. "Tell him everything that you told me."

She nodded. "I took up with him when I was just a kid. He picked me up at the counter. When I told him that I was going to dancing school he got really interested. That's the way it started. He took me up to his apartment he had on Seventh Avenue and wanted me to dance for him. He said he knew many producers that he could introduce me to. And I believed him. So I began dancing. Then he wanted me to take my clothes off. So I did. Naked, I kept dancing and sat down when I was out of breath and sweating. He gave me a Coca-Cola and he talked so sweet to me that I let him lay me right there on the floor. Then he laid me again on the bed. I didn't know it then, but he had knocked me up." She continued as she emptied her glass of champagne. "My throat is dry," she said, and smiled.

Julian, who was still behind the bar listening to her story, took her glass quickly and filled it. "I don't think anybody will miss this champagne," he said, and smiled at her.

"Thank you," she said.

"My pleasure, miss," he returned, and gently handed her the glass.

"Then what happened?" I asked.

"I'm Catholic," she said. "By the time I was living with him I knew I was pregnant. Harry screamed and wanted me to have an abortion, but I yelled back at him. No way would I have an abortion and the chance to die in hell. He said he was going to throw me out on the street. So I went to Father O'Bannion at my church. The father went with me to talk to Harry. The priest laid the word on him. I was under seventeen at the time and the church would turn him in to the police. Harry could spend a long time in jail. But he was even more frightened that his wife would find out than he was of jail. He was afraid that Lila would divorce him and the whole world would know what he did. I had the baby in a Harlem hospital and the church took the child to its orphanage. I never saw the baby, but Harry paid all of the expenses. Then he took me back in and I lived in his apartment until he took up with your girl. But I didn't care by that time. I was making my own money and I had my own career and he could go fuck himself for all I cared. Then when I heard he got married, I sent him a couple of pictures of us fucking, for a wedding present. He got crazy again because I also sent him a copy of the baby's birth certificate with his name as father on it. He sent me a thousand dollars to give him the negatives and the birth certificate, but I never sent it to him."

"Jesus!" I said.

Buddy turned to me. "I didn't know any of this about a baby until she told me. But I always told you that he was a real prick."

"It's too late now," I answered. Then I turned to Rosey. "Thanks for telling me about him."

"Maybe I can help you," she said. "I'll give you all the negatives and a copy of the birth certificate. That will get him crazy. Especially since Kitty is about to have a baby in the next few days. I heard that from the super in his apartment, who is a friend of mine. He always keeps in touch with me and tells me the scoop on Harry."

"What could it do for me even if I have it?" I asked.

"Don't be stupid," Buddy said. "Take it. You'll never know when it might come in handy."

I looked at Rosey again. "Thank you. Thank you very much."

"You don't have to thank me," she said. "Just make sure you and Buddy take me out to dinner tonight. I know the best barbecue restaurant in town."

"You've got a date!" Buddy said quickly before I could speak.

"I'm with you," I said.

10

Our work had become monotonous. Every three months a new platoon appeared at the factory door and Buddy and I would teach them the same thing. We were both hoping we would be shipped overseas, but the army always did it their way. We requested a transfer, but we were both ordered to stay in Detroit. Apparently the major in the so-called repair school for jeeps thought we were the best teachers he had ever found here. I never knew that Buddy had given the major a twenty-five percent override on his winnings in crap games and poker, as well as horse-racing bets. It wasn't until the major was promoted to lieutenant colonel that we got an asshole captain who took over. He didn't think we were so great, but it took him a little time to ship us out. Almost two years.

Buddy thought that we would be shipped to Pearl Harbor, but he was wrong. Our former CO, the major, pulled a few strings and we were transferred to Paris under his command. By September of 1944 de Gaulle had everything under control in France. We had a two-week advance shipping notice so we decided that we should have a good-bye party.

Leroy thought it was a great idea. He said he would do it up right, and he did. He invited our entire platoon for a barbecue dinner, free beer, and a show at the club. It was good publicity for him and the club. He arranged for the party to be over by eleven o'clock and he promised the captain that all of the soldiers would be out of the club by 11:30 P.M., because he needed the space for his regular crowd at midnight. Leroy knew where his money came from. He put an ad in the *Amsterdam News* telling all the black world that he was behind our fighting men. Leroy's Stage Door, he called the club in the ad. He didn't let anyone know that it was just for one night. He laughed when he showed us the ad in the New York paper. "What the hell," he said. "Nobody in New York knows anything about Detroit. They think we're just some small town."

I had the Saturday off before the party, a one-day leave. I called Carolyn in Grosse Pointe to tell her that I really wanted to see her before I left.

She purred into the phone. "Maybe you can meet me at my apartment out here. Leroy told me that he was working at the club tonight. I'll let him know that I won't be home tonight, since I have so much paperwork to catch up on."

"You sure it's safe?" I asked.

"Don't be such a baby." She laughed. "You don't believe that Leroy is really working? He's going to audition some out-of-town whore. That's the only way he can get his rocks off."

I was silent for a moment. It's a crazy world. She cut into my thoughts. "Besides, I know you're going to Paris. I worked there for three years. One of my best friends owns one of the biggest strip cabarets in Clichy. He's French but he speaks English perfectly and he can really show you around."

"I don't give a damn about him," I said into the phone, almost able to feel the hotness of her breath.

She laughed. "Okay, but I'll still give his name to you and the name of his club. You never know when you'll need a friend there."

It was after nine o'clock when I knocked on her door. I had picked up a bottle of Dom Pérignon from the liquor store near her apartment. The store was very classy. The bottle was in an ice bucket with a red-ribboned bow tied around with a cellophane cover to keep the ice from falling out. That was Grosse Pointe for you. In downtown Detroit there was not a chance that you could find Dom Pérignon, only American or Cook's, and never would they give you a decorated ice bucket.

The door opened. I could never tell you what the gown looked like. But there was one thing I knew. It was nothing you could wear out in public. You could see through the sheer silk from the red nipples on her breasts to the winking belly button and the soft curls of her silken auburn hair over her pussy. My hands were shaking and I almost came as she took the ice bucket and her soft warm hands touched mine.

I had been to the apartment before, but I always felt like a millionaire surrounded by the beautiful paintings, delicate antique furnishings, and Persian rugs. On top of it all, there was the heavenly aroma of a sirloin steak.

She kissed me as I came in. "You didn't have to bring champagne. Especially Dom Pérignon. Fifty dollars is more than the army pays a month."

I laughed. "I've saved up my money down here. There's nothing to do but go to the movies sometimes and have a beer."

"But I hear that Clarence is doing well. He's in the club almost every weekend. Leroy says he's become a pretty good gambler. He says most of the time he leaves with winnings." She smiled at me as she opened the bottle and the cork popped off and the champagne bubbled over and onto her hands before she could pour it in the glass. "I'm not really good at this. Leroy usually opens the bottle."

"I've never opened a bottle of champagne," I said, holding my glass toward her.

She poured the champagne into our two glasses. "I'll miss you," I said.

"I'll miss you, too," she said, sipping from her glass. "Steak and *pommes frites*. We'll eat first and then we'll make love."

It was nearly six o'clock in the morning when I came back to the barracks. It was Sunday and most of the platoon was already at breakfast. After breakfast was church. Then men who did not go to church took the bus into Detroit and walked around or went to the movies and tried to pick up a girl. There was a way to do this. You waited on the corner outside the church. There were mostly girls at church and their boyfriends and husbands were away at war. There was always one of the girls who would talk to a serviceman. They too were lonely and they wanted to go somewhere on Sunday afternoon.

I was surprised to find Buddy sitting on the edge of his bunk. "What are you doing here now?" I asked. "I thought that you stayed the night with Rosey."

He shook his head. "I was lucky at the tables. I never made it to Rosey's. I made a lot of money and I don't think that Cousin Leroy liked it very much. It's okay if I win a couple of hundred bucks, but I took out over three grand. Now I don't know what to do."

"There's only one thing that you can do," I said. "Give it back to him.

Tell him that you were only playing for fun. You were not trying to take his money."

"If I did that he would kill me," Buddy said. "He's got too much pride. Leroy is real sensitive."

I thought for a moment. "Then tell him that since you're shipping out now, you would like for him to take this money and invest it for you. Tell him that you never had that much money and you don't know how to take care of it."

Buddy looked up at me. "Do you think he would go for it?"

"He'll go for it," I said. "After all, you are his cousin and he loves you. You do that and he'll respect that you are a real man."

"But three grand," Buddy said, agonizing over parting with his wealth.

"You'll get over it," I said. "Carolyn gave me a connection in Paris. She told me that he would take care of us. And this Frenchman owns a strip club in Clichy, like Leroy."

Buddy looked up at me quizzically. "When did she tell you about that?"

"Some time ago," I said. I knew right away that I had slipped. "I don't remember when."

"When did you see her last?" Buddy asked. He was on the trail. I knew him—he was really smart.

"I don't remember," I said. But my face was burning red with my own guilt.

"Rosey told me that you were banging Carolyn but I didn't believe her. She even told me that Julian had told her about that first night you stayed at Leroy's place," Buddy said, still surprised. "What kind of an asshole are you? Don't you know that if Leroy caught you he would eat both of you alive, and maybe me, too?"

"I'm sorry," I said, and that was the truth. I kept my eyes on him. "I didn't mean any harm."

Buddy began to sound like a preacher. "That's what Adam said when the Lord kicked him out of Eden."

"But he left with Eve." I laughed. "I'm not taking her with me. Leroy still has his Garden of Eden."

"You are a number one prick." Buddy finally laughed. "And I kept thinking that you were just a little kike asshole." He stood up from his bunk. "How about some breakfast?"

We had dinner the next weekend with Leroy, Carolyn, and Rosey, and two days later we went to Philadelphia to board a troop ship to Europe.

BOOK THREE

FRANCE
THREE FRANCS A LITER

1

November in Paris was nothing like the songs I had heard. It was raining and cold. It was miserable; there were times when the snow would turn to half sleet and half snow. As it came down, it felt like little needles piercing your skin. In the States it was either snow or rain. I had never been so cold in my life.

But, as it turned out, I had no reason to complain. As the cold months passed by, we were in the warm barracks and not out in the freezing snow that we saw in the newsreels of the battles being fought with the Germans.

We knew that things were bad at the front from all the jeeps that were being shipped to us for repair. We worked three shifts, night and day, to get them into good condition and send them back. But many of the jeeps were beyond repair. These jeeps were retired to a large dumping ground behind the camp.

Buddy with his master sergeant stripes that he had earned took over the recreation program in the barracks. It wasn't long before a floating crap game was going on every night, and next to it was a large table for those who preferred poker. The games were straight. That was something that he had learned from his cousin Leroy. He didn't play any of the games; he took five percent from the winners. There were more than two hundred soldiers in the camp, so it turned into a very big business.

One morning Buddy came to my bunk before breakfast. He had been with the master sergeant who had brought us over the night before. He said he was going to pay him twenty-five percent of his part of the winnings.

He laughed and said that everybody in camp had been talking about the games and the master sergeant had heard about it and threatened to stop the games. Buddy made him part of the deal. So nobody stopped the games. Everybody just had a good time and Buddy and the master sergeant made a good living.

I found a new world. I met the man that Carolyn had told me to get in touch with, Paul Renard. He was very much like his name, Renard, which I found out meant "fox" in French. He was a fox. Paul was everything that Carolyn said he would be. Bright and always quick to find new opportunities. He and Carolyn had met when he was the manager of the Moulin Rouge. On the side he managed many of the girls' lives. They all trusted him because he was one of them. He was homosexual. It was he who introduced Carolyn to Leroy. When Carolyn first met Leroy she was worried that it would be difficult for them to live together. It was Renard who assured her that it would be very good. He knew how connected Leroy was and how wealthy he was and because of this the racial issue could be overcome. After all, in France, Josephine Baker loved and lived with many men, both white and black, and she loved them all. In the world of entertainment in France, black and white made no difference. He said that Leroy would give her anything that she wanted. If she married him, she would see all of her dreams come true. They had remained friends and Carolyn had written him about me and told him that I would be contacting him.

War for him was only opportunities. He left his job with the Moulin Rouge and found two profitable cabarets to buy from proprietors who had been drafted into the French army. One was in Clichy and the other was in Montmartre. He changed them quickly from family-oriented cabarets into his own styles of entertainment. One club was renamed the Montmartre Sophisticate and catered to the new tourist trade, which was all soldiers now. The cabaret show was a strip show. And the girls who served hustled the tables for champagne and sex.

The other cabaret was in Clichy and was oriented to a homosexual clientele, the world in which Paul lived. The show was very much like that of the club in Montmartre, but here the girls were more beautiful and brighter. They hustled the champagne but never sex, because this was a more respectable clientele. He renamed this cabaret the Blue Note. He was the first person to play records between the cabaret acts. As the records were playing, he encouraged the boys, men, and girls to dance. Men could dance together, women could dance together, or men and women could dance together without censure from the police. It wasn't until the American soldiers came into the club from the Citröen factory where all of the jeeps were repaired to be sent back into battle that Paul Renard made a change in the club. Most of the Americans did not know that it was a gay club so, in preparation for the Americans, Paul simply split the room into halves. Up the center of the club was a runway that went from the entrance to the stage. The gay world was on the left of the runway. The straight world was on the right of the runway. And Paul allowed the clientele to choose their own world. Sex or not. He was very tolerant.

I didn't meet Paul until early in December. Buddy and I had our first weekend pass in Paris. We drove around through Paris and stopped a few times in the afternoon at different bistros and bars. The first thing I found out was that it was very expensive. Working girls were everywhere. American soldiers were their pigeons. To them all Americans were rich and stupid.

Stupid meant that we couldn't speak the language. The girls approached us at each bar we went to, and seductively spoke English to us with their cute French accents, but all they could talk about was buying champagne and sex. We would all laugh as the waiter would bring a bottle of champagne and we would tell him that we wanted beer. Of course, they would bring the beer, but at champagne prices. When we ordered cigarettes they were five times the normal price of what they would charge the Frenchmen.

We went up and down the Champs-Elysées all day, and in the evening we went back to Clichy. It was then I opened the note that Carolyn had sent for Paul Renard. Fortunately, she had included the address of the Blue Note. It was 2200 hours by the time we found the club. We pulled up in front of the club and the doorman gave us a hearty English greeting and said he would park the car for us. I handed him a hundred-franc note and said I would give him more when I came back. A one hundred-franc note sounds like a lot of money, but it was only about forty dollars in American money.

Inside, I gave the maître d' Carolyn's note and asked him to take it to his patron. Buddy and I went to the bar and ordered two beers. A few minutes later, Paul rushed over to us with his hands outstretched. I shook his hand and told him that Buddy was Leroy's cousin.

He seated us at a table that was close to the runway and stage. We stayed with our beers and he ordered a whiskey and soda. He was very curious about how Carolyn was getting along in the States. It was obvious that he loved her very much. It was at this time that we learned that Leroy had given him twenty-five percent of the money to buy the Blue Note and

Montmartre Sophisticate. I told him how successful Carolyn was in her decorating business, and he was genuinely happy for her. I told him all about Leroy's successful clubs and that his nightclub was the most popular in Detroit.

Paul shook his head and sighed. "Leroy is very lucky," he said. "He is lucky that he can have gambling in his club. We could never get away with it in France. Gambling is only allowed in the casinos owned by rich Frenchmen, and run by the Greeks or the Corsicans. But I'm not complaining," the little Frenchman said happily. "After all, I've never had any problem with the policemen."

I found out later that the reason he was never bothered by the police was because several of his clients were important men of the government. He also neglected to tell us that they happened to be homosexual, like himself.

He continued to tell us the simple rules of his club. The girls in the show also hustled liquor for the clientele, but no sex was allowed with the clientele. If someone wanted more than a companion at the table, he would send them by taxi, at his expense, to the Montmartre Sophisticate, where the girls were on the turf.

"This is a petite Moulin Rouge, very high-class strippers who not only take it off but make a little scenario. To segue the stripper acts, we have clowns, jugglers, and acrobats. And we don't charge admission for the shows like they do at the Moulin Rouge, the Lido, or the Folies Bergère. The clientele can just enjoy themselves at the table with a bottle of our champagne. Standing at the bar is a two-drink minimum. We have two shows each night, at twenty-three-hundred hours and oh-one-hundred hours. Then the club is open until oh-five-hundred for dancing."

"I bet Leroy loves this club," Buddy said.

"Oui. Is this similar to Leroy's club in Detroit?" Paul asked.

Buddy started to answer, but I spoke first. "In a kind of way," I said. "You both give your customers more than they expect."

Paul smiled. "I would like you to see the early show. It will give me enough time to order *entrecôtes* and *pommes frites lyonnaise* for your dinner."

I smiled. "I'm starved. Thank you very much."

Buddy laughed. "I am hungry too, but I would still like to meet a pretty girl tonight."

Paul smiled at him. "After you have dinner and see the show, I will have my personal chauffeur take you to meet one of my many beautiful girls at Montmartre. And you will be my guest. No charge." He turned to me. "And you?" he asked. "Would you like to go with Buddy?"

"I'm happy here," I said. "I'll stay here for a while and then go back to the barracks."

2

The day before Christmas I received a present. It was from Fat Rita and her brother, Eddie. It was a two-foot-long cardboard box, about four inches square, sealed tightly with shipping paper tape. Buddy and I stared at it. We had no idea what could be in the package.

Buddy laughed. "I think Fat Rita caught your Uncle Harry, cut his cock off, and stuffed it!"

"You're crazy, Buddy," I said, laughing. "Look at the label. She mailed it from California."

"What could it be?" Buddy said.

By this time some of the other soldiers had come over to look at the package. All of them made a wild guess. Only one of them was right, a soldier who used to work at a delicatessen in Brooklyn. "A salami," he said. "I know."

"Why don't you open it?" Buddy asked.

"I don't know, maybe I should wait until Christmas Day," I said.

"Suit yourself," said Buddy. "It's your gift."

"I'll open it for you. If it's a salami, we can all have some," Sammy, the deli man, said. He leaned over and smelled the package. "I can smell it through the cardboard."

"Okay," I said. "You know so much. Open it."

He looked up at Buddy. "Lend me your knife."

Buddy held the knife to him, and in only seconds Sammy had the pack-

192

age open. It was a kosher salami. He held it up over his head. "A genuine kosher salami!" he announced.

Buddy looked up at it. "Maybe it *was* your Uncle Harry. It's so wrinkled." Buddy laughed. "Anyway, it's a hell of a Christmas present," he said to me. "It smells up the whole barracks."

Sammy stared at him. "You get me two dozen eggs and a half a pound of butter and I'll make the whole barracks the greatest deli omelette you've ever had in your life."

Buddy laughed. "I can get the goods for you, but you'll have to throw in some onions with it. And I'll get a couple of big baguettes as well."

"I'm with you," Sammy said. "We'll use the stoves over at the mess hall and have one hell of a deli Christmas Eve dinner."

I looked at both of them. "What are you guys doing? Remember, it's my Christmas present."

Sammy laughed as he put the salami under his arm. "This is for Hanukkah, not Christmas!" He cut off a small slice of salami and threw it to me. "Taste it. It's like heaven. You'll never find anything like this in France."

I bit into it. It was as hard as a rock. I nodded to Sammy. "Make your omelette. It's got to be better than eating it raw."

The Blue Note became my second home. Paul was a good friend. Every weekend when I had a pass, I would go to a French movie. Though I didn't understand the dialogue being spoken, I began to learn some French.

After the movie I would go to a local restaurant and practice more French as I ordered dinner. I also acquired a taste for French red wines. They were light, nothing like the Manischewitz my father used at home when I was a kid and we had a special dinner. By the time February came around, I was a regular at the Blue Note. I was able to speak a little pidgin French to the girls.

Buddy came to the Blue Note one evening. It was about 0200 hours when he suddenly appeared at my table, which was now known in the club as the "Special Americans" table. He looked exhausted. He sat down and looked at me. "Are you alone?"

I looked back at him. He could see there was no one else sitting at the table. "Yes," I answered.

"I'm in trouble," he said.

"What happened?"

"The colonel and I used to go to a special club and the MPs raided the place tonight. The colonel got out in time, but they nailed me." He wiped his forehead. "I need a drink."

I gestured to the waitress. "Double whiskey and soda for my friend." I waited until Buddy had a chance to gulp his drink. "What kind of club were you at?"

"A sex club. Crazy, S and M, anything-goes kind of place. Whips, chains, leather. The girls were crazy. They were all drinking absinthe, which is illegal in France. And this place is strictly off-limits for American soldiers."

"I never heard of this place. How did you get into it?" I asked.

"It was the colonel's idea. Every time I was ready to give him his split of the winnings from the games he wanted me to meet him there. He never wanted to take the money while we were on the base."

Buddy's drink was empty. He motioned to the girl to give him another one.

"You're going to be smashed," I said.

"So what else can go wrong?" he said. "We have to make plans."

"What are you talking about?" I asked.

"The colonel is going to ship me out with a platoon that is going to Norway to take over the repairs garage there," he said. He began to drink a little more slowly. "He says that this is the only way I can stay out of trouble. He says the minute the police report gets into headquarters I will wind up in the can."

"Then what can I do about it?" I asked.

"Nothing about the transfer, but maybe you can take over the games for me. There's a lot of money in it. I can talk to the colonel about splitting his half of the take and you can take some and you can send the rest to me." Buddy looked at me pleadingly. "Somebody will move on it the minute I'm gone. I'd like you to take it on. After all, we're friends."

I laughed. "Oh, shit, Buddy. Thanks, but no thanks. I couldn't handle that kind of action. I'd fuck it all up. Besides, once the army starts checking on you, the both of you will be fucked. The colonel is smart. He gets you out of the way, and he'll be clear."

"Maybe you can come with me," he said. "I think I could talk the colonel into it. After all, I've done a lot of things for him."

I shook my head. "I like it here," I said. "I don't want to go anywhere except home. But we can stay in touch, Buddy."

Buddy got up out of his chair. "I'll have to go back to the base."

"What's the rush?" I asked. "You're in the shithouse already. You can't get into any more trouble."

"I have the old man in the car," he said. "I'm his chauffeur. That's the only way he could get me out of the base after the shit hit the fan."

"Fuck it," I said. "Bring him in. He's safe here."

3

The colonel moved quickly when he had something in mind, especially his ass being on the line. Buddy didn't even have enough time to pick up his money from the crap games. In two days he was on his way to Norway.

I went to the mess hall with him the morning he left and we had coffee. "I'll miss you, Buddy," I said.

"We'll manage," he said philosophically. "This war won't go on forever. The gossip over at the colonel's office is that it's goin' to be over by May."

"I don't know anything," I said. "All I know is what I read in the *Stars and Stripes* or what I see on the newsreels. As long as we're getting those jeeps it's still war. I just hope you're right."

"I want to come back here before it's over," he said. "I've seen pictures of Norway—it's always snowing and freezing. Besides, I like the French, especially the women." He laughed.

"I'll be here." I smiled and stood up. "You just take care of yourself." Awkwardly we shook hands. It was like we had known each other too long to do that. I lit a cigarette as he left the mess hall. And I began to wonder. The world changes right around you. And it did. The very next day.

I was called into the colonel's office the very next morning. "Cooper." He said my name as if he had never even met me before, even though we had drunk a bottle of champagne at the Blue Note the night before. "I've been reading your records," he said very authoritatively. "You have a good record and I think you can take over the job that has been vacated by the master sergeant."

I stared at him. I didn't know what he was talking about. I never knew what Buddy was doing besides hustling the crap games and poker tables. "What is that, sir?" I asked.

"Master sergeant, son," he boomed. "I'm promoting you into Buddy's rank. We need a master sergeant in this platoon. Especially since we are going to become a smaller operation. This location and setup is being returned to the French. But we have a very good location just a few blocks away from here. There's only one problem."

"What's that, sir?" I asked.

"You'll have two platoons. Sergeant Felder will be under you in charge of repairs and getting the jeeps back into shape. But we have barracks only large enough for one platoon. You'll have to find a room near our location." He looked at me with a smile. "I'm moving over to Montmartre and I'll be depending on you to keep our workforce in good shape."

"Renting a room around here is pretty expensive, sir," I said.

"I realize that." He smiled. "I've cut orders so that you will be given the money to cover the necessary expenses." He took a cigarette out. I lit it for him. It was a really fancy French cigarette, Gitane. It stank. French cigarettes always do.

"Thank you, sir," I said. "But you do realize, sir, that I don't know how to handle some of the other projects that Buddy was in charge of."

"I know that, Cooper," he said. "But there will be other opportunities that will come up." He picked up his telephone and spoke into it. "Give Sergeant Cooper an overall pass so that he can leave the base at his discretion. Also I want a jeep assigned to him that he can use as necessary."

I stared at him. I didn't know what to say. This was like a gift from heaven.

The colonel looked at me. "The company clerk will cut your orders, Cooper," he said. "I want to congratulate you on your promotion. You have done very good work and the army appreciates it."

"Thank you, sir," I said.

He snapped a salute at me. "Thank you, Sergeant," he said. "You're dismissed."

4

Three weeks passed before we were able to move into our new garage and barracks. I still hadn't found a place to live. The barracks we were moving into was an old building of stone and wood and the platoon was more comfortable in this barracks than the cold Quonset hut that we were in before. I stayed in the barracks until everything was settled and then I went over to the Blue Note to talk to Paul about a place to live.

Paul was always glad to see me when I came in. I hadn't been in for a while and I told him that the platoon had been moving. I also told him my problem. I needed a place to live immediately. He offered to help me. He wanted to know where the new location was. Maybe he could open a bar close by. Paul was always looking for an opportunity.

"I know of a nice two-bedroom apartment near here if you don't mind sharing it," he finally said after thinking about my dilemma. "The price would be reasonable."

I looked at him. "I don't know," I said. "I've never shared a place with a homosexual."

Paul began laughing. "You are very funny. I would not put you in with one of the fairies. You would share the apartment with a girl who works here in the club. She is a girl from my hometown, Lyons, and I've known her since she was a child."

I was curious. I knew he never had affairs with women. "How come a girl you knew as a child comes here to be a stripper? You get her into it?"

"No, my friend," he said disapprovingly. "I am friends with her family.

She began working in Lyons as a stripper, until there was a little problem, and she came to Paris. I wanted her here because in a big city she could be lost."

"What was she running away from?" I asked.

"The Gestapo," he said. "Her sister had been in love with a German officer and she told Giselle about certain important information. Then that Giselle would pass the information to the French underground. Her sister learned from her lover that the Nazis were going after Giselle. It was then that Giselle came here."

"That's a hell of a story," I said. "How come I never met her?"

"Because after the show, I have her working on the fairies' side of the runway. She is bright and they like her because she never hustled them for more champagne. So, of course, then they ordered more than ever." He laughed again. "You'll like her. But just remember she's a good girl, not a whore."

"You seem to worry about her," I said.

"She is a brave girl as well," he said. "And I don't want her to be hurt."

And that was the way I met Giselle. Paul told me to wait until she had finished the show. He pointed her out to me. She was beautiful and naked. I turned to Paul. "I don't know if I can handle it," I said.

"Just remember that you are a gentleman." He smiled. "And I promised her father that I would take care of her."

An hour later, he brought her over to the table and introduced us to each other. Much to my surprise she spoke very good English. I smiled at her as we shook hands French style, formally. Two shakes up, two shakes down. "I enjoyed your act," I said. "You are really a very talented dancer."

She laughed. "Jerry, the only talent you need in this show is how you look naked."

"That, too," I said. "But you had a good act."

"Paul taught me how to do that." She smiled. "He said that a girl has to have what you call a gimmick."

"You have that, too," I said.

She nodded. "Paul told me that you are looking to share an apartment."

"Actually all I need is a room. Most of my time will be spent in the garage. All of my meals will be in the army mess hall," I said. "I won't be any trouble."

"I want a roommate, not a lover," she said. "Paul said that you would agree to that."

"Yes, ma'am," I said. "I'm not looking for any ties. When the war is over I want to go home."

She looked at me. "The rent will be one hundred twenty-five dollars a month."

"That's more money than I get paid by the army," I answered.

"Paul said he would find you a way to earn extra money," she said.

"I don't know anything about that," I said. "He hasn't mentioned it."

"Well, let's see what he has in mind," she said quietly.

Paul was a fixer. He knew the way to do anything. The first thing he did was take me over to Giselle's apartment with her after her show ended at three o'clock in the morning. It was three blocks from the club, in an old-fashioned brownstone house. The apartment was on the fifth floor. It was a walk-up, no elevator. But the apartment was very nice. It had a kitchen which also served as a dining room, two bedrooms, and a small living room. The large bedroom was Giselle's. It was very comfortably furnished. The double bed had down-filled pillows and a large down blanket. There were also a dresser and an armoire and two chairs.

The other room was smaller. A single bed, simple pillow, and a wool blanket. A narrow armoire and a small table on which there was a large bowl and pitcher and towel rack attached. Over the table was an oval mirror, which you used to wash and shave. The bathroom was between the rooms. It was completely furnished with running water for the sink and bathtub and bidet. Hot water was from a simple water heater attached to the sink and tub. In the corner of the bathroom was a closet which housed the toilet and gave complete privacy.

Paul looked at me. "What do you think?"

"It's fine," I said. "The only problem is, I can't afford it."

"I have an idea that might help you," he said. "Can I meet you at your garage tomorrow morning?"

"I can arrange a pass for you," I answered.

"Good," he said. "Then we will discuss my proposition. If you would like you can spend the night here and I will pick you up in the morning."

I turned to Giselle. "Is that all right with you?"

"It's okay with me," she said. "After all, Paul owns this apartment and if it's good with him, it's okay with me."

I was right—it was Paul's apartment. "I appreciate what you are both doing, but I think it would be better if I went back to the barracks tonight," I said. Then I turned to Paul. "We will meet in the morning. I'll need to give you directions."

Paul laughed. "I know where you are. After all, I am French and I know everything that goes on in my territory."

"Your territory?" I asked curiously.

"I'm Corsican," he said. "Everything is always fine with us."

I turned to Giselle. "Are you Corsican also?"

She laughed. "No, I am Lyonnaise. That's real French."

I held out my hand to her. "I'm just curious. Who will be my landlord, you or Paul?"

Paul interrupted. "She will, of course."

I still held out my hand. "Then, I thank you, madame." I didn't know it then, but later I learned that the Corsicans in France were like the Mafia at home. They were in control of almost everything.

Paul met me the next morning at the garage. He was very interested in the way we repaired the jeeps. He wanted to know if they looked like new when they were repainted. I took him to the field where we stored many of the jeeps we had cannibalized for parts when we were restoring the better jeeps.

He turned to me. "Jerry, who is in charge of all the jeeps you use to restore the others?"

"Actually the colonel is in charge," I said. "He stays in Paris most of the time at the American headquarters. He just signs the junking orders that I send him."

"That is the officer that your friend Buddy brought into my club?" he asked.

I was surprised. It was true he knew everything that went on in his club. "Yes," I said.

"Then he will not be in your way," he said with authority. "I know many men who need cars for their business. If you could arrange to repair some of those jeeps we can get a good price for them."

"I'll have to use some of the specialists in the platoon, but Sergeant Felder is in charge of that and he is a friend of mine," I said.

"With twelve thousand francs for each car you'll be able to persuade the ones you need."

I looked at him. Twelve thousand francs was equal to two thousand dollars. "And what would you get out of it?"

"Twenty-five thousand a car." He smiled. "But you probably should be able to keep most of the money for yourself. And then you can afford Giselle's apartment."

I laughed. "I like the idea. I just don't want to get caught."

"You can't get caught," he said. "I will arrange all the contacts with the customers. They're French. They don't talk to anyone, especially about contraband."

"I'll check it out," I said. "If everyone is in agreement, I'll let you know. Then I can move into the apartment."

Paul pressed my arm with his hand. "You can move into the apartment without any problem. We are friends. We don't need a business affair to stand between us."

"Thank you," I said to him. "But I'll feel better if I can pay my share of the apartment. As soon as I can put everything together I'll let you know."

He smiled and he walked down the street. I watched him until he turned the corner. But there was something in the way he pressed my arm that worried me. Maybe it was because I knew that he was queer that it worried me. I didn't want him to have any ideas about me.

5

The first jeep was ready for sale in less than two weeks. It wasn't easy. We had to file off all the numbers on the parts so they could not be traced. Sergeant Felder, who was in charge of the junked jeep field, told me if I could get him two more men to help him he could repair one jeep each week.

"You're a real Henry Kaiser," I said, and laughed.

"More like Henry Ford." He laughed. "Now I want to work with you, but I'm not getting enough for the risk I am taking. I might get my ass in a sling."

"There's not going to be a problem," I said. "We are giving each of the men twenty thousand francs. When you add two more men, we have to pay more money. That adds up to eighty thousand francs. We can't get enough money to go around."

"I want fifty thousand francs for myself. I take all the responsibility. Besides, I'm not stupid. The French are hungry for cars. They'll pay any price. They are desperate."

I looked at him. "Felder, you're a schmuck. You might blow the whole deal."

"I don't give a shit," he said. "I can get that money just selling parts to the frogs."

"Yeah," I said. "And you'll really wind up in the can."

"Then how much do you think I can get?" he asked.

I was glad. At least he was bargaining. That's something I learned from

203

Buddy. If they are ready to bargain, you have the upper hand. "Let me see what we can get for the first car," I said. "Then we'll know better how we can split it up."

I drove the first jeep off the base about midnight. Only Felder and I were there. We wanted to make sure that no one else would see us. Felder padlocked the gate behind me. "Be careful," he said. "There's no army license plates on the car. Watch out for MPs."

I took the dark, narrow back streets to the back door of the Blue Note. I left the car in the alley and knocked on the door.

A big Frenchman opened the door. "Who are you?" he asked in passable English.

"I want to see Monsieur Renard," I said.

He looked at me. "Monsieur Renard doesn't see anyone at the stage door."

I took out a five-hundred-franc note and passed it to him. "He'll see me," I said.

Just that moment Giselle came down the circular stairway from the dressing room. "Jerry!" she exclaimed. "What are you doing back here?"

"I'm supposed to meet Paul here," I said. "But maybe he has forgotten about it."

Giselle nodded and turned to the doorman. She spoke quickly in French to him. He nodded his head and ran off.

She looked at me. "I'm going on stage in a few minutes. You will be able to watch me."

"I'm sure I will be able to stay. As soon as I finish my business with Paul," I said.

"Is it the jeep?" she asked.

"You know?" I asked.

"Paul told me. He likes you." She laughed. "Can I see the car?"

"Of course," I said. "But it's cold outside." I looked at her costume. What there was of it was not enough to keep her warm.

Paul appeared with the fat man right behind him. "You have the car?" he asked excitedly.

"The first one we finished," I answered.

Giselle spoke to him. "Can I see it?"

"Get her a cape," Paul said to the fat man.

There was a rack near the door. The fat man took a cape from a group of overcoats and placed it around Giselle's shoulders. Then we all went out to look at the car.

"It's beautiful," Giselle said. "I never saw a white jeep before."

"We're painting the jeeps different colors," I said. "We don't want them to look like they are still army property."

Paul turned to the fat man. "Cover the car with a canvas. I don't want anyone to see it without my okay. Before the morning put it in the garage next door."

"Oui, monsieur," the fat man answered, and opened the door to let us go back into the club.

Paul smiled. "Come into the club."

Giselle laughed. "I'm going on in a few minutes. I'll be disappointed if you are not in the audience."

"He'll be there," Paul said to her, and then he turned to me. "Let's go in and have a drink."

I followed him through the hallway which led into the club. I looked around. It was Tuesday and the club was not very busy. Only the homosexual side of the runway was fairly filled up. Paul's table was set so that he could observe everything going on in the room. He ordered a pastis and I had a beer.

He looked at me. "Were there any problems?"

"Only money. Felder wants more money for himself and wants me to assign two more men to him. He says that he can turn out a car a week."

"What did you tell him?" he asked.

"I told him that the money is tight. But he knows the market because he sells parts to auto mechanics." I took a swig of my beer. "But if we give him what he wants there won't be that much left for us."

"We can do it," Paul said. "We just charge more for the cars. If the cars all look as good as the white one, there will be no problem."

"There's only one other problem," I said. "We're Americans. They all want dollars."

Paul stared at me. "That's not easy. Everybody wants to keep the dollars for themselves."

"If they want a car bad enough, the money will not be important," I said, feeling confident. I knew that he took in a lot of dollars. After all, half of his clients at both of his clubs were American soldiers.

"We'll work on it," he said. Then he smiled at me. "Giselle is coming on. Watch her. She is really very beautiful."

I didn't realize that they put on a different show at one o'clock in the morning than they put on at eleven at night. Paul explained that to me. "In the early show, there are more straight couples. At this later show the homosexuals want something more exciting. You will see why they love Giselle so much."

The music began and I watched her entrance. It was wild. She wore leather everything. A leather truck-driver cap, a tiny leather brassiere with brass and diamondlike stones outlining her breasts, a short, short skirt almost up to her hips which almost revealed a diamond-studded leather bikini underneath it. Black opera stockings with seams that began from the heel of her six-inch-stiletto-heeled shoes, which were also diamond-studded.

The music reached a rhythmic crescendo just as she stopped at the brass pole and posed seductively with one knee up and slightly open to the audience. The queers went crazy. They screamed and applauded and threw money on the stage before she even began to dance. From the darkness of the floor beneath her she picked up a long snakelike whip. Each time she would crack the whip another piece of clothing would come off. By the time she laid down the whip she was completely nude except for a diamond on each nipple and a big diamond on the high point of her shaven pussy. Then the queers really went crazy, calling her back many times for an encore. But all she did was come out and smile and bow to the audience in appreciation. After a while, when she would no longer return, the audience quieted down. Then the show was over and the music started and the dancing for the audience began.

The French dancing was different than the Americans'. Queers would be dancing together. Some of the men and women would just be dancing by themselves. And then the straight couples joined in with everyone on the stage. It was another world.

Paul placed his hand on my arm. "Jerry," he said, smiling, "isn't she marvelous?"

I smiled at him. "Do they react to her every night like that?"

He nodded.

"She is something else," I said.

"She's a good girl," he said, lowering his voice. "She's not a whore." He lit a cigarette. "That's why we love her. She does not try to change us."

I looked at him. "Why are you telling me so much about her?"

He looked serious for a moment. "Because she likes you," he said. "I don't want you to hurt her. After the war I want to give her back to her family as good as when she came here."

"Maybe I shouldn't move into the apartment with her," I said. "But she said she didn't want a lover."

"Women can change their mind, no?" he said. "She likes you, and I like you; we both trust you."

"But I look at her," I said. "I don't know if I can be with her and not get crazy."

He laughed. "You Americans are crazy. You all think that if you fuck you are in trouble." He ordered another pastis for himself and a beer for me. "She's a healthy girl. A fuck would be good for her, as well as for you."

"You're really a pimp, Paul," I said.

He laughed. "I just want my friends to be happy." He held up his glass to me. "À votre santé."

I held up my beer. "Cheers."

"Giselle will be here in a few minutes," he said. "She is expecting you to go home with her."

"But I haven't said anything to her," I said.

"Yes, you did. She heard what you said before. You said you would move into the apartment when you could afford it," he said. "Well, you can afford it now. One car a week will make you a rich man."

6

When the show was over, Giselle sat down at a table on the other side of the runway. I turned to Paul. "She's going over there with that table of guys."

"They're all queer," he said. "They are big fans of Giselle and she always sits with them for a while after the show. It's good for business. It's not only the money they throw on stage, but when she sits down they start ordering bottle after bottle of champagne."

I looked at my watch. It was a quarter after two. "How long does she stay with them? Don't forget I have to be at the garage at seven in the morning."

He shrugged his shoulders. "It depends on her. When they are buying she stays around. When the night is slow, then she leaves earlier."

"Then her job is really hustling the wine?" I asked calmly.

He laughed. "Don't be so American. It is a job. All of the girls do that. They know that whatever they do after hours is their own time. In this club I do not take any of the girls' extra money."

"But Giselle said she doesn't go out after hours. She is always with the fags," I said. "What does she do for extra money?"

"She doesn't want extra money. All she wants is the war to be over so she can go home," he said.

"If she doesn't need money, then why does she want me to move into the apartment?" I asked.

"She is a very honest girl and the rent is high," he said. "I told her she could have it for nothing, but she insists that she pay me."

"Does she really want to share the apartment with me?" I asked. "Or is this your idea?"

"Let's say it is both our idea," he said, and smiled. "She saw you several times in the club. She liked the way you looked. And I am a businessman, but I liked you, too. I knew you were not in my game, so business is business. This way everybody is happy."

"I need a real drink. Do you have a real whiskey?" I asked. "I still really don't have an understanding of the French world."

He ordered me a double scotch and soda. By the time I drank that, I didn't care what time it was. Giselle finally came to the table and we walked from the club to the apartment. It was almost four o'clock in the morning. I was glad the apartment was only three blocks away. I followed her up the stairs. I watched her open the door with a key. I went into the apartment and walked directly to my room. I fell on the bed with my clothes on and passed out.

"Jerry, Jerry!" I heard her voice in my ear. It sounded like "Chéri," the way she pronounced it. I heard her again. Slowly, I rolled over and sat up. I was still dressed.

"What is it?" I asked, still half-asleep.

"It is six o'clock," she answered. "I heard you had to be at the garage at seven. I have café au lait and baguettes."

I sat up straight now and looked at her. She was wearing an old-fashioned flannel nightgown. But it looked as if it were molded to her body. And the body was pure sex. Not like the average French girl, skinny and flat-chested. "You look beautiful," I said groggily. It was the only thing I could think when I looked at her. "Did you get any sleep?"

"A little," she said. "But once we get into a routine, you'll be able to go to work and I will sleep till my normal time. Noon."

I went to the bathroom and splashed some water on my face. I didn't look very good. I needed a shave and a change of uniform before I would look normal. Then I went into the kitchen and had my coffee and bread and jam. I checked my watch. Six-fifteen.

I got out of the chair. "I'll have to run. It will take me a half hour to get to the base."

"When you get off duties," she said with her French pronunciation, "you can bring your things over here."

"I'm off at seven o'clock," I said. "I don't want to bother you."

She smiled. "I'll be here. I do not go to the club until ten o'clock."

"Thank you," I said. Then the doorbell rang. I looked at her. "Who is it?"

She shrugged her shoulders. "Probably Paul. He told me that he wanted to see you in the morning."

It was Paul. He entered smiling. "Ah, my children, did you get a good night's sleep?"

"You have to be out of your fucking mind," I said. "We didn't get back here until after four in the morning. I passed out the minute I walked through the door."

He looked at Giselle. "Americans," he said, and shrugged. "I have not slept at all," he said excitedly. "I was working all night for you." He took out his wallet from the inside of his jacket pocket. Dramatically he took out the money. Importantly, he counted each bill out one at a time. There was twenty-five hundred dollars.

I stared at him speechless for a moment, then found my voice. "Dollars," I said. "How did you get it?"

"A Corsican friend of mine. He loved the car and he wants two more of them," he said. Then he picked up the money again and began to share it. "One hundred twenty-five dollars to Giselle," he said. "Now you have paid your rent for the month." He took his share out. "Six hundred twenty-five dollars for me. The rest is yours," he said. "I hope this will satisfy your friends."

"I'm sure they will be happy," I said, picking up the money and putting it in the pocket of my shirt and buttoning it. "I'm glad you caught me. I was just on my way to the garage. I want to really thank you for everything you have done."

"It is good for all of us." He smiled. "I have my car downstairs. I can give you a lift."

"Thanks again," I said, and turned to Giselle. "I'll be back a little after seven."

She nodded. "I will be here."

Walking down the steps, Paul smiled at me. "She likes you."

"I'm glad," I said, feeling good about everything.

"There is one thing I forgot to tell you," he said. "The man who bought the car is Moroccan. He is shipping this car to Morocco. But he wants the other two cars to be black."

"Okay," I answered. "Any reason for that color?"

"He imports hashish here and he doesn't want the cars to be conspicuous." We came to the street in front of his old Renault. "He wants you to always be very careful that all the numbers on the car and its parts have been filed off so they cannot be traced to him in any way."

I smiled at him. "Tell him not to worry. The numbers have not only been filed off but we have acid to really bring them down."

We got into the car. He had his fat man drive. We both sat in the back of the Renault. The fat man was really his bodyguard and chauffeur. He said nothing to me, but he knew where the barracks and the garage were, and he dropped me off a block away.

Paul leaned out from the car. "You will be at the club tonight?" he asked.

"I don't know," I said. "I have to move my things into the apartment."

"That will be no problem," he said confidently. "She's a French girl, she'll help you." Then he made a gesture to the fat man and the car took off.

I looked after them and thought for a moment. It couldn't be just the money in the cars that he was interested in. He did good with his clubs. And it also wasn't the extra money he got from my share of Giselle's apartment. It came to me as I walked to the garage. It was the hashish. He had to be making a share of the drug money. It was the Mafia all over, only here it was the Corsicans.

Felder was waiting for me when I went into the garage. He looked at me. "You look like hell," he said.

I rubbed my chin for a minute. "I've been busy," I answered.

"How much money did we get?" he asked.

"I got what you wanted," I said to him. "But they were pissed off. They said that we didn't keep our end of the deal."

"They took the car, didn't they?" he said arrogantly.

"They took it," I answered.

"Then fuck 'em," Felder said. "They know they ain't going to get cars anywhere else. The French factories aren't yet working. But we are."

"You're a real Henry Ford," I snapped. "I'm being nice to you and you think you're in charge of everything. Well, you can fuck yourself. I'm going in to the company clerk and have him cut orders to move you out!"

"You wouldn't do that," Felder said, backing up. "We've been working together a long time, ever since we got to France, Cooper."

"Then you remember who brought you into this deal," I said flatly. "I can stop it just as easy."

"I've already got another car almost half ready," he said.

"Okay," I said. "From now on paint them black, just like Henry Ford used to. I'll pay you the money in the barracks before we go to lunch."

"Yes, sir," he said.

I laughed. "Don't be a putz. Don't kiss my ass. Just do your job."

7

I never realized how much junk and clothing I had collected since I had been stationed in Paris. Then I remembered that Buddy had left some of his things with me. I was carrying two loaded duffel bags when I finally dragged up the stairs to Giselle's apartment. I was out of breath when I knocked on the door.

Her voice came through the closed door. "Jerree?"

"Yes," I answered.

She opened the door. She looked so young without her stage makeup that she wore at the club. "I was worried," she said. "When you were late I didn't know what might have happened."

"I had a lot of packing to do," I said, pulling the duffel bags into the apartment behind me. I looked at her. "If it's too much to keep here, I can send some of the things back to the barracks."

"We'll make room," she said, and followed me into my room. "Did you have dinner?" she asked.

"Not yet," I said as I threw the duffel bags on the bed. "I thought we could have dinner at some restaurant before we go to the club."

"I have already made dinner for you," she said. "We can eat and then you can unpack after I go to work."

I didn't argue. I was starving. We walked into the dining room and she served me a delicious dinner. French-style roast chicken that she had basted with olive oil and Burgundy wine. I had never had a chicken pre-pared like this, but it wasn't bad, especially the roasted potatoes and thin string beans. We had the usual baguettes, and red wine to drink. She had also gotten a few bottles of beer, in case I preferred that over the wine.

"This is really delicious," I said. "But I didn't want you to go to so much trouble."

She laughed. "I really can't cook. Everything comes from the charcuterie. All I had to do was put the chicken into a pot and add a little wine and oil."

I laughed. "I still think it's lovely of you to have a dinner prepared for me."

She brought coffee cups for each of us from the kitchen. After she had poured the coffee, she added a small shot of cognac. "This will keep you up enough to unpack some of your things."

"You're great." I laughed. "What time will you be finished with your last show? I can pick you up and bring you home."

"You don't have to do that," she answered. "You know sometimes I have to sit with certain clients. I never really know when I will be able to leave."

Quickly, she washed the dishes and changed from her housedress to a simple white blouse and black skirt. I sat there and watched her as she carefully pulled up her black-seamed silk stockings, making sure that the seams were straight. She then stepped into her black high-heeled shoes. She turned to me. "Didn't you ever see a girl pull on her stockings before?"

I laughed. "No."

"Why are you laughing?" she asked, slightly annoyed.

"I was not watching your stockings," I said. "I was looking at your shaved pussy. The white skin around it made me think it was your panties."

She laughed, too. "I never wear panties—only when I'm working on stage."

"And after that?" I asked.

"No panties. Even when I sit down at the table with our clients. But it is no problem since I only sit with the queers at the club. They love me. I am their favorite since I do the sadomasochistic act." She smiled. "Some of them are very nice men and from good families that are very rich."

"Do they give you money?" I asked.

"Of course. And we get a commission on every bottle of champagne that is sold to our clients. I am very lucky. The gay boys are more generous than the others." She looked at me. "And I don't have to have sex with them."

"What about the other girls at the club?" I asked. "Does Paul get extra money for the girls' extra services?"

She laughed. "You Americans are naive. The Blue Note doesn't allow any 'extra services.' Paul sends those customers who want extra services over to his club in Montmartre."

"And you? Do you have any ties to anyone? Any special men friends?" I asked.

"I did, some years ago in Lyons. But he went into the army and was killed in action. After that, I came to Paul in Paris. And here I am."

"Are you happy here?" I asked.

"I am alive. The Boche haven't gotten me. And Paul gives me protection. Yes, I am happy." She nodded. "As happy as I can be until this terrible war is over and I can go home."

"I think all of us want the same thing. Just to go home." I smiled. I looked at my Ingersoll. It was almost ten o'clock. I looked at her as she went to the door. "Do you want me to walk over to the club with you? You should have protection on the dark streets," I said.

She laughed. "No, thank you, Jerree. The doorman from the club picks me up every night."

"Okay," I said. "I was just trying to help."

"Thank you again," she said. "Paul is an old friend of my papa. This is why he is my protector."

I watched as she closed the door behind her. Then I looked around. Maybe I could do something to fix up the apartment. Then it dawned on me. I could put something in her apartment that very few people in France had: a radio. The PX had the best radios in the world. In France you couldn't even buy a radio, you had to get it on the black market and it would cost an arm and a leg. I didn't bother to unpack. I headed straight for the PX and picked up the biggest worldwide-band radio they had and brought it back to the apartment. I placed it in the middle of the dining table, where she would see it as soon as she came home. By this time I was too tired to unpack. I dropped into bed and fell asleep. There would be time to unpack in the morning.

8

My small alarm clock buzzed me awake at 6:30 A.M. It was still dark. I turned on the light and went to the bathroom in my BVDs and barefoot so I wouldn't make any noise and wake her up. On the way I peeked into the dining room. The radio which I had placed on the table was gone. I smiled to myself. It was the right gift.

By the time I had shaved and washed, I could hear music coming from the kitchen. I came out of the bathroom, holding a towel over my BVDs. She was sitting at the dinner table, the radio in the center, listening to the music while she smoked a cigarette.

She turned and smiled. "Thank you for such a wonderful gift. It is something that I wanted."

"I'm glad," I said. "I'll get dressed. I feel stupid standing here in my BVDs."

"I made fresh coffee for you and there are some fresh croissants for you." She smiled. "And don't worry about your underwear. My father and my brother were always in their long johns at breakfast."

I dropped the towel and sat down at the table. She served me a café au lait. Coffee and milk, French style. I took a teaspoonful of sugar and began to stir. "I didn't know that you had a brother," I said.

"He was the baby of the family. He was only eighteen when he went into the army. He was killed when the Boche rolled over the Maginot Line."

"I'm sorry," I said.

"It was four years ago. It was sad, but it is something that many French families had to live through." She shook her head. "Now you Americans are here and it is better—finally the Germans are losing. In a few months the war may be over."

She rose from the table and brought back some brioche, croissants, and orange marmalade. "I am sorry but we have no butter. We cannot buy it in the stores."

"Maybe I can bring some from the mess hall and also coffee and canned milk."

She laughed. "We will be living like millionaires."

"Close to it," I said. I looked at her. "Is there some way that I can take you to dinner tonight?"

"I'd like that," she said. "But it would have to be early. I have to be at work by ten o'clock."

"I know that," I said. "But you will have to pick a restaurant because I don't know any restaurants here."

"I know all of them," she said. "Seven o'clock tonight, if it's okay with you."

"Perfect," I said as I got up. "I have to get dressed now. I apologize that I haven't unpacked yet, but I will do that tonight after we've had dinner."

"No problem," she said, rising from the table. She picked up my cup and plate. "I'll help you."

I stared at her. With a cup in one hand and a plate in the other, her morning kimono fell open. Tits, belly, and pussy. It was beautiful. I felt myself getting hard.

She laughed at me. "Don't get embarrassed. I always go around the apartment like this."

"That's great," I said. "But I will need at least a few cold showers each day."

"You are funny, Jerree." She smiled. "And very sweet." She placed the dishes in the sink and looked over her shoulder at me. "You better get dressed, soldier," she said. "Or you'll really be late for work."

9

Paul was waiting for me on the street in front of the apartment. *"Bonjour."*
He smiled.

"Good morning," I answered. "What brings you out this early? Don't
you ever sleep?"

Paul laughed. "Corsicans never sleep," he said, and took my arm. "I
have my car around the corner and I brought two men with me who want
to do business with you."

"Can't it be this evening? I have to go to work," I said.

"These men are very important. It is necessary that you speak with them
now," he said. "Let's hurry." Paul still holding my arm, we turned the
corner. I could see two men sitting in the backseat. He opened the car
door and he pushed me into it. As soon as he sat down next to me, the
chauffeur started to move the car out into the lane of traffic.

I looked at Paul. "What's all this bullshit about? What kind of business
do these men want to talk to me about?" I looked in the back at the two
men. Their eyes did not meet mine.

Paul spoke almost apologetically. "We cannot be seen with these gentlemen. Everything said here must be held in confidence. I will not mention
any names, but one of the gentlemen here is one of the chiefs of the Paris
Sûreté."

I couldn't believe my ears. "Great," I said, shaking my head. "What
could they want me for? Outside of throwing me in the can."

"You Americans have a very funny sense of humor," Paul said. Then his voice became stern. "The gentlemen only want to make you rich."

I raised my eyebrows. "How are they going to do that?"

The man in the gray business suit leaned toward me. He spoke in perfect English, British style. "Sergeant," he said in a voice accustomed to authority. "It has come to our attention that you are in charge of repairing army jeeps that have been damaged. I understand also that you are able to move some of them into civilian hands."

"That's right," I said. "But only those jeeps that headquarters has ordered to be destroyed because they are too expensive to repair. Unfortunately, we don't have enough of them to meet the demand."

The other man, who was wearing a dark blue suit, spoke also in British English. "What if you had ten jeeps a week to repair, could you handle that?"

"I'd need more men," I said. "But, yes. I can handle it. But there is no way I will move that many of them into the civilian market. That many jeeps will stick out like a sore thumb. Then I really would wind up in the can."

"You are a funny man, Sergeant," the gray suit said. "First, we must have names so that you can address us. I am Jack and my confrere is Peter. Of course, they are not our real names, but that is not important."

"Yes, sir," I said. By this time, I figured out that the gray suit was the French general. But I was smart enough not to salute him.

The gray suit nodded. "Now I have a connection with the U.S. Army that will supply you with at least ten jeeps that have the official papers for their destruction."

"We still can't dump that many cars on the street without being tagged," I said.

Peter, the blue suit, smiled. "We are not dumping them into the streets of Paris. As a matter of fact, the jeeps will not even remain in France. You deliver us the jeeps and that is all you have to worry about. You do your work and you get your money. And it will be more money than you are getting in black-marketing the jeeps here."

"How will all of this be arranged?" I asked.

"You didn't ask how much money you would be receiving," Jack, the gray suit, said.

"I am not a businessman; I will be happy if Paul would take care of that for me. I am sure he will be completely fair," I said. "But here is one other problem. I will need more personnel."

Jack gray suit smiled. "We will arrange for that also. When you need the help just send your request to your commanding officer. He will have orders from headquarters to give you anything you need."

I turned to Paul. "Look, this is big business. Wholesaling. But what about the man that bought the first car and ordered two more?"

"You can deliver them to him," Paul said.

"It will be fine," Peter blue suit said. "It will take us at least two weeks to have everything in place."

Jack gray suit smiled and handed me an envelope. "Here is an advance on your work."

I looked at the package of bills he put in my hand. It was U.S. one-hundred-dollar bills. I turned to Paul and gave him the money. "I would like Paul to hold the money until some of the work is done."

Peter blue suit leaned toward me. "That's five thousand dollars, Sergeant. It is yours to keep."

"Thank you, gentlemen," I said. "I have confidence that Paul will take care of the money until I feel that it's right to receive it."

Paul took his small leather bag that all classy Frenchmen carried and placed the money in the bag. He looked at me. "Do you want me to drop you off at your barracks?"

"I think it will be better if I walk. It will be more discreet." I held my hand out to Jack gray suit and Peter blue suit. "Thank you, gentlemen," I said, and shook hands French style, one pump up and one pump down.

10

Sergeant Felder was at the barracks garage when I came in. He looked smilingly at me. "I heard you took an apartment with a stripper working at the Blue Note."

"That's right," I said. "Jesus, is that all you guys have to do, watch what I'm doing?"

"A couple of the guys saw you going out with her." He laughed. "Does your rent include fucking privileges? She is a hot-looking cunt."

"It's a rental, not a romance," I said. "Her boss at the club owns the apartment and rented me half of it."

"Some guys have all the luck." Felder smiled.

"That's enough of the bullshit," I said. "Any new cars come in?"

"Only those that we've had in the past few weeks. Nothing new just now. We can finish off the two cars that we promised. But after that we're fucked."

"What if we had ten cars a week—could we ship out that many a week?" I looked at him.

"To finish out ten cars a week . . ." He thought for a few moments. "We would have to have fourteen cars in stock so that we could use them for repair parts. And we would need twice as many mechanics here to do that much work."

I looked at him silently.

He stared at me. "You have an idea?"

"I can set it up," I said, nodding. "You just give me a list of personnel that we need and I will send the request up to headquarters."

"You'll get it, just like that." He was impressed. "What do you know that I don't?"

"Connections." I laughed. "Now get on it. We'll all make some loot over this."

I walked over to the company clerk's office. I looked at him working. He was a college man and thought he knew better than any of us because he was a business major in college, but as far as I was concerned he was nothing but a schmuck secretary. "The old man in yet?" I asked.

"He doesn't come in until eleven hundred hours," he said.

"Would you call me when he shows up?" I asked.

"Sure, Cooper," he said. "Hey, I heard you shacked up with the stripper from the Blue Note."

"There are no damn secrets around here." I laughed. "But don't worry, I'm not going to ask the old man to give me marrying papers."

"Is she hot?" he asked.

"They're all hot," I said. "Don't forget there's been a war on for a long time."

"I wish I had your luck," he said. "The only thing I get is paid pussy. And half the time I'm afraid I'll wind up with the clap."

"You don't send French letters through the mail, you know." I laughed. "Just remember to check with me when the old man gets in."

When it meant money Felder was right on the job. By the time I got back to his desk, he had a list of ten mechanics, all specialists in rebuilding jeeps. They had worked with him at different times during the last six months. "They are all that I can think of," he said. "I could use maybe another six men."

"Maybe we could draft unskilled workers to help us," I said. Then I had the right idea. Buddy. He was a hustler and he could get the new workers and teach them at the same time. The only problem might be the colonel. He'd had Buddy shipped out the minute he thought there might be trouble.

It was thirteen hundred hours before I got the call that the colonel would see me. He was smiling and his face was flushed when I walked into his office. At least I knew he had drunk his lunch. "What's on your mind, Sergeant?" he asked after I saluted him.

"I got word that they're shipping a large amount of jeeps for us to repair

and I have a list of men that I would like to bring here to do the job, sir."
I handed him the paper.

He hardly glanced at the paper. "Well, Sergeant, if we need them, we
need them. No need to worry. I'll have the company clerk order the req-
uisitions." Then he stopped as he read down to the bottom of the page,
where I had written Buddy's name. He was silent for a moment as he lit a
cigarette. Suddenly, I was his buddy, Jerry. "Jerry," he asked, "do you think
it might stir up a little problem? After all, we have only shipped Buddy to
Norway three months ago. They might need him there."

I looked straight ahead as I spoke to the colonel. "We need him here
more than they do in Norway, sir," I said. "And I'll keep him under wraps
so there'll be no flap about him. And sir, don't forget how very loyal he is
to you personally."

He looked at me for a moment. "But he'll understand that he is under
your orders."

"We'll have no problem about that, sir," I said.

"Okay, Jerry," he said. "I'm depending on you. This is really an important assignment for us and I don't want anything to go wrong with it."

"It will be fine, Colonel," I said. By now I knew that he was in on the
scam and they were all in the same business.

"Dismissed, Sergeant," he said suddenly, back to being official.

"Thank you, Colonel." I saluted and left.

11

She brought me to a small restaurant around the corner from the apartment house. There were only ten tables that seated four persons each. The floor was wooden and it creaked under the weight of my army boots. The kitchen was at the rear and open to the entire restaurant. I quickly learned that it was a Papa and Mama operation and that Papa was the chef and Mama was the waitress. The settings were simple: white tablecloths and napkins and stainless steel cutlery. But the menu was not simple. Roast chicken basted with olive oil and garlic; beef tenderloin, bleu, marinated in Burgundy wine; and pigeon roasted on the open fire and then stuffed with chopped browned mushrooms and raisins. Fresh baguettes with butter. Wine or beer refrigerated.

Mama and Papa were very sweet. They knew Giselle very well. She introduced me to them as her friend and I soon learned that they were cousins of her father.

She ordered pigeon and I ordered beef tenderloin. It didn't take long to arrive at the table. I was starved and it was delicious. After I had finished, Giselle told me that the beef tenderloin was really *cheval*. But it was the war, she explained. Most of the cattle were shipped to Germany. I could not taste the difference. Anyway, it was better than the Jewish beef stew I remembered from home. Dessert was flan, and we had small espressos after our dessert. The biggest surprise was the check. It came to twenty dollars in American money.

We walked to the apartment. She wanted to change her dress before she went to work. She put on a plain cotton dress. "Why?" I asked. "The dress you have on is beautiful."

She laughed. "That was silk and it was Chanel. One does not go to work in clothes like that."

"Why not?"

"It's too expensive. I wear them only on special occasions," she said. "I can afford but one nice dress and one nice suit."

"I can afford to give you some nice clothes," I said. "After all, you are so kind to me and you have opened your life to me."

"I liked you before I met you." She smiled. "Paul told me about you."

"Nobody had to tell me that you are beautiful." I laughed. "I found that out on my own." I looked at my wristwatch. It was nine-thirty. "I'll go back to the club with you."

"You don't have to," she answered. "The driver will be here any moment."

"I'd still like to go with you. I'd like to walk if it's okay with you. This has been the nicest evening I have had since I came here and I don't want it to end."

She looked up at me and then came close to me. "I like you very much."

I put my arms around her and kissed her. Her mouth was sweet and warm. She kissed me again. Then I stopped and caught my breath. "We're running late," I said. "I don't want to have Paul angry at me for taking you to dinner and being late."

"Paul will not be angry. He is a romantic," she said. "He has already told me that he would not be surprised that we would fall in love."

I laughed. "He's right. I think I'm already falling." I took her by the arm. "Let's get going," I said. "I'm taking you to the club."

12

We went into the club by the stage door. I didn't know how Paul knew we would come in this way, but he was right at the door as we came in. He was smiling. "Monsieur, would you join me for a drink?"

I looked at him, then at her. "I wasn't planning to stay. I was going back to finish my unpacking."

"That's not important," he said, and looked at Giselle. "Jerry and I will be at my table while you do the first show; then you both can go home because I am letting you off for the second show." She looked at me, then at him, and went up the staircase to the dressing rooms.

Paul took my arm and led me to his table. M. Gray Suit was sitting waiting for us. He was holding a cognac snifter between the palms of both hands warming the liquor. He spoke quickly. "Sergeant."

He was a general, that was for sure. "Yes, sir," I answered just as succinctly. I kept my hand from saluting him.

"Have you requisitioned your new personnel?" he asked.

"I have, sir," I said.

"Did you have any problem with your colonel?"

"No, sir," I answered. "He sent in the request to headquarters immediately."

"How soon do you think the new soldiers will be here?"

"I don't know, sir," I answered. "I hope soon so that we can begin work."

Gray suit shook his head. "I hope they are faster than the French to follow orders. If the personnel don't arrive here quickly, the war will be over before we can get into business."

"Really, sir?" I said.

Paul spoke to the gray suit in French, then turned to me. "They have just learned this afternoon that the war will possibly be over by May. That gives us really only two months to ship our forty cars. If that can be done, we will all be satisfied."

"Forty cars is easy if I get the help," I said.

"You will also be rich." Paul smiled.

Gray suit rose from the table. He held out his hand and I took it. His grip was firm and we shook in French style. "Thank you, sir," I said. "I will do my best for all of us."

Gray suit nodded and left the club. I noticed that two men followed him out. I turned to Paul. "Bodyguards?"

Paul nodded. "All important men in France now have to have bodyguards because we are not sure who will be in charge of the government when this is all over."

"I thought de Gaulle would take over," I said.

"There are very important politicians who do not believe an army general should be either the president or the premier of France," he explained to me. "And our general is a Gaullist."

"Then he will be okay," I said.

"We will not know until the war is over and meanwhile we must pick the fruit as soon as it is ripe."

"I didn't know that you were a philosopher," I said.

"I am not a philosopher, I am a pragmatist." He smiled. "I believe that the name of the game is money. If you have money you will go the way you want and nobody will bother you."

"Is that what the French believe?" I asked.

He laughed. "I cannot speak for the French. I am Corsican. Now have a cognac and enjoy yourself." He got up and left the table. "I have something to take care of, but I will be back to see Giselle."

I had three cognacs while I was waiting for Giselle to come on stage. She was beautiful and I applauded like crazy when she finished. Paul slipped into a chair at the table. "She is lovely, isn't she?" he said.

I nodded. "More than that," I said. "She is unbelievable. And it's not the cognac I drank speaking."

He put his hand on my shoulder. "Jerry, I will have my chauffeur drive you and Giselle home."

13

It was after midnight by the time we got to the apartment. "I will make some coffee," she said.

"I'm okay," I said. "I'm not drunk."

She laughed. "I know but I need to talk to you so that you will be alive when you have finished your work and the war is over."

I looked at her. Now I was sober. "You know something that I do not?"

"You must remember that they are Corsicans," she said.

"Even the general?" I asked.

"Especially the general. He is an important Corsican in France. He is in the French army because he believes that de Gaulle will support him in allowing Corsica to secede from France and become a separate country."

"I guess I don't understand French politics. What if de Gaulle doesn't support him?" I said.

"Another underground war. The Corsicans will try to get away from France any way that they can. Now that you are working with the Corsicans to give them cars you are going to be in trouble at the end of it. If the French do not throw you into jail, the Corsicans will kill you because you know about what they have done."

"Jesus!" I said. I looked at her. "Why are you telling me about this? You might be in danger."

She laughed. "I'm a stripper, not a Mata Hari. And because I'm not a part of their plan."

"But you have told me everything about them."

She looked at me. "I am a fool. I am just like my sister. She fell in love with a German and I am falling in love with an American."

I reached for her hand. She came very close to me. "I know that you are not in love with me," she whispered. "But I don't care. I am in love with you and that is all that is important to me."

"I don't understand you," I said.

"I am French," she said softly. "There is nothing you have to understand. We love together as long as we are here."

I kissed her mouth. Her lips were soft and trembling. "Will you love me sometime?" she asked.

"I love you now," I said.

She was beautiful. But not in the way she was beautiful on stage. There she seemed to be larger than life, bigger breasts, fuller belly, heavy hips and ass, and longer, slimmer legs. But here in the bedroom she felt smaller. Real. A young girl. Her eyes were luminous and blue. Her face was young and trusting. Her breasts seemed smaller, and surprisingly, her whole body seemed smaller. And because she was a dancer, her beautiful pussy was shaven, with only a small thin line of light auburn hair around her cunt.

As she stood naked in front of me, she smiled softly. "French girls are not as big as American girls. Are you surprised?"

"No," I said as I touched her soft and supple skin. "Only that you look different on stage."

"I am the same girl," she said. "Only on stage the costumes are padded and built up so when we take off our clothes, they only see what they believed before."

"I guess I'm innocent. I think you are even more beautiful here next to me than you are on stage."

She pressed my face between her breasts, then moved me slowly down across her belly, and then finally she buried me in her pussy. I felt her clit grow hard in my mouth and then suddenly she screamed. "I can't hold it! I can't hold it!" She held my face tightly in her hands between her legs so that her hot pee poured over my face.

She held me tightly until her hips stopped bucking. Then she looked down at me. "Are you angry?" she asked.

"No," I said. "But, I want a towel and the right to give you the same golden shower that you gave me."

"I love you," she said, and delicately lapped the pee off of my face. "You have the right to do anything you want."

"Good," I said. "Then, now can we fuck?"

14

It was strange. I had never really lived with a girl before. Even when I was with Kitty, we were in heat. Either one or the other of us was tearing our clothes off. But we never lived together. I had my apartment. She lived with her father. We were together, but not really together. We had hungers. For sex. For money. But it was not until now that I understood that my hunger was different than her hunger. She was greedy. For sex, money, power. I was growing up and dreaming about all that life has to offer. That was why it was so easy for her to move on to Harry. I was just a step on her road.

I wondered why I couldn't understand then. Unfortunately, I didn't see what Fat Rita or Buddy saw. And even if they had told me about her then I wouldn't have believed it.

Giselle was like no one I had ever known. She loved. She didn't seek money or power. The only thing that mattered to her was the love she gave and the love she needed. Sex was our expression. Despite the difficult world we lived in.

We had finished the first of the two cars that Paul wanted to be painted black when the new batch of jeeps began trickling in. I began to sweat every day I saw a new one arrive. The cars began piling up and I was worried that we wouldn't have enough room to store them. I checked with head-

quarters. The colonel sent back orders telling me not to worry. New personnel would show up in another week.

It was the middle of the week. Giselle had gone to work and I was sitting
in the apartment listening to the Voice of America near midnight. There
was a knock at the door. It was a strange knock. And I hadn't heard it in
a long time. One knock, one knock, and then two quick knocks followed
by one more. I didn't have to open the door to know who was there.
"Buddy!" I smiled.

There he was. Tall, and skinnier than he had been in France. We
hugged, and as I looked over his shoulder there was a blue-eyed blonde girl
standing behind him.

His face had a big, happy grin. "Jerry, I'd like you to meet my wife,
Ulla."

I stared at him almost in shock. "You're married?"

"It has to happen sometime and she picked me."

I reached for her hand. She smiled nervously. "Ulla," I said. "Welcome.
Please come in."

Buddy dragged his two duffel bags into the apartment. I gestured to them.
"Please sit down. I'll have some coffee ready for you in a moment."

"Ulla will have a coffee; I'll have a beer if you have one." Buddy smiled.

I gave him a bottle of beer and turned on the gas burner to warm up
the coffee. "Jesus!" I exclaimed. "When did you get in? When did you get
married? Why didn't you let me know?"

Buddy took a swig from his beer and laughed at me. "Okay. One question
at a time. Ulla and I got married a month ago at her father's church in
Oslo. We got into Paris about two hours ago. I never got time to write you.
I went straight to the club to ask Paul if he knew a place for us to stay. I
met Giselle and she invited us to come up here."

I stared at him. Something was different. Then I realized that he had
lost his stripes—he was back to being a private. "Are you okay?" I asked.

"I'm okay now," he said. "Giselle said that we could use the extra bedroom until we got settled in our own place."

"Fine," I said. "I'll move my things out of the armoire in that bedroom
in the morning."

"And what about you and Giselle? Serious?" Buddy asked.

"I guess so," I said. "I've never felt like this with anyone before."

Ulla smiled at me. "I was surprised when I saw you. I always thought
that you were like Buddy."

"You mean black?" I asked.

"Yes," she said.

"We are very much alike," I laughed. "Only he's black and I'm a Jew."

"We don't have any Jews in my town. It's a very small town," she said. "We are mostly Protestant. My father is a Lutheran minister."

I was curious. "Do you have any blacks in your town?"

She smiled. "Only traveling jazz bands and in the movies. But in Oslo, it's a much bigger city; there are many Jews and blacks."

Buddy gave me a broad smile.

By this time the coffee was ready. I gave her a mug. *"Au lait?* We also have some baguettes and Gruyère."

"Just coffee will be fine. All I really want is some sleep. The trip was tiring," she said.

"Bring your coffee and you can go to the bedroom and I'll show you where the lavatory is at the end of the hall," I said, leading her to the doorway. "Just make yourself comfortable."

I took out another two beers, one for myself and the other for Buddy. "She's beautiful," I said to him after she had gone into the bedroom. "Are you really married?"

He took out a folded formal sheet of paper. "Legitimate. Signed, sealed, and delivered."

I looked at it. It was in Norwegian. In the corner of the paper was a picture of the king of Norway, with writing on lines below. It was Buddy and Ulla's names signed next to each other. I gave him back the paper. "I wouldn't have guessed it in a million years. Buddy, a married man."

He was serious. "When the war is over I want to take her home."

"It's not going to be easy for her. Harlem ain't Norway," I said.

"I'm not planning to go back to Harlem. I want to go out west. Maybe Los Angeles or San Francisco. We're planning to have a family," he said.

"Isn't it a little too soon to start thinking about that?" I asked.

"Not really." He laughed. "She's already knocked up."

"You have a family," I said. "You're going to need to make some money."

He smiled at me. "That's where you come in. When I got the orders signed from the old man that you were in charge of a special project, I knew there was money coming my way."

I nodded to him. "Tonight you get some rest. There will be time enough in the morning to fill you in."

He stood up and took my hand. "I really love her," he said. "And I want to thank you for both of us."

15

Paul found a studio apartment for Buddy the next day. He also gave Ulla a waitress job at the Blue Note. Buddy was really pleased. He only had one problem. The money we were making wasn't enough for him. He wanted more action. In a week, he was back into his old gambling games that he had run before he was transferred to Norway.

Sergeant Felder, who was in charge of the work detail repairing the jeeps, was pissed off at Buddy. He came to me complaining that Buddy was hustling the others into gambling and they not only lost their money, but they also lost time at work.

I called Buddy on it. What he was doing was hurting all of us. I didn't ask to get him back here to get us in trouble.

Buddy stared at me. "I can get more money in the card and crap games in a day than we can make all week. I'll cut you in for twenty-five percent. That's as much as I give the old man."

"You're being stupid," I told him. "This isn't just the old man's game, it's the French and Corsicans." I reached for a cigarette. "You're a married man now. Your wife is working for Paul. Paul is a Corsican; he's the one that got me into this deal. Corsicans are like the Mafia—they control practically everything. They gave the orders for the old man to go ahead on this deal. Otherwise, there would have been no deal. You want to kill it? We all get killed."

"I've dealt with the Mafia. The Mafia ain't so tough. The niggers in Harlem keep them in their place," Buddy snapped.

"You're becoming more stupid by the minute," I said. "First of all, you got no niggers to back you up here in Paris. They're Africans and they work as street cleaners and pearl divers in restaurants. The French don't even let them in the army. And second, remember—here, you're white."

"What if I don't let our soldiers in the game? I have enough players that are French."

"Just as long as you keep your work up here," I said.

"I'll still give you your share," he said.

"I have enough trouble," I said. "You just keep it away from here. I want nothing of it."

"The old man is taking his share," Buddy said, smiling.

"I don't give a shit," I said. "He can go fuck himself for all I care!"

Giselle and I had set up a routine. Monday through Thursday were slow days for the gay clientele at the club. So I waited for her to come home early. Friday, Saturday, and Sunday were busy nights for her. They all loved her and she worked late on those nights. After her late show she spent time at everyone's table. I tried staying up late to wait for her, but four or five in the morning was too much for me. I still had to get up and go to work at seven in the morning.

Once again Paul came through for us. He agreed that Giselle could go home after the first show at midnight. It worked great for us. I would stay at the club until she was finished and then we went home together.

By the end of February the factory was going full blast. I was delivering blue suit a jeep each day and gray suit one every other day. Buddy and Felder were going crazy trying to figure out who I was really delivering these cars to. But Paul and I had a special system. I delivered the car to Paul at the club at night. Then the fat man would direct me to a different location for each car. When I reached that location there was a French one-striper private who I would hand the car keys. In return, he always handed me a brown envelope with my payment enclosed. Words were never exchanged. In a moment the fat man would arrive and take me back to the club in an old *deux chevaux*. On the nights that Giselle and I came home early, I waited until the morning to put the envelopes in the safe. On the weekends I always delivered them to the garage and put them in the safe.

In the first week of April I opened the safe and counted my share of the money. I had twelve thousand dollars. Sergeant Felder and the others had about the same. Buddy had gotten almost as much as I, but I never knew what he did with his money. His crap games and the poker games seemed to be profitable. I had once heard him mention that he had put together almost twenty grand and was planning on sending Ulla with the money to Norway when she was ready to have the baby.

The word was everywhere that the Germans were falling back every day and the war would be over soon. But you wouldn't believe it if you saw the broken-down jeeps that came to us.

One evening when Giselle and I were having dinner at the Papa and Mama restaurant she began talking about what we would do after the war was over.

"I will go home to Lyons," she said. "The life in Paris is not for me." She looked at me. "Are you planning to go back to the States?"

I shrugged my shoulders. "I guess so. The army will send us back to the States for discharge."

"You can stay in France," she said. "I would like to be with you."

I looked at her. "I want to be with you, too," I said. "But what could I do here? I don't even speak French."

"Maybe you can take me to the States with you," she said. "I speak English."

"We both have problems," I said. "I love you, but my world is uncertain. Let's not worry about our future until the war is over. Then we can really decide what we want to do."

She reached across the table for my hand. "I love you, Jerry. I don't want to lose you."

I kissed her hand. "And I don't want to lose you, Giselle."

16

I was sitting at the small desk in the back of the garage. The last shipment of the jeeps for the week had been shipped and all the money had been paid to the men. I checked my share. Seventeen thousand dollars. I stared in awe at it. I didn't know what to do with it. I was fucked. If I declared it, the army would have me thrown in the can. And if I tried to take it back to the States when I was discharged I would be picked up by customs, who would want to know how I got the money.

It was nearly 1800 hours when Buddy sat down in the chair across my desk. "We're getting near the end here," he said.

"That's what everybody is saying," I answered.

"What do you plan to be doing, then?" he asked.

"They discharge me, I go home," I said.

"I heard they'll be shipping many of us to the Pacific. Japan is still fighting and they don't think that it will be over for a long time."

"I don't know," I said kiddingly. "The president hasn't given me his plans yet."

"I don't trust Truman," Buddy said. "At least with Roosevelt we knew where we were going."

I laughed. "We knew shit. They're all over our heads."

"One thing I do know," he said. "I don't want to go be in another war with Japan."

"You're full of shit," I said. "We've never even been in any war. All we

236

did was work behind the lines fixing jeeps. We never fought anything more than getting the grease off our hands!"

"When did you become such a hero?" he asked sarcastically.

"I'm not," I said. "But I saw the newspapers and the newsreels. I think we've been pretty lucky."

"The minute it's over here," he said, "I want to go home and get my discharge money and papers. I don't want to be the last one to leave here, I want to be the first."

"What about Ulla?" I asked. "I thought you were going to bring her home with you."

"I checked it out," he said. "The only way I can bring her into the States is on a Norwegian visa, with immigration papers."

"You're kidding. Even though you are married to her?" I asked.

"They're pricks," he said. "Immigration said there are too many foreign girls marrying American soldiers just to get into the country."

"What are you going to do, then?" I asked.

"She wants to go home to have the baby. The baby will be an American citizen since I'm the father; we'll register the baby at the American consulate. Then it will be easier to get her into the States."

"You check all of this out?" I asked.

"Lawyers at the American consulate and army headquarters in Paris. They say it's the way to go."

"Then you have it all worked out. Congratulations!" I said.

"I still need your help," he said. "I want you to have the old man okay my discharge papers as soon as this shit war is over."

"I can send the orders to him, but there will be no guarantee that he will sign them," I answered.

Buddy took a fat envelope from the inside of his shirt pocket. "There's ten grand in here. Give it to him and tell him that it is his if he signs the orders."

I couldn't believe Buddy sometimes. "You mean you want *me* to walk into the old man's headquarters and show him this envelope with the money and tell him that it's his if he bails you out?"

"I can't go into his office. Every asshole in the place knows that I was in the shithouse with him. Besides, he wouldn't trust me to give him this money. He'd think I was setting him up. Every time I pay him for the action, he gives me a different meeting place."

I shook my head. "No way for me to help you on this. I'm in enough trouble right now. If I get caught with this car deal, I'll be in the can for life."

"I'll throw five grand in for you, too," he said.

"What the fuck are you? A millionaire?" I asked.

"I been doing pretty good," he said. "French love the action."

"How much have you got?" I asked.

"I'm sending Ulla back to Norway with sixty grand. We're putting the money in an account for the baby. When Ulla and the baby get to the States we'll have enough to get settled." He smiled at me. "Ulla's honest. She doesn't think the way that we think."

"As long as she's not like Kitty you're way ahead," I said.

"But you will send out the discharge papers for me?" he asked again. "You don't have to take the money to him. I'll find another way to get with him on this."

"I'll sign the papers," I said. "But I won't date it until the war is over. But you will be the first I send up."

He looked at me. "You really scared, ain't you?"

"You bet your ass I am. And if you're as smart as I think you are, you should be scared, too!" I answered. "Don't forget, you're not alone anymore. You've got a family."

17

It was April 20 when Paul came to the table where I was waiting for Giselle to finish her performance. He didn't look happy. "Jerry," he said. "We're all fucked."

"They're on to us?" I asked, my stomach a little knotted.

"Not that," he said irritably. "I've just heard from the blue suit that they have all of the cars they need from us. The order is to shut everything down."

"We've only given them fifty cars," I said. "That's all they need?"

"They're all shipped to Corsica. It's a small island. That's a lot of cars for them."

"But I have fifteen jeeps in the garage that we are ready to repair. And what about the extra men we brought back for them?" I asked.

"Blue suit says you should send orders to ship them back to their original units. He says it's already taken care of and it won't be any problem for you. He said that they all made a lot of money. None of them will complain." He looked at me. "Now we can go back to our original idea. We'll be able to sell those fifteen cars in a minute."

I lit a cigarette. "I'm not worried about the cars. I'm worried about the men. What can I tell them?"

"Tell them the truth. They'll shut up and leave. They know they can't talk about it; otherwise, they will wind up in big trouble too."

"You know, Paul," I said, "you're talking like an American. Where did you get that?"

"In my business. I had to learn and think like an American, as a Frenchman. It's not easy!" He laughed. "Let's have a cognac. We'll make everything right." He gestured to a waitress, who brought our cognacs without a word. "What is your plan after all of this is over? Are you and Giselle marrying?"

We clinked our glasses. *"Salut."* I smiled at him. "Giselle and I want to be together, but neither of us has spoken about marriage."

"Après la guerre," he said, "you can stay here in France. There are many things you can do. Many opportunities."

"But I don't speak French," I said. "What kind of work or job would I be able to do? Nobody could understand me."

"You'll be able to learn to speak French quickly enough," he said. "And if you stay here after the war I'll help you."

"Paul," I asked, "Do you have something in mind?"

"I have a few ideas," he answered. "But we must wait until the time is right."

I looked at him for a moment. "Meanwhile, I still have fifteen jeeps I'll need to get rid of," I said. "And I'll be losing more than fifty percent of my workers."

"We can get them sold the same way that we did before. We can sell at least two a week." Paul smiled. "There will still be a shortage of cars for the average Frenchman and I can get in touch with the right people to move the cars." He looked down at his watch. "Giselle will be coming down soon. Just relax and go home. Everything will be fine."

The next morning I told the men the bad news. Much to my surprise, most of them didn't complain. They were looking to go back to their own army groups. They all had seniority in their division and the word was that they would be the first to be shipped home for discharge.

Buddy was the only one who was pissed off. He had planned to go home from France, even though Ulla was going back to Norway; he didn't want to be with his division because of his low discharge priority.

"You have to get to the colonel," Buddy said desperately. "I don't care how much it costs. I have to get home before Ulla and the baby get there."

"What are you so hot about?" I asked. "Maybe it will be better if you can all go home together."

Buddy lit a cigarette and shook his head at me. "You're an asshole," he said. "Do you think if it wasn't important that I would be this hot?" He took a deep lungful of smoke and then let it come out slowly. "I have a girl that I married in Harlem before I went into the army. I thought it would get me out of the draft, but I was stupid. I've got nothing but grief from that cunt. Now I have to get divorced from her or kill her before Ulla gets to the States."

I stared at him. "And I thought I was in the shithouse."

"Then you'll go to the old man?" he asked.

I nodded. "I'll go."

He put his hand on my shoulder and squeezed gently. "We've been friends a long time," he said. "I appreciate you for helping me out. You know that anything that I can do for you, all you have to do is say the word."

Late that night after Giselle and I had gone back to the apartment we sat at the table having a coffee. "Paul told me what was going on."

"He talks a lot to you," I said.

"I told you we go back with family," she said. "He wants you to stay in France. Do you want to?"

"I don't know," I said. "The only thing I know is that I want to be with you. But I don't know what I can do here."

"Paul said that he will help your friend Buddy to stay in France and go from here to the States, if you will stay here in France after your discharge." She looked as if she were close to tears. "I want you to stay here, Jerry. I know you can find something to do."

I leaned across the table and cupped her face in my hands. "I will try, Giselle." Then I kissed her warm lips and we went into the bedroom.

Quickly, we threw our clothes on the floor and, naked, rolled onto the bed. With my fingers I opened her pussy. My cock was already dripping as I drove into her.

She gasped. "Jerree! Give me your baby! Come inside and make many children inside me. I love you, I love you!"

I felt her fingernails tearing into my buttocks. Then I felt my body shuddering and I opened my mouth to gasp in air as my orgasm tore through me and I felt my life essence pouring into her. "My God! My God!" I collapsed like dead weight on top of her. Our bodies were pouring sweat.

She pulled my face to her and kissed me. "I really love you, Jerree," she whispered. Her tears were wet on my face.

18

It was almost a week later that I had my last meeting with blue suit and gray suit. It was in a small curtained-off corner table in the Blue Note. This was different than any other meeting. The Frenchmen were in uniform. The gray suit was dressed in the French army brigadier general's uniform and the blue suit was in the gray Sûreté police uniform with a hard round hat and two braids on the shoulder. Paul brought me to their table. This was a section of the club in which I never sat. It was the homos' side of the runway.

When Paul brought me to the table the two Frenchmen stayed in their chairs. I saluted them and "yes sir'd" them to death. There was a bottle of cognac on the table before them, and the general poured a drink for Paul and myself. *"Salut!"* he toasted.

"Salut!" we answered.

The policeman looked at me. "We are very pleased with your assignment. It went very well."

"Thank you, sir," I said.

The general spoke to me. "Have all your extra personnel returned to their divisions?"

"Yes, sir," I said. "All except one. He was in my platoon since before we came to France."

The policeman looked at me. "The one who had been transferred to Norway?"

242

"Yes, sir," I said.

"Why didn't you send him back to Norway?" the general asked.

"He wanted to stay here," I said, looking to Paul for help. "He was originally transferred because he had a problem with the MPs while driving our commanding officer to an off-limits club."

The policeman smiled. "Your friend was sent to Norway to cover up the incident?"

"Yes, sir," I said.

"Did you arrange that transfer?"

"No, sir," I answered. "That was not my jurisdiction at the time."

"But you knew that your commanding officer arranged for the transfer?" the general asked.

"Yes, sir," I said.

"Do you think that your friend is trustworthy and can keep his mouth shut?" the policeman asked.

"Yes, sir," I said.

They turned to Paul. "What do you think?" the general asked.

"Jerry and he have been friends since long before the war started," he said. "I have no doubt that they can both be trusted."

This time it was the policeman who poured the drinks. "*Salut!*"

"*Salut!*" I returned and toasted.

The general then pushed an envelope across the table to me. "This is a bonus in appreciation for a job well done."

I picked up the envelope. It felt full and thick with banknotes. "It is not necessary, but I thank you for your generosity, gentlemen."

The policeman smiled. "And I want you to know that you will not be bothered by any of the authorities if you choose to sell the rest of the jeeps on the street."

"Thank you, sir," I answered.

We all stood up and shook hands formally as they left. Paul and I returned to our chairs. The envelope was still lying on the table.

I picked it up and opened it. I counted the bills. Five thousand U.S. dollars in one-hundred-dollar bills. I looked at Paul. "I think they meant for half of this to go to you."

He shook his head. "I've been taken care of already. This money is all yours."

I whistled softly. "This is crazy," I said. "This will make over twenty-five thousand dollars from the time we started to now."

"Let me assure you," Paul said. "There was a lot of money made for those two if you made that much. You owe them nothing. You are safe; they will not forget your help."

"I don't know how to hide this from the American authorities," I said.

"Why not do the same thing Buddy did?" Paul asked.

"But he's married. He's covered it by giving it to his wife," I said.

"Giselle could hide it for you," Paul said.

"But we're not married," I said.

"Giselle loves you—the money makes no difference to her. She'll hide it for you and protect you." Paul smiled.

I thought about Kitty and how she had protected me.

"I'd offer to hold it for you, but that would not be safe. I'm Corsican and too many people in the French government know that I'm close to the separatist movement. If there is ever a problem, they'll wipe me out and I'll lose everything."

"Christ," I said sympathetically. "I don't understand it."

Paul nodded. "That is the way of the world. The Irish fight the English. The Jews fight the Arabs. There will always be people fighting for their own country. They always believe that it will bring them freedom. Even your own Civil War should tell that to you."

"Great," I said sarcastically. "Thanks for the history lesson, but that has nothing to do with my money. I still don't know how to hide my money."

"You could always be honest about it." He laughed. "Tell them you got the money gambling. Then you can pay your taxes and there will be no problem. Of course, you may not have much money afterward, but you will be honest."

"Shit," I said. "You're laughing at me."

"Of course I am," he said. "If you can't trust Giselle there is no one in the world you can trust." He got up from the table. "If you want my advice, talk to Giselle tonight."

I stared after him as he walked through the club to the backstage area. The son of a bitch was right. There was nothing else I could do. I didn't want to be cleaned out like I was when Uncle Harry and Kitty did their number on me. Giselle was the only person I could trust.

19

It was the end of April. Exactly April 30. It was eleven at night and I was sitting at the Blue Note at Paul's table waiting until Giselle did her turn and we could go home. I was nursing a beer when a voice came from behind me. "Sergeant Cooper."

I knew the voice. I stood up and saluted. "Colonel."

"At ease, Sergeant," he said, and sat down.

"Yes, sir," I said, also sitting. "May I offer you a drink, sir?"

"Thank you, Cooper," he answered. "Do you think they have any Canadian rye in this place?"

"I can ask," I answered, gesturing to a waitress. But Paul was faster. He came quickly from backstage before the waitress could come to the table.

"Colonel." He smiled. "I'm happy to see you again."

Paul was great. He hadn't seen the colonel since Buddy brought him into the club months ago. "The colonel wants to know if you have any Canadian rye whiskey," I said.

Paul was apologetic. "No, sir. But I do have American bourbon."

"Okay," the colonel answered. "Thank you. Also some ginger ale."

"Right away, sir," Paul answered.

The colonel looked at him. "I have to talk with the sergeant privately."

"My office is at your service, Colonel." Paul bowed. "No one will bother you there."

Five minutes later we were sitting in Paul's office. I had never seen it before. It was a small room but tastefully furnished. An antique desk, partly covered in leather with a chair to match. Across from the desk was a two-cushion leather couch. On the wall hung a few French theatrical prints and clown paintings.

The colonel took over the desk and its chair. Paul had placed a bottle of bourbon in front of him with a glass, ice, and ginger ale. He made himself a highball and then leaned over to me. "The war is almost over," he said to me as though I had never heard anything about it.

"Yes, sir," I said.

"I have orders to close down this whole operation," he said, making himself another drink.

I was silent.

"I know you still have about eleven jeeps that can be salvaged, as well as a few others that can only be used for extra parts." He looked at me. "Have you any ideas about how we can use them?" he asked.

"I haven't thought about it, sir," I lied. I wasn't about to tell him that I had already received permission from the Corsicans to sell them on the black market.

"I don't know, either," he said, again pouring himself another drink. "I've been transferred back to Detroit to set up the discharge headquarters for the platoon so we can get everybody out as fast as we got them in."

"Yes, sir," I said.

"I can take you back to the States with me, Sergeant," he said. "I've received permission to bring certain help with me. I thought that you might be interested because you've done a good job with me and I wanted to show my appreciation."

I looked at him. By this time his face was flushed and he was on the way to getting completely pissed. I was not that stupid. I knew the only reason he wanted to bring me back to the States was to make sure I couldn't talk about the operation here after he left. Besides, I didn't trust him. He drank too much and I couldn't be sure that he would take me to the States.

"I appreciate your consideration, sir," I said. "But I was planning on staying in France after the war."

"You have a girl?" he asked.

"Yes, sir," I said. "But, Colonel, Buddy knows as much about the division as I do, and I know that he wants to go home as soon as he can. Especially with you, sir. He has a great deal of respect for you."

The colonel thought for a moment and poured another drink. "Then what will you do?" he asked.

"Just leave me the discharge papers dated the day the war is officially

over and I'll be okay," I answered. "I'm sure that I can get a job here." I
held my breath while he thought about my idea.

Again, he poured another shot of bourbon into his glass. He looked into
the bottom of the glass. "Okay, Sergeant," he said. "You send the private
over to see me. I know that he's bright enough to handle the job. I'll sign
your discharge papers and you can send them into headquarters whenever
you are ready. And I will give you junk orders for the jeeps you have left.
Make sure you get some money out of them."

"Thank you, sir," I said, standing and saluting.

He stood straight up from his chair and began to salute, but he didn't
quite make it. He started to fall forward across the desk, knocking the
bottle of bourbon and his empty glass onto the floor.

I don't know how, but Paul must have had a sixth sense. He was in the
office in only a few moments. He looked at the colonel. "He can't hold
his liquor."

Frenchmen are funny even when they don't mean to be funny. "Stupid,"
I said. "Get the fat man to help me straighten him up. I'll run over and
get Buddy to take him back to the colonel's apartment."

"What was it he needed to tell you?" he asked.

I smiled at him. "I guess you'll have me around awhile. I'm getting my
discharge papers. And by the way, tell blue suit and gray suit that Buddy
will be leaving with the colonel."

20

Suddenly everything changed. Two days later, May 2, Buddy put Ulla on the train to Norway and picked up his duffel bags from my office in the garage. "I'm meeting the old man in Paris," he said. "Tomorrow we're going to the States."

"Okay," I said.

"That's all you have to say?" he asked, looking at me. "Aren't you even going to say 'Good luck'?"

I smiled at him. "Buddy, I never knew you were so sentimental! You were always 'Mr. Cool-man' all the time."

"Jerry," he said, "I was never like that with you. You were always my friend and I felt like we were brothers."

"We are," I said. "But we're taking a different road now. I'm going to miss you, but I'll have to get used to it."

"I'll miss you, too," he said.

I looked at him. There were tears on his cheeks. "You're crying," I said.

"Niggers don't cry," he said, embracing me. "You're just a crazy Jew boy."

I hugged him back. "You're my best friend, you son of a bitch. The best friend I have in the world. Now let go of me or people will think that we're queers."

He stepped back, took out a cigarette, and lit it. "I suppose you couldn't grab a jeep and drive me to headquarters?"

I took out a cigarette of my own and lit it. "You haven't changed." I laughed. "I was beginning to think you had really just come to say good-bye."

He laughed, too, and let the smoke trail out of his nostrils. "That is what I came for," he said. "But I thought it wasn't a bad idea if you took me into Paris. Being best friends and all of that."

"You are a prick." I grabbed his hand. "You're a rich man. You can take a taxi into Paris."

He shook my hand. Each of us was holding his cigarette in the other hand. "When am I going to see you again?"

"I don't know," I answered. "I'll be hanging around here."

"After the war?"

"Yes, after the war," I replied.

"How can I get in touch with you?"

I thought for a moment. "Reach me through Paul at his club. He'll always know where I am."

"Will you be able to keep in touch with Ulla?" he asked.

"I will," I said. "Besides, Giselle likes her; they've already arranged to keep in touch."

He looked at his watch. "I'm running late. I better get going."

I took his hand again. "Good luck, Buddy."

He smiled at me. "And you, too." Then he turned and walked out of the office.

Five days later, May 7, the war was over in Europe. Paris became nothing but a party town. The American soldiers were heroes. Wine, champagne, and beer flowed freely. The girls, married or not, were all caught up in the fever. Couples were fucking in the park in the daylight, in the hallways and stairways of the apartment houses. Love was everywhere.

The Blue Note was jammed from the minute it opened until the last closing drink. The homosexuals were no different than anyone else. Both sides of the runway were crowded, every table jammed, with champagne corks popping and the wine flowing. I couldn't get a place at my usual table, so I waited backstage so that I could see what was going on.

Paul came up behind me and tapped my shoulder. "What do you think?" he asked.

"The war is really over," I said. "I never thought I would see this kind of happiness."

"It's been many years," Paul said. "It's like climbing out of hell. So much death. So much destruction."

"I had it easy," I said. "I didn't go through any of it, really. Maybe I should be ashamed of myself."

"You are human," he said. "You had no choice of what the army would have you go and do. It might just as well have been that they sent you to the front. Who knows in this life?"

"I don't know," I said. "For me the war turned into a business."

"That was what the army gave you to do," he said. "The extra was there for anyone to pick up. You are a good soldier. You did what you were told to do."

"Were the French like that?" I asked.

"They were like all the others. They stole, they lied, they collaborated with the enemy, they turned on their own French Jews. And many of them made money because of it. Much more money than you can ever dream about. At the end of it, the bureaucrats will own the country, not the patriots who risked their lives for victory."

I stared at him. "You have no respect for any of them."

"Why should I?" he asked. "They gave up half of Asia, a quarter of Africa, and fifteen percent of the Middle East because they bled everything they could from them and then shit them out. Yet, Corsica is still held prisoner because they still have use for it."

"Since the war is over," I said, "what will happen with the clubs?"

He laughed. "The clubs will do all right. Maybe they will not make as much money, since the American soldiers will be leaving, but Paris is a city that all the world comes to for entertainment and excitement."

"I'm beginning to wonder if I did the right thing. I still am uncertain about what I will be doing here," I said.

"Relax," he said. "You have celebrating to do now. Later we will worry about what you can do." He turned and looked at what was happening in the club. The pandemonium was deafening. He turned back to me. "I'm going to cancel the shows for tonight. There's enough going on here. I'll send the girls home. I don't want any of them to be raped here."

It was eleven o'clock when Giselle and I walked home. The streets were crowded with people happy with victory. Even with Giselle holding my arm, the American uniform was like a magnet. People would stop me and kiss me on both cheeks, shouting wonderful things about the Americans.

We finally made our way into the apartment. I was out of breath even before we started climbing the stairs to the apartment. "I felt like everybody was so happy and excited, they were ready to devour me."

She smiled as she unlocked the door. "They are happy because this is the first time they feel safe. The war has destroyed all of our confidence in ourselves."

"It's over now," I said as we walked into the apartment. "Now we will begin to forget it."

"We will never forget," she said. She dropped her coat on a chair. She turned and placed her hands on my face. "I love you," she said. "I was not afraid before because you were here with me. Now, I am afraid."

I looked into her eyes; they were deep blue with a hint of tears. "Why now, Giselle? We are staying together."

"For how long?" she whispered. "Sooner or later, you'll have to go home and I will be left alone. Like my sister was when her lover left her."

"I am staying here, you know that. My discharge papers have already been approved. When my work is over at the garage I'm out of the army and free," I said, and held her close to me. "If I do go back to the States, you will come with me."

She looked up at me. "Do you really mean that? Not just because I am upset now?"

I kissed her gently. "I promise."

We went into the bedroom. I had undressed before she did, so I brought the radio into the bedroom and put it on the night table. I turned on the Voice of America program. It was mid-afternoon in New York and the announcer was broadcasting from Times Square.

I could hardly hear his voice over the noise of the crowds in the square. It was the first time I had heard the words in English. *"The war in Europe is over. It's VE day!"* Then they cut to Kate Smith singing "God Bless America." Then I began to cry. I couldn't believe it. The world had turned upside down, again.

My eyes were still blurry from the tears as she came into the bedroom and stood at the door, saluting. She was completely naked. And I don't know how she did it, but she had taped a paper American flag just above her pussy, and held a bottle of champagne and two glasses in her other hand.

21

It was two weeks later when the discharge papers came down. Not only for me, but for the whole platoon. Sergeant Felder came to me. He held his transfer orders in his hand. "I thought they told you we would have time to get rid of the jeeps."

"So did I," I said. "But they fucked me. That's the way of the army."

"We've got seven cars left," he insisted. "We're losing a lot of money."

"You're going home," I said. "Don't complain about it. At least you're not going to the Pacific."

"I heard that they're sending another officer over here to make sure everything is wrapped up correctly," he said.

"Felder, don't be a pain in the ass," I said. "It's over. You got pretty good money for it. Now take it home and maybe you can settle down with your wife and kids. You have enough to open an automobile repair place if you want. And I'm sure your wife will be happy to have you home again."

"I don't know how happy she's going to be. I still have the clap," he said.

"Christ!" I said. "You have had that for six months. Didn't you take care of it?"

"I seen a doctor three times. Each time he said I was cured. But I wasn't." He looked back at me dejectedly.

"That doesn't make any sense," I said. "Everybody else got over it in just a little time."

He looked at me. "I was a schmuck," he said. "I was hot for this girl and I always went back to her."

"Schmuck is right." I laughed. "At least now you can get over it. Don't go see this girl anymore. Let the doctor straighten you out before you get discharged and go home."

He sat shaking his head. "How could I have been so stupid?"

"It takes practice." I laughed. "There's just one thing I want before you leave. I want to get a car fixed up for me. And I want it finished in three days and then I'll take off. I want it to be like brand-new. You do that and I'll sign your discharge papers with a commendation."

Felder had the car finished ahead of schedule. It took him only two days. That night I took the jeep into one of Paul's hidden garages. It was just in time. That morning we moved the other jeeps that could be saved into another garage that was owned by a Corsican friend of Paul's.

Late that same afternoon the door of my garage office opened and a second lieutenant stood in front of me. "Sergeant Cooper?" he questioned.

I stood up and saluted. "Yes, sir."

"Lieutenant Johnson." He returned the salute. "I've been ordered down here to move the squad back to headquarters."

"Yes, sir," I said. "We've been expecting you, sir."

"You have nine men?" he asked.

I nodded. "Yes, sir."

"Are they ready to move out this afternoon?" he asked.

"They are all in their quarters, sir," I answered.

"I have a bus ready to take them to headquarters," he said. He looked around the garage and junkyard as we walked back to the squad's quarters. "You have a hell of a lot of junk jeeps here. Weren't any of them able to be repaired?"

"We have destruction orders for each of them, sir," I said. "We used them for parts to repair the cars that we were fixing."

"Didn't any of these get sold to junk dealers?" he asked.

"That's not my responsibility, sir," I said. "Any orders like that have to come from headquarters."

"Strange," he said. "I should think that they would have taken care of that."

I was silent.

"I saw from the orders that you're being discharged here in France," he said. "Is there any reason you didn't want to go home?"

"My parents are gone, sir," I said. "And I have no other family to go home to."

"You have a girl?" he asked.

"Yes, sir," I said.

He nodded. "I thought so, Sergeant. That's the reason most of the soldiers who want to stay here do."

I didn't answer. I looked at him. He seemed a young man, no older that I. "Have you been here long, sir?" I asked.

"Not really, Sergeant," he answered. "I was just transferred here directly from West Point three weeks ago."

Again I was silent.

He looked at me. "You know, Sergeant. I'm jealous of you. I didn't get to see anything of the war like you did. You must have seen many things. I wanted them to transfer me to the Pacific, but they wanted me here."

"There's an important job to do here, sir," I said. Schmuck, I thought. He missed nothing except getting killed.

"From here I'm being transferred to Berlin," he said. "That should be interesting. I've seen all those movies with Marlene Dietrich. The German girls have to be great."

By this time we were at the barracks door. I opened and called out in an official sergeant voice, "Attention!"

22

It was not until the end of June that I finished the work on the jeeps that I had hidden in Paul's friend's garage. Without Felder and some of the other men, I had to find a few French mechanics who could work for me. Paul knew them all. They were older men whom the French had not drafted into the army. But there was one good thing about them. They knew their work and I found out that they had spent their lives working on automobiles. They were like artists.

There were times during the day that I couldn't explain to them what I needed them to do because of the language. My French was pitiful and they didn't understand a word of English. Finally Giselle came to the garage with me for a few hours each day and translated what I needed. With her help we managed to finish.

Then I had to pay them for their work. That took nine thousand dollars of my savings, which left me with seventeen grand. But it was worth it. The cars looked better than the day they were delivered new. Now, although the war was over and the French automobile companies were in production, it would be some time before they had cars to deliver. But a lot of our customers were willing to wait for their French autos.

Fortunately, Paul was on my side. There were still enough hustlers who would buy the jeeps. But the money was not as good as before. On July 25 I sold the last jeep. I wound up with twenty thousand of my own and a really perfect jeep, with an all-canvas top and Plexiglas clear windows on the side.

That summer in Paris was hell. It was hot and humid. But everybody was glad to go back to work. And as soon as everybody was back to work in a normal routine, then came vacation time. I never knew that in France vacation time was like religion. Everyone in Paris leaves town. When I would walk around I would see more American uniforms and Englishmen than French.

I sat at the table in the club with Paul. "What goes on with this? It doesn't make sense. Doesn't anyone want to get back to normal and stay normal?"

He laughed. "This is normal. Even during the war the French took their vacations."

The fat man who covered the stage door and acted as bouncer came over to Paul and started speaking excitedly. "The radio in your office!" he exclaimed.

Paul gestured for me to follow him. We walked into the office. The announcer was also speaking excitedly. He spoke so fast that I couldn't understand a word that he was saying.

After a moment, Paul turned to me. He was so excited that he scrambled his English with his French. From what I could understand, it was something about the Americans having dropped an atomic bomb in Japan, and that thousands of people had been killed.

He looked at me. I had never seen an expression of shock like his. "That's terrible. So many people dead. Just innocent people who had nothing to do with the war. What is this kind of bomb that could do such horrible things?"

I shook my head. "I don't know. I never heard of anything like that before. Turn to the Voice of America; maybe they will tell us."

He spun the dial quickly and picked up BBC. The British newscaster was as frantic as the others. "The Americans dropped an atomic bomb over Hiroshima in Japan. President Harry S. Truman while speaking to the American Congress said that this bomb will end the war in the Pacific and save many of the Americans who have had to fight from island to island to reach Japan."

Paul turned off the radio before I could hear any more. "An atomic bomb? What kind of bomb is that?"

"I don't know," I said. "But if it stops the war, I guess it is a good thing."

"Politics!" he spat out. "The Socialists are trying to push de Gaulle out of power now that the war is over and they have no more use for him. The British kicked Churchill out the minute the war was over. French Socialists, the British Labor are all Communists. In the end, Russia will control all of Europe."

Later that night when Giselle and I were at home, I talked to her about what Paul had said and thought, and whether all the French felt like that.

She smiled. "I don't think so. Paul is a Corsican and very excitable and emotional. After all, it's on the other side of the world. It can't bother us here."

I took a beer and sat down at the table until she came out from the bathroom. She laughed. "Why don't you come to bed. The war is really over now."

23

It was the middle of August, two-thirty in the morning, and Giselle and I were sleeping when Paul woke us up. This was the first time I had ever seen him nervous. He slumped into a chair at the kitchen table. I quickly gave him a cognac while Giselle made coffee.

He drained his glass in one big swig and filled his glass again. He looked at us. "We're in trouble," he said.

"Tell me why?" I asked.

"The army found the jeeps in Corsica. They tracked them to our friends. Now the general and the inspector in the Sûreté are under house arrest. Our friends won't talk, but the French army police are not stupid. They are already aware that that number of jeeps could only have come out of Paris." He finished his cognac and took a sip of his coffee.

"What are you so upset about?" I asked. "You're not in the army. They can't touch you."

"I'm Corsican," he said. "They know that the police inspector is my brother. And they also know that we have been in touch with your commanding officer, who was in charge of jeep repairs."

"He's in the fucking States," I said. "There's no way they can reach him. And the whole platoon has returned to the States. They've got nothing to grab."

"Jerry," he said. "Don't be a fool. We are still here and they can grab us."

"They don't have any evidence, there's nothing to find. All the cars are gone and I'm an American citizen. They can't hold me for anything."

"You still have your own jeep," he said. "Don't forget, French and American law are very different. They can hold you without having a reason." He reached for a cigarette. "My advice to you is to get out of Paris as quickly as you can. I'm on the way to Corsica in the morning."

"You're just leaving the clubs"—I snapped my fingers—"just like that!"

For the first time since he had walked in the door he laughed. "I'm Corsican. That means I'm not stupid. I have my own people to run them until I return."

I took a cup of coffee and sat down next to Giselle. "Where am I supposed to go? I'm American and I stick out like a sore thumb."

"You get into civilian clothes and you'll look like everyone else." He turned to Giselle. "The two of you had better begin packing. I think you should go to Lyons and see your parents. You will give them my affection and tell them I hope to see them soon." He took out an envelope from his breast pocket and gave it to her. "This note will introduce you to the manager of the club that I own in Nice and he will put you to work immediately."

He then turned to me. "I am also giving another note to you. You will give it to a close friend of mine who also knows Giselle. He is Monsieur Jean Pierre Martin, a former colonel on de Gaulle's staff. He is a homosexual as I am, but we became very good friends because I helped him with some problems with the American that he lives with now in the south of France. He is from a very rich French social family and they own Plescassier, one of the two biggest bottled-water companies in France. He likes Americans because he went to school in the States as a boy and a young man. You talk to him. There is a good chance that he will find you a position in his company. He is planning to expand his company to England and the United States."

"Paul," I said. "This is wonderful of you to do this for me. And I am very grateful, but why me?"

"You have done for my brother and me more than you realize. Besides, we are friends. And being a good friend is sometimes worth more than being a lover." He put down his cigarette and finished his coffee. He stood up and embraced Giselle. He kissed her on both cheeks and then turned to me. "You should be lucky that I am gay or you would never have found this girl."

I laughed. "Paul, please, you have to take care of yourself."

"I will, my friend." He embraced me and kissed me on each cheek. "I have to go now." He went to the door and turned to Giselle. "When you leave the apartment, leave the keys with the concierge, who will know how to take care of everything."

We watched him leave as he closed the door. Then I looked at Giselle. "Will he be okay?" I asked.

She took my hand. "He will be safe," she said. "Now we better start packing. Let's try to have everything packed and in the car before daylight. That way no one will see us leaving."

"How much time will it take for us to drive to Lyons?" I asked.

"It depends on how bad the roads are from the war. Maybe between seven and ten hours." She laughed. "It will not be a honeymoon trip."

24

I don't know how we did it, but we did! We were packed and on the road a little after 6:00 A.M. The faint gray light was just beginning to creep up from the east. It was humid and cloudy as we drove out of Paris. The jeep drove smoothly, the engine hummed along easily, and there was no problem. But I had a problem. No road map. Giselle said she knew the way home. It was not easy driving for me. All the road signs were in kilometers and my jeep had an American mileage speedometer dial. But Giselle was not worried. She was happy. She was going home. What was the difference if it was 400 kilometers or 240 miles? It was all the same distance, she said.

I figured that at an average of thirty miles an hour, it would take us about eight hours to get to Lyons if we didn't have to make any stops. But there were stops. Lots of them. Pee stops, lunch stops, gasoline stops, detour stops. And the most important stop of all for Giselle. We had to stop in a city so that I could buy a civilian suit.

She explained to me that her parents were "antiforeigners." Especially soldiers. Ever since the German soldier had left her sister pregnant and outcast. Therese had to have an abortion and her parents never forgave Therese or her lover.

"The clothes won't make any difference," I said. "Your parents had to know that I was an American soldier."

"I know," she said. "But it will make them and me more comfortable. If they see you in a suit, at least they will feel that you're staying in France instead of leaving me alone."

"There is another difference," I said. "He was on the other side against France; remember, I was on your side."

It didn't matter. I got a new gray light wool suit and a few white shirts. French suits were not like American suits. The French have narrower shoulders, lower asses, and shorter legs. The suit I found that fit was a large French size, but it would have been a medium size in the States.

It was five in the afternoon by the time we arrived at her parents' house. Her mother opened the door. She called out to her husband. "Giselle is home!" She held her daughter and she was crying. "My baby is home!"

Giselle's father came to the door. He hugged her and kissed her on both cheeks. "Giselle, why didn't you let us know that you were coming?"

They were all chattering away in French while we walked into the house, talking so fast I didn't understand much of what they were saying.

Finally, her father turned and looked at me. "American?" he asked.

"Oui, Papa," she answered.

I held out my hand. "I am happy to meet you, sir."

He looked at my hand and ignored it.

"My father doesn't understand any English," Giselle said apologetically.

I looked at her. "He also doesn't have any manners," I said. "I'll go outside and wait in the car."

"Calm down," she said to me; then she turned to her father and spoke very rapidly. I managed to pick out a few of the French words that I could understand. "A war hero. He is rich. My fiancé. And great love."

Her mother turned and took my hand. I followed her to the table and sat down. Her father was still dour faced, but finally he held out his hand to me in a polite shake. Then he took out a bottle of wine and poured a small glass for each of us. "*Salut*," he said. I nodded and replied. We tasted the wine.

A few minutes later Therese showed up. The sisters hugged and kissed each other. I watched their father. He didn't seem to be as nice to Therese as he was with Giselle. Therese turned and smiled at me. "I feel I know you," she said in English. "Giselle wrote me several times a month while she was away."

"She told me about you," I answered. "It is good to meet you at last."

"I am sorry about my father," she apologized. "It's my fault really. My father didn't like my lover."

"It is your choice," I answered. "Your father has no right to interfere."

"It is over now." She shrugged. "Now that the war is over, maybe all of the old hatreds and angers will be over, too."

"I hope so," I said.

Giselle smiled at me. "Don't you think my sister is beautiful?"

"You both are," I said. "I am sorry that your father is angry about the past."

"It will take time," Giselle said. "Meanwhile, Therese, you and I will go to dinner at a restaurant that a very good friend of mine owns. My parents eat very French style. They had their big meal at midday and in the evening they have just cheese, baguette, and a glass of wine."

"That's nice," I said.

"There is one other thing." Giselle smiled. "My parents are very old-fashioned. They want me to stay with them tonight, but there is only one extra bedroom and you can't sleep here with me."

"Okay," I said. "I can find a hotel room."

"You don't have to do that," she said. "Therese said that she could put you up for the night."

I looked at Therese. "It wouldn't be any trouble?"

Therese smiled. "It will be my pleasure."

I looked at Giselle, and she nodded in agreement.

I never knew that Lyons had a reputation for having the finest cuisine in all of France. And as far as I could tell, the best in the world. The patron was a close friend of the sisters, though I noticed he was a little cool to Therese. Then I saw the ribbon in his boutonniere. It was the war. He had a Légion d'honneur, and Therese had crossed the line. She had slept with the enemy. But he was also a gentleman. He said nothing and welcomed our company in the restaurant.

After dinner, Giselle drove us to her sister's apartment. She gave me my small valise that she had packed for me with my toiletries and pajamas. She laughed and kissed my cheek. "Now be a nice boy with my sister."

"Of course," I said. I looked at Therese, who was smiling at her sister; then they kissed cheeks and Giselle put the car into gear. "I'll pick you up at nine," she said, and drove off. I followed Therese into her apartment.

She showed me to the bathroom and then the bedroom. There was only one double bed there. I looked at her. "Don't you have another bedroom?" I asked.

She shook her head smiling. "No."

"Then am I supposed to sleep on the sofa?"

She laughed again. "No."

I looked at her.

She was still smiling. "It is a big bed. I am sure there is room enough in it for both of us to be comfortable."

I gestured to her. "Together?"

"Of course," she said. "I am not a virgin, and after all Giselle and I are sisters—we all share together."

This was a custom of the French I had never known about. When I came back from the bathroom Therese was already naked in the bed. It took her only twenty seconds to tear off my pajamas. Then she pressed me down in the bed on my back and sat on my face. Her pussy was already wet and pouring as her left hand reached behind her and grabbed my prick. Quickly, she rhythmically pulled on it as she continued bucking her hips into my face. She laughed aloud as I came all over her back and ass. "*Je suis montais au cheval!*" she screamed as she came all over my face, mouth, and eyes until I thought I had gone blind.

25

At nine o'clock in the morning I was standing on the sidewalk in front of Therese's apartment house as Giselle turned the corner and pulled the jeep up in front of me. Silently, I picked up my small valise and threw it in the backseat of the car.

She moved over from the driver's seat to the passenger side. I got in behind the wheel and looked at her. She was smiling.

"Bitch!" I said.

"Didn't you like my little sister?" She spoke innocently, but smiled mischievously.

"You set me up. I'm lucky she didn't fuck me to death!" I snapped.

"Therese has been alone too long," she said. "My sister needed a man."

I looked across the car at her. "When you told me that you and your sister shared everything, I didn't know that included lovers."

She leaned over and kissed my cheek. "Only good lovers." She laughed.

"I'm lucky you don't have any more sisters." I smiled. "Otherwise, I'd be dead for sure."

She kissed me again. "I love you, Jerree."

I shook my head. "I don't understand it. Is this a usual French custom?"

"I think we better get going," she said. "The best route for us is to go down to Marseilles and then go to RN Seven, to Cannes, and then to Nice."

"How long should that take us?" I asked.

"About the same time that it took us to get here from Paris," she answered. "But we will have to find a hotel to stay in. I have no family to stay with in Nice." She added with a mischievous smile, "Not even another sister."

It was after seven at night by the time we checked into a small hotel in Nice. We had a good dinner at a restaurant that Giselle knew about. This was the Mediterranean and the special all along the coast was fresh fish. I usually don't like fish, but this was good. A whole bottle of Provençal didn't hurt.

It was a French double bed in the hotel. Just wide enough for the two of us, but a little short for my legs. But that didn't bother Giselle. She was ready that night to show me who was boss. And she did. I was lucky I didn't wind up unconscious on the floor that night.

It was a nice hotel, but unfortunately, there was no restaurant. The room was already beginning to get warm from the heat of the summer sun. I opened the heavy shutters that covered the windows, like every apartment I'd had ever seen in France. I opened the windows, but the windows were on the same wall and there was no cross-ventilation.

I watched Giselle as she came out of the tub. She looked beautiful and cool with the water dripping from her smooth skin onto her towel. "Is it always like this?" I asked.

"This is the south of France," she said. "It is because of this weather that all of Europe comes to the Côte d'Azur."

"Even in winter?" I asked.

"It is comfortable then, but not like now." She turned her back to me and gave me the towel. "Dry my back."

I patted her dry. "What next?" I asked.

She slipped into her brassiere and she put her stockings on very carefully so they didn't run. Silk stockings were very hard to get even with the war being over. Finally, she slipped a light white cotton dress that you could almost see through over her head. "It is too early for me to see the manager of the club here," she said. "So I thought we would drive to Cannes and see Jean Pierre Martin. He's the man Paul wanted you to meet."

"Okay," I said. "But what about breakfast?"

"Of course, breakfast," she said. "But then after that we have to get you some light cotton pants and a shirt, or by noon you will be cooked."

I hadn't realized it, but Nice was one of the biggest cities in France. She took me to a large department store, very much like those in the States, and we went directly to the men's department. Giselle went clothes-happy for me. Pants: two white, one pink, one pastel blue. Then light see-through cotton shirts that I had to wear without my army T-shirt, and a navy blue blazer to top it off.

She nodded and looked at me in the mirror with approval. "How do you feel now?" She smiled.

"I feel like a pimp," I said. "I never wore clothes like this."

"You look like a gentleman now," she said. "Remember, Jean Pierre is a rich man. He even had his uniforms especially made by one of the best tailors in France. The same tailor made uniforms for de Gaulle and when Jean Pierre fell in love with his American officer he had the tailor make his uniforms, too."

"I still don't know why you think a man like him will bother with me," I said.

She spoke as if I were stupid. "First, J. P. owes Paul for many favors he has done for him. The Corsicans kept labor working in J. P.'s enterprise, war or no war. Second, Paul protected J. P. when the police and the army were going to expose him with his American lover in their hideout, both in London and Paris, and Cannes."

"That doesn't mean that he would give me a job," I said.

"Paul didn't say that he would," she said. "He only said that you should meet him and that he might have something that you could do."

"And what about your relationship with him?" I asked. "Did you fuck him?"

She laughed and shook her head. "J. P.'s homosexual. He comes from a family of homosexuals. He knows no other way to live. He hasn't even got a bisexual bone in his body."

"That's about him," I said. "You didn't answer my question. Did you fuck him?"

"No," she said flatly, then looked at me. "Are you jealous?"

"Yes, I am," I said. "I'm not French, I don't understand all of the customs."

She put her arm under mine. "I'm glad," she said. "I'm going to call J. P. and see if he could see us this afternoon."

"Do you think he will?" I asked.

"I'm sure that he will," she said confidently. "I know that by now Paul has spoken to him."

And as usual she was right. He invited us to lunch at his villa in Cannes.

26

She knew the way. It was up a big hill before you drove into Cannes. As we drove up, I saw homes being built along the road. She told me they would all be villas; this was an expensive area, no little houses. Finally, we made it to the top of the hill. There was a large roundabout so that you could turn around to go back down the hill. But on the far side of the road there was a large iron gate with a fence going down each side of the property for protection. On the center of the gates was DOMAINE DE MARTIN written in gold. Behind the gate and off to the side was a small guardhouse.

A Frenchman wearing blue farmer's clothing spoke to us through the gates. "*Vos nommes, s'il vous plaît.*"

Giselle gave him our names. He went into the guardhouse, and through its window we saw him pick up a telephone. A moment later, he came out and opened the gate and gestured for us to go further up the roadway to the villa.

We pulled up in front of the place. It wasn't a villa, it was a palace. I looked at Giselle. She looked as impressed as I. A large entrance door opened and the butler stepped out.

He looked at my car and almost seemed to sniff. He faggily gestured his hand that I should move away from the two Rolls-Royces and the Cadillac.

Giselle started to move the car. I stopped her. I took the keys from the ignition. "You want the car moved, you do it," I said to him through the window.

The butler stared at me, horrified. A man who was standing in the doorway began to laugh. He said something in French to the butler and the butler almost bent to the ground, slinking almost like a cat through the doorway behind him.

The Frenchman was tall, with almost blond hair, a mustache, and brilliant blue eyes. He was wearing shorts and had a fantastic tan. He hugged Giselle and kissed her on both cheeks, then turned to me and held out his hand. "Jean Pierre Martin," he said.

I shook his hand. It was firm and good. "Jerry Cooper," I said. On the sign on the gate it spelled Martin, but the French pronounce it "Martan."

"*Bienvenue*," he said. "Come in."

We followed him into the villa. I, again, had never seen a home furnished like this except in the movies. We went into a living room that was almost fifty feet long, with giant windows on the far end that gave you a view of all the city below and the sea and marina filled with boats and yachts next to it.

"Would you like a drink?" he asked. "We have scotch whiskey. I know Americans like it."

I smiled. "Thank you, but I'm a beer drinker myself."

"And you, my dear?" he asked Giselle.

"A small white wine, Jean Pierre," she answered. "But I don't usually drink anything but water at lunch." Then she smiled. "Preferably Plescassier, if it's available."

He laughed. "That we have." He gestured and we followed past the large windows into his garden. The luncheon table was set beside the pool. A good-looking young man was already seated at the table. Jean Pierre introduced us. The young man already knew Giselle. He hugged her and kissed her cheeks.

"Jack Cochran." He smiled, holding his hand out to me.

I shook it and smiled. "Jerry Cooper," I answered.

"Enough of this bullshit," Jack said. "We're all friends here."

Giselle looked at him. "No tricks, Jack. He's mine."

Jean Pierre laughed. "Jack thinks every guy is a trick. Sooner or later, he'll learn."

Jack shrugged off the kidding. "You should know, honey." He winked. "I was in Eisenhower's headquarters; then, when we transferred to Paris, I met J. P."

"I was running an auto repair garage in Clichy," I said. "I was nowhere near those headquarters."

I hadn't noticed, but J. P. must have ordered the drinks. My beer was already on the table. I saw that the two of them were drinking pastis; Giselle had a glass of wine and a bottle of water sitting in front of her. We all held up our glasses. "Cheers," I said.

The butler and a maid placed a platter of cold cuts and cheese and a second platter of biscuits and bread. I followed Giselle as she ate and copied her. The food was good. For dessert we were served coffee and petits fours.

I looked at Jean Pierre. "Thank you. It was a great luncheon."

He smiled at me. "It's not like an American delicatessen."

"I didn't expect that." I smiled. "This is France."

Jean Pierre turned to Giselle. "Paul said you will be working in a club of his in Nice."

"Yes," she said. "I'm sure it will be a good club since Paul is sending me there. But I haven't seen it yet. They will not be open until this evening."

"I have some good friends who are club owners here in Cannes. I'm sure that you would be happier in Cannes than in Nice. Nice is a difficult town."

"But the money," Giselle said. "Nice is a less expensive place than Cannes. The apartments are almost half as much. And for shopping, everything is cheaper."

"But I can get you a job in a good club, and the apartment would only be a nominal amount for you. I own the apartment building. The only thing you would have to put up with is that most of the apartments are either owned or rented by gays. Sometimes they make a lot of noise."

Giselle looked at me. "What do you think, Jerree?"

"I don't know," I said. "I don't know anything about Cannes. The homosexuals don't bother me. But I am worried about getting a job here. I know it is hard for a foreigner to get working papers in France."

"Paul told me that you were very clever and thought I could find a place for you," Jean Pierre said. "But I don't know anything about what you would like to do. All he told me was the same thing you told me, that you were running an auto repair shop for jeeps while you were in the army."

Jack Cochran smiled. "Maybe if you told J. P. a little about yourself before you were in the army, it might help."

"When I was in the States I owned a seltzer company. I bought it with the money that my father left for me. I sold special soda water in spritz bottles. We called it Coney Island Seltzer and we sold from door to door. Most of our customers were regular users. It was like delivering milk."

Jack interrupted me to fill J. P. in on the seltzer business in New York. "Seltzer bottles were usually sold to the old-fashioned Jews who didn't trust New York water," he said.

"I also worked in a soda fountain that sold drinks over the counter. We served two cents plain, egg creams, and Coca-Colas," I said.

"What is 'two cents plain'?" Jean Pierre asked.

"A plain glass of soda water," I said.

"Was that bottled soda water that you dispensed?" J. P. asked.

"No," I answered. "We had tanks of gas that we tied into the water lines to make the soda."

"Then it wasn't natural carbonated spring water that you sold?"

I shook my head. "No, sir."

"Did anyone ever want natural carbonated spring water?" he asked.

"Not that I ever knew of," I said. "The only thing that might be close was Canada Dry soda that we sold in bottles."

"That's what the bars and hotels gave you when you ordered scotch and soda. The highballs were rye whiskey with ginger ale," Jack filled him in.

J. P. turned back to me. "Do you think natural spring water in bottles would sell well in the States?"

"I don't know," I answered. "I think it would be a good idea. Especially with a lot of advertising behind it, and maybe a word about how the army soldier in Europe lived on it."

"But it's not actually true." J. P. smiled.

"Who would know?" I asked.

J. P. looked at me and then smiled. "I have a job for you, Jerry," J. P. said. "I want to go worldwide with my water, particularly in England and the States first. But I want someone that knows about Plescassier from the bottom up. I think that it will take about four or five years to get the company set up for it, but meanwhile, I'll pay you five hundred francs a month to learn the business."

I stared at him. That was not much money. Only two hundred U.S. dollars. A good salary in France, but shit in the States.

Giselle looked at me. "I'll be working. We can manage all right."

"I don't want you to have to go whoring for our living," I said.

"She won't have to," J. P. said. "I'll make sure that she gets into a decent club to work. Giselle is my very good friend. Also, this could make you a very wealthy man."

I looked at her again. I still had almost twenty grand socked away. If there were any problems, we could run. I turned to J. P. and held out my hand. "Thank you," I said. "I hope I'll be good for you."

BOOK FOUR

AMERICA
TWO DOLLARS A QUART

1

"J. P. is still under his father's thumb," I said. I was watching Giselle getting ready for dinner. J. P. was having one of his famous parties. Or maybe it was Jack Cochran, J. P.'s lover, who set all the parties up. J. P. had a beautiful 130-foot yacht in the marina at Cannes. That was where the party was going to be. This was a big party; Jack had been arranging things for almost three days. But it was no problem for Jack, who always stayed in Cannes while J. P. flew his two-engine Cessna to his office in Paris, Plescassier Springs, and the bottling plant in the Alpes Maritime.

Giselle looked at me. "You can't risk saying anything about it. J. P. is very close to his father."

"But it doesn't make any sense," I said. "I've been here more than four years now and there is nothing more that I can do for him. Remember, right after I came to work for him, I tried to get him to take the distribution for Pepsi-Cola in France and Europe, but no! His father said the French would never drink that cola over beer and wine. So there you are, Pepsi and Coke are the biggest-selling soft drinks in Europe."

"So there was nothing you could do about it," Giselle answered.

"Finally his father allowed him to take over some other cola. Green River. I told J. P. that it was a dog, and just as I said, it went out of business." Jerry lit a cigarette.

"But J. P. set up a flavored-cola company. He has all kinds. Orange, cherry, strawberry. You name them and he has them. And they're doing

275

pretty good," Giselle said. "So stop complaining—he's listened and learned from you. That's why you are paid ten thousand francs a month now."

"But the original idea was to go to the States. He has not even tried to get into the States yet," I said. "When we met he said he wanted to make Plescassier into a worldwide bottled water."

"He still has his father to deal with," Giselle said. "Give him time, he will get there."

"I'm on the front line," I answered. "I hear what's going on. Perrier and Evian are already talking about setting up an operation in the States. If he takes too long they will all be in there before us. They will take the cream off the market first!"

Giselle turned to him. "Why don't you just tell him?"

"I have," I said sadly. "A dozen times. But he always says, 'It's not time yet.'" I looked at her. "I think that he's waiting for his father to die before he makes a move."

She was silent.

"What do you think?"

She smiled at me and kissed me. "Don't forget that it's his business and his ball game."

I finished tying the black bow tie. "What is so important? Every time they have a big party, we have to put on formal evening clothes."

"Because this is a very special party," Giselle answered. "J. P. is inviting people who are either in the government or have international contacts. He needs them when he tries to bring his business into the States."

"It's kind of crazy," I said. "Because half of them will wind up in a homosexual orgy."

"But that's after the real party is over," Giselle said.

"Maybe that's when the real party begins," I teased.

"You're very provincial, maybe, because you are American." She laughed. "Maybe it would be better if they had an orgy that you could join in on."

"You know I don't need that," I said. "You're all the orgy I need."

J. P. arrived at the yacht directly from the airport in Nice. Jack was already setting the place cards on the large dining table on the rear deck.

J. P. walked toward him, and they kissed, much like an old married couple. "How's it going?" he asked.

"Fine," Jack answered. "But I do have problems seating some of the Americans. Estée Lauder would be a joy to anyone, but her husband, Joe is another story."

J. P. smiled. "That shouldn't be any trouble. Sit him next to Princess Troubestkoy. Marcia is American, and on the other side of him seat Giselle. She speaks English and a pretty girl won't hurt anything."

"Then I'll sit Jerry next to Mrs. Lauder and Count Di Stefano on the other side," J. P. said.

"Ernesto will bullshit her up to her ears," Jack said.

"But the ladies always like him," J. P. said. "Be sure and sit Madame d'Estaing next to me. Too bad her husband won't be with us. Sooner or later he'll be the president of France."

"We have plenty of friends here whom we will enjoy later," J. P. answered. He turned and walked away, and then turned around and came back. "There's a young American lawyer that will be here with his wife. It's the first time for either of them to be at one of our parties. So be careful, and take care of them. He's an assistant to the new secretary of commerce in the Eisenhower administration. He's straight and honest, but he likes us and is willing to help us set up Plescassier in the States."

"I'll make sure that they are taken care of." Jack smiled.

J. P. laughed. "Just don't try to seduce him. Especially in front of his wife." He started off again and then called back to Jack. "Tell Jerry to come see me in my cabin before the party. I want to let him know what we are doing."

J. P. was drinking a scotch on the rocks when I knocked on the door of the small living room in the master cabin. "You wanted me, J. P.?" I asked.

J. P. was sitting comfortably in his shorts, one leg hanging over the side of the leather couch. He looked up at me. "Do you still want to take Plescassier into the States?"

"That's what I've been waiting for," I answered. "That is why I have studied and worked all over your company so I could know the business."

J. P. smiled at me. Then he gestured down to his penis and testicles, slightly showing out of one leg of his shorts. "Enough to suck me?"

I looked at him. "You're joking."

"You'd wind up making a lot of money," J. P. said. "Jack would give his life for a chance like this."

"I'm sure he would," I answered. "But he'd blow a lot of money as well as your cock. Jack is nothing but a playboy acting like a housewife."

J. P. looked at me. "You don't like Jack, do you?"

"He's okay as your lover, not mine," I answered.

"You love Giselle?" J. P. asked.

"Yes."

"Enough to take her to the States with you?"

"Yes," I answered.

"Marry her?" J. P. asked.

"We never thought about it," I answered. "Maybe in time."

J. P. fixed another drink for himself and offered me one. I shook his head. "Scotch is too heavy this early. Besides, why did you ask me to come down here?"

J. P. nodded. "I've decided to send Plescassier to the States and I think that you are the right man for the job."

I looked at him. "You mean that?"

J. P. said seriously, "I do."

I took a deep breath. "I think I'll have that scotch now."

J. P. shook my hand. "We'll work out the details next week. I'll want you to meet my father."

"That makes me nervous," I said. "What if your father doesn't like me?"

"My father already knows everything about you," J. P. answered. "He likes the way that you worked through the business."

"But he was angry with me when I didn't agree on the Green River colas," I said.

"And you were right. That was yesterday and it's over," J. P. answered. "I've already talked to my father. He thinks you'll be right."

"And Jack?" I asked. "He might be pissed off. He might think that he should take over this operation."

"Well, like you say, Jack is a playboy acting like a housewife." He shook his head. "He won't complain about it. I've built a villa down the hill for him near mine. I've made him a rich man. And I don't even give a damn that he has his own boyfriend down there living with him."

I took a sip of the scotch. "You're in another world. I don't understand it."

"You don't have to understand that world," J. P. said. "As long as you understand the business we are in, that's all you need. I like you. Even more important, I trust you. And I think that we are friends." He held out his hand again.

I shook his hand. "Yes, we are friends. Thank you."

2

It was two weeks later that I met J. P. and his father, in their house in Paris. Jacques Martin was proud of his son. Jean Pierre was everything he had wanted him to be. He had completely proved himself in the business. It was Jean Pierre alone who had built Plescassier into the second highest selling water in France behind Evian and Perrier. But there was only one problem with Jean Pierre as far as his father was concerned: Jean Pierre had an attachment for American men. But to Jacques, all American men were whores. He had been angry when J. P. gave so much to the American, Brad, he had picked up in London. One million francs. Brad had exchanged it into American dollars and had it wired to the States. Then he arranged to have himself transferred back to the U.S. Once he got there, Jean Pierre never heard from him again.

It wasn't long after that that the Allies had moved their offices to Paris. Jean Pierre fell in love with another American. Jack Cochran. But Jacques approved of him. He was nothing but a playboy. He loved parties and good times, and also had a talent for interior decoration, which made France very interesting for him. Jack had no desire to return to the States permanently. That made Jacques feel at ease.

Now there was another problem. Me. Not only was I an American, I was a Jew. Jacques didn't like the Jews. It was not because he was anti-Semitic, but he had always fallen into unfair business agreements. He had made a partnership with an important Jewish industrialist. The partnership involved an investment of two million francs to build up Plescassier. The industrialist promised Jacques that Plescassier would be the number one bottled water in France. But when he went over the agreement with his advocate he discovered at the end of it that a Jew would have control of the company and finally own it. Jacques wanted to kill him, but he didn't have to. All he did was wait until the Germans came into France and then he turned him over to the Nazis.

Jacques was seventy-two when he met me. But he still had an astute understanding of men. The first thing he knew was that I was straight. He was heterosexual and would not become jealous of J. P.'s relationship with Jack. Neither did Jack and I live in the same world. Jack liked everything to do with society and I seemed to care nothing about it. All I was interested in was business and was loyal to J. P. because he had given me an opportunity.

I was surprised at how much J. P. and his father resembled each other. Maybe his old man was a queer, but there had to have been at least one time that he was straight.

Jacques looked across the table at me. "How do you plan to market Plescassier in the States?"

I looked back across the table at J. P. and then over at the old man. "Very much the same way you do in France. Half-liter and liter bottles, as in France, shipped to the States. Then we will begin an advertising and publicity campaign so the American public will recognize and at least try the water in the beginning. Newspapers, magazines, radio, and the new television stations are all necessary for success."

"That means we are going to have to make a large investment," Monsieur Martin said.

"America is a giant, untapped market," I said. "There are two hundred million people we have to reach. Four times the population of France."

Jacques shook his head. "I feel that it would be expensive to send these bottles to the States because of the shipping weight and space. I feel that we should ship the water in five-liter bottles and then rebottle in smaller bottles once we get to the States. You can buy bottles cheaper there and labeling would be no problem."

"I'm sorry, Monsieur Martin, I don't agree. The Americans are sometimes very skeptical. They won't believe it's French water if it doesn't have a French label that says it's bottled in France," I said, and looked at J. P. "What do you think?"

"You are talking about a great deal of money," he said. "Maybe we would be better just to start it in New York. We'll bottle it there, and try it there first."

Jacques looked at me. "I don't want you to lose your enthusiasm for the project, but it will be safer if we start in New York." He looked at his son and then back to me. "Because we realize that you are from New York, I'm sure that you will know the right way to make it successful."

J. P. spoke across the table. "I just want to get there before any of the other waters."

"We'll make it, son," Jacques said confidently.

I had nothing more to say. It was their company.

J. P. spoke to me as they got into the car to drop him at his hotel. "What do you think of my father?"

"Your father has his own ideas," I said.

"Don't put it down," J. P. said. "My father has been right more times than he's been wrong."

3

"When do you think we'll go to the States?" Giselle asked.

I was stretched out on the bed looking at the *Herald Tribune*. "I don't really know," I answered. "I didn't get any more information since we spoke with J. P.'s father. Maybe they are down on it. Maybe I spoke too soon. I was talking to them about a lot of money."

Giselle smiled. "I don't think it's the money. I think the old man is looking for a partner."

"You mean he's trying to hedge his bet?" I asked.

"The French always want to do that. They like to bet a little on each side. This way they feel they are safe." Giselle stretched out on the bed next to me. "Maybe we can find someone to go in with him," she said.

"Like who?" I asked.

"Paul," she said. "He has a lot of money in the States now. Maybe he would want to take a piece of it."

"Paul?" I looked at her. "Do you think the Martins would want to get involved with outside money?"

"Why not?" she asked. "Money has no family ties."

"Can you get in touch with him in Corsica?" I asked.

"I know how to get in touch with him," she said. "But there'll be one thing. You'll have to ship the water over on one of his freighters."

"He has ships?" I asked.

"He's also tied in with the Greeks. But the shipping will have to go out

282

of Marseilles. The Corsicans control the port there. They can't ship out of Le Havre." She looked at me. "What do you think?"

"How do you know so much about him?" I asked.

"I told you a long time ago that we're family," she answered.

"I think I better talk about it with J. P. first. Maybe his father wouldn't want to do business with the Corsicans."

"He shouldn't have any complaints," she answered. "After all, the Corsicans kept his labor under control during the war."

Buddy didn't get to California. He found a better deal in Harlem. He was running numbers from 110th Street down to 59th Street between Central Park West and the East River. Buddy and I had kept in touch. I knew that he had more than twenty runners and they reported to him at a used car dealership on St. Nicholas Avenue. Buddy and Ulla had a son. When he was baptized, they named him Jerome. I saw pictures of the child; he was fair skinned and good-looking. They didn't live in Harlem; instead, they had a fairly new apartment on 80th Street and West End Avenue.

I called him at home. It was the only telephone number I had because Giselle and Ulla kept in touch by phone. New York was six hours behind us and I knew that Buddy always got home late. I called him at six in the morning, which was midnight in New York.

"I'm coming home, Buddy," I said loudly into the phone. "The Plescassier company is going to bring their bottled water into the States."

"That's balls," he said. "Why should anybody in New York pay for French bottled water when they get it free from the tap?"

I smiled into the phone. "Does Ulla wash her pussy in tap water?"

"No," he answered. "She uses plain bottled water from the A & P."

"French water is better," I said. "I bet Ulla would buy it if she could get it."

"I don't know," Buddy said doubtfully.

I laughed. "Don't be a schmuck. Giselle even has got me washing my balls in Plescassier."

"Okay," he said. "So what do you want me to do?"

"I'll need a big storage place or warehouse near the Brooklyn docks. Don't forget I'm moving a lot of bottles of water and I don't want the breakage to put me out of business."

"The only place you can go to is Bush Terminal. But the Brooklyn waterfront is controlled by the Randazzo family. You'd have to make a deal with them." He laughed. "And they're tough—they'll want a piece of the action."

"Who do I have to deal with?" I asked.

"I have a good friend who I met when I was working in the navy yard. Phil Cioffi. They put him in charge of the whole terminal."

"How do I get in touch with him?" I asked.

"You don't," Buddy said. "My boss is close with the Randazzo family. Albert Anastasia is the capo down in Brooklyn. They'll put me in touch with Cioffi. You tell me what you want and I'll find out how much it's going to cost you."

"Thanks," I said. "Nothing really changes, does it, Buddy?"

Buddy laughed. "Not really. Only your Uncle Harry's gone up in the world. He and Kitty have two kids. He's got the franchises for White Tower nickel hamburgers, maybe three hundred stores. He's also got a bottling contract for Royal Crown Cola in the East and a bottling plant in New Jersey. And he and Kitty live in a big house in Westchester."

"Jesus," I said. "That son of a bitch!"

"Fuck him!" Buddy said. "The two of them are yesterday for you. You're doing okay. Giselle coming in with you?"

"Of course," I answered.

"Married yet?" Buddy asked.

"We're waiting for the time," I answered.

"Ulla says you shouldn't wait too long or you'll lose her."

"I'll think on it," I said. "Meanwhile, put a rush on it. I have to get Plescassier into the States."

4

There were fifty gallons of Plescassier water in each of the barrels that we shipped to the States, on an old Greek ship leaving from Marseilles that would take about twenty days to arrive in New York. One hundred thousand gallons in all being shipped to the Bush Terminal in Brooklyn.

Meanwhile, one month before, Giselle and I took the *Leonardo da Vinci* from Genoa. We landed in New York eight days later. Giselle loved it, but I didn't care much for the ocean. I spent most of the time being seasick, and I almost kissed the ground on Fifty-first Street when we came off the ship.

Buddy and Ulla were there waiting for us. They had everything planned for us. We would stay at their apartment until we could find our own place. The two girls would look for an apartment while Buddy was taking me to meet Phil Cioffi at the terminal offices.

Buddy and I walked into the terminal offices. We were right on time. The secretary asked us to wait a moment. She went inside the office behind her desk. In a moment, both she and a tall man with a mustache came out. Buddy stood up and introduced me.

"Mr. Cioffi, this is my friend, Jerry Cooper," he said. I had never seen Buddy so formal.

Mr. Cioffi stretched out his hand. "How you doing, Jerry?"

"Just fine," I answered. He seemed like a nice enough man.

We went inside the office and started talking about what I needed. After a while, Mr. Cioffi stood up and said he would need to bring Mr. Albert

Anastasia into the meeting. He said that Anastasia was the only one who could approve this kind of deal.

Buddy and I looked at each other.

Soon enough, Cioffi came back in the room with a man that was about five feet ten and very heavy, and had thin strands of hair crossing his bald head. He had a long cigar that he always kept in his mouth when he was talking.

After we all sat down, I spoke first. "Mr. Anastasia, I'm bringing in Plescassier water from France. I've got one hundred thousand gallons in fifty-gallon barrels."

He puffed away on his cigar. "That's a hell of a lot of water!" He paused for a minute. "That's about thirty thousand square feet of storage. Jesus! That's stacking them four barrels high. Hell of a lot of space!"

It was a lot of space. I nodded in agreement.

"What the hell do I need this for? I'd have to charge you ten thousand dollars a month."

"Mr. Anastasia," I said politely. "You know I'll never be able to pay that kind of rent. We're just starting out."

"You from New York?" Anastasia asked me.

"Originally. I served in the army in France and I just got back," I answered.

"Those frogs think their water is pretty good?"

"It sells good in France," I answered.

"Okay, Cooper, I'll take three thousand dollars a month for the first six months. Later, we'll renegotiate," he said gruffly, and puffed proudly on his cigar. "Only because you served our country. And I'm a very patriotic man."

"That includes heat enough to keep the water from freezing?" I asked.

Phil Cioffi nodded.

"How you going to bottle this water?" Anastasia asked.

"I owned a seltzer bottling company before the war. I'm going to try and see if it's still in business."

Anastasia leaned back in his chair. "What do you Jews know about bottling soda? There's only one or two seltzer companies still in business and they are only selling two or three hundred bottles a week. Now, we have a bottling plant in Long Island. We can bottle anything. We already bottle American Cola and all the fruit-flavored sodas. We can do it in any kind of bottle that you want and it's a lot cheaper than you can do it yourself."

I looked at him. His cigar was stinking up the room. "That sounds good, but how much will that cost? My people in France really have control of all the money."

Anastasia waved his cigar. "We're reasonable. Not only do we do the bottling, we can also set you up with salesmen to reach the stores and make a deal with the Teamsters union to deliver."

"Okay," I said. "How much?"

Anastasia looked down at the desk. He scribbled some numbers on a notepad. He looked at it for a few minutes. Then he threw his pencil onto the desk. "Fuck it!" he said. "This is nothing but a pain in the ass. Tell you what I'm gonna do. I'll give you the best goddamn deal of your lifetime. You set up a company and give us fifty percent of it and then all you have to do is rake in the money."

"I'll still have to clear it with the French," I said. "But thank you, Mr. Anastasia."

He smiled broadly and offered me one of his cigars. "Just call me Al," he said.

5

J. P. was angry. "Everything in the United States is Mafia. The warehouse is controlled by the Mafia. The bottling is controlled by the Mafia, the selling and distributing is Mafia. And they take fifty percent of everything! And what do we have? We pay for the shipping, we pay for the barrels, and one month personnel at the springs for the water. Then we have nothing left but one sou a liter."

"We still need advertising if we're going to sell to the stores. I've already talked to some of the big grocery markets. They want advertising if they use space for the bottles. Wholesalers won't sell to the restaurants unless they get one hundred percent markup on each bottle," I said. "Other European businesses are making money in the States. Cosmetics, perfumes, many canned foods. We can sell Plescassier here, but we have to invest to make it happen."

"My father doesn't want to invest that kind of money. Period," J. P. said. "You'll have to find a way to get us out."

"Five-liter bottles," I answered. "That's what your father wanted, and that's what we're going to have to do. But it will not make any money and it certainly won't add to the Plescassier name."

"I don't have the choice," J. P. said. "Do what you can." And he hung up the phone.

Giselle looked at me. "You don't look very happy."

We had been in our little furnished apartment on East 64th Street for almost a month. "I'm not happy. In two days the water arrives in Bush Terminal and I haven't got a deal with anyone to buy Plescassier. J. P. thinks the Mafia is too expensive, his father won't invest money to advertise, and at the end of it, I'm the one who is fucked."

She crossed the room and sat on the couch next to me. "If it doesn't work," she said, "we can always go back to France."

"And what is that for me? A shitty job for no real money and no future," I said. I looked at her. "I'm sorry, darling, but I'm American and this is where I should be. In France, I'm still a foreigner."

"I am a foreigner here," she said. "But I am happy to be with you."

"I am happy to be with you, too, dear," I said. "But I'm a man. I want to take care of you. I don't know how long J. P. will want me once I go back. Then I'm just a gigolo living on your back."

She took my hand. "Jerree, just give yourself time. We'll find a way out."

I kissed her. "You're wonderful. You always believe in me."

She laughed and got to her feet. "Take a shower. I'll wash you. Then we can go to bed and make love. You'll forget all about your problems."

"You forgot about dinner," I said.

"After," she said.

In the morning Buddy woke me up. "I got a hot deal for you," he said.

I groaned. "I've not been lucky with good deals," I said.

"Don't be a schmuck," he said. "This is really hot."

"What?" I asked.

"A Roadmaster right off the line," he said. "And you can get it for peanuts."

"It's hot?" I said.

"So?" he answered. "We get it from the used-car dealer. Everything's been taken care of. You even get legitimate papers."

"My business is going into the shithouse and you want to talk to me about hot deals," I said.

"You pay a grand," he said. "It's forty-five hundred off the showroom floor. Keep it a couple of months and you can get twenty-five hundred for it."

"I'm not in the car business," I said.

"You need a car," he said. "Your taxicabs cost that much in a month. Besides, Giselle needs a car. Subways and buses are not her style."

"Okay," I said. "Where do you want me to go to get it?"

"I'll pick you up about noon," he said. "It's at a Buick dealership up on St. Nicholas Avenue."

I took Giselle with me to get the car. She stared at it. "Mon Dieu," she said. "It's a giant."

Buddy and I laughed. "It's a great car," I said. "This is the first year they came in with air-conditioning."

"Why do you need an air conditioner in an automobile?" she asked. "Just open the windows and you get all the air you need."

"Wait until the heat of summer," I said.

"The windows are electric, too," Buddy said. "You don't have to crank them up."

"It's too big," Giselle said. "I would like a small car."

"You get used to it and you'll love it," Buddy said. "Ulla felt the same way when we came here."

Buddy and I took Giselle home and then we went over the Brooklyn Bridge to the terminal. On the way I told Buddy the deal. He sympathized with me, but he had no answers for me. I drove to the terminal offices and walked into Cioffi's office.

He was smiling. "Everything okay?"

"No," I said. "Can you get me a meeting with Al?"

"I'll call him," Cioffi said, picking up the phone. "He did say he would be down here sometime this afternoon."

"If it's okay with you, then, I'll wait here for him." I turned to Buddy. "You take the car and go home," I told him. "We'll see you both for dinner."

I waited in the office until it was almost six o'clock before Anastasia showed up. I looked out the window and saw his Cadillac and two body-guards waiting for him.

"Hi ya, Jerry." Anastasia smiled. "You talk to the frogs yet?"

"I spoke to them, Al," I replied. "They're not ready to do a big setup yet. They said they haven't the money to support it."

He looked at me. "You got a fuckin' lot of water," he said. "What are you goin' to do with it? Stick it up your ass like a giant enema?"

I laughed. "I checked out a few supermarket operators. They said they could use three-gallon and five-gallon bottles of pure French water. Of course, they won't pay much for it, and they don't care about the name. They only want it because it's cheap."

"What do you think you can get for it?" he asked.

"Two dollars for the three-gallon, and three dollars for the five-gallon bottles," I said.

"That won't give us very much," he said. "It'll cost us seventy cents a bottle to service it. Well, this changes things. We'll have to get more than fifty-fifty."

"It's your ball game, Al," I said. "You tell me. Just remember, I get nothing out of this. All the money goes to the French."

"I don't care," Anastasia said. "Fuck the French. You keep what you want and they won't know the difference."

"That wasn't my deal with them," I said. "They'll get all their money."

6

It was six months before I got rid of all the water. That made it late April 1956 before I could send all the money to France. Twenty thousand dollars. That meant that I got nothing for the work I had done. On top of that, I used up almost nine grand of my own money to live on. I really felt stupid. I did my best to promote the goddamn Plescassier and they gave me nothing. They didn't help me and they didn't help themselves.

I stared at the account books on the table I had set up in the apartment. I looked across the room at Giselle. "They really fucked me, my French friends," I said sarcastically.

"Why do you say that?" she asked. "They tried to give you a chance."

"They gave me a chance," I snapped. "But they kept a leash around my neck so that I couldn't go too far."

"They put up a lot of money to ship the water into the States," she said.

I looked at her. "Not that much," I said. "Don't forget I worked a long time inside Plescassier and I know all their costs. I know how much it cost to barrel and ship the water. The twenty grand I sent back to them pays for all their costs and a little more."

She didn't say anything to me.

I slammed the account books on the floor. "Fuck them! I know they have a two-million-dollar advertising program for their water in France. Why in the hell did they think it wouldn't cost at least that much money here? The Americans weren't waiting with open arms to embrace Plescassier!"

"Why don't you talk to J. P. about it again?" she asked. "He's not stupid."

"Maybe he's not," I answered. "But his father is. Besides, talking to J. P. on the phone won't do a damn thing. Over the phone, neither of us understands the other's accent."

"Then why don't you go to France and see him?" she asked.

"I couldn't take another eight days of seasickness," I said.

"There are already three airlines flying jets between Europe and the States. You will be there in one day." She smiled.

I looked at her. "Will you fly with me?"

She was still smiling. "Anywhere with you."

"You're crazy!" Buddy said. "You go back to France, you're fucked!"

"What am I goin' to do here?" I asked. "I've never done anything but work in Uncle Harry's fountain and learn a little about the seltzer business from Rita and Eddie. And I wasn't very smart about that—the minute I went into the army, my fuckin' uncle and girlfriend screwed me out of it."

"But in the army you learned about running an auto repair and service factory. There's a lot of car dealers looking for a man to run their service department. There's been a lot of schmucks out there who know nothing about the work they do and they're doin' all right."

I looked at him. "What do you mean they're doing well, Buddy?" I asked. "They make nine or ten grand a year. That's shit. You're booking forty grand a year with what you do. I can't even keep the cheap apartment that I live in on that kind of money."

"You gonna do better in France?" he asked.

"Maybe," I said. "Better living there is cheaper than here. I'll make more money with Plescassier than I would working in a service department at an automobile dealer's showroom."

"Giselle talk you into it?" he asked. "I know she wants to go home."

"This is my decision, not hers," I said. "Don't forget Plescassier isn't the only bottled water in France. Evian and Perrier are way in front of them. And I know that they are planning on going into the States. Maybe I can get a job with one of them."

"That's a long shot," Buddy said.

"I got nothing to lose," I said. "Everything's in the shithouse already."

"I can get you seventeen fifty for your Buick," he said. "You can't use it over there."

I laughed at him. "When I bought it, you told me I could get twenty-five hundred for it."

"But that was if you kept it for just a few months." He smiled. "But you got it almost eight months now. The new-year models will be coming out soon."

"Okay, you son of a bitch." I laughed at him. "But someday, I'll get even with you."

7

The airlines only went to three cities in Europe from the States: Pan American to London, TWA to Rome, and KLM, the Dutch airlines, to Amsterdam. I decided to go to London. At least they spoke English. We had to take a small Air France plane to Paris.

In Paris we had a surprise. Paul met us when we arrived at Orly. He gave us a normal French greeting. First he kissed Giselle on both cheeks, then gave an extra kiss for good luck on her right cheek. Then he hugged me and kissed me on the cheek, and we shook hands French style.

He looked at Giselle. "You look more beautiful than ever. Very American." Then he turned to me. "Don't you think?"

I smiled. "She looks French to me."

Paul gestured and took my arm. "When the *porteur* brings your luggage to the car, I will drive you to the nice apartment that I have for you."

I looked at him. "I haven't heard from J. P. at the office in the last two days since we took off for here. I thought that he and his father would at least want to have a meeting with me."

Paul looked at us. "You've not heard the news?"

"What news?" I asked.

"*Monsieur Martin est mort*," he said. "That's why I met you. He told me to tell you that he would see you as soon as the mourning period is over. The family is very religious French Huguenot so they go the whole period. That means J. P. will not do any business for almost a month."

Paul had one of the new D.S. 21 Citroëns. It was the largest automobile

295

they built in France. They only made them in black. He told me that now only politicians, the noveaux riches, and the gangsters could afford it. I laughed at him. "And where do you fit into that crowd?"

He smiled. "I'm a Corsican. We are in a class of our own."

Giselle and I sat in the backseat of the car. "I want to take some time to see my family."

Paul nodded. "That's already arranged. Next week you will go to Lyons."

"Will my sister be there, too?" she asked.

"Of course; she will be coming from Brittany with her new husband," he answered.

I looked at Giselle. "You didn't tell me that Therese got married."

"I didn't think it was important for you," she answered. "Besides, I had so much to learn in the States, I forgot all about it."

Paul looked back at us from the front passenger's seat. It wasn't until then that I realized the fat man was still chauffeuring for him. I reached over the seat and extended my hand to him. He smiled and looked at Giselle. "*Bienvenue, mademoiselle.*"

She laughed and leaned forward and kissed him on his cheek. "*Ma cher ami,*" she said.

I sat back and spoke to Paul. "So I'm fucked. I wish I had known about the old man before we took off. Now what the hell am I going to do while I'm waiting here in Paris for a month?"

"We won't be staying in Paris." Paul laughed. "We'll be going to the film festival in Cannes. It's beginning on May twelfth and I have to be there a few days ahead."

"What the hell do you have to do with a film festival?" I asked.

"You have not been in touch," he said. "I am a very important artists' manager now. Many of my clients are in films that will be shown at Cannes."

"So you are a busy man," I said. "What am I supposed to do?"

"Take the sun." He smiled. "See some of the interesting films and look at all the beautiful girls on the beaches."

Giselle looked over at him. "Jerree is not watching the pretty girls without me being there."

"Of course," Paul said. "And not only that. Jack Cochran, J. P.'s friend, has invited both of you to stay at his villa."

8

Paul owned an apartment building on the George V, across from the famous hotel. His building was almost thirty years old. Paul had bought it when real estate in Paris was at its ebb, just after the war. Before the war ended, the Germans had used the building as officers' apartment housing. When the Germans had left, the building was completely gutted. The valuable gold-finished faucets and bathroom fixtures were taken; oriental rugs, French tapestries decorating the important entryways and halls, and even copies of French art and sculpture had been stolen. He paid next to nothing for the property, claiming that this was one of the spoils of war. Paul told us that it had taken more than a year to restore the building, but, he said, smiling, he was Corsican and Corsicans knew how to get things done. His building was one of the first ever to be completed.

He was also very clever. He turned the lower three floors into office space and the nine floors above were apartments. Of course, he kept the penthouse apartment for himself. And, at the same time, he managed to get control of several of the important cabaret theaters. Through the artists he had working in the theaters he began to manage their careers. He found them a great deal of work in the French film industry, which was just recovering from the destruction of war. It was only a short time before he became one of the most important artists' managers in the film industry. He had the most beautiful girls at his beck and call, culled from his cabarets and clubs, and it didn't hurt that most of them did their best work on their backs. The male dancers, most of them being gay, were all very bright.

They had physical beauty, and they could act. It wasn't long until he realized that the real opportunities were in the film industry. He still kept his clubs, but he turned them over to his Corsican employees, who he knew could give him a straight count. And on the first floor of the building he opened his offices.

PAUL RENARD—ARTISTS' AGENCY AND REPRESENTATION

The apartment he gave us to stay in was a very comfortably decorated living room, bedroom, and kitchen with the newest appliances found in France. Giselle loved it. She smiled at me. "I could live here forever," she said.

"It's kind of tight," I said.

"An apartment like this would cost much more than the larger apartment we had in New York," she said. "This would cost us two thousand dollars a month, compared with the five fifty we were paying there."

I stared at her. "But I thought it would be cheaper for us in France than in the States."

"Avenue George V is like Fifth Avenue or Park Avenue in New York," she said. "I've checked apartments there and I know. If we had an apartment on one of those streets in New York it would be just as expensive as here."

"I don't know how we are going to live here, in that case," I said.

"Don't be stupid." She laughed. "Who says we have to live like this?"

Jack Cochran called me at the apartment the second day that we were there. "Hi, Jerry," he said. "Everything okay? Is Giselle happy?"

"We're all good, Jack," I said. "Thank you for calling."

"I thought that we could have dinner this evening," he said.

"Is J. P. in Paris?" I asked.

"No," Jack answered. "He's staying in the original family home in Plescassier. He's going to stay there for a month. It's a family custom."

"Then where are you, Jack?" I asked. "I thought you would be in Cannes."

He laughed. "I'm right across the street from you in the hotel. I thought we all could have a few laughs and some fun after dinner."

"I have Giselle with me," I said.

"I know," he said. "She's coming with us. I'm also bringing one of my friends with me. He's an English comedian and he's also done a few French movies. You'll both like him."

"Sounds great to me," I said. "I just have to check with Paul. I want to make sure he doesn't have anything planned."

"I already checked with him," he answered. "It's okay."

"Then it's okay. Thank you," I said. "Just one word. What about J. P.? I know that he was close with his father. Is he okay?"

"He's fine," Jack replied. "He also sends his regards to you and Giselle. Let's meet in the bar at the hotel at eight."

"Eight o'clock," I said. "See you then."

9

"Dark suit," Giselle admonished me. "This is Paris."

"At least I don't have to wear a tux," I said.

She laughed. "That depends. If you were going to dinner at Maxim's and you didn't wear a tuxedo, they might not let you in, or if they did, you would be seated next to the kitchen."

"That's crazy," I said. "And I remember that during the war we were happy to dress any way that we wanted and we were happy to eat horse meat."

"The world has changed a lot in the ten years since the war," she said. She looked at me. "And we've grown older, too."

"Not you," I said. "You still look like the kid I first met. But I'm beginning to lose a little of my hair."

"You look fine," she said. "Maybe if you went gray then you'd look distinguished. You are very handsome. You have nothing to worry about."

We did not go to Maxim's for dinner. We went to a great restaurant I had never even heard about and we didn't get seated anywhere near the kitchen. Everyone in the restaurant knew Jack. Monsieur Cochran was known by everyone. The doorman, the hatcheck girl, the bartender, the maître d', and the sommelier. Even the *patron* came to the table to greet him.

Jack ordered the wine; I had my usual beer. Jack looked at us. "I know the menu," he said. "Would you like for me to order the dinner?"

"Fine, Jack," Giselle answered, glancing at me.

I nodded. "Great," I said.

Even Archie, Jack's English friend, went along with all of us. And Jack wasn't stupid. He had great taste and it was a superb dinner. I looked at him. Gay or not, he knew the finer things in life.

It was almost midnight by the time we finished dinner. Then Jack piled us into his silver Rolls and ordered the chauffeur to take us to the most exclusive cabaret in town. The word was that even the president of France could not get in because he was not gay and would not appear in public with any of the gay men who worked in the government.

It was the Folies Bergère transvestites of the year. I couldn't believe it after we sat down for the show. I looked at Giselle and she smiled at me. "Aren't they more beautiful than any line of showgirls or actresses you've ever seen?"

"But they don't have any pussies!" I whispered into her ear.

"Some of them do," she whispered back to me. "They've gone to Denmark and had the operation."

I turned back to watch the show. I still couldn't believe it. But they were really good. Apparently they all knew the Englishman. "Archie! Archie!" they called him up to the stage.

He ran up on stage with them. First he joined the chorus line as they all kicked up with their legs as if they were the Radio City Music Hall Rockettes in New York. They they let him do a turn on his own. He was taller than most of them and spoke perfect French. He began talking and the audience fell apart laughing. I didn't understand most of it even though Giselle tried to catch me up to what was being said. Then he stood silently in the spotlight. Quickly, with one hand he took out his four front teeth and with the other hand brought a large dildo from his back pocket and began sucking it. Everybody screamed.

Jack leaned toward me, his eyes tearing with laughter. "That's what he always does. He always says he's the best cocksucker in the world because he can fit any cock, no matter how big, in between his teeth."

I looked at him. "Jesus!" I said.

Jack laughed. "You tell anybody in the States about this. They won't believe you."

When we got back to the apartment, I looked at Giselle. "What do you think about all of that?"

"Jerree," she said. "That's their world!"

10

It was the weekend when I put Giselle on the train to Lyons to see her family. I hadn't paid any attention at the time, but she had brought three valises from the States. Only one of them contained her things. The other two were gifts and clothing for Therese and their parents that were half the cost of what they would be in France.

I followed the *porteur* with her baggage to a small private cabin on the train. I tipped the *porteur* and watched her sit down. She smiled at me. "This is not expensive. I even have my own bidet and washroom."

"I'm not complaining." I looked at her. "It's just that they never had anything like this in the subways."

"Neither do they have in the Paris Metro." She patted the small couch beside her. "Sit. We'll have a *coupe* of champagne before the train leaves." She pressed a button and immediately a waiter came to the door.

He was experienced. We did not have to order anything. He already had a bottle of champagne and glasses in front of us. He spoke to Giselle in French, but it was too fast for me to understand. As I paid for the drinks and the tip, he had already opened the bottle and filled our glasses. Then he left, closing the door behind him.

We clinked our glasses. "Have a happy trip," I said.

"I wish you were coming with me," she said wistfully.

"I think they will be happier that you came alone," I said. We sipped our champagne. We both knew how they felt about foreigners. "Besides, it will be only two weeks and you'll be with me in Cannes."

"I'm just worried that one of the homos will seduce you," she said. "I know how they work. Drink. Hashish. Ginseng."

I started to laugh. "They don't have a chance. I'm a beer and Lucky Strike man."

"Then there will be starlets that will flock to the film festival," she said. "They're just looking for an American to—"

I interrupted her. "You're being stupid. Nobody will give a damn. I'm not in the entertainment business. For them I'm just a guy who is hanging out with the gays."

She leaned toward me and kissed me. "Promise?" she asked.

"Promise," I answered. Then the waiter came back to the door. It was time to go. We kissed again and I stepped off the train.

Jack was waiting at Paul's office when I returned from the train station. Through the window on the ground-floor offices he saw me get out of the car after the fat man opened the door. We met in the entrance hall. "Giselle leave to see her parents already?" he said as a greeting.

"Jack," I said. "That's right."

"What are you planning to do? With nothing to do for two weeks?" he asked.

"I haven't really thought about it. I'm waiting for Paul. He said he has to be in Cannes early. He says he'll have work to do before everyone arrives," I said.

"He'll be staying here for another week. I know that he is going to Cannes only a week before the festival," he said.

"I thought I'd probably go down with him," I said.

"He told you that you and Giselle will be staying at my place in Cannes? I'm taking the Rolls with Archie and I thought you might like to join us. We'll have some fun down there before the crowds get too big," he said. "Anyway, J. P. thought that you'd go down with us. Paul's got nothing to do here but work."

"I'll talk to Paul," I said. "I don't know whether he was expecting me to go with him."

"I spoke to Paul already," Jack replied. "Paul said that it's your call, he has nothing for you to do."

"Okay, Jack," I said. "Thanks. When are you planning to drive down?"

"Monday," he said. "After the weekend traffic rush."

"You got a deal." I laughed.

"There's just one thing you will need down there," he said. "In many films that will be shown you must wear a tuxedo."

"Shit!" I said. "I haven't had a tuxedo on since I left France. I never needed any in the States."

"Do you still have it?" he asked.

I shook my head. "I lost it a long time ago."

"We'll check with Paul," he said. "I'm sure he has a tailor who works fast. They need them in Paul's world."

He was right. Paul sent me right over to a tailor and he had an almost-finished tuxedo that he could send over the next morning. I found evening shirts in white and blue Egyptian cotton and black bow ties at Sulka down the street on George V.

I called Giselle at her parents' house and told her what I was planning to do. Then suddenly she began to cry into the telephone. "I knew it! I knew it!" she said. "The minute I turned my back they were planning to go up yours."

"My God!" I said. "Giselle, what's goin' on with you? Do you really think those assholes control the world? If they do, they don't control me. I'm straight and if you don't know it by now, you'll never know."

"But we never try to make a baby!" she wailed.

"What do you think we are doing when we are fucking? Playing solitaire?" I asked.

She went silent for a moment. Then she spoke. "I'm sorry. I never wanted a baby before and maybe I still don't want one." She took a deep breath. "It's just that I found out that Therese is having a baby; maybe I was a little jealous."

"Don't be jealous," I said. "We're still young and we have all the time in the world that we need to have babies."

11

It only took seven hours to drive down to Cannes in the big silver Rolls convertible. Seven hours and six bottles of Dom Pérignon and a kilo of Malassol caviar. Jack and Archie were on their own diet. They didn't even get out of the car to piss. There were special urinal bottles, on which were engraved J. P. that were stowed away in a large rubber-lined compartment under the convertible top.

I couldn't believe it. They thought it was a lark and were betting between themselves how long I could hold it back. I fooled both of them when they had to stop for gasoline, just before we got to Cannes. It was the longest piss I had ever had.

When I went back to the car, they were standing up and applauding. Then Jack placed a ribbon on my neck which held a gold-plated medal. The Number One Pisser in the World. He kissed me French style on each cheek. "You are now an honorary fag!" Then they fell back into their seats laughing, and seemed to fall asleep.

I was seated in the passenger's side next to the chauffeur. We looked at each other. "They're having fun." He smiled as he spoke in English.

"Is it always like this?" I asked, taking the medal off.

"Not as much when J. P. is around," he answered. I looked at the back-seat. They were gone. I turned around and took out a cigarette. I offered one to the chauffeur. He shook his head as he held the lighter from the dash toward me. "I can't smoke while I'm on duty," he said politely.

There was nothing we had to say until we reached Jack's villa. Then the chauffeur went into the house and came back with two burly housemen. Jack and Archie were still out when the men threw them like sacks of potatoes over their shoulders and took them to their rooms.

I walked into the entrance hall and then the living room. It was just another palace, not as grand as J. P.'s, but something important enough to blow my mind. I walked to the windows. The view was the same as J. P.'s but from lower on the hill. Cannes was starting to slip into night and the lights were coming on both in the town and on the yachts in the marina, turning into a picture that only an artist can paint.

A woman's voice came from behind me. "*Bienvenue*, Monsieur Jerry. The Villa Jocko is at your command."

I turned. She was a very well dressed lady about forty and very attractive. "I am Arlene," she said. "I am the hostess for Jack. May I offer you a drink?"

"No, thank you," I said. "But I would like to go to my room and clean up."

"No problem," she said, and clapped her hands sharply. One of the housemen who had caried Jack into the house nodded. She spoke briefly in French. "Monsieur Jerry will have the blue room." She turned back to me and spoke in English. "Dinner will be at nine this evening."

"Thank you, Arlene," I said, and followed the houseman up the staircase. I wasn't surprised that my luggage was already in the room.

The houseman spoke to me in English. "I am also your valet," he said. "May I unpack you, sir?"

I had never been in Cannes at the time of the film festival. Now that it was almost ten days before the opening, the excitement was already building. There were billboards and signs hung outside the entrances to all of the big hotels. They were advertising movies from many countries and many languages. Only a few of them were in English.

I would sit during the morning at a table of the Festivale, a restaurant that was located catercorner to the Palais de Festivale. It was there that all of the participants of the festival had to register and collect the tickets for the motion pictures that were being shown. In addition to the films being shown at the festival, there were at least fifty or more other movies trying to be sold and distributed in other countries around the world.

That was the morning. At luncheon I moved down to the beach restaurant of the Hotel Carlton. There were the most beautiful starlets in the world here, and influential producers and directors who controlled the flesh market. And they, too, men and women, came from all over the world. And these were not the most important actors and actresses, producers and directors that were competing in the festival. That was yet to come. But it didn't matter. This was where the action was.

I thought it was like a dream. But Jack and Archie didn't give a damn. They had been through it too many times before. At night they had their own cabarets and discos. I would have dinner at the villa with them and then I would try to find English newspapers and magazines to read. Then everything changed. First Paul appeared. Two days later, Giselle came down. And finally, a week later, J. P. returned.

12

Giselle was very excited about the festival. She told me that several girls that she had known while working with Paul were in the movies now. Not really stars but important enough for them to be recognized by the paparazzi. The result was that their photographs would end up in movie magazines, tabloids, and newspapers around the world.

Paul pushed his "girls," as he called them, into more and more photograph opportunities with well-known stars. One of the best stories he told was about his publicity stunt he planned in the festival of 1954. Simone Silva, an actress with small movie credits, did a striptease on the steps of the Palais de Festivale. She did it while the most important producers and artists were entering the theater to watch one of the most important movies of the festival.

The next day, of course, she was banished from Cannes. Paul didn't give a damn. He had photographs of her being published all around the world. Very soon, he had a contract from one of the smaller studios in Hollywood for three movies. This finally cemented Paul's reputation as an artists' agent and manager. It was at this time that he signed some male actors as well as the "girls."

In 1955, he took over the career of one of the most physically attractive stars of the Italian cinema, "Atlas." As Atlas, he played the world's fastest man in the costume drama of the Greek *Odyssey*. Paul immediately changed the actor's name to an American-sounding name: George Niagara.

In one year, he made three of the most popular movies in the world. Children in all countries adored him. He became an idol.

Paul was lunching with Giselle and me at the Carlton when he pointed out George Niagara signing autographs on the beach. Paul looked at us and shook his head. "I have just one problem with him. Even though he speaks perfect English, since he was educated in Great Britain, I cannot get him a movie in Hollywood. They think that he's foreign and that they would have to dub him in English."

"Maybe they don't think he can act," I said. "Look at him—he's nothing but muscle. He could put Mr. Universe to shame. All they watch him do in his movies is run until he can catch the bad guys and beat them up."

"There still has to be a way," Paul said.

Giselle saw someone whom she knew. She waved and called to a girl, who came over to the table. A beautiful blonde, blue-eyed, bikinied beauty. Giselle introduced her to me. "Annette Duvallier, mon ami, Jerry."

I nodded and smiled. Paul asked her to sit down with us. He knew her even though she was not one of his clients. Giselle later told me that despite the name she used now, she was English and she was one of the Blue Bell showgirls from the Lido. She had already had several good parts in French movies.

"It's warm," she said.

"Let me get you a drink," I offered.

She smiled. "Thank you, but I can take care of myself." Then I watched her as she took a liter bottle of Plescassier from her bag and began to sprinkle the water over her face and shoulders.

I looked at her, then at Giselle. Giselle knew what I was thinking. "Can I ask her?" I asked Giselle.

She laughed. "Annette and I are old friends. You can ask her."

I turned to Annette. But she too knew what I had been thinking. "Yes." She laughed. "On my pussy too."

I turned to Paul. "It's a new world. I have an idea that I want to talk to J. P. about."

"Will it need artists? Maybe I could have a place in this idea?"

I looked at Annette. "Do you have an agent?"

"Not really," she said. "All of my jobs have come from friends."

"Then you sign with me," Paul said. "Then you will have a real career."

Giselle looked at me. "What are you thinking about?"

"There is one thing I will need," I said to Paul. "Is George available for promotions?"

"For money he'll do anything," Paul said.

"Good," I said. "Then tonight I will talk to J. P.; maybe this is the right time to get back into business."

13

Jack had moved up the hill to Villa Plescassier to be with J. P. when he returned to Cannes. That left Giselle, Archie, and me to stay in his villa. But we still went up the hill to have dinner with J. P. every day. J. P. looked well, but he still wore the black mourning band on his sleeve. Giselle had told me that the old family kept that on for six months.

Earlier, when I had sent back the twenty thousand to J. P., I had spoken to him about why we had failed and given him all the reasons. I was very careful not to complain about any of his father's plans to sell the water in the States. He had known how I felt about that even before we left for the States. Now I had to find out if he still wanted to go into the States with Plescassier.

That night I had the opportunity to talk to him about trying again. It was now only a question of time before other water companies would start going into the market before us. I looked at him. "The last time we went unprepared. The wrong packaging, very little advertising, but most of all we didn't tell them of the many wonderful qualities that Plescassier has."

J. P. looked at me. "You're talking about a lot of money again."

I stared at him. "And you're talking like your father again. And whether you like it or not, that's why we bombed the last time. Believe me, Evian and Perrier won't make the mistakes that we made."

"What's your plan besides the money?" J. P. asked.

"I remember that some time ago during the war you were stationed in London. You also knew an important army officer, Colonel Matthew Fox, who was on Eisenhower's public relations staff."

J. P. looked at me. "What has this got to do with selling the waters in the States?"

"Colonel Fox was in the motion picture business and the early beginnings of television advertising in the States. He and an associate bought advertising time on many television stations. They promoted a cleaning product of their own and made it the biggest household product in the United States." I looked across the table at him. "I can use that same idea to sell Plescassier waters in America."

"But that was many years ago. TV advertising is more expensive now," J. P. answered.

"George Niagara, who plays Atlas in the movies, is one of the most handsome men in the world. He drinks Plescassier only for his health. He drinks it when he exercises. There's a well-known actress, Annette Duvallier. The world thinks she is French, but she is really British. She has a body that doesn't stop, and a gorgeous face to match. All I need is Niagara and Duvallier in the tiniest bikinis coming out of the water on the beach of Cannes, each of them drinking and pouring a bottle of Plescassier over their beautiful bodies." By this time, I was almost out of breath.

"It's exciting," J. P. said. "But then how do we follow it up?"

"I'm going to have TV exercising clips of them, together and separately, talking about their health and beauty exercises and Plescassier," I said.

"And how much do you think that will take?" he asked.

"The film clips are cheap. We'll make them here in Europe. TV advertising in the States, maybe one million dollars. Shipping half-liter and liter bottles of Plescassier to Los Angeles won't be that much. And we would bring the two stars to Hollywood for an important promotion." I looked at him. "You have the money. I know you are spending more than two million dollars in advertising alone in France."

"You know a lot about Plescassier's business," he said.

"Working for almost five years with you, J. P.," I answered, "I had to learn something."

"Why don't you want to begin in New York again?" he asked. "It's the biggest market in the States."

"We were a loser there," I said. "They don't forget. Besides, the Mafia and the unions control everything there."

J. P. sat silently for a while. I watched him. Finally I couldn't wait any longer. "Do you still want to go into the States or don't you?"

He looked at me. "It will be almost a two-million-dollar investment, not one million."

"But the market," I answered. "If you win, you will cover the world."

14

I hadn't realized that J. P. had so many friends at the film festival. I also hadn't known that J. P. had financed several of the smaller films and one of them was accepted in the competition. On the weekend before the festival finished, J. P. had a large, extravagant party on Saturday night. He invited over one hundred guests for a buffet dinner and dance on his yacht. He ordered that the yacht sail out of the marina and anchor in the bay to show all the lights along the Croisette and behind Cannes.

I had been busy in the last few days before the party, trying to get the promotion for Plescassier water planned for the States, so I had not had time to be with Giselle. She told me that she was helping J. P. with the party. On the night of the party she told me that J. P. had asked her to act as hostess with him. I thought that was really nice to give her that honor, even if it meant that she would have to go early in the afternoon to the yacht.

I was curious. "What's happening with Jack?"

"There are many political men coming to the party, especially Monsieur Mitterrand, who is minister of information and really controls the festival. There are a lot of rumors that he may become president of France in time." She turned to me. "It's a real honor for me," she said. "This means that I am accepted in French society."

"Where does that leave me?" I asked.

"You're American. It doesn't change anything. At the film festival they only care about American stars. Kim Novak and Susan Hayward will be at the party and they will be seated on each side of Mitterrand like a sandwich," she said, laughing.

"I don't know what is so great about stars. It's just movies and the people that work in that business," I said.

"There is also a lot of business going on here. You would never have met George Niagara or Annette and you would have never had your promotion idea for Plescassier," she replied.

"Where am I going to sit if you're next to J. P.?" I asked.

"I have had Paul arrange everything. You will be seated with him and George and Annette in a special corner where the paparazzi will be taking a lot of pictures." She smiled. "And just for your information, Jack will be seated next to me with J. P. on my other side and a little French starlet, Brigitte Bardot, on the other side of Jack and then Archie on her other side."

I laughed. "I hope he won't take out his teeth and dildo at dinner. If he does, it'll blow the ship out of the water."

She laughed with me. "It would be funny, but it won't happen. He's a real professional and there are several producers that will be there that are interested in using him for a movie."

"Does anyone know yet who is going to win the prize at the festival?" I asked.

"Nobody really knows. The jury has Preminger and Buñuel on it and their lips are sealed. But the favorite is Susan Hayward for *I'll Cry Tomommow*," she replied.

"But that's an American movie. I thought they were all against it."

She smiled. "It's a jury," she said. "Like in a courtroom, anything could happen."

But, it was a great party, I heard. Of course, the moment the motors on the yacht were turned on, I became seasick, and I spent the whole of the night in one of the cabins in the toilet. It was about one in the morning when Paul got me off the yacht and up to Jack's villa.

I looked at Paul. "Where's Giselle?"

"They are having the party go on to the Playgirl disco. Everybody will be there all night," he answered. "Why don't you freshen up and we'll go down to the party."

My head was splitting. "All I need now is some aspirin and sleep," I said.

I closed the door behind me as I walked into the entrance hall. Arlene was standing there. "Are you all right?" she asked.

"I need some aspirin," I said, and started up the staircase to the bedroom.

"I'll bring some to you in your room," she said. "I'm sorry, both the housemen are doing guard duty at the party."

"Okay," I said. "I'll manage."

I did until the room and then the world began spinning around again. When Arlene came into the room I was half on and half off the bed. "Let me help," she said. I didn't know until now how strong she was. She lifted me up onto the bed with her hands under my armpits. Then she quickly took off my jacket and shirt. "Still dizzy?" she asked.

"A little," I said, looking up at her. "You act like a real expert."

She laughed. "I spent ten years being a nurse in the American Hospital in Paris."

I shook my head. "I never would have known."

She gave me two pastilles and dropped them into a glass of Plescassier water. The pastilles began to fizz in the water. I looked up at her. "This reminds me of Alka-Seltzer in the States."

"The same idea," she said. "But this is just aspirin." She smiled, looking down at me. "Can I help you take off your shoes and trousers, so you can get into bed?"

I smiled. "That's real service."

"That's what I'm here for," she said. "Now lean back and try to get some sleep. If you need any help later, just call."

I spent the rest of the festival setting up filming of the commercials for the States. Luckily, Paul knew one of the American directors who made commercials as well as films. He knew exactly what we needed. But everything took more time than I had expected, because we also had to rework a complete bottling plant for the American market.

It was February of '57 when I finally called Buddy in New York.

"What are you tryin' to do now?" Buddy asked. "Don't you think you took enough of a beating the last time?"

"Buddy, it's a new ball game," I told him. "And I need your help with it. We're moving it to Los Angeles."

"Why Los Angeles?" he asked.

"Two reasons," I answered. "We're doing big promotion this time. TV commercials, and exercise programs with Mr. Atlas and Miss France. We are publicizing their physical beauty and our water. It goes together, hand in hand."

"You got that already," Buddy said. "Why do you need me?"

"Distribution," I said. "You still have the connections with the Teamsters and the other unions who we need to deliver our water into the marketplace."

"But I got a good deal here," he said. "What makes it better for me out there?"

"One, sooner or later, they are going to nail you with the numbers game and you know they don't like you. Especially since you are black and married with a white girl," I said.

"You're right there," he said.

"I read in the papers they blew Anastasia away in a barber's chair next to the Carnegie Delicatessen. How long do you think it'll be before Cioffi has to get out or is killed, and you'll have no protection?"

"Cioffi already quit," he said. "He moved to Scottsdale, Arizona."

"Okay," I said. "Then you can become completely legitimate. Vice president of distribution of Plescassier America. I got you down for thirty grand plus expenses for the first year. We do better, you'll do better."

He was silent for a moment. "What do I have to do first?"

"Get us both a place to live," I said. "Then find a warehouse near the L.A. waterfront where I can store the water. And this time we don't do any bottling. All the bottles, half-liters and liters, will be bottled and labeled in France. It's now the real McCoy."

"How much time do I have?" he asked.

"We want to be set up by the fall," I said. "So are you going to shake your ass?"

"And money?" he asked. "When I see some. I have expenses, too. Moving and everything."

"I'll send you ten grand tomorrow morning," I said. "Is that okay?"

"That'll help to start," he answered.

"Good," I said. "Let's get going. And don't get greedy. The Frenchman ain't no asshole."

15

It was early in the fall of 1957 that we finally got Plescassier's promotion and new packaging into the States. In many ways, Paul had been a big help with the promotion of the television commercials because he had his clients make personal appearances on live shows and talk about their exercise and beauty regimens. By the time October came around probably everybody in the U.S. had either heard or seen the exercise pamphlet that had been written under their names. Of course, the key was Plescassier water. No sodium. No sugar. No fat. Nothing but Plescassier could keep a body clean and healthy.

We did not do the first big promotion in Los Angeles or New York. Because of Paul's connections to the Stardust, which had the Lido show from Paris, we were able to use this magnificent show to start our promotion in the U.S. Plescassier was being served at every table and food counter in the hotel. And the hotel comped every star we had obtained to come to Vegas for the national radio and TV programs. Of course, George and Annette, one or the other or both, were in the lobby to greet each guest and present them with their own signed bottle of Plescassier water.

It was really the greatest promotion that had ever been for water. God himself could not have poured more water on the earth in order to float Noah's Ark than we did for Plescassier. I couldn't believe that so many people had pitched in to make Plescassier a household name.

I was flying high. Everything I had always dreamed about was happening and coming true. And all the time I was losing everything: Giselle.

I didn't know how, but it seemed that I was always working. She kept staying with J. P. as his hostess, because he was involved more and more with business dinners and social invitations. I didn't realize then what it meant. Finally, as the last night of the Plescassier promotion in Las Vegas began, J. P. and Giselle came in from France. They asked me to meet them at the Sands Hotel at six in the evening. I was still stupid. I didn't understand why they didn't stay at the Stardust, where all the action was. But at six o'clock I went to the Sands.

Jack Cochran was in the lobby waiting for me. I shook his hand. "Congratulations!" He smiled. "You've really done it. Nobody really believed that the States would accept Plescassier."

"I wasn't alone," I said. "I had a lot of help along the way."

He looked at me. "Do you know why J. P. wanted you to come here today?"

"Not really," I answered. "I thought maybe he wanted to get in on some of the fun."

Jack shook his head. "Not really."

I looked at him. "Then what?"

Jack looked into my eyes. "He wants to get married."

"Here?" I asked. "Why not in France?"

"It takes thirty days for the banns to be posted in France," he said. "And he has to be married now."

"So what's the rush?" I asked.

"Under French law he needs a male heir in order for him to keep the company in the family. Without a male child, seventy-five percent of the company and the inheritance would be taken over by the French government." Jack watched me closely. "That's almost like ninety million dollars now."

"Okay," I said. "So he gets married here, that's no problem. He still hasn't got an heir yet."

"You still don't understand, do you?" Jack asked.

I stared at him. Then lights began going off in my head. "No!" I said. "Not Giselle!"

Jack spoke softly. "She's already pregnant."

I couldn't speak. All I could do was stare at him.

He took me by the arm. "We better go to the bar and have a drink."

I followed him in silence. I was almost in shock. He ordered both of us a double scotch on the rocks.

"Drink it," he said. "We both need it."

The scotch burned its way down my throat, but I didn't give a damn. I gestured for another. "But Giselle's my girl. We love each other."

The second scotches were set on the table. Jack picked up his glass. "J. P. and I are lovers. We love each other, too." He swallowed his drink. "But, Jerry, we're American, they're French. They have their own ways that we don't even understand."

"Yes," I said. "But I don't understand why they even bothered to come here and tell me."

"Giselle still loves you. J. P. respects you. She wants you to give her away in marriage and J. P. wants me to be the best man." He suddenly began to laugh. "It's crazy. Really crazy." He looked at me. "What the hell! Let's go upstairs and congratulate them."

They had the biggest suite in the Sands Hotel. Three bedrooms, living room, dining room, kitchen, and four bathrooms. It was half of the floor at the top of the Sands. One of J. P.'s housemen from France was acting as the butler. He nodded at me as we came in the door and went into the living room. J. P. and Giselle were seated side by side on the couch. There was an ice bucket with a bottle of Dom Pérignon on the coffee table in front of them.

J. P. rose to his feet and held out his hand to me. "Hello, Jerry," he said.

I shook his outstretched hand, but I couldn't speak. I was looking at Giselle. She had never looked more beautiful. I tried to remember how old we were when we met. It was in 1944. I was twenty-one when we had been transferred to Paris. I remembered her birthday. July the fourth, American Independence Day, she was going to be twenty-two. Maybe she was only a few months older than I was, but I always felt she was younger, she was just so beautiful.

She looked up at me as I stood in front of them. "Hello, Jerree. Please sit down."

Jack and I sat down in the chairs in front of them. J. P. poured the champagne. "*Salut!*" he toasted.

I didn't raise my glass. I was still silent, watching her.

J. P. spoke to me. "You really did everything you said you would do in America. I thank you for what you have done. We would not have been able to do this without you."

I didn't answer.

"I want us to be friends," J. P. said. "There are difficult things ahead to overcome. Both for Giselle and me. But we still feel the same about you and Jack as our lovers. Love and friendship do not have to die because of circumstances. The world does not accept Jack's and my lifestyle. We all have to make sacrifices."

I turned to Giselle. "And how do you feel?"

There were tears in the corners of her eyes. "I love you, Jerree," she whispered huskily. "I will always love you; you will have to believe that."

"But you're going to marry him, and you will move to France and live with him. We will not be together. I love you, Giselle, but I don't understand your kind of love." I felt tears coming into the corners of my own eyes.

"Love me," she said. "And give me away in marriage with love, Jerree, please." She reached for my hand. She held my hand for a moment and looked at me and then she kissed my hand.

It was then that I knew it would never be the same. It would again be a whole new world. I turned over her hand to her palm and kissed it. "Congratulations and love, my darling," I said. "I am going to get in touch with Buddy right now and we will give you the greatest wedding that Las Vegas has ever had." Then I turned to J. P. "I can never thank you enough, but I want you to know that I really appreciate everything that you've done for me. I have only one wish for you."

"Tell me," he said shaking my hand and then kissing both of my cheeks, French style.

"May all of your children be boys."

16

By the end of 1959 we were grossing ten million dollars a year from Plescassier. J. P. was keeping two million dollars for the share that the French company owned. Sixty-five percent was Plescassier America profit. And I had thirty-five percent of the company. I was making almost one million dollars for myself. By now, Evian and other French waters had begun coming into the States. They, too, were promotional-minded companies.

J. P. and Giselle had been having promotions of their own. Two girls. One in 1958, the second in 1959. I sent them congratulations and sent a diamond and gold necklace for each of the babies.

Jack called me from Cannes. "J. P. is disappointed. He needs a male heir."

"I'm sure they are both working on it," I said.

"That doesn't mean anything," Jack said. "Don't forget, J. P. is a Frenchman. He's not going to blow his fortune because all he has is daughters."

"If that's what Giselle has, he has no choice. They are his children, his family. He can't just throw them away," I said.

"You're forgetting one thing, Jerry. J. P. is still gay. He'll sell his company and keep all the money rather than give it away to the government. You know the French tax laws," Jack replied. "That way he keeps it all. His family and his money. He's big now in French society; it'll be easy for him to move into an important government position."

"And then what happens to you?" I asked.

Jack laughed. "I'll manage. I've got a lot of stock property, both in

France and the United States. But, most important, J. P. and I will stay together."

"Okay," I said. "I'm glad everything is fine with you. Just keep in touch." I wondered at the time if Giselle would be in or out. But Giselle had made her own choices.

And, of course, again in 1960 Giselle and J. P. had another baby girl. They called to tell me the news. What no one had told me was that J. P. was planning to sell his company now. That was in November and there was a new excitement in the air. John F. Kennedy won the election for president in the U.S. It was a breakthrough in America's belief that only a Protestant could be elected to the highest office in the land. Kennedy was a Catholic and a World War II veteran. It was really a feeling that a new generation had taken over the government, and along with this it gave America a new hope.

Since I had been a New York Democrat, I called Annette to ask her to dinner for my own private celebration.

I wanted to go to Nicky Felder's Restaurant on Sunset Boulevard. I had a great deal with Nicky. In Paris during the war he was my sergeant when we were running the jeep hustle. After the war, he had gone into his own family business, so when his father passed away, Nicky moved his restaurant to Los Angeles. His New York–style restaurant was a big success in Los Angeles. Annette already had plans, but I went to dinner anyway.

I made a U-turn just as the light turned red at Sunset Boulevard. I drove the car a half block and pulled up in front of Nicky Felder's. The parking valet opened my door.

"Slick U-turn, Mr. Cooper." He smiled. "The cops were at that light just two minutes before you."

"I'm a lucky man." I laughed, slipping him a fiver. "Don't scratch it up. I haven't paid for it." Nicky's valet guys were notorious for dings and scratches.

The doorman opened the glass doors and I walked into the restaurant. The restaurant was jammed. Nicky moved through the crowd toward me.

"Hi, Jerry, you alone for dinner?" he asked as he greeted me.

I nodded.

He looked out toward the dining area. "Give me a few minutes," he said. "Have a drink on me at the bar."

I looked at him. "You forgot something."

Nicky looked puzzled for a moment, then caught on. "It got busy early, Jerry. I'll get it straightened out in five minutes."

"We had an agreement, Nicky," I said. "I gave you twenty grand to put a bottle of Plescassier on each table. You've got twenty cases a day to keep you supplied, and it doesn't cost you or your patrons one dime."

"Relax, relax, it's my mistake." Nicky patted me on the shoulder. "Calm down, have yourself a drink, and I'll get everything straightened out."

I watched him as he moved into the dining room. Nicky could take one look at the room and know who needed water, who was getting impatient waiting for food. It was like radar that only a professional had. The restaurant business was rough, but Nicky Felder's was the hottest place in town. But it's not easy when you're on top. Nicky told me to relax, but his face was tense, and a fine patina of perspiration almost hid his greeter's smile. I shrugged and·squeezed my way toward the bar and got myself a Glenmorangie, neat.

Nicky was a genius in stacking his bar. From five-thirty until midnight, the bar and the cocktail tables were filled with the greatest-looking hookers in town. Nothing but eights, nines, and tens. If you could throw them on any baccarat table in Monte Carlo you would be a millionaire just picking up the naturals.

I leaned my right elbow on the polished mahogany bar. I lit a cigarette and drew the smoke into my lungs. Jesus, this was the life, I thought to myself. As I looked around at the beautiful women I thought about Giselle. I'd come a long way from after the war in Clichy, France. Life was a ball breaker then. No money. Everything was a hustle. If it had not been for Giselle and J. P. I guess I would have been on the street running numbers with Buddy.

A girl's voice came from behind my shoulder. "Do you have a menthol?" It was a husky voice and I always liked husky voices.

I turned to look at her. Beautiful hair and lovely eyes. Nine and a half. I held up my pack of cigarettes. "Only Dunhills," I said.

"Sorry," she said, and began to turn away.

"What's your brand?" I asked.

"Anything cool," she answered.

I flagged one of the bartenders. "Give the lady a package of Dunhill menthols, on me."

The bartender was a schmuck. He pointed at a pack half open in front of her. They were Kools.

"Asshole," I said to him, picking up the half-empty package of Kools and throwing them behind the bar. "I think those have gotten stale. Now give her a fresh pack of Dunhill menthols and just for good luck a fresh pack of Kools, and the lady can take her choice."

He stared at me, then moved like a flash. Two packs, both opened and held for the lady's choice. She took the Dunhill and he lit it for her.

I smiled at him. "Now you're being a gentleman." I slipped him a twenty. I watched as he nodded his thanks and moved down the bar.

She let the smoke drift slowly from her nostrils. "You must be somebody. You've got a lot of style. Thank you."

"I'm nobody," I said. "But you're a beautiful lady."

"Are you eating alone?" she questioned.

"Not if you join me for dinner," I said.

I watched her nod and smile, then held up my hand to catch Nicky's eye. It took a few minutes for Nicky to show up. He was seating a few large tables. I could see that the one-liter iced bottles of Plescassier were already at each of the tables and were being poured into iced glasses for the patrons. I was satisfied.

Nicky was smiling when he got to me. He kissed the girl's cheek. Nicky was famous now for his kisses on every girl's cheek. He also made sure that every girl in the bar was tabbed for drinks and dinner just in case she didn't connect with someone. He made a smooth introduction. "Jerry, Sue Ellen. Sue Ellen, Jerry." Then he turned to business. "Dinner in the dining room or the Sweethearts table in the bar?"

"You know the table I like," I said. "The corner banquette in the cocktail room, you got it available?"

Nicky waved his hand grandly. "It'll be ready in three minutes."

Sue Ellen smiled and watched him walk off. "He's a sweet man," she said. "It looks like you've known each other for a long time."

"We were in the army during the war together," I said. "And that has been a long time. Tell me about yourself, Sue Ellen."

"Not much to tell," she answered. "I was a beauty queen out of the heart of America, straight off a farm. I used to watch the planes that used to fly overhead when we were kids. I dreamed about California or New York. So I took my shot. And I found out that I was like a thousand other girls who had the same dream but without the talent to back it up."

"You're looking good," I said. "That's not so bad."

Nicky quickly appeared and led us to the table. He smiled as I nodded in appreciation at the Plescassier bottle in the center of the table in front of us. I turned to Sue Ellen as Nicky took off and the sommelier took his place.

"May I offer you something to drink?" asked the sommelier.

"What's your pleasure, Sue Ellen?" I asked.

She laughed and leaned over toward me. "I'm a hooker. What do you think hookers at Nicky's order?" She laughed.

I turned to the sommelier. "A cold bottle of Dom Pérignon for the lady and a Glenmorangie neat." I took a sip of the Plescassier that had been poured for me. It was right. Cool but not freezing.

All sommeliers are full of shit. They all think they are contenders for the Oscar. This one thought he was Paul Newman. It didn't work, though; the real one was sitting at one of the larger tables in the center of the dining room. With a flourish he placed two tulip champagne glasses in front of us. As he raised his eyebrow he placed the opened bottle of Cristale in front of us. He poured a small amount in my glass. I tasted the Dom Pérignon and nodded in approval. He then poured Sue Ellen a glass and then placed the Glenmorangie in front of me. He then turned and left with a happy swish.

17

I turned to her as she took a sip. "Like it, Sue Ellen?"

"What's not to like?" She smiled. "Thank you."

Dinner was simple. Each of us had Caesar salad. She had a New York, prime, medium rare. I had linguine with fresh clam sauce. We both ate as though we hadn't eaten all day. As a matter of fact, I hadn't and she probably hadn't either.

"This steak is delicious," she said.

"Nicky always brags about his steaks. He says he orders them from a butcher in New York." I smiled. "I thought L.A. girls always ordered fish or chicken."

"My roots give me away. We used to have cattle and my daddy even butchered our own meat. We always had a freezer full of a side of beef." She laughed. "After all, you ordered linguine, but you don't look Italian."

"My specialty when I was a kid growing up in New York was a kosher hot dog with sauerkraut and Pepsi. In those years Pepsi came in a big bottle for a nickel. Coca-Cola was the same price, but came only in a small bottle."

She laughed. "We're funny. Both from different parts of the country but here we are in L.A."

"That's life," I said, keeping my eye on the door. It was a bad habit I'd had for a long time. You never knew what was coming in the door.

Sue Ellen was a bright lady. She watched me checking the door. "You're nervous?" she asked.

"No," I said. "Just careful."

"Maybe a wife or a girlfriend might be coming in?" she asked discreetly.

I laughed. "No, nothing like that," I answered honestly. I gestured for a waiter. "Would you like coffee and a brandy?" I asked.

She nodded.

"Two coffees, and Hennessey XO." I motioned for both of us to the waiter.

"So what are you looking out for, Jerry?" she asked playfully.

"You're a nosy cunt," I said.

"I'm not a nosy cunt," she said. "I just like to know more about a client I like."

"I'm glad you like me," I said. "But I'm not a client."

She smiled. "Sorry. One C for dinner."

"That's cheap," I said. "I'm giving you five Cs."

I heard a man's voice come from the front of our table. Intuition and instinct paid off. I saw the glint of the gun and rolled myself and Sue Ellen off the banquette. I kicked the table and it knocked the gun sideways as it hit the man's arm. I felt the shot go off, but he had a silencer and it wasn't heard. But I felt the bullet burn as it traveled along my left shoulder. I reached for the small .25 caliber that I always wore in my Italian boots. I shot the son of a bitch in the balls. He screamed and ran for the door, his hands cupping his crotch with blood dripping between his fingers. His feet barely touched the floor. He was out the door before anyone could stop him.

I bent over and helped Sue Ellen up from under the table. "You okay, baby?" I asked.

"I'm okay," she said, her face pale. "But you're bleeding through your jacket sleeve."

"I'm okay, it's only a surface wound," I said.

Nicky was right next to us before a crowd could begin to develop. A couple of waiters were with him. "Let's get you into my office, and I've got my doctor in the restaurant now. I'll bring him over."

"Good," I said. "Give Sue Ellen a grand. Let your boys take her out the back way. Make sure that nobody gets any pictures of her." I turned to her. "Don't worry, you'll be okay. Just don't let anybody know that you were here."

She looked at me. Her mascara was beginning to run down her cheek. "Won't I ever get to see you again?"

"In time," I answered. "Right now you gotta get out of here before the cops show up and bring you into it."

Nicky told the two waiters to get her out. He then led me to his office. He closed the door behind us. "Now, before the cops get here, what's this all about?"

"Water," I said. "Believe it or not. Water is hotter than booze now."

18

Nicky's doctor was having dinner at the restaurant. The doctor was in Nicky's office before the police got there. He helped me off with my jacket and shirt. "The jacket's going to need some reweaving," he said.

"You a doctor or a tailor?" I snapped. My arm didn't feel too good. It burned.

"Calm down," the doctor said, smiling. "My father was a tailor. I always check out the patient's clothing. If it's expensive I know they can afford me."

"Who are you?" I asked.

"I'm Dr. Kramer. I'm a surgeon," he answered as he felt the flesh on my arm. He turned to Nicky. "Do you have a first aid kit?"

"In the kitchen," Nicky said. "I'll get it."

After Nicky went for the first aid kit, the doctor looked down at me. "You're lucky," he said. "The bullet only grazed the fatty back part of your arm. If it had gone into the muscle you would really be unhappy."

In no time, Nicky was back with the first aid kit. Quickly, the doctor peroxided me, iodined me, held the edges of the wound tight, and wrapped the gauze and tape around my arm. "That'll hold," the doctor said. He gave me a card from his wallet. "I'll be in surgery in the morning," he said. "But I'll be in the office after one o'clock. Come in then and I'll change the dressing."

I looked down at the card. Dr. Kramer. Obstetrics and gynecology. I turned and looked up at him. "You're a woman's doctor," I said.

He laughed. "If you're worried, come to my office in drag."

I laughed. "Thank you, Doctor. I'll see you tomorrow."

The doctor left and I turned to Nicky. "How come you told me that was your doctor?"

"It's my business," he said. "You can't believe how many of the girls ask me for a doctor. Who the hell knew I'd need a doctor for you tonight?"

The police knocked on the door. Nicky let them in. Detectives Randall and Schultz. I showed them my driver's license, gun permit, and business card.

"It says on your card that you're president of a water-distributing company," Detective Schultz said. "What kind of water do you sell?"

"French bottled water. We sell to restaurants, supermarkets, convenience stores."

"You mean something like Canada Dry?" Detective Randall asked.

"Something like that," I answered.

"Is that why somebody wanted to pop you?" Detective Schultz asked. "For fucking bottles of water?"

I looked at him. He didn't know how right he was. "No," I said. "Everybody knows I always carry a bundle of cash with me. That's why I was given a gun permit."

"But the guy went after you in the middle of a restaurant," said Detective Schultz. "Christ"—he motioned toward the restaurant—"in this place he could have hit any table and come up with big cash."

"It was his hard luck," I answered. "If he had been polite I might have just given the money to him."

The telephone rang and Nicky answered it. He handed it over to Detective Randall. Randall listened for a moment, then put the telephone down and looked at me. "We just heard from the emergency room at Cedars; they took a guy in who has one of his testicles shot off."

"So?" I asked.

"Did you do it?" Schultz asked.

"What would you do if a guy was shooting at you?" I asked.

"Give me your gun," Randall said. He looked down at the gun, then back at me. "He's lucky you didn't have a magnum. In that case he would have lost both balls and his prick."

A uniformed policeman came into the office. He held up a small cellophane bag. "I just dug this out of the back of the leather banquette. It looks like a thirty-eight bullet."

"I didn't know that you were an expert," Schultz said, annoyed. He took it from the policeman, who left; he then turned to me. "With a bullet like that, the guy meant business. You sure you don't know of anything he might have been after?"

"No," I said flatly. "You've got him in custody, why don't you find out what he has to say."

Randall turned to me. "We'd appreciate it if you could stop in at the station tomorrow and give us a statement. By that time, we'll probably be able to give you back your gun."

"I'll be there," I said.

Nicky and I watched the policemen leave; then he turned to me. "I'll drive you home, if you'd like."

"I'm okay," I said. "But I want to make sure that neither the bartender or the sommelier says anything about the girl."

"My staff is smart," Nicky said. "There will be no problems about that." He hesitated a moment. "But someone is after you—what are you going to do?"

"I'll take care of it," I said. Nicky gave me one of his shirts to wear. It was tight but I slipped on my jacket. "Give me the bill for the repairs."

"Forget it," he said. "That's what insurance is for. Besides, you've already given me twenty grand."

I looked at my watch. It was a few minutes to nine. "I'm going home," I said to Nicky. "If there's any calls for me tell them that I've already left."

"Check," Nicky said. "Sure you're okay to drive?"

"I'm okay, thanks." I started out the door.

Nicky held up his hand. "Maybe you should go out the private entrance. It's on the side street. I'll have the parking attendant bring your car over to you."

I looked at Nicky. He was smart. It was a big enough problem that there had been a shooting inside the restaurant. It would be too much if I got splattered at the entrance of the restaurant. Nicky didn't want to take any chances. I started to laugh. "Nicky," I said. "You haven't changed."

He laughed and led me to the back door of his office. I followed him down the side of the lobby of the office building where the restaurant was located. Nicky took out a set of keys and opened one of the doors. "The building side doors are always locked at night. Just wait here and I'll send the car over," he said.

The car was there in a few minutes. It was the same valet who had taken the car from me when I pulled up earlier. "Here you are, Mr. Cooper, no dings or scratches on the car."

I slipped him another twenty. The car didn't have a scratch and I wished that I didn't have one. The arm was sore.

19

I drove down the hill from Sunset Boulevard to Santa Monica Boulevard. I picked up the telephone in the case under my seat and called the Plescassier warehouse. I would have liked to go down there and make sure everything was okay, but I was in a Rolls. The warehouse was in Watts and that was not the right neighborhood to park a Rolls.

A heavy voice answered the phone. "Plessycassy Company."

"Joe," I said, recognizing the voice of our night watchman. I almost laughed: he could never pronounce the name of our company. "Buddy around?"

"He left about seven, Jerry," he answered.

"All the trucks in? Everything locked up?" I asked.

"Everything okay here, Jerry," he answered. "Is there anything wrong?"

"I don't think so, Joe," I said. "Just make sure you have the place locked up good. I'm gonna call Buddy at home and have him get you some extra men at night."

"Don't worry, Jerry," he said in a reassuring voice. "I got everything under control. I've got my ol' police positive right here with me."

"Good," I said, and put down the phone. I had forgotten that Joe was a retired policeman. I picked up the phone again to call Buddy.

Buddy's wife, Ulla, answered. "Buddy's gone out," she said. "I think he was on his way to see you."

"If you hear from him, let him know I'm on my way home," I said.

"Okay, Jerry," she said. "Don't forget, I've invited you for Norwegian dinner. You haven't seen your godchildren for several months. They're getting bigger every day."

"I won't forget. As soon as things slow down a little bit, I'll take you up on dinner. You know I love your cooking."

I turned off the telephone and put it back under the seat and got into the lane to turn west onto Fountain.

Even at this hour Santa Monica was jammed. Gridlock at nine in the evening. The light changed and I turned down Fountain to Wilshire and made it home in about ten minutes.

Buddy was sitting in the lobby waiting for me when I came into the high-rise apartment building. He looked at me worriedly. "Are you okay?" he asked.

"I'm okay," I said. "Let's get up to the apartment." We got into the elevator and I pressed the sixteenth floor. I had one of the four penthouse apartments in the building. It was a good setup. Maid and laundry service. They had an in-house restaurant that delivered by reservation to your apartment. Bar service twenty-four hours a day. Plus each apartment had a complete gourmet kitchen.

We went into the apartment and headed straight for the bar. I fixed us both a scotch on the rocks. "Some shithead took a pop at me in Nicky's restaurant."

"I know," Buddy said. "I called Nicky. He told me what happened."

"Ulla said you were on your way to talk to me. What's going on?" I asked.

"We have trouble with the distributors," he answered. "It was like an earthquake today. Every one of the distributors, all twenty of them, called in this afternoon."

"What's the problem?" I asked.

"Muscle," Buddy said flatly.

"What are you talking about?" I asked.

"Every one of the distributors said that two men came to their warehouses and told them that there was enough French waters on the market and they were replacing them with Italian water, something called 'Dolce Alps.' Outside they had a small truck and without another word they had their helpers bring in the Italian water and take out all of the cases of Plescassier."

"That's it?" I said. "None of the distributors gave them an argument. Did they think we had sent them?"

"They didn't know what was happening. They're salesmen, not goons. They said it all happened so fast," Buddy said.

I shook my head in confusion.

"Here's the really strange thing. It all happened within the same hour. That means that it is a big operation. It took at least sixty to eighty men to hit everybody at once."

"That means they also had a list of all of our distributors," I said. "Somebody must have gotten into our files." I poured another drink for myself. "A big operation," I said. "And also someone may be after my ass."

"You might have a few guys after you," Buddy said annoyingly.

I looked at him. "Any of the distributors get a tag number on any of these trucks?"

"Two of them," he answered. "Rental trucks. Budget and Ryder. All with Nevada plates."

"Okay," I said. "I'll call Moe in Vegas tomorrow and find out who rented the trucks. Meanwhile, let's get the vans out first thing in the morning to replace the bottles of Plescassier and pull out the Italian water and dump it in the city dump."

"We don't have enough people working for us to get it done," Buddy answered.

"There's enough unemployed in Watts to fill every job in Los Angeles. And I also want some muscle boys left at the plant in case we have any trouble there," I said.

"I'm going to need a lot of currency," he said.

"That's no problem, I've got plenty of cash," I answered.

"That's not the tough one to cover. The big currency is cocaine," he said.

"Do whatever you have to do," I said to Buddy. "Pay for it. But cover your ass. Also, let's get your wife and kids out of town. Let her go to her mother's home in Norway for a month. I'm sure the kids would want to go."

"You think it's going to get that rough?" Buddy asked.

"Could be," I said.

"Sounds like the old days." Buddy smiled.

"Yeah," I said. "First thing I have to do is call Jimmy Hoffa. He'll talk to Giancana in Chicago. They all have big investments in Vegas."

"Hoffa's on our side. They set up all the arrangements for us in L.A."

"That's what I want to hear," I said. "If they are still on my side or not."

"What if they are out?" Buddy asked.

"Then I'm out of business," I said. "I'll have to go back to Europe, then to France, and then over to Sicily to find out where the problem is. I've always been straight with them. If there is a problem here they will have to straighten it out for me."

"And if they don't?" Buddy asked.

"I'm fucked," I answered. "Then I'm back in the used-car business."

"That's a long time ago. We ain't done that since after the war," Buddy said.

"That's right," I said, and poured us both another drink.

20

It was seven in the morning when the telephone rang. I rolled over in my bed and picked up the phone. "Hello," I growled.

"Mr. Cooper?" It was a strange voice.

"Yes," I said.

"Detective Schultz out of the West Side Station," he said. "I'm one of the detectives who talked to you at Felder's restaurant."

"I remember," I said, still groggy.

"The guy whose balls you popped off is still in the hospital. He ain't very happy," Detective Schultz said.

"Fuck him," I said. "I don't give a shit about him."

"We found out who he is," Detective Schultz said. "He's a hood out from New York. Johnny Terrazano. A wiseguy from the Carlino family back there in the East."

"So, what about him?" I asked.

"You know him?" the detective asked.

"Never saw him in my life," I said.

"Did you ever have any business with the Carlino family?"

"No," I answered. "I'm in the bottled-water business. That's got nothing to do with the rackets."

"You have any idea why he'd want to fire a bullet at you?" he asked.

"None at all," I answered.

There was a long silence on the phone.

"We still have your gun," he said. "You'll have to come down to the station house so that you can sign for it."

"Thank you, Detective," I said. "I'll come around for it in a day or so."

"You're not worried that some other wiseguy might want to take a shot at you?" He laughed.

"What the hell for?" I said. "I got nothing they want."

I put down the phone. I knew what they wanted, but it didn't make any sense to me why they went after me with a gun. All they had to do was talk to me. We could always make a deal. I swung my feet off the bed and picked the phone back up and called Buddy.

"The cop just called me and told me where the guy came from. He's out of the Carlinos," I said. "I still don't understand why they want to take me out."

"I've been on the phone, too," Buddy said. "I think I know why it's all happening. Last night I called Cioffi in Scottsdale. He told me that the Carlinos were unhappy that you didn't give them Plescassier when you brought it back into the States. They complained that you made the deal with Anastasia, and all they got from it was a lot of grief and they lost money. They say you've been making a lot of money out here with the water, and when you started you gave them nothing."

"That's bullshit!" I said. "If anybody made any money out of it the first time, it was them. They sold everything out whether I liked it or not. I was just lucky enough to have enough to pay J. P. back. I used my own money to live on. I got nothing for all my work. Those greedy bastards."

"What the hell can you do about it? Argue with them?" he said. "They're not in the business of arguments. They want the whole ball game."

"They still can't own the name Plescassier unless they buy it from me. And that stupid wop water that they try to sell won't make them a cent. Nobody even knows about it."

I thought for a little bit and then I had an idea. "Buddy, didn't you hear that my Uncle Harry had a big bottling and distribution setup that covers the East?"

"That's right!" Buddy said. "Damn, I should have had this one figured out. Uncle Harry was always in with the Carlinos. Even years ago, when he gave them his betting and numbers business. Then they had to have backed him in his bottling business, after he ripped it off from you."

"The son of a bitch!" I said. "I bet he's doing pretty good."

"He's a millionaire, from what I hear," Buddy said. "I know a lot of people that keep in touch with him. He and his wife are pretty big in Jewish society."

I sat there on the side of the bed, tapping my toe, while I thought. Finally I spoke again to Buddy. "You just get our bottles back on the shelves of the distributors. Hire bodyguards for every one of the places. Meanwhile, I'm going to get in touch with the Frenchman. I have an idea."

21

The next morning I was in Paris. I checked into the George V and called Paul at his office. Fortunately, he was in town. We decided that we would have lunch in the hotel. It was easy for him. His office was just across the street. And it would give me a little extra time to rest; the nine-hour time difference had me exhausted.

We sat down for lunch at noon. I didn't waste any time. Quickly, I told him what had happened and the ideas that I had to keep me from losing my ass.

Paul smiled. He was Corsican. There was nothing better for a Corsican than being able to screw someone who is getting ready to screw you. They call that justice.

I asked him if he thought J. P. would give me the okay. Paul nodded. "All you can do is ask him," he said. "Right now he will be in the Plescassier offices on the Champs-Elysées. I'll call him immediately. I have his private number."

"Thank you, Paul," I said. "Have you seen Giselle? I've always wanted to give her a call, but I didn't know if that would have been the proper thing to do."

Paul looked at me for a moment. "You did right," he said. "My niece is a very sensitive girl, and I know that her relationship with you was always on her mind."

"She never told me that she was your niece," I said. "All she ever told me was that you were a friend of the family."

"Her mother is my sister," he said. "But in Lyons nobody was supposed to know that she was Corsican. Because in Lyons, the Corsicans are not accepted."

"I can't believe that. After all of these years, they still don't like to talk about it?"

Paul laughed. "My brother-in-law still does not even speak to me." He lit a Gitane. "I can never even go into my sister's home."

I lit up a Lucky. "Do you think we'll be able to see J. P. this afternoon?"

"Of course," he said, then smiled. "It's like you say in America. I have clout." And he left the table to use the telephone.

I had never been in J. P.'s office in Paris. He had the same office that his father and grandfather had before him. The single large penthouse, nine stories above the Champs-Elysées, with large windows facing the Arc de Triomphe. The furnishings were cherry mahogany, with leather and glass. J. P. held out his hand and greeted me warmly. "*Bienvenue*," he said as we shook hands.

I looked at him. He looked well, still a very handsome man, even though he had taken on a little weight. "How are you?" I asked. "And Giselle and the children?"

"They are all very fine," he said. "I'm sorry that they are not here to see you, but they are in Cannes. This winter has been terrible in Paris."

"I'm sorry, too, that I can't see them. But maybe some other time," I replied.

He waved me to the chair opposite his desk. "Now, tell me what brings you back to Paris."

I told him succinctly what had happened. Then I gave him the picture as I saw it in the States. "The Mafia wants Plescassier out of the States. They think they can sell their own so-called Italian water in its place."

"They're never going to be able to do it!" J. P. said angrily. "They don't know it yet, but even if they knock out Plescassier, that won't be the end of their problems. All the French waters are already into the States. Perrier. Evian. Volvic. Contrex and many others. The French water already has the reputation that we have made for all of them."

"I won't argue with that," I said. "But Plescassier is still a large invest-ment in America. It won't be good for your company's reputation if Ples-cassier falls out of the American market."

He leaned back in his chair and took a large cigar from the box on his

342

desk. Carefully he snipped the end so that he could place it in his mouth; then he took out a Zippo lighter, probably a war souvenir. He rolled the cigar gently around until it was comfortably lit. Then he let out a large smoke ring and, through it, looked at me. "And what do you think we should do?"

"The first thing I have to know is what you are planning to do. I heard that you would like to sell Plescassier to a Swiss company. True or false?" I asked.

He smiled. "Yes and no. I am in negotiation with another company, but it is nowhere near being completed. But you are right. If we lose the States, part of the value of Plescassier will be less."

"I would like to sell Plescassier America to the Mafia. If you okay the sale, they would pay me and I'm out of their way. But, of course, they wind up fucked, because you have sixty-five percent of the company and you sell them the water. If you sell your complete company, then nobody has to sell them the water."

J. P. watched me as I spoke and I could see the wheels in his head turning. "You have a buyer?" he asked.

"Yes," I said. "The man who wanted my life, whatever I did. If he thinks that I have to sell Plescassier to him, he'll be in heaven."

"Who is he?" J. P. asked. "And does he have the money?"

"He is my uncle who screwed me out of my father's life savings that he left for me," I said. "He is a real millionaire and a partner in the biggest bottling plant on the East Coast of the United States with the Carlino family. One of the five important Sicilian Mafia families in the United States."

"And how do you know about all of this?" J. P. asked.

"I started working for him selling carbonated water over the counter before the war," I answered.

He sat there silently again for a moment, then nodded. "You do it," he said. "I will be behind you all the way."

"Thank you," I said.

He laughed. "Don't thank me. Just have dinner tonight with the four musketeers. Jack, Paul, you, and me. And believe me, we'll pour you on the plane for your return trip to the States in the morning. You still have a lot of work to do."

22

It was snowing in New York when I landed at Idlewild Airport just before noon. I took a cab to the Plaza. I checked into a room and fell into bed and slept. I couldn't handle the nightlife with the Frenchmen. I couldn't keep up. J. P., Paul, Jack, and I had gone into every cabaret in Paris and Dom Pérignon never stopped being poured. J. P. was right, they did pour me onto my flight to New York. But I had to sleep now because I was supposed to meet Buddy at eight o'clock for dinner.

I was rested, shaved, showered, and waiting for him when he arrived. "Let's go to the Palms on Second Avenue for dinner," I said. "I've been waiting for a good sirloin steak for a long time."

Buddy looked at me. "How can you be hungry with all the shit that's flying around?"

"We'll make it," I said. "Where's Ulla and the kids?"

"I left them in L.A. I put a blanket around the house," he said. "Nobody's going to get near them."

I called the Palms and we went downstairs to get a cab. On the way, I filled him in on my talk with J. P. and I leaned back in the dirty cab and looked at him. "Now you've got to make a connection that can take me to Uncle Harry and at the same time get me next to one of the capos in the Carlino family to straighten everything out."

Buddy looked at me. "And when do you expect me to do all that?"

"By tomorrow morning," I said as we walked into the restaurant.

The steaks were great. You didn't get steaks like this anywhere except

New York. In California, they call them New Yorks, but they don't com-
pare. Charolais in France are too soft and mushy. Black Angus out of
Scotland are not too bad. But this is New York. The sirloin top of the
world.

Buddy wiped his mouth when he finished his steak. "You're right," he
said. "I really prefer barbecued ribs, but this is something else."

"Where are you staying?" I asked. "Just in case I have to get you in the
morning."

"I'll be in the St. Therese on St. Nicholas Avenue in Harlem. I'll be
getting up early in the morning. I have to catch some of my old policy
books so they can give me all the lowdown on Uncle Harry."

I stared at him. "How will they know about him now? He's a rich man."

"Your Uncle Harry may be seventy-two years old, but he's never
changed. He still likes a bit of black ass every now and then." He laughed.
"Still the same old prick."

I shook my head. "But what about Kitty?"

"She's running his business. She's got him, not only by his balls, she's
also got him by his bank accounts."

We both laughed.

It was eleven in the morning that Buddy called me for the first meeting.
He said it would be in an Italian restaurant on Lexington Avenue, not far
from Bloomingdale's. I didn't know then, but that was the midtown meeting place for all the families. Our meeting was with a capo from the Carlino
family and a wiseguy from the Colombo family.

But this was not the important meeting. This was an "arrange the
important meeting" meeting. It was decided at this meeting that I would
meet with Frank Costello in the corner of the Norse Room of the Waldorf-
Astoria for lunch at twelve-thirty the next day. Costello had his own table
every day at lunch in the far corner from the entrance. There would be
only one person seated at the table with him. Miss LaJunta White, a friend
of Mr. Costello. And I was supposed to go alone. No Buddy, no niggers
with me. I was also supposed to explain the deal in detail to Mr. Costello
and show him the agreements, proving that I was legitimate.

Lunch this time was linguine with fresh clams. Dessert was cannolis and
espresso. And for the first time, I had the feeling that the whole deal was
going to work, because the wiseguy picked up the check.

The Norse Room in the Waldorf-Astoria Hotel was a very large, high-

ceiling dining room whose thin tall windows looked onto Lexington
Avenue. The maître d' held a pen in his hand and pointed to me.

"I'm Mr. Cooper," I said. "I have an—"

The maître d' nodded quickly, interrupting me. "I know, sir," he said.
"Please follow me."

He took me to the table in the far corner. Costello was not a very tall
man. He had a nice golden suntan and black hair with gray at the temples.
Miss White was an attractive lady with platinum blond hair and a bright
smile. She had a glass of champagne in front of her; he had red wine, and
I ordered a beer. Mr. Costello came right to the point. "Miss White is my
friend and a confidante. You can speak freely in front of her."

I nodded. "Yes, sir."

Costello looked at me. "You are the president of Plescassier Water
America," he said. "You have the rights to sell Plescassier in the States by
contracts and partnership with the original company in France."

"That's right," I said.

"Then, what do you want from me?" he asked directly.

I looked at him. "A few days ago in Los Angeles, a man tried to shoot
me, but he missed and lost one of his balls in consequence."

Mr. Costello and Miss White looked at each other and began to laugh.
"I've heard about that," Costello said.

"On this same day, a number of goons entered my distributors' businesses
and removed Plescassier from their shelves and replaced them with another
supposedly Italian water. Which we have since found out was simply
Brooklyn tap water. I arranged immediately for my people to get rid of the
phony water and put our water back in place." I looked at him and took
a breath. "This bullshit operation ended up costing me over one hundred
thousand dollars."

Mr. Costello looked at me casually. "Do you know who was behind
this?"

"The police told me the wiseguy that shot at me came from the Carlino
family in New York. I was able, by another source, to find out that the
phony bottled water came from a bottling plant owned by a relative of
mine who has a number of partnerships with the Carlino family." I looked
at Miss White. "May I smoke?"

"Be my guest." She smiled.

I lit up a Lucky. Mr. Costello thought for a moment. "You haven't
ordered lunch yet."

"I was waiting for you, sir," I answered.

"Miss White and I usually have Caesar salads and that's all," he said.

"Fine." I smiled. "I'll just have ham and eggs."

The service was special. Apparently everyone there knew Frank Costello. They didn't want any problems. We ate quickly. He didn't talk very much. She did most of the talking. She spoke mostly about President Kennedy and the First Lady, Jacqueline. By the time she finished I knew everything about the Kennedys. The only thing Costello said about the president was that he knew his father had been in the liquor business in Canada. I told them he was a Democrat and that was fine with me.

Then lunch was over and Mr. Costello spoke up again. "I notice you have brought a briefcase."

"Yes," I answered. "I have all the contracts and agreements we need to complete the deal. All I need is someone to take the papers and make the deal."

"How much are you asking for it?" he asked.

"Two million dollars to me for Plescassier America," I answered.

"Does that include the contracts for the water from the French company?" he asked.

"That, too, is signed and sealed," I replied.

He nodded. "Just turn them over to me. I'll get in touch with you as soon as I find out if they like the deal."

I picked up the briefcase and gave it to him. "Everything's in there. All you have to do is call me and I'll sign the papers."

He looked at me. "Do you have an attorney here?"

"Yes," I said. "Former Judge Eugene Cage."

Miss White laughed. "You may not know it," she told me in confidence. "Most of Frank's associates call him 'the Judge.' "

"I can appreciate that," I said. "He said that Mr. Costello would have a real grasp of this situation." I got up. "It's been a pleasure to meet you, Miss White, and thank you for lunch, Mr. Costello. You can reach me at the Plaza Hotel. I will be waiting for your call."

They didn't call him "the Judge" for nothing. The word around town was that the families used him to straighten up any of their problems that could be negotiated. Apparently, it also was true with the Carlinos and the Colombos. It was only two days later that I was called to Uncle Harry's bottling company offices on Madison Avenue. I was told to bring Judge Cage.

Uncle Harry was in his seventies now, but he seemed to be exactly the same. Kitty was sitting off to the side. I looked at her. She seemed to look a lot older. She had lines around her mouth that made her look very hard. She would not meet my eyes.

We said hello, but we did not shake hands. Uncle Harry smiled at me. "How are you? Feeling well?"

"I'm okay," I answered.

He kept rattling. "Kitty and I have two sons. They're bright, all going to college," he said.

"That's great," I said agreeably. "Who do they look like, you or Kitty?"

"It's funny," Harry said. "They don't look like either of us. Our oldest looks more like your mother, but that doesn't make any sense."

"Nothing makes any sense, Uncle Harry." I looked at Kitty, and for one tiny second our eyes met. I knew. Kitty was fucking me just before they got married.

"My lawyer is waiting for us," Harry said. "What do you say we get this thing done?"

"I'm ready," I said. "I want Buddy to come in here while the papers are being signed. He can be one of the witnesses when we sign."

Harry looked at Buddy as he walked into the room. "You never change," he said.

"Some things never do." Buddy laughed.

Then the two lawyers spread out the papers and we signed them all and it was all over except for one thing. Harry had to hand me the check.

I looked at the check in my hand. It was a cashier's check for two million dollars payable to me. I looked at him and suddenly I began to laugh.

"Thank you, Uncle Harry!" I said, my eyes tearing with laughter. "Thank you for everything!"